Star of
DELIVERANCE

Star of DELIVERANCE

MANDY MADSON VOISIN

SWEETWATER
BOOKS

An Imprint of Cedar Fort, Inc.
Springville, Utah

ISBN 13: 978-1-4621-1454-2

Published by Sweetwater Books, an imprint of Cedar Fort, Inc.
2373 W. 700 S., Springville, UT 84663
Distributed by Cedar Fort, Inc., www.cedarfort.com

LIBRARY OF CONGRESS CATALOGING-IN-PUBLICATION DATA

   Voisin, Mandy Madson, 1988- author.
   Star of deliverance / Mandy Madson Voisin.
      pages cm
   Summary: Emi, a Savian girl born into a war-ravaged country, has been raised to be the next healer for her deprived and malnourished people, but when a young boy stumbles into their clinic with an untreatable disease, Emi goes out to find a cure despite the dangers of her country.
   ISBN 978-1-4621-1454-2 (perfect : alk. paper)
   [1. Healers--Fiction. 2. Orphans--Fiction. 3. Diseases--Fiction. 4. Epidemics--Fiction. 5. Fantasy.]
   I. Title.
   PZ7.V8825St 2014
   [Fic]--dc23
                         2014013411

Cover design by Kristen Reeves
Cover design © 2014 by Lyle Mortimer
Edited and typeset by Melissa J. Caldwell

Printed in the United States of America

10 9 8 7 6 5 4 3 2 1

Printed on acid-free paper

For Jessica, the bravest one

"For if thou altogether holdest thy peace at this time, then shall there enlargement and deliverance arise to the Jews from another place; but thou and thy father's house shall be destroyed: and who knoweth whether thou art come to the kingdom for such a time as this?"

— ESTHER 4:14

My Dear Child,

They will tell you many things. They will tell you that because you were born into bondage, you are theirs. They will tell you that you are weak, even when you feel the strongest. They will tell you that peace cannot endure.

They will instill fear in many forms and I ask you to welcome this fear—even embrace it—because fear is the greatest gift they could give you. Only when we tremble can we defy and act. There is no courage without fear. There is no cause to be brave without it.

They are coming for me now. My soul is bursting with words, but I will leave you with this: I have heard it said that to have courage is to tell your story with your whole heart.

So tell it.

Mom

1

I woke to the sound of horse hooves. The ground trembled beneath my body with a steady rhythm. *Soldiers!* I scolded myself as I brushed fallen leaves off my face and tunic. *How long have I been asleep?* The waning light confirmed my fears: it was well past curfew, the moon already spreading its dull glow through the trees.

The thundering hooves continued to rattle through the orchard and instinctively I pulled myself against the tree I had sat under to read several hours before. One of our patients had traded us treatment for an old Sansikwan book of proverbs, but my eyelids were so heavy from long hours in the clinic that I must have dozed off.

The moon cast a dull glow on the branches of the trees, and flecks of light from the stars penetrated the deep shadows. "Nowhere in the world are there stars like those in the West Deshan orchards," Cen told me once. For the first time, I wished they weren't quite so bright.

As I sat up, I became aware that the soldiers were close—almost close enough to hear my heart pounding in my chest. Even in this low light, they could easily discover me. A shadowy dust hung in the air around me, spurred from the heels of the horses, whose rumbling hooves were getting closer to my resting spot. Peering around the tree I saw five or six Brockan soldiers approaching on tall, black steeds. I burrowed deeper into the tall grass, my pulse throbbing, hoping they would not catch me here outside the village gates after hours. The punishment for a Savian being out past curfew was two days in the valley prison with no food and only water—and even then, only when the guards were feeling generous.

Circling together in this private space, the steeds huffed and snorted while their riders dismounted, stopping a row of trees away from me. I inhaled, squeezing my eyes tightly, as a tear fell to my jaw. Even though the sun had gone down hours before, the hot summer air penetrated my skin, the hair on my long braid sticking to the sweat on my neck. The soldiers bantered back and forth with one another until finally one cleared his throat, resulting in complete silence.

Should I run? I might be able to slip away without being noticed. I was known as the fastest girl in the village, but it would be reckless to believe that I could ever beat their horses. The only sounds I heard were the chorus of crickets, the heavy panting of the horses, and the pounding of my own heart that pulsed from my toes to my ears. My palms dripped sweat into the grass, and I wiped them on my leggings, every nerve in my body charged.

"Are you going to tell us why you dragged us out 'ere then?" one soldier whined, his high voice breaking the quiet. I could not see their faces, and after nestling into the tall grass, I didn't dare raise my head out to look.

A bolder voice spoke, his tones echoing through the clearing against the bark of the trees. "Yes, gentlemen. Before I could give you the latest information, we needed the cover of night . . . and to be a comfortable distance from listening ears." I could see why he waited to get out of the city gates. With his voice, anything he said there would not remain a secret for long. "Today I received some information directly from the palace. King Jairus has fallen ill." He paused. "The plan has begun."

"Does that mean I'm goin' to be the next king?" I heard the same whiney voice reply. The other soldiers laughed.

"You're far too short to rule!" another voice called out, this one softer. "I'll be the next king!" A louder chorus of laughter ensued. I squeezed my eyelids and inhaled deeply. Brockan soldiers joking about the king's death? I should not be hearing this.

"Quiet!" yelled the strong voice, silencing the laughter. "You are all fools!"

Stillness settled into the orchard at his reprimand. Even the crickets seemed to hush with the power of the strong voice. Impulsively I sat up against the tree to hear better. As I did, a twig snapped beneath me. My stomach heaved as the sound rang through the trees.

"Wait a minute, Chief," the whiney voice spoke again. "I don't think we're alone. Give me a minute to check 'er out." The other men sighed but didn't protest.

Footsteps approached me, the soldier's heavy boots breaking the branches that littered the orchard ground. I could feel him circling, going out to examine the next set of trees, somehow passing over me. At one point I could see him standing just inches from my body, but the tall grass kept me out of sight. One more stride toward the tree though, and he'd step right on me. I pressed my hands hard against the sides of my legs, willing him to move in the opposite direction.

His red hair glowed in the moonlight, whiskers patchy from the shadows cast on his face. His filthy hands swung by his side right next to his glistening sword. I knew then that my punishment for overhearing this conversation would be far worse than just two days in the prison. Savians were often killed for no reason at all—as a girl alone in the orchard past curfew overhearing an important, private conversation, my fate would be sealed. I'd never get to say good-bye to Cen.

I closed my eyes tightly, silently reciting the hymn all Savians sing in times of fear. It was so old that no one really knew where it originated. It was a piece of us—as old as the Fathers themselves.

Ring out the bells,
Pull up your boots,
Sing out your voice
Steady and true.

Have heart in the fear
And faith in the new,
Heaven's stars are fighting
Their battles for you.

I dared open my eyes to look at him, digging my nails into my clammy palms. While he backed away I recited the words again, my muscles cramping from holding so still.

"Musta been all in my head," the soldier finally called out to his group, turning around and brushing against the grass surrounding me. "Creepy orchards," he muttered.

I gently released the breath I was keeping captive in my chest, my muscles still clenched from fear. I had had close calls before since curfew was a law that was difficult for me to follow, but I had never been this close to being caught.

"Are you finished, Collier?" the strong voice spoke, clearly annoyed by the interruption.

"Yes, sir. Sorry, Chief," he muttered.

A new voice spoke, "Out with it then, Samson. None of us here are much good at guessing games. I wasn't aware that the king croaking was part of the plan. It's not as though that prince is ready to rule. Why, I almost see this as a bad thing. There's no chance of change if we don't have an active king. Everything in the government seems to freeze."

The other men seemed to be in agreement, a few of them muttering through the dark orchard. One said, "This isn't what I signed up for."

Samson's loud voice spoke softer now, a powerful soft—piercing and even. "You are all missing the point. Men, what it is that prevents us from becoming the most powerful nation in the world?"

The orchard was still for a moment as the men considered Samson's question. So still I could hear the distant sounds of the village closing up for the night: friends calling to each other and doors shutting. What I would give to be inside the gates right now. When no one spoke up, Samson answered it himself. "Three-fourths of our military force is allotted to control the dirty Savians. We are stationed among them, making sure they do not flee; yet they may as well run. They are good for nothing now that we get most of our food from Sansikwa. We run the risk of their blood mixing with ours and tainting the Brockan race every day we allow them to live in this kingdom!"

Several men spat at Samson's declaration. I almost forgot my predicament and stood up to spit back at them. Good men and women of my village died regularly to serve these pompous Brockans. I sat as still as I could, though I flushed from head to toe in anger.

"The Savians have caused our country trouble from day one. They cannot be trusted among our own women and children and we certainly can't educate those stupid people—why, they are better use to our country dead than alive." Samson's voice became louder as he neared the end of his speech.

"Men, the death of the king means that Marley will gain more power. The young prince is no match for the team of advisors Marley has implemented. He is too naïve, too inexperienced in the ways of the world. Why, he has never even ventured out of the palace gates! And Marley has made it clear to me and the rest of his loyal followers that he wants the Savians gone." Samson's voice grew quiet. "He has a plan that will end them. And because you few have been loyal to Marley since the beginning, he felt I should inform you that it has begun. Further instructions will follow."

"But what *is* the plan?" another voice spoke, "What could he possibly do to wipe out all of them? Every last one?" Tingles raced up my legs. These were my people they were talking about—my family, my friends, my neighbors, and my patients. Everyone I loved.

Samson paused before answering him. "You will see soon enough. It has already begun thanks to Marley's careful planning and influence in the court. Now that the king has *conveniently* fallen ill, Marley will take the opportunity to have full reign to whisper in the young prince's ear. From there, the Savians will be gone for good and we will be able to move on with our lives. We will be free to pursue other conquests. To expand our armies, and rise in power as the countries around us fold to our mighty strength!" His voice amplified as he continued, "Instead of playing guard to those dirty scoundrels, we will be free. What of that, men?"

At his statement the men cheered and clapped their hands, stomping their feet and whistling. Their ruckus began to shake the trunks of the cherry trees and fruit tumbled to the earth, each one thump-thump-thumping onto the grass I lay in. Cherries were a rare delicacy for us, but I didn't dare take the fruit. Tomorrow, some Savian would be punished when the fruit on the ground was discovered. Who would be accused of sneaking into the orchard to rob from the king? Which homes would be searched for extra rations? All the soldiers would find is empty cupboards and empty bellies. They were always empty.

After their hollering subsided, Samson spoke again, "Say nothing of this meeting, men. Difficult times may be ahead for the kingdom, but our rewards are closer than ever."

With that, the men whistled for their horses and rode into the night, the stars above sharing their bright light with traveler and soldier alike.

I waited until I could no longer hear the horse hooves before sitting up, feeling my cheeks flush—not from heat but from fear, my knuckles sore from clenching my fingers against my sides. I rose slowly. Then I gathered my books and began to run.

2

*P*inch your fingers together like this," Cen explained, crossing one finger over the other and pressing down firmly until new wrinkles formed on his leathery hands. "Then lift the needle and weave in and out. The stitch should look like the fletching on an arrow. Don't pull too hard unless you know where you want it to go." He demonstrated on an old rag. "Now you practice." Turning away to walk downstairs to the clinic, he called behind him, "I'll be back to inspect your work!"

I wove in and out, perfecting the stitch, occasionally pulling out my work and starting over when there was a pucker or tear. Most girls practiced needlework for embroidery and quilting. I practiced mine before sewing up wounds.

Cen had taught me to read as soon as I could speak, and once I was reading everything I could, he began teaching me everything he knew about medicine. "Who will be here to run the clinic when I am gone? Our people will need you." Cen was right; someone would need to be the Kalvos village healer when he was

7

gone, and I was the only one for the job—a thought that both terrified and thrilled me.

That realization became even more solid as I watched Cen get older. His hair was completely white now, not even a speck of gray left. He had a harder time getting up from his bed or from chairs, often reaching out to me. "Emi, give me a boost, will you?" he would ask. Cen was very thin, but no one could call him frail. His muscles were strong, even if his bones were timeworn.

My childhood memories weren't filled with dolls or braiding baskets or playing with other girls my age. Instead, Cen taught me which herbs soothed toothaches and brought down fevers. He taught me how to wrap a bandage so that the ends would stay tucked in without chafing the skin beneath. He taught me how to tell if a baby was head first or feet first just by the shape of the mother's belly. We spent hours after the clinic closed identifying different types of burns and which route to take to treat them. He loved to teach me about the skin, explaining that it is made of layers, ready and waiting to grow back and protect us. Cen showed me how to get a splinter out from under a fingernail without causing more pain. It was a useful skill to have when so many of our patients picked fruit in an orchard all day. I learned what to do when a person's body went limp and how to prevent shock. "The cause of shock is fear, so your job is to diminish fear," Cen often said.

We had old books and scrolls on every possible topic from healing practices to herbology and ancient remedies—gathered from Cen's ancestors over the years. Cen's knowledge far exceeded mine but he was a patient teacher.

Most Savians were unable to pay us with money, so they found other ways. Often we woke to a doorstep full of their form of payment. A handful of dried figs wrapped in a coarse leather strip; a small, hand-woven scarf to protect our heads from the summer heat; a dozen fresh eggs speckled with brown and white spots that were easily fried for breakfast or a late-night meal. I once protested, "If they can't pay, why do we treat them?" I was feeling irritable about having cornmeal cakes for three mornings in a row without milk or honey.

"We all do the best we can," Cen answered. "There is not one idle Savian hand. We do what we can with the skills we are given." He was right of course, although I did not recognize it at such a young age. Now, however, I saw the respect and admiration that so many of the Savians in Kalvos felt toward Cen. Our neighbors and friends did not overlook his generosity and constant diligence. Almost daily, I heard some praise or story about Cen's kindness. From hours of stitching sutures and delivering the orchard workers' children, Cen knew everyone, and everyone loved him.

As I grew older, my neighbors began to recognize me as a source of medical knowledge, an expectation that both flattered and terrified me. I often wondered what would happen if something were to happen to Cen. I still had so much to learn, and I worried—as I watched him stumble up the stairs or forget that he put a pot on to boil—that something would happen before I had the chance to complete my training. As a result, I studied late into the night, and Cen often found me curled up on the exam bed, a candle slowly flickering out and a heavy book of healer's terminology sprawled across my lap.

Cen came back upstairs to inspect my stitch, interrupting my musings. "Very nice! Try it again here with smaller stitches while I stew an antidote." This particular day in the clinic was slow, and I was in a talkative mood.

"Tell me about my mother," I said to Cen as he sifted minerals for the medicine.

"Oh Emi," he murmured, stirring vigorously. "It's such a sad story. Why don't I tell you about that time I revived that man's heart? It was stopped completely, not a pulse to be found! It's important for you to know that."

"I already know that story, Cen. You've shared it a dozen times. I want to hear about my mother today. Please." I had seen a woman and her two daughters at the well that morning as I drew water for the day—the three of them singing softly as the sun came over the small orchard hill. She patted them each on the head before they turned to walk home. That one simple act stung me. Sometimes I forgot I had a mother to begin with. Hearing Cen's story made her real again.

"She was brought to the clinic by four soldiers, her stomach swollen and bursting," he told me. "She'd escaped from her imprisonment and was attempting to cross Deshan's borders in order to save your life and hers. One soldier explained in low tones to me that the king himself gave them orders to kill her, but that they would spare her unborn child as an act of mercy. They did not tell me where your mother came from, what crime she committed, or who the father was," Cen whispered. It didn't matter how many times he told me the story, tears always welled up in his eyes. "The soldiers gave us some privacy for her delivery, and that is when she told me all about her hopes for you—her only distraction from the pain.

"She begged me to raise you myself; apparently she had no friends or relatives who would be able to take you in. She told me that I must raise you to be brave and good and kind.

"I did everything I could to save her, Emi," Cen told me, and I knew he was speaking the truth. He pleaded with the soldiers to spare her life, he begged on his knees, offering payment, services, and silence if they would let her go—but they shook their heads repeating again and again, "We have orders from the crown." So Cen kept me as his own, despite his old age, raising me to become his replacement as the village healer.

"And all she left me is that letter?" I asked. "Just that one letter?" I knew what his response would be. He'd seen me search her letter hundreds of times. It was so worn out that the parchment was soft to the touch and most of the words were beginning to fade. It didn't matter if they faded. It didn't matter if they disappeared completely. I knew every one. Every curve of every S, the distance between each word—the beautiful ferocity of her tone.

"Yes, that's all she left besides you." He winced when he said that, often avoiding my eye for hours after. I knew that he wished he had something else to offer.

We turned back to our work, the mood more somber now. I asked him to tell me about my mother often because occasionally he would provide a new detail, an embellishment I hadn't heard before. I knew the story so well I could picture it in my head—sweat soaking her hair, her teeth gritted in pain. Those few precious moments she held me in her arms. I always asked him if I looked like her, but I could never get a direct response from him about that. "I didn't see her long. But you have her skin. She had beautiful skin." He was avoiding the obvious response. I knew I didn't look like my mother, a Savian. The girls in the village made certain to tease me for my light skin and blue eyes behind my back. Although we all descended from the same forefathers, many believed that Brockans had paler skin and eyes, while Savians sported darker features. As for me, I didn't see much of a difference. I turned back to my stitches and thought about my mother—about her being a Savian.

That much I was reminded of on a daily basis. I am reminded that my mother was a Savian every day I see a Brockan soldier beat one of my neighbors in the streets of the village. I know she was a Savian because of where I live—on the outskirts of the capital, in an orchard village—just one of the many that surround the kingdom of Deshan, patrolled by Brockan soldiers that whip us for sneaking one cherry, one olive, one fig into our hungry mouths.

Every day my neighbors in the village work in the orchards, the fruit of our labor belonging to the king. We get a meager allowance once a month of cornmeal and milk, some beans if we are lucky, and the old fruit that has gone bad before it gets to the capital. There is a village well where we draw water to drink and bathe and cook with. Most of us tend to a small plot of soil outside our homes; it's the only way we can feed our empty bellies.

At a moment's notice, our fathers, mothers, brothers, and sisters—if we are lucky enough to still have them—could be killed for a minor infraction, innocent or not. We are watched carefully and not allowed to venture outside of the village perimeter. The night I heard the conversation in the orchard very well could have ended my life. There would have been no trial; no explanation given to Cen. Every judge and every soldier is Brockan, leaving us no one to turn to with our pleas. We live by mercy, although very little is offered. The king's guards patrol our cities night and day, and we as Savians know our place as slaves to the Brockan king of Deshan.

* * * * *

"I'm going out," I told Cen the next evening. We had treated only two patients all day, and one of them had come in for a nosebleed. Besides, Cen had been yawning since dinner. "I need to draw some water at the well for tomorrow's treatments. I'll go now so you can get some sleep." He eyed me curiously. Since that night in the orchard, I had been afraid to venture out on my own, preferring to stick close to home, especially as dusk approached.

"You're sure?" In the past, he argued with me when I told him I would stay up and monitor the clinic. These days, he was so tired that he welcomed any opportunity he was given to sleep. "Be safe," he warned, as he headed up the stairs to the loft. "I'll prep for tomorrow while you're out. I love you!"

"I love you more!" I yelled back, walking out to the makeshift stable behind the clinic. It housed our horse, Lexon, a gray, spotted, straggly steed. He wasn't the finest horse, but he was faster than he looked and we were lucky to have him. Since we sometimes have to make emergency visits around the village, the Brockan soldiers allow us to keep him—so long as we keep him fed and out of their way.

The trip to the well wasn't far, but still he whinnied softly as I entered, eager to get out. I understood. It had been days since I left the clinic without Cen, and weeks since I'd ridden Lexon. And it was hot tonight—but then again, every night was hot in Deshan.

The main well was crowded when I got there, a swarm gathered to draw water for their bathing and cooking. Some patients nodded toward me, but no one said a word. Soldiers monitored the area, making sure no family drew more than their allotted two buckets.

I was told that the well used to be a place of conversation and cama-raderie. For as long as I could remember, though, it has been heavily monitored. After waiting in line and retrieving my buckets, Lexon and I meandered back to the clinic, passing several soldiers who pushed their uniforms aside to show the knives on their belts. I didn't have to spur Lexon to make our walk past them faster.

After unloading the water into the storage buckets I drew the shades, settling in to read up on natural cures for insect bites.

I was reading about fatal bee stings when the knock came. It was so weak I ignored it, thinking it was the wind or someone knocking on the neighbor's door, but then it came again, this time even fainter than the first. It had been hours since I had returned from the well and it was late now—too late for someone to come for healing. Unless it was an emergency, the soldiers would never allow someone to be on the streets at this hour. I set my book down, plac-ing the marker in it, and walked to the door. "Who is it?" I called cautiously through the wood.

When there was no response, I cracked the door open a little until it was stopped suddenly by something. Not by a tree or a rock though—a body. I moved through the small gap and almost stepped onto a boy lying on the rocky dirt in front of the door, his arm strewn limply across his small frame. I dropped to my knees, reaching to find his pulse. It was there, but barely, and his breaths were uneven. "Cen!" I called loudly. The boy was not tall, and he was so thin I could probably have carried him in myself but I remembered what Cen told me about head injuries. *Do not move them if you can help it. It may do more harm than good.*

Cen rushed down moments later, his ratty brown robe tied hastily around his frail shoulders. "What is it?" he exclaimed, rub-bing his eyes. "Who's there?"

"A boy!" I shouted back. "I need your help to get him inside."

Cen sprang to life, racing toward the door where I knelt, his knobbly knees more spry than they looked. "Take his feet," he ordered as he firmly cradled his head. He was lighter than most patients we had to lift, so we easily hoisted him inside and up on the exam bed—a makeshift mat woven together with hay bales and covered with a coarse cloth. "Get my kit," Cen said with a grim face as I rushed to retrieve it from the cupboard. With squinting eyes, Cen examined the boy's face in the flickering candlelight. That was the first time I had the chance to really observe him.

He was small but wiry, with dark hair that fell like a hood around his face—definitely a Savian. I guessed that he was a few years younger than me, not older than fourteen. His clothes were filthy; dirt and sweat mingled with what smelled like a bad infection. It was the first time I had ever seen him, which meant he was not from Kalvos. There were a few villages not too far from here, but there was no way of traveling across villages this late at night unless it was through the forest, and the forest at night wasn't safe for anyone—especially a Savian after curfew.

"His leg," Cen murmured. "Clean it while I treat his fever." He began to rub jusen on the boy's temples, massaging the green cream in a circular motion. I sprang forward, examining his right leg, which looked less like a leg and more like a skinny tree trunk. Huge scratches intertwined around each other, blood and infection weeping from open sores. I set a pot of water on to boil and scrapped some bandages. While the water boiled I grated olint root into it, infusing the air with a sweet, woody scent.

Cen stood with his face close to the boy's, examining his breathing. "His fever is extreme," he mused, concerned. "There's something very wrong if the jusen won't improve it at all."

I began to dip bandages into the boiling pot. "He's not from Kalvos. He must have come through the forest. But how did he make it here? He had enough strength to knock but when I opened the door he was already unconscious."

Cen frowned. "If he came through the woods, it was very foolish, especially in his condition. He may have soldiers following him. If that is the case, we must be especially careful." He stood up and locked the door, pressing the bolt in with a rattled click. We both knew that flimsy door wouldn't protect us though. If the situation weren't so serious we might have laughed at Cen's precaution.

I brought the pot to the table and began to lay the bandage strips gently on the boy's tattered legs. He shook when I placed the first one, and Cen reached for his head to keep it steady. With each strip I placed, he twitched, moans escaping from his lips. "Can you understand me?" Cen asked him, speaking softly into his ear. "If you can understand me, shake your head." There was no movement from the boy, but as I wrapped the leg tightly with fresh cloth, his breathing seemed to become stronger.

"His chest," I observed to Cen, who murmured in acquiescence, watching his breaths intently.

"He's responding to the root. But what else is wrong?" Cen considered, rubbing his jaw with his knuckles.

I stood back with Cen, watching the boy's chest rise and fall. There was no more movement after I finished with his leg. No more twitching or moaning either. I racked my mind with his symptoms—fever, infection, and unconsciousness. His head seemed intact, with no injuries sustained there.

"Garmin pox?" I suggested, but I ruled it out before Cen even shook his head. Sores would be all over his body if that were the case, instead of just on his legs.

Cen stood over my shoulder, his hands stroking his chin nervously. "Kiusjna?" he proposed doubtfully a few minutes later.

"Yes," I agreed. "His feet. We need to check his feet."

Carefully, we removed his boots, pulling them off so as not to disturb his bandages. A pair of threadbare socks, tattered with holes were resting halfway off in the boot. As soon as we removed the socks, Cen gasped aloud. Rings of purple rippled across the soles of his feet, both pulsing so hard we could see the throbbing. The stench was putrid.

I ran to the cupboard to rummage for carmine ointment. We made batches of it at a time, since it was the cure-all for most rashes. "Emi, carmine won't fix it," Cen protested. "It's more than a rash. Kiusjna is internal—it affects more than just the infected area. And who knows how long he has been sick? I've never seen someone become unconscious from kiusjna."

I frowned, twitching my lip anxiously. "You're right. His legs are too scraped up to tell if the rash spread there, but tomorrow when we remove the bandages we will have a better idea."

Cen nodded. "Right. All we can do at this point is wait and see how far the rings spread."

I frowned, observing the boy. His chest was still rising and falling, which was a relief, but his feet were extremely swollen. I wondered how long he walked before arriving at our clinic—how he even knew about our clinic. Cen was the best healer in Kalvos, of course—the only healer, besides the one who treated the soldiers at their barracks. We sometimes had a few patients come from neighboring villages, but it was rare. Often they had to have a permit and a soldier escort.

"You can go to bed," I offered. I was too awake now to even think about sleep, and although Cen was attentive now, I worried about him. He pushed himself too hard, working long hours in the clinic, rarely taking a break even when we had the time. "I'll stay up with him. I'm not tired anyway," I lied.

"No, I'll stay up. I already had some sleep. Besides, I need to observe his progress and I am concerned that there may be soldiers looking for him. What if they came while I was asleep upstairs? I could never do that to you." I knew he was thinking about my incident in the orchard just a couple weeks before. Looming olive trees and ferocious soldiers that morphed into dogs or other creatures had haunted my dreams lately. And that was if I was lucky enough to fall asleep to begin with.

"Please let me, Cen. It would be a relief not to have to sleep tonight."

He sighed, raising his unruly, gray eyebrows. "Are you still having dreams? About the soldiers?"

I shrugged. Of course Cen knew about my nightmares. With just the two of us here in the clinic, we knew everything about each other. He heard my screams in my sleep and often woke with me to calm me down, his hands stroking my back as I sobbed. We never talked about the nightmares though, carrying on in the morning like nothing happened, opening the clinic, feeding Lexon, making

scones, or stewing an antidote. I think Cen wanted me to feel safe
while I was awake, even though reality was just as chilling as the
nightmares that burrowed their way into my dreams. I changed the
subject, "If there are soldiers following him . . . what will happen to
us? Could we be punished for treating him?"

Cen nodded, pursing his lips. "Yes. We could be punished."

I swallowed. If this boy was a fugitive, sheltering and aiding
him would be considered treason. Even if he were just an average
citizen we could be punished for treating someone from a neighboring village without reporting it to them. "But the king hasn't died
yet, so there are still rules for the soldiers, right, Cen?" I wanted so
badly to feel safe. "I mean, we couldn't be punished for just taking
in a sick person, especially a young boy."

Cen exhaled slowly. "It doesn't matter what their rules are or
what the punishment will be. We are healers, so we do what we
can to help our people regardless of the potential punishment." He
paused. "And that includes this boy."

I looked down at the boy's distressed face, the fever far from
breaking, and the steady pulsing in his feet. I understood then. It
didn't matter how much danger we would be in for treating him or
any other person who came to us. We were healers. We would do
it anyway.

*　*　*　*

"Hello?" came a weak voice as the sun rose the next morning,
breaking through the rough glass of the clinic windows.

I stood up suddenly, letting my book fall with a heavy clunk to
the floor, its pages spread open. "You're awake!" I exclaimed, "Or
you're conscious, I mean. How are you feeling? How did you get
here? What's your name?" I was so absorbed by my book that I
didn't realize the sun was fighting its way over the Deshan Mountains and my candle was nothing more than a puddle of wax.

The boy grimaced as he looked down at his leg, struggling to sit
up. "First, could I bother you for some tea? My throat is parched,
and I feel I could stomach it." I eyed him. It looked like he could

use a lot more than just tea. His bones threatened to erupt from his thin skin, and his cheeks were sallow and sunken in. Starvation wasn't a hard diagnosis.

I pulled several logs from under the kiln and tossed them in before mixing together an herb blend that is good for those with weak stomachs. A dash of piorn, a scoop of thyen, and a few drops of honey mixed with water. If he could keep the tea down, I would make him some corn cakes—maybe even the scraps of bacon that we were saving. "What a relief to see you awake," I said as the fire stoked, its flames snapping and breaking down the logs. "Cen and I were worried about you last night."

He perked up boyishly. "Cen? Cen the healer? I hoped I would find him."

"How did you hear about Cen? And were you followed?" I asked, which seemed to be the most important question of all. If soldiers did pursue him, it wouldn't be long before we received a visit.

He grimaced again in pain, his teeth grinding together. "Some soldiers and dogs hunted me through the woods, but they lost track of me. Once I got to your village I asked a local where the clinic was."

"You were foolish to travel so far in your condition," I scolded him as I poured the boiling tea into a ceramic mug. "You could have sent a messenger. Cen might have been able to come to you— or at least tell your healer how to treat it."

He almost gulped the hot tea. It made me cringe a little thinking about him burning his throat but I understood. I knew the desperate ache of hunger, the body's way of shutting down without food. Things like the temperature of the food or drink were never important when you were that hollow. "I couldn't . . . have sent a messenger," he stammered out, draining what was left of the tea.

Before I got the chance to ask him what he meant, Cen walked around the corner from the loft, his white hair sticking out in tufts like a bird's feathers. "Ah, good, you're awake! You gave us a scare last night! Now, tell us everything. How you got here, how long you have suffered, what village you are from, if you are being followed, and on and on." Cen waved his hands as he spoke, a habit I acquired from him.

The boy smiled weakly, setting his empty cup on the table near the bed. "I will tell you everything. But first, could I bother you for something to eat?" He eyed the pantry door. There wasn't much inside—some meal and flour, maybe some wafers—but I had the feeling that he wouldn't be too particular.

Cen nodded. "Yes, please start at the beginning, and while you talk, I'll make us all some breakfast. A patient dropped by some bacon yesterday as repayment for a toothache I treated last month. It's not much, just some scraps he was able to trade the soldiers for, but your awakening calls for a celebration."

I sat back to listen with a smile while Cen pulled the bacon from the cupboard. Bacon was a treat even for us, but the boy looked like he might cry at the mention of it.

He scowled in pain as he propped himself up. "First, let me say thank you . . . I don't remember much from last night, but I think you saved my life. Believe me when I say that I will do anything in my power to repay you."

Cen nodded; we were used to hearing speeches like this one. The people we treated were grateful, sincerely grateful. However, once they regained their strength it was often easy for them to forget the pain or discomfort they were in before. Most patients never came back to pay until another issue arose. The money we did receive we used to buy more supplies for the clinic, and we lived off the gifts that were not monetary. We were used to healing for free. "It is our privilege to heal our people," Cen reminded me anytime I complained.

"My name is Maddock. I come from the southeast orchard village, Collina, just two over from yours. The large forest to the east and several miles are all that separate us." Cen nodded as if he knew of the village, but I would have no way of knowing. The only place I had ever been to was the market at the capital to purchase supplies—but we needed a permit from the soldiers to even do that, and we were punished if we were late for curfew, so we never stayed long. The boy continued, "I noticed the illness coming on a few weeks ago. It started with feelings of dizziness and chills of hot and cold. My feet were sore, but I didn't notice the rings around the bottom of them until a few days ago when they kept going numb."

Cen wrinkled his forehead in confusion. "You should have come sooner. Doesn't Collina have a healer?"

Maddock looked down. "Not anymore," he replied after some hesitation. Creases formed along his brow, deeper than they should have been for a boy his age.

"But what happened to your healer?" I asked, "Surely they must have a replacement . . . All villages are supposed to have one."

Maddock kept his eyes on the ground then whispered, "He's dead . . . So many are dead."

Cen looked up at me sharply and walked over to Maddock's bed, kneeling with great effort. "Maddock, I know you are afraid," he offered compassionately. "But I need you to tell us what is going on. We can't help you if we don't know everything."

Maddock shook his head, his lower lip quivering. "My whole village," he croaked out, "they're all sick. Many have died already. They locked us up—set up gates so we can't get out. I ran away to find you . . . They said you could help."

His eyes filled with tears, ready to spill over at any minute. He opened his mouth again, but a knock at the door kept him from saying anything more.

3

*O*pen the door, healer!" the voice called out. The knocking shook the doorframe, and dust fell from the eaves.

Frantically, I searched for somewhere to hide Maddock.

"Pantry," Cen mouthed to me, his eyes electrified as he called out to the soldiers at the door. "I'm coming! Just a moment."

We each took an arm and a leg, heaving Maddock across the room and into the pantry. Cen positioned him on a bucket of oats and with shaking arms, cleared a shelf to elevate his leg. "Not a sound," he whispered to Maddock, closing the door gently.

I yanked an apron around my waist and turned to the kiln, rotating the bacon that was beginning to heat, its woody scent filling the clinic air, crackling loudly in the pan.

Cen slid the latch and opened the door. I didn't dare turn around, but I could tell there were several soldiers by the sound of their swords all being drawn out of their sheaths.

"Gentlemen," Cen greeted, "what can I do for you?" His voice was steady. "Do one of you require treatment?"

A voice spoke up. "No. We are looking for someone. A boy about this tall. He escaped from prison a few villages over last night and a neighbor of yours mentioned some suspiciously loud noises coming from your clinic. We wondered if you'd seen him. He's got . . ." The soldier paused. "He's got a disease. We don't want anyone else to pick it up." If I weren't afraid I would have laughed. The soldiers had never cared about our well-being before; why would they mind if Maddock spread his disease to our village?

I lifted my eyes from the smoking bacon and dared to look at the soldiers. One was eyeing me curiously from the doorway, his hair streaked with dirt from the long trek he must have taken through the forest. For a moment I imagined that he was there in the orchard all of those nights before—one of the men plotting against the king. Then I realized that these were not our soldiers. They must have come from Maddock's village after pursuing him through the night.

Cen looked at me sharply and then spoke up. "Yes, there was a bit of noise. You see, we had a patient come in with a severe fever, nothing that couldn't be treated. Unfortunately, it was not a boy, but a young girl. Her cries must have alerted the neighbors."

I looked back at the doorway. The dirt-streaked soldier was definitely looking at me now. "You," he spat, "girl. Come here."

I looked at Cen desperately, who nodded calmly in reassurance. Before I went to the door I removed the tray from the kiln with a rag and then edged closer, making sure to stand behind Cen. "Yes, sir?" I asked, feeling my voice shake.

He grunted. "You're an able-bodied Savian and you're not in the orchards. What are you doing here at this hour?"

Cen put his arm on mine protectively. "We received permission years ago for her to stay with me. She is my assistant, learning how to become the village healer. It is a position that takes a lifetime to learn, which is why she does not work in the orchards with the rest of the Savians her age."

Another soldier spoke up, "I thought those exceptions were just for the Capital Savians—the servants in the palace and vendors in the market. Do you have documentation on her? Written documentation?"

Cen nodded. "Yes, of course. Allow me to retrieve it."

"And you won't mind if we search the place while you do." The gruff soldier who spoke to me first barged in. "This boy is important. We must find him." I couldn't help but tense up as he mentioned Maddock. How could a sick young boy be so important to them?

Cen shrugged coolly. "Look around if you must. Just please, no touching anything if you can. There are some sterile instruments I would like to remain that way." His composure always astounded me. He walked over to his cupboard full of papers while the soldiers, their swords still drawn, stomped in and began to poke around. With all of them in here, the clinic was crowded. Clumsily, they bumped into each other as their boots hit the wooden floor.

I eyed the pantry door. It was mere feet away from the gruff soldier, who was shorter up close than he looked outside. To send this many soldiers to pursue one Savian boy was strange. What did they want from him? He tapped closer to the pantry door, kneeling on the ground to inspect the floorboards. If I weren't so terrified of them finding Maddock, I would have laughed at his thoroughness. There had never been anything to hide in the clinic I realized— until now.

The soldier reached for the handle of the pantry just as Cen spun around and shouted, "Ahh! Here is my documentation. I apologize for the delay. I should really keep this parchment handy, but it has been so long since I was asked for it."

The soldier eyed the pantry door and stepped toward Cen, reaching his hand out. After examining it he looked at me, as though to verify my age and handed the paper back to Cen. "Very well then, I think we've seen all we need to see here, men. Nothing more to be done." I glanced at Cen. No one else would have noticed, but I knew him well enough to see that he was digging his nails into his palms—something he did rarely and only when he was afraid.

"We'll be back," the gruff soldier called out. The dirt-streaked one looked at me a little longer, shaking his head. Then, almost as an afterthought, he walked toward me and lifted the entire tray of bacon with his gloved hand, gnawing on the first piece before he even shut the door. All he left behind was the briny scent.

I peered out the window to make sure they were actually leaving, their white cloaks trailing behind them. Only then did I release the breath that I was subconsciously holding. We were safe for now. All three of us.

✳ ✳ ✳ ✳

As soon as the soldiers left, we constructed a makeshift room for Maddock in the loft so that he was somewhat separated from Cen and me but still out of the open clinic. I lifted a tattered blanket over his cot in our loft, draping it like a child's backyard fort. It wasn't much, but it did offer him a little more privacy.

For the next several days, Cen made it my responsibility to take care of his fluctuating fever and observe the rash that seemed to grow further up his legs, twisting like a vine. "Once it reaches his heart, it stops," Cen told me one night, while Maddock snored softly in the corner. "We have to find a cure before then."

As a result, anytime I wasn't downstairs with Cen, I was researching kiusjna in our stacks of books. It was such an old disease that it was strange how quickly Cen made his diagnosis. Then again, Cen was gifted. He seemed to know absolutely everything. We had never treated it before, but Cen was hopeful that a cure existed. Hope was the only tool we had.

In the evenings Maddock told us long, wild stories about the village he came from. He said Brockan soldiers had killed both of his parents for minor transgressions, and with no one to take care of him and his younger brother, Levi, they were thrown into prison for wandering the streets to beg for food. It was in prison that he discovered the rings on Levi's feet. Levi lay awake many nights with fever, and Maddock pleaded with the guards to offer him some treatment to no avail.

"There were others, too, who began to show signs of the disease," Maddock explained. "The old and weak contracted it first, but soon enough there was not one prisoner who did not have the rings on their feet and the feverish nightmares that accompanied them." His voice hushed as he spoke about his time in prison, closing his eyes for long periods of time before continuing.

It was in prison that he first heard about Cen. "There was a man there who called himself Rodmin. He said that Cen treated his father years and years ago. He told me that the only way to cure this was to find him—that he was some kind of miracle healer. Our village healer died years ago and no one was left to take his place." Maddock shook his head. "A few weeks later I woke up with the rings myself. I thought it was all over then."

Maddock was only fourteen, but he carried himself much more maturely, the kind of maturity that was evidence of a life of grief. "When we got released," he continued, "Rodmin told us to go to his house. It was empty and we had nothing else. So Levi and I lived there for a week, taking care of each other and trying to figure out what to do next. We boiled roots we dug up from the forest to eat. That was all we had." That explained his emaciated face—his scraggy limbs.

"While we were in prison, the guards built iron gates tall enough to hold us all inside the village—inside with the plague that was killing us." His eyes grew distant. "The wailing was unbearable."

Cen shuddered. "I've never heard of such a thing. A plague to destroy an entire village. And with no healer!" He rested his hand on my back, rubbing it lightly while I hunched over on the bed, wanting to know but, at the same time, not wanting to know the horrors my people were experiencing. There had been epidemics before of course, pox and the flu—but nothing like this.

Maddock nodded, as though he couldn't really believe it either. "One morning, after I had spent most of the night tending to Levi's fever and nightmares, I realized I would lose him next, just like so many had already lost. So I gathered water for him, enough to last for weeks. I scavenged for food and spent the last of our savings on some bread and meat. Then I scaled the iron walls to find you like

Rodmin said." He shrugged. "I didn't realize that anyone would notice, but the soldiers must have seen me running and sent men after me. They tracked me all the way here with their dogs. I'm not sure why my life even matters to them, but clearly they didn't want any of us to get out of our village."

A few tears slid down his face, and Cen reached for his hand. He was never one to shy away from compassionate gestures. "Levi is still there," Maddock murmured, "all alone."

Cen attempted a smile. "We will take care of Levi," he said, "as soon as we figure out how to get you well."

Maddock's shoulders shook as another tear slid down his cheek. "Just get me better, and I'll be on my way. There is so much to be done," he said, then repeated, "so very, very much to be done."

*　✳︎　*　✳︎　*

The rain didn't fall often in Deshan, but when it did it was warm and humid—the air heavy and thick. It was a rainy after-noon when I finally found a reference to kiusjna in our books.

Kiusjna is sometimes referred to as the silver plague, because of the shiny rings of silver around the purple rash. The rash takes the form of a ring, much like what is found in a tree stump, and spreads from the feet toward the heart.

"Yes!" I exclaimed, startling Maddock, who was standing over my shoulder, steadying himself with a cane.

"Did you find my cure?" he asked shyly, a sad smile creeping over his face.

I shook my head, "Not yet—but I did find some interesting information. Apparently it used to be called 'The Silver Plague,' because of—"

"The rings of silver around the purple rash," Maddock inter-rupted. "I already found that. Cen lent me some books to read while you see patients." He shrugged. "It gets a little boring just sitting around and waiting to die." I knew he meant it as a joke, but neither of us laughed.

"You can read then?" I asked, trying to change the subject.

Cen taught me to read when I was young, but most Savians are never taught.

"My mother taught me," he replied with a solemn look. "Both me and Levi. We used to practice our letters when she got home from the orchard. We never had this many books though." He gestured to my stack on the floor.

This new information gave me an idea. I pushed my braid around my shoulder. "If you can read, you can help," I said as gently as I could. "You have more time than I do. You can read while I treat patients. Maybe you'll find something."

He offered a sad smile before returning back to bed. "It's too hard," he said, pausing, "to search for something that's not there. Besides, I'm tired." He had been standing for less than five minutes. I marveled at the fact that he made it through the forest to our clinic a few weeks prior, when now just a couple of steps could wear him out so completely.

I continued searching while he slept. My nightmares were the same since the incident in the orchard. Even after I went to bed, I tossed and turned—waking to Maddock's snores mingled with two words he repeated again and again.

"Gates," he muttered, twisting in his blanket feverishly. "Run."

4

The weeks of Maddock's sickness were their own universe. With the change of seasons we experienced an influx of patients needing treatment for difficulty breathing, swollen throats, and excessive heat. Whenever we weren't in the clinic, we were studying or experimenting with treatments and stepping upstairs to tend to Maddock even when we had several patients waiting. It felt at times that all of life would stop when his did. We lived for Maddock, somehow believing that our hope could save him—until one morning. The universe shifted, never to be the same again.

I woke to loud voices blaring from the clinic below. "Fix this! And do it now!" I rubbed my eyes and sat up slowly, blearily trying to make out the conversation. The voice was angry. When Cen replied to it, he sounded almost hostile.

"I'm sorry but I cannot heal this infection," Cen said. "I have a line of patients already forming outside my door. There are women and children who need attention. Please, sir, there is a clinic for Brockan soldiers in the barracks just over the hill."

"You will treat the infection now," the voice demanded. "I've heard that you are the best healer in Kalvos. Far better than the fool in the barracks. Man doesn't even know where to begin with this! Besides, you have no say in whether you treat it or not. How dare you defy orders from me? A superior!"

I pulled my worn leather pants on over my sleeping tunic and buttoned them as I tiptoed down the stairs that led into the clinic. I carefully dodged the fifth step from the bottom—it squeaked, and I'd had years of practice sneaking out of the house to ride Lexon early in the mornings.

"I could treat it," Cen responded slowly, clearly attempting to mediate the conversation with careful words. "However, I do not feel completely comfortable treating it since you cannot tell me what it is from. You said you underwent a procedure at the palace? Perhaps they could treat it there. I wouldn't want to interfere with what the Royal Healer did."

The Brockan butted in. "My commanding officer won't give me leave to go to the palace for another week. Who knows what could happen to me by then? You'll take care of it, and you'll do it now!"

I dared to peek around the corner where I was concealed and caught a glimpse of the man. He had black hair and a smattering of black freckles. His booming voice seemed oddly familiar. I wondered if he was in the orchard that night a few months before, or maybe he came in to search the clinic after Maddock arrived? I couldn't be sure. All of the soldiers seemed the same to me, as I'm sure we all seemed the same to them. There was a dirty white bandage dangling from the skin near his collarbone, just above his heart.

Cen cleared his throat. "I am not sure how to treat this infection, but I will do what I can. Please allow me to retrieve my daughter from upstairs—she can treat the other patients who are waiting and will be expected at the orchards soon."

"Get on it with it then!" the soldier spat out, kicking Cen's stool to the ground, where it fell with a dull thud.

I concealed myself against the corner, reaching out to him as he rounded the corner. With a finger to his lips, he motioned for me to go upstairs. Softly, we walked to the top of the loft. "Treat Maddock first," he said in a hushed whisper. "Then come down."

I nodded, not realizing I was shaking until Cen enveloped me in his frail embrace. I could feel his heart thumping in his chest as I nuzzled my head against it. It seemed faint, but for the first time I was grateful for that heartbeat of his. He was all I had. After releasing me, he didn't say another word before turning around again and hobbling down the narrow steps.

The clinic door swung open. I could hear the cluster of individuals, all forming a line to see us even if I couldn't see them. They hushed, I'm assuming, when they saw a soldier standing in the doorway. "Clinic's closed until I'm treated," the soldier yelled out. "From now on, soldiers receive first priority at this clinic and you lot will not be treated until every Brockan soldier is taken care of first. Now get to the orchards!" He slammed the door, and I stood with my eyes closed, trembling at the rage in his voice.

I crouched beside Maddock, who was sweating wildly; his forehead trickled with beads that ran in rivers down his face. "What's happening?" he asked, pushing himself up. "Who's there?"

I mopped up the sweat with a damp rag and began to rub jusen into his temples. "It's a soldier," I whispered back. "He's here for an infection. You'll have to be quiet."

He nodded in acknowledgment and lay back down. Fortunately I'd set out some pre-dipped bandages the night before to make this morning smoother. Quietly, I replaced the soiled bandages with clean ones. The rings were creeping up, so high that they almost reached his waist. Only a week ago they were at his knee. We were running out of time, if we were going to save him at all.

I walked down the stairs when Maddock was finished, just as Cen gathered his materials to create a remedy. "Who's this?" the soldier snarled, looking me up and down. "Your daughter?"

Cen nodded. "Yes. She is a fine healer."

I held my head high as I approached the soldier, careful not to show any signs of fear. "What is the matter?" I asked, motioning to the spot near his collarbone, controlling my voice. "A wound? An infection?"

The soldier curled his beefy lips up in a pout. "Not sure really. A few weeks back, all of us soldiers were summoned to the capital. It seems there is a new disease spreading around. The healer there cut open this hole," he explained, gesturing to the wound, "then he poured some kind of fiery liquid inside. Hurt like you wouldn't believe. Weeks later, here I am, and the cut they made turned into this grisly mess." He frowned. "They said it might happen, but that it was rare. Course it happened to me, considering my luck."

"Can I see it? Do you mind?" I asked, more to Cen than to the soldier. Cen nodded nervously, and the soldier pulled his white uniform down to expose the infection a little more. There was an incision about the size of my pinky finger running across his upper chest. It was red and puffy, with white spots of discharge. "Did they tell you," I asked pointedly as I reached for a towel to clean up the weeping infection, "what the new disease is?"

Cen looked at me crossly as he stirred, but I had to know. What if it was kiusjna?

"Not sure," the soldier replied. "It's supposed to be a secret but I heard rumors that it's something to do with bad water and feet. That's all I know, and they made us stand in a long line during the hottest part of the day." He looked up at me warily. "Why? You seen anything like it?" He blinked, and I noticed his hazel eyes. They seemed kind maybe, underneath his gruff exterior. I wondered if all of the soldiers were really as cruel as they made themselves out to be.

I shook my head, "No, I've never seen it before."

We treated him in silence after that, and he left less than an hour later, his infection completely cleared. The wound on his chest was just a scratch now, a permanent stripe above his heart. If you weren't looking for it, you might not even notice it was there.

* * * * *

The day I found a treatment for Maddock's disease was the same day we received news of the king's death. A fever, they said, the soldiers gathering the whole village in the square to inform us.

It was the hottest day we had seen that year. Heat choked the air, dense and heavy as though the sun's rays were wedged in between heaven and earth. Although he was a Brockan king, we as Savians were still his subjects and forced to mourn his loss. The village flags were flown at half-mast, and no soldiers ventured into the clinic, perhaps more from an effort to stay out of the heat than respect for the king. Since there were no patients to treat, I finally had time to research.

I sat on the wooden floor, piles of books behind me. I'd scoured every inch of them, their words and pages worn from my use and the healers before me. I reached up for an old medicine book I knew well, fanning myself with a scrap of parchment. It was old—so old that there were occasional Sansikwan words thrown in with our Brockan/Savian dialect. I rolled my eyes at some of the treatments suggested for well-known illnesses. Kifa bark for heat rash, and sarng for the pox was laughable. No one used those anymore. Just as I was about to put the book aside, I flipped through the pages as a last effort and passed an illustration of what looked like kiusjna. Fanning back, I found the page. Rings of purple were depicted snaking up a leg. "Yes!" I exclaimed loudly, waking Maddock.

"What?" he whispered frantically, sitting up in bed.

I brought the book over to him eagerly. "I think I've found it! I can't believe I didn't realize that we've been looking under the wrong name. Kiusjna is what we call it now, ever since our languages blended after the second Great War. But this book is older, much older than that. Vox is what they call kiusjna—or what they used to call it at least . . . It hasn't been a problem in Deshan in years. No doubt they didn't feel it important to include it in more recent healing books."

"Vox? Is there a cure?" he asked excited, his puffy eyes lighting up.

Cen came in the door then, "I heard your scream. Is everything all right?" He was holding a large stick behind his back, and Maddock and I erupted in laughter before Cen held a finger to his lips. Sheepishly, he set it down with a shrug. "We can't be too careful."

"I think we found it!" I told Cen with a smile so wide it almost hurt. "We've been looking under the wrong name. Vox is what we should have been looking for."

Cen dropped the stick with a thud, and flew to my side, taking the book from me. "Vox . . . of course. My father mentioned . . ." He stroked the page, reading each word with furrowed brows and then handed it back to me with a fallen countenance. "But is there a cure?"

I grabbed the book back and began to read, trying to interpret the old language. "To temporarily relieve the vox, farknon and lucius must be ground together to form a paste-like liquid. The paste should be ingested twice a day for a fortnight." I set the book down. "Temporary relief? We don't want to temporarily heal it." I looked at Maddock, who bit his lip as if he were about to cry.

Cen's eyes lowered to the book. "Does it mention anything permanent?"

I scanned over the page again, shaking my head. "No, nothing," I replied softly. There was a faint outline near the bottom where it looked as though someone had written in the book. I turned the book at an angle, trying to decipher the scrawl, but it was in Sansikwan and so faint I could barely see what was there.

"Look here!" I motioned to Cen. "Someone tried to write something in it."

Cen took the book from me, squinting as he observed the page. "Ninety-one," he murmured. "Ninety-one what?" I took the book from him and saw the number scrawled on the edge of the page. Ninety-one. There were some other symbols, too, written faintly, but nothing I could decipher. Just then the clinic door rattled and Cen gave a shrug, then left to hobble down the steps.

Maddock sat with his fist almost buried in his mouth. "This is unbelievable," he murmured. "The one thing that could save my life . . . That could allow me to save my brother—it's hopeless." His voice broke. "It's probably too late for him anyway," he spat bitterly. "He's probably already gone. I left him alone. He died alone."

I shook my head, tears forming in my eyes. "All is not lost. We will find another way. Another cure will exist."

But when the words came out of my mouth they felt like a lie.

Together, Cen and I formed the paste the book suggested, feeding it to Maddock with a spoon. He shuddered as it went down and promptly fell asleep.

We gave him the paste for two weeks, just like the book suggested, but nothing really changed.

One night I went to check on him before bed and saw that he had flung his tunic off, no doubt from the heat of his fever finally breaking. But the rings were still there, resting right below his rib cage now. This treatment route was hopeless—something had to be done. And with Cen as weak and frail as he was, I was the one who would have to do it.

5

I left in the night before anyone could stop me. Cen would try, that I knew, and recently the soldiers had become stricter than ever about curfew. Fortunately, I knew of a back road out of the village that was rarely guarded. I dressed in an old yellow dress a patient had traded for treatment, and my riding boots. Usually I wore leather pants and a tunic, but if I was going to the palace, I had to look my best.

Silently, I braided my hair, securing it with a torn piece of bandage. Then with a creak, I lifted the floorboard downstairs that kept my savings—five finla wrapped tightly in a piece of leather. I also gathered a small pouch with a few old figs and a crust of dried-out bread.

Hastily, I scrawled a note in the dark and left it for Cen to find.

Cen,

> *I went to the capital to find a cure. There are*
> *vendors in the marketplace there that might know*
> *what to do. It's not just for Maddock. It's for his entire*

village—for everyone in the future we could treat if we
knew how. My entire life I have been told I could pass for
a Brockan, so now is my chance to try.

Please forgive me for leaving you like this. I just
couldn't bear to let Maddock die without trying abso-
lutely everything.

I love you always and I will be back soon.

Emi

Their snores bid me farewell.

Lexon was excited to see me even at this hour, stomping his hind legs and searching my pack for a carrot that wasn't there. Poor horse—we rarely had treats to share with him. I shushed him in the dark, stroking his broad forehead, praying that his whinnies would not wake any neighbors. I let him lick my fingers for a few seconds, until he finally realized there was nothing to be had and snorted into the patchy grass behind the clinic. "Shhh. We're going on an adventure. I need your help on this one," I whispered.

Carefully, I tucked my money into the pouch at my waist and guided Lexon out on foot. I sang to him softly, certain that only the two of us would hear. If the song worked for me in my times of fear and doubt, perhaps it would also work for him. And I could use a little extra courage too.

Ring out the bells,
Pull up your boots,
Sing out your voice
Steady and true.

Have heart in the fear
And faith in the new,
Heaven's stars are fighting
Their battles for you.

The village was eerie at night without the usual soldiers marching around or chatting with their backs against their doors. No bakers selling day-old bread, no vendors attempting to barter the rotten fruits and vegetables that they scavenged from the orchard floors. For a moment I considered turning back—Cen would be so hurt knowing that I left without telling him. Then I thought of the rings on Maddock's chest, so close to his heart—of the tears he wept for his brother. I kept walking.

When I made it outside of the village gates, I mounted Lexon and whispered softly in his ear, "To the capital." I would go to the marketplace first. I'd never been without Cen but remembered the way. Surely someone there would be able to help me. Lexon paused for a moment but then trotted along the dark, dusty road. Only one road led to the capital, and he knew the way from going with us to buy supplies. "Take me to the capital, boy," I reaffirmed as we raced on, the moonlight guiding our path.

* ✳ * ✳ *

We arrived at the capital just as the sun came up. It was a relief to have traveled without incident; there had been no bandits or, worse, soldiers to stop me. I saw the occasional nomad walking the path alone, but no one gave me any trouble. It was eerie riding in the dark with only the sound of horse hooves, the path lit by a brilliant moon.

The capital's marketplace was not entirely unfamiliar to me, but it seemed that each time I went, there was something strange or new to see. Anything could be purchased at the marketplace: live animals in cages, smoked salmon, leather boots, and headscarves, which often hung on posts twirling in the breeze.

Even early in the morning, foods of all kind were being sold from vendors: Rods with roasted pigs, squirrels, and lamb, the smoke settling stubbornly in the sticky air. Pickles as long as a man's arm and hot buttery scones that dissolved the instant they touched your tongue, as though made of air. Honeycomb cut fresh from the hive, the sides sticky, amber, and intoxicatingly sweet, served with large slabs of thick, hot bread. Fish along an entire row, their slithery silver and pink bodies naked on icy crates, which melted into mini rivers that spread like veins across the stony ground of the capital courtyard.

Rows of vendors sold figs, olives, nuts, dates, cherries, and warm bread, each calling out their costs, promising a better bargain than their neighbors mere inches away. Old women with missing teeth sat on stools calling out, "Braid? Lemme braid your hair, girl. Lemme braid your hair. Only half finla. Half finla only." Brockans mingled with Savians, and old men haggled with buyers. Little children with sad eyes and hollow stomachs scampered around, some stealing money, and others attempting desperately to lead more traffic to their parents' stands. These children's parents were personal slaves to the Brockan merchants, placed in the marketplace to sell their master's wares. I wondered how different their lives were from those of us in the orchards and fields.

The castle loomed above it all, its domes sparkling in the heat, reflecting the sun that it seemed so close to. Trees surrounded the enormous golden gates, as though the elements themselves were protecting the royal court from outsiders—Savians like me.

I rode Lexon through the city gates, stopping so that he could take a much-deserved drink of water from the outside well. Once we arrived, I tied him to a wooden post, guarded by two heavy men. The post was on the edge of the square, next to some crude huts. I could see a woman and two children sleeping inside. "Two finla for the day, or we can't promise your horse will be here when you return," one of them told me with a slanted eye.

"Two finla?" I protested. I only had five with me. Two finla would leave me with only three to pay for the supplies—or information—I needed. "Before it was less. Half a finla," I offered, remembering the cost when Cen and I came last.

"Half is the regular rate. Today's a special occasion. No promises your horse will be here when you return if you pay less," the slanted eye man spoke again, eyeing Lexon up and down. "We'll get more than enough business on a day like this one. And from the looks of it, your horse looks like he's worth a bit more than two finla, although not much." He laughed, stroking his broad belly.

"Fine," I replied, rolling my eyes and then rummaging in my satchel for the money. "I don't believe that today is different than any other, but I'm warning you: if he's not well fed and kept in the shade when I return, I expect my money back." I felt brave today. Perhaps it was the way I made it out of the village and to the capital by myself. Maybe it was my determination to find a cure. Either way, it felt good.

Unfazed by my weak threat, the man nodded, clearly amused, and held out his hand to retrieve the money. "I'll return as soon as I can," I whispered to Lexon. I kissed his nose before entering the marketplace, already overwhelmed by the smells. Children skittered around my feet as I walked, and I inhaled slowly, looking around for anyone, anything, that might provide some answers.

It was already hot, even though the sun had just risen over the mountains behind the castle. I wandered up and down the aisles as vendors shouted to me, "Dried figs! You won't find them fresher anywhere else!" or "Rare Goldfish! Real gold! Only thirteen finla an ounce!"

The herbs and other medicines were kept on the row right over from the fish. I approached a quiet vendor at the edge of the row, whose wares were covered in baskets. He was a Savian with a black turban on his head and deep, tanned wrinkles that overwhelmed his face. "What do you have there, sir?" I asked, curious.

He smiled up at me, displaying a scattering of teeth and gums. "Is there something in particular you are searching for?" His voice was raspy and he curled his fingers in front of his face, beckoning me to come closer.

I nodded, lifting my hand to shield the sun from my face. "Yes. Are you aware of any healers in the marketplace? Anyone who could help me locate some information? There's a disease . . . ," I stumbled, trying to find the right words. "My friend is very sick, and I must speak to a healer."

The man's face fell, and he stood quickly, getting uncomfortably close to me. "What is this disease you speak of?" he whispered, looking around the square nervously.

I stammered. What was making this man so anxious? I leaned closer to him. "Vox."

His eyes grew wide and he backed away from me. "I will have none of that!" he yelled, his hands stretched out as if to ward me off. "I will not hear another mention of that!" His eyes darted back and forth. "Not on such a day as this! Not outside the royal gates!"

I flushed, swiveling my head nervously. Other vendors and shoppers were beginning to look at us strangely. "I . . . ," I stammered. "I'm sorry, sir." I walked backward, hoping to get away from him and the unwanted attention.

I spent the next several morning hours looking for a healer or a cure, but many had the same reaction as the first man. Vox was being talked about in the marketplace, that was certain. The only problem is no one wanted to talk to a stranger about it, and no one seemed to know any more than I did about it. My heart sunk as I stumbled away from the stench of the fish rows and the perfume of the herbs. I was so close to the cure I could feel it. So close to saving Maddock. I walked over to the gates, pressing my face against their golden turrets. I stood for several minutes at those gates, looking up at the vast, white castle looming on the hill just beyond my reach before a soldier waved me away politely. "Please, miss, no one can touch the gates," he said jovially. Then almost as an afterthought, he piped up, "But that is a brilliant dress."

I stepped back, my first instinct to be afraid, until I realized that he was truly flattering me. He thought I was a Brockan girl. "My apologies," I murmured with a smile at his kindness. He couldn't have been much older than I was, with dark hair that hung across his forehead beneath the soldier's cap. I began to step away, but as I turned I saw something—a flash of white peeking out of the soldier's uniform. A bandage. I wondered if it covered a wound right above his heart, the same placement as the soldier from the clinic.

He locked eyes with me for a moment when I refused to look away, clearly flattered, "Is there something I can do for you, miss?" he asked with a wide, toothy grin.

"I was just noticing the bandage peeking out of your uniform," I said with a forced giggle. "I hope you were not wounded in battle." I sucked in a deep breath.

The young soldier offered a grin. "It was not from battle, unfortunately." He rolled his eyes, gesturing to the palace. "I'm just finishing training so I spend most of my time here, although I am being transferred to monitor some villages shortly. Hopefully I'll see some more action there."

I nodded, uninterested in his transfer. "What is your wound from?" I asked, trying to mimic the girls from my village and the way they flirted with boys our age. I had no experience of my own. The only boys I spoke to were patients, and most were young children or old men.

He frowned, squinting into the sunlight. "Every Brockan soldier who is sent to the outer villages is required to have one. Some sort of protection, they say, from the dirty Savians and their maladies." He laughed, looking to me for a reaction, and I feigned a smile even though his insult made my stomach churn.

"I see," I replied, turning to go.

"Are you here to see the procession?" he asked before I could step away, his voice eager. "There's quite a crowd gathering, as you can see. It's going to be a busy day for us. They are sending extra reinforcements in for it." He leaned casually against the gates, brushing back his hair.

I ignored him and scanned the square. It always seemed crowded to me compared to the village, but he was right. Today it was busier than usual, large groups clustering around the gates. There were Brockan men, women, and children, cooling themselves with elaborate silk fans, watching the square but not purchasing anything. "Yes," I replied, squinting at the reflection coming off the golden gates. "I wouldn't miss it." His commander called for him. "Kye! Transfer!" He gave me a wink before turning to go.

I sat down on a wall near the gates and pulled my knees up, resting my head on them. The vendors' reaction to my mention of the vox, the soldiers who wore matching bandages only when being deported to the villages . . . I scanned my memory thinking of the information the soldier in the clinic gave me the day we treated him. What had he said about the disease? "Bad water," he had said. "Bad water and—" But what came after the "and"?

I sat for what felt like hours, trying to think of the word. I lifted my eyes and scanned the crowd. "Bad water and . . ." How could my mind fail me like this? A makeshift ball of rags and string rolled toward me and interrupted my thoughts. I squinted into the sunlight as a scrawny Savian child ran to retrieve it. His face was alight with joy and sun, but there was something wrong too. He ran slower than he should have and seemed out of breath. My gaze went to his feet, which were bare and covered in rings. Vox. It wasn't just in Maddock's village. It was here. That was why the man had such a violent reaction. The word sprang into my mind almost immediately. "Bad water and feet," I repeated aloud, as I picked up the ball and held it out to the boy.

"I'm sorry, miss. Master brought me today from our village and told me to be a good boy. Please don't be angry," he begged. With my dress and pale skin, evidently I appeared to be a Brockan woman. Up close I noticed the beads of sweat racing down his forehead. His disease was new, but it wouldn't take long for a boy that small. His heart was already close to his feet. Tears pricked my eyes as I handed the ball back to him.

"Take these," I said, offering him the three finla left in my pouch. That money would do me no good here. It was information I needed. With a shout, he thanked me and ran off.

As I sat in the humming marketplace, I pieced together the information I had. Vox had to be the disease the soldier at the gates was talking about, which meant that whatever procedure the soldier's were getting on their chests was an antidote. Or a future prevention—something to protect the soldiers stationed at villages from contracting it too. Without that knowledge of what was in the antidote I would never be able to save Maddock or the rest of his village. But how could I retrieve it? Who would be willing to give a poor Savian girl information that seemed so carefully guarded by the capital? I closed my eyes and prayed, knowing it would take much, much more than a simple Savian girl like me could do to find a cure.

Amid the usual chaos, I suddenly heard a large commotion near the east gates, interrupting my thoughts. A horn blew from within the palace, but the hustle occurred here in the market. All at once, the sound of the market seemed to dull, all eyes turning toward a group of Brockan guards marching with their hands on the hilts of the swords they kept gleaming at their waists, ready to pull out at a moment's notice. Marching guards were a common occurrence in the marketplace, but this time was different.

In the middle of the guards was a cluster of girls that looked about my same age. This must be the procession the soldier spoke of. Each girl wore a scarf tied around her head the same way I always did, and they were wearing long dresses and braids. I thought that they would look frightened with soldiers standing on every side of them, but they looked almost happy. I could tell that all of the girls were Brockan, with their ornate dresses and jewelry. One thing was certain—every girl was undeniably beautiful. I could tell from the hush in the marketplace that my fellow market-goers thought so too. Each girl seemed more beautiful than the next, yet I could never have chosen whose features, whose structure was the best. They all seemed to outdo each other, their long hair cascading down their backs in intricate braids under the scarves; their faces glowed in the sunlight yet none of them squinted at the sun. They all smiled, revealing perfect teeth and delicate faces.

The guard at the front took a sharp right, and the entire line turned and walked to the gate near me. I heard it open behind me, its golden hinges creaking gently. The gate was opening for them— these girls were going inside the palace. And all at once, I knew what had to be done.

I got down from the wall and walked quickly to keep in line with them, pushing against the crowd that was trying to get a good look. Some of the people held white handkerchiefs out, waving them eagerly in the girls' direction. I stepped quickly, trying to get as close as possible to the group. A few men and women elbowed me out of the way, but I persisted. They were getting so close to the gate. I saw my opportunity at the back of the line. I elbowed through the crowd, my teeth gritted, and pushed forward until I fell hard, right in the middle of the group.

My knees hit the ground forcefully, tearing my skirt, and I felt gravel pierce my palms. I could see the soldier boots around me as I panted on my hands and knees, too afraid to look up. I wasn't sure what to do next. Someone pulled me gently to my feet, "My sincere apologies, miss," I heard a soldier speak, but I was certain he was not speaking to me. "I didn't see you there." I dared to look up, and his eyes met mine. The entire group had stopped at the gates as the soldier pulled me to my feet. "I'm a bit clumsy, you see. I must have stepped on the back of your gown. Please forgive me."

I forced a smile, feeling my legs shake under my skirts. "That's quite fine. Thank you for helping me up. I'm afraid I am the clumsy one."

He nodded ahead to the soldier at the front of the group, and they moved forward again. I lifted my skirts to keep up with the rest of the girls, who were all a few steps ahead of me. Some of them had turned around, waving and blowing kisses to the admiring crowd that cheered for them as we entered. I heard the clang of the castle gates close and looked up at the sparkling building ahead of me—ominous and looming. It had never seemed as threatening before as it did at that very moment, but surely a place as grand as this harbored secrets. Maybe even answers for the disease that was ravaging a whole village.

My heart seemed to pound in my throat, and I could barely put one foot in front of the other, almost completely paralyzed with fear. As we marched up the front steps of the palace, my muscles lost all feeling, going completely numb. I realized that each step I took in was another I would have to take out.

I wondered how many Savians had ever come out of these gates alive.

6

We climbed the seemingly endless stone steps to the entrance, the crowd cheering us wildly and still waving white handkerchiefs in our direction. I was the last girl to step into the palace. Sweat, caused more from fear than heat, pooled across my hairline. A legion of soldiers greeted us inside, bowing their heads respectfully as we strolled into the marble foyer. A gasp escaped my throat, my nerves electrified.

I had never seen anything like the inside of the palace—not even the drawings in my books could adequately depict what it felt like to step inside such a grand place. If I were not in so much danger, it might have seemed beautiful. In my current state, however, everything was stark. We stood in the foyer at the steps of the white staircase. Everything was white—white walls that seemed to disappear into the sky itself, white marbled floors with gold specks that glittered in the sunlight, and white drapes that stretched to heaven. Art hung on the walls, huge pieces that lent the only color to the entryway. They depicted warriors, black horses, and women with long hair that wrapped around entire paintings. Most of the other girls seemed as enthralled by the palace interior as me, although some were biting their nails or tapping their feet nervously. I wondered what they had to be worried about. There was no way we were here to be slaves. They were Brockans and dressed far too fine. Perhaps this was a palace tour, some kind of reward for the upper class Brockan girls. We waited as a group in silence until a sound echoed through the hall—the clack-clack of shoes approaching.

A woman emerged, her thick, silver braid swooshing back and forth as her heels continued to clack-clack, the only sound I could hear. Even though the market was just a few hundred yards from the palace gates, it was completely silent except for the footsteps on the marble. Four soldiers flanked the silver-haired woman, and she offered us a kind smile before walking up the marble staircase in the center of the foyer. After walking up a few steps, she turned around to face us, her white skirts so long they grazed the step beneath her.

As soon as the woman turned, the girl directly in front of me sunk into a low curtsy, and the others in the group followed suite, kneeling first, and then prostrating onto the cold marble. I looked around at them, feeling my own knees bend. *This woman is the queen,* I finally grasped. *I am a Savian girl, and I am standing in front of the queen.* My mind was thick with fear. As I bowed I realized that she was *their* queen, not mine. I did not feel any respect for her. She had never done anything for me, yet I knelt, knowing I had no choice.

After I knelt with my face on the cool floor for several seconds, the woman murmured, "Rise," and I rose slowly with the other girls, assessing their reactions. Every face I saw was beaming, their eyes locked onto the queen. "Ladies, it is wonderful to have you here," she said, her kind eyes searching the crowd. When her eyes caught mine, I quickly averted them. *She knows I am a Savian. She is going to have me killed.* My legs shook uncontrollably beneath my skirt.

"As you know, my dear husband, King Jairus, passed away just a few weeks ago, which is why you have all been gathered here: to participate in the most important program this nation has." I felt a rush of blood from my face and wished for a moment that Cen were here. He could fix my horrible mistake. He always did.

The girls nodded in solemnity, all of their once-beaming faces lined with sadness now. "My scouts gathered the most eligible girls from the finest Brockan families in the kingdom. You are the most talented, most educated, most beautiful girls in Deshan. You have left your families, your homes, everything—in the hopes that you will someday become the next queen of your people." My cheeks flushed. No wonder everyone in the marketplace cheered them on and waved handkerchiefs at them. They knew that one of these girls was their future queen. I looked down at my faded dress and scuffed riding boots, the dirt buried beneath my nails. What seemed so fine this morning now seemed embarrassing and strange. I didn't belong here. Even if I were Brockan I wouldn't have fit in.

"As you know, it is traditional for the queen to be chosen in this way. You will be placed in the south mansion on the castle grounds away from the main palace. You will reside in the home for a year—learning philosophy, history, and foreign languages. You'll be tutored on household management, poise, and conversation, and above all, you'll have supervised visits in the form of six balls with my son, Prince Corban—the future king of Deshan." She spoke these last words proudly, as though his title was as precious as he evidently was to her. The girls around me smiled at the mention of the prince, some of them giggling and others tilting their heads higher, their faces intent on the queen's.

"You will be given further instruction on the rules of the program, but I will emphasize a few for you now. First of all, you must stay in the mansion at all times, unless a soldier escorts you to a class or another building on the premises. There will be no wandering around the palace grounds. Second, visits with family members or friends will not be allowed for the entirety of the year. Letters may be written, but the palace advisors will censor even those. I apologize for that, but we cannot be too careful in these dangerous and uncertain times." I wondered what she meant by that—if she knew about what the soldiers spoke of in the orchards.

Her countenance changed suddenly, and her voice rose in tone and precision. "This is how the queens were chosen anciently. This is also," she said, softening, "how I was chosen. This process should be treated with respect and taken very seriously. Every one of us is eager to find the best-suited queen to reign over Deshan. Because the world outside the palace provides a distraction to you young girls, you will be supervised night and day by the soldiers who surround you now." I looked around me at the Brockan soldiers who had escorted us in. Many looked around proudly at their good fortune to guard a group of young women for a year. I kept myself from shuddering—eventually I would have to go around them to make my escape.

"Now, I will say this once and only once," the queen said, her voice echoing against the white walls. "*Do not* leave the house unaccompanied by a guard. There are many who would like to hurt you. One of you is the future queen, making each of you extremely valuable commodities to this kingdom. Be selective about your associations here, and be careful about your actions at all times. We desire for you to return safely to your families at the end of this year." I dared to look up and saw that she was looking directly at me. She held my gaze for several moments. I thought at first that she was staring at my gown, but it was my eyes that she was so intently focused on. I held hers and, hoping not to seem obvious, offered a smile. She looked away and abruptly clapped twice. A hefty middle-aged woman with stark features and a long, pointed nose stepped out from a corner and walked briskly toward us. "This is Hortense. She is in charge of the program and I chose her to look after you. Please treat her with the respect she deserves. She will give you further instructions. Farewell for now. I will see you again at our first ball." Hortense bowed her head solemnly, and the queen walked up the staircase, disappearing around a corner.

Hortense looked us up and down with a smirk. Her nose was so long that it almost fell to her lips. She finally nodded. "Follow me then."

She led us briskly through the palace. At first I tried to make sense of all of the twists and turns so I could find my way out, but the halls seemed to continue endlessly and I soon lost track. Everything in the palace was white or gold. White floors with specks of gold in the marble and white walls and furnishings with gold metallic accents lit up the rooms we passed. We followed her in silence, and once we exited the palace, we were led through gardens that were more beautiful than anything I had ever imagined—perfectly hedged bushes, exotic flowers, and crystal blue pools spouted water from ceramic dolphin mouths. White cabanas with sheer curtains dotted the gardens, sporting lush furniture and purple satin pillows. Bright colored birds walked around the grounds freely in clusters. I think I even saw a zebra peeking out of a bush.

I squinted my eyes at the beauty of it all and for a moment I forgot that I was a Savian girl in a Brockan castle, intruding on this group of girls, one of whom would be my future queen. Perhaps I could stay. Then I thought of Maddock and his suffering, the rings closing in on his heart. I could not forget my purpose.

Hortense led us silently past a series of gardens and pools until we reached a large, white stone house in the back corner of the palace grounds. The mountain behind the palace provided shade at this hour. Palms bowed in front of the porch and orange lilies bloomed cheerfully from flowerbeds. Two soldiers stood on either side of the entrance, their expressions stoic, their swords drawn and held in front of their faces. Hortense whispered something to the one on the left, and he nodded his head, letting us enter.

The house was a smaller version of the palace, with white plaster walls and marbled floors. We were led through the main floor that sported a common room with several large sofas and chairs, a classroom, a library, a dining room, and a dance hall. There was also a large kitchen, although no one was preparing food at the time. The entire upstairs was one giant room with two dozen white beds lined up on either side. The beds were canopied, and beside each was a washstand with white towels folded neatly on top.

"This will be your home for the next year," Hortense said, turning to face us. "You may each choose a bed, and then we will commence our tour." Shyly, we all stood where we were, waiting for others to choose. Hortense spoke coarsely, "Go on! We have a very tight schedule."

I waited while the twenty girls chose their beds—some of them grasping each other's hands and whispering about the castle, the grounds, and the prince. I eyed a bed that no one drifted to in the far corner of the room near a window and the doors to the balcony. I had to get out of here, and that bed might provide the best escape route. I walked timidly outside to the balcony to observe the height of the wall and the kind of landing I would sustain when I did escape. Deep rivets lined the stone and a pool lay directly below the balcony. The stone looked easier to scale than the smooth mud walls at home, and although landing in the pool might be loud, at least I wouldn't break my legs if I did fall. I exhaled anxiously and turned around to enter the room again, only to come face-to-face with a girl I had not seen standing with the group before.

Her features were sharp and stunning, with high cheekbones and a delicate nose. Her long auburn hair fell freely to her waist, with a thick braid wrapping around the crown of her head. She had radiant olive skin and piercing green eyes that seemed to smile along with the rest of her face. "I'm Younda," she offered with a smile, "from the capital. What's your name? I've never seen you before at any events. Are you new to Deshan?" Her voice was extraordinarily sweet.

I smiled tensely. Why hadn't I thought of an identity sooner? Of course I would be asked this question. Most of these girls probably ran in the same circles in upper class Deshan, and I would bet that several had met the queen before as well.

Searching my memory for places I could be from, I thanked the heavens that Cen had made geography a focus of my studies.

"I was born in Canton," I said finally, naming a region in south Deshan known for its excellent cattle, steep mountain roads, and ugly women. "My father is very protective and I don't get out much."

Surely none of the other girls were from Canton; it was probably a safe choice.

She eyed me suspiciously but smiled, seeming to believe my story. "Wonderful. I have never had the pleasure of visiting Canton, although I hear their livestock is excellent. I did not expect anyone from Canton to be here." She eyed my clothing curiously. Even in my finest dress, I was still wearing my dirty riding boots, and my dress looked like rags compared to the luxurious dress she wore. I placed my hand awkwardly over a stain on the hip. "And what is your name?" she asked, smoothing her violet skirts down.

I scoured my mind for a name. Any name. "Larken," I replied finally, meeting her eyes. "Larken of Canton." It was a name I read once in a book of tales. Larken was a fairy that outwitted humans by transforming into a bird every time one of them saw her. It was not the best name I could have thought of, but it was certainly much better than my real name: Emi of Kalvos the orchard village, healer's apprentice and Savian orphan.

Hortense clapped twice and cleared her throat behind Younda, who was smiling strangely at me, her head cocked to the side. "It is wonderful to have met you, Larken of Canton," she whispered, as we reentered the room to join the rest of the girls. "I am eager to get to know you even better." The voice that sounded so sweet moments ago now seemed almost hostile.

We stood around Hortense as she carried on a long speech about respecting the royal family by respecting their palace grounds, but I barely heard a word. The sun was beginning to set outside, and pinks and oranges were fusing across the sky. Seeing those colors made me think desperately of Cen pacing the floors at the clinic, struggling to treat the patients while he was wild with worry for me. Would he have the energy to do it alone? I pictured him running to our neighbors' homes after the patients had all gone, asking them if they saw me leave, if they knew anything. I thought of Lexon still tied to that awful man's post, certain to be sold in the morning if I did not reach him first. Last of all I thought of Maddock and wondered if the rings had spread, wondered if Cen could treat his fever while also taking care of the other patients and soldiers who came to the clinic.

I needed to find the treatment and go home to Cen, Maddock, and the rest of my village. I was their healer. These other girls—these rich Brockan girls—could afford to stay here for a year and compete for the prince and his heart, but not me. Every moment I was here was another ring, another second of Maddock's short life—and of Cen's fear and worry. When I get home I would promise to never leave him again.

That moment was the first time I realized what a terrible, desperate mistake it had been to throw myself into that crowd of girls. But it would not be the last.

* * * * *

They fed us in the large dining room under a dozen small gold chandeliers that spanned the length of the table. There was more food on one table than I had ever seen in my life: mounds of fresh white fish peppered with something red and sweet, a green salad with figs and cheese, and piping hot rolls drizzled with nectar. I ate until I was sick, oblivious to the fact that the other girls seemed to just pick at their food. When I finally looked up from my plate, my eyes met with a dozen others, their owners staring at me open mouthed. I smiled weakly with my mouth still full, swallowed, and nodded toward the plates of food. "Delicious, isn't it?"

Silence filled the room and Hortense patted her lips with a napkin. "Quite delicious," she replied, her eyes assessing my scrawny frame and thin face. I knew she must have been wondering how I stayed so thin when I ate so much. What she didn't know was that this was the first time I ever remembered eating until I was full. It was the most wonderful feeling in the world.

"Madame Hortense?" I asked, trying to fill the silence. Besides my comment on the food, it was the first time I had said anything at dinner. Now I had the whole table looking at me expectantly. Some of the girls whispered to each other—no doubt about my dress or my eating habits. Probably both.

"Yes?" she asked disdainfully, her nose in the air as she sipped her tea.

"I wondered if you could tell me where the healer is located within the palace?"

She coughed into her cup. "Excuse me, Miss Larken? Why is it that you need to visit the healer so soon? Do you have an injury or an illness that I should be aware of?"

I forced a smile. "Not exactly. It was more out of curiosity. I wondered where it was located. In case I did become ill." It was a weak explanation, and I could tell she thought so too. I forced myself to breathe deeply, picturing myself reuniting with Cen and sleeping in my own bed above the clinic the following night.

She shook her head. "You will learn your way around the grounds soon enough. Also, you will never go anywhere without an escort by a guard. You would know that if you were listening to Her Majesty's speech earlier." Some of the girls giggled, including Younda, the girl who had spoken to me on the balcony.

I flushed in embarrassment and turned back to my plate, not expecting her to say another word. The rest of the girls whispered to each other again, and then Hortense spoke up. "But if you must know, the healer is located on the west side of the palace grounds in a house not unlike this one."

I looked up gratefully, attempting to ignore the stares that were continuing to come my way. "Thank you, madame."

That night I pretended to prepare for bed with the other girls, who had not spoken to me since before dinner, but in actuality I was preparing to pay a visit to the palace clinic. I braided my hair in a tight knot and tucked my headscarf into my boots. The other girls had almost ten trunks each, brought up by the royal valets. They opened them to reveal elaborately printed silks and cottons in deep purples, pinks, and blues. I heard one girl mumble to another, "The queen wore white. I was told that blues were in this season."

Her friend hissed back at her, "White is always in style, Olia. It is the royal color! Did you not notice the castle? All white."

Hortense noticed that I had arrived with no luggage. She impatiently asked a valet where my trunks were. He told Hortense that they must have gotten lost en route. "I'll do my best to find them, miss," he repeated to me over and over, his face red with embarrassment.

I smiled nervously and responded, "I'm sure they'll turn up somewhere. Canton is far away; it is easy to see how they might be misplaced. Until then I will have to make do with what I have."

Hortense glanced down at my dirty boots and tattered skirt suspiciously. When no one offered to lend me a nightdress or a hairbrush, she took me downstairs to a linen cupboard with a dozen folded white nightgowns and conjured up a hairbrush for me as well. The nightgown was more beautiful than anything I had ever worn, with silk ribbon lacing the bodice and tied in a wide bow across the chest. I put it on in the corner, with my back turned to the rest of the girls, who chatted with excitement to each other about being in the castle grounds for a year. Occasionally I heard a shriek of excitement and a chorus of giggles. I climbed under the covers with the nightdress and boots while the other girls finished dressing. Facing the wall as though I were sleeping, I stared out the window at the moon, praying that it would stay bright tonight—just long enough for me to find my way to the healer and then find my way home.

7

y fear kept me awake. The fear of all of those soldiers watching the mansion. The fear of going home with no answers. The fear of Cen's broken heart. It seemed like hours until all of the girls finally went to bed, and though my tired eyes begged for sleep, I knew I couldn't wait another day. This was my chance, and I had to take it.

Soon enough I was left with only the sounds of breathing and the occasional sleepy sigh. Someone in the far corner was snoring loudly, and I wished for a moment that I knew who it was so I could thank her for masking the sound of my footsteps on the marble floor. I reminded myself that if everything went as planned; I would never get the chance to thank her.

I tiptoed toward the balcony, praying that no soldiers were pacing the courtyard below. But as I turned the lock to get outside, I heard a gasp directly behind me.

Anxiously, I turned to see a girl sitting up in her bed just a few over from mine, her face buried in her hands. Fortunately Hortense had drawn the curtains before we went to sleep, and I was close enough to them to conceal myself. I doubted she could see through them, even with the moonlight. Through the curtain I could see her sobbing into her nightdress sleeve, trying to catch her breath. She stood up slowly, carefully putting on her slippers and to my horror, pitter-pattered toward my hiding place in the curtains.

Up close I recognized her from dinner. She had been seated across from me and to the left one seat. Her hair was thick and plaited with gold leaves and her pale rose dress was the finest of any of the girls' apparel. She had a pretty face with blushed cheeks and large amber eyes. An array of freckles splattered her face. I watched her turn the handle to the balcony and step out into the darkness, leaving the door propped open slightly, inviting in the warm desert air that seemed even drier at night.

I had two choices: turn back to my bed at the risk of alarming her and waking the other girls, or stay where I was. I quickly ruled out the second option. If she turned around to get back inside, she would see me through the window. A thought came to my mind—it was the last thing I wanted to do, but I knew if I could comfort her and get her back to bed, I could make my escape.

"You couldn't sleep either?" I asked her in a whisper, gently closing the door behind me so as not to wake the other girls.

She gasped and turned around, clasping her hands to her heart. "Oh! You frightened me!" She held onto the edge of the balcony. "How long have you been awake? Oh, I look so awful! I'm sorry! I couldn't sleep and I couldn't stop thinking about home. Not that the palace isn't lovely and perfect, because it is but I . . . I . . ." Her voice trailed off, and she burst into sobs, burying her face in her nightdress sleeve again, her shoulders shaking with emotion.

I stepped toward her to grab her free hand. One thing I had learned from working at the clinic is that the power of touch must not be underestimated.

"It's hard, I know," I said softly. She nodded, her face still buried in her sleeve. "Don't you . . . want to be the queen?" I prodded when she still refused to speak. I barely knew how to speak to girls my age. Occasionally the girls in my village would host sewing parties or dances, but I was rarely invited and seldom went even if I was. I didn't have much free time, and the precious free time I did have I spent riding Lexon.

Minutes passed before she let her red, splotchy eyes meet mine. "Are you homesick?" I tried again, eager to get moving.

She nodded and then buried her face into her hands again to sob even more. Her shoulders heaved up and down, and I began to feel a little homesick just watching her. "It's hard, I know," I said again, thinking of how frightened I would feel leaving home for a full year. I was frightened enough after being here for a matter of hours.

She sobbed for several minutes but eventually caught her breath and raised her head out of her hands to face me. Our eyes met, and she forced a smile through her tears. "I'm Jessra of Roding," she finally offered. Her voice sounded funny, her nose still stuffed from crying.

"Em—I'm Larken," I told her. "Of Canton." She raised her eyebrows faintly when I stumbled through my name, but did not comment on it, leaning against the railing of the balcony, rubbing her eyes with her fingers, and struggling to gain her composure.

While she did that I scoured the surroundings. From here I saw a hanging lantern and two soldiers standing at attention on the sidewall, their silhouettes lengthening and shortening as they shifted their weight. They were laughing softly. A dog lounged nearby them. I knew I could get around the soldiers, but the dog? It would definitely sniff me out—certainly the palace dogs were trained to sense an intruder from miles away. I couldn't see any more soldiers; although with the number of trees surrounding the mansion, there had to be more nearby.

"Larken, I am terribly sorry to have woken you with my silly behavior," Jessra said, breaking my observations of the mansion's property. "It was not fair to you. I just . . . miss home already, and being here in the palace with all of these other girls who are so wonderful and charming . . . it's all a bit overwhelming."

You have no idea, I thought.

"It's getting so late, so I should head to bed. I want to be ready for classes tomorrow. But thank you for your kindness. I can already see that you are a good friend." She offered a quick curtsy with her nightdress before turning around to open the door, disappearing behind the curtains into the room of slumbering girls.

I released a sigh of relief. Finally, it was time.

Before I began, I made sure Jessra actually went to bed. I saw her climb in and turn on her side with her back toward me, her long braid falling off the bed and dusting the floor. Then I mapped my plan out in my head: Climb down the vine and get to the group of palms about forty paces from the pool. If I could get there, I hoped to see the wall just beyond. From there, I could walk around the perimeter, traveling west until I found the clinic—and the healer. I hoped that he was a kind man who would help me. If not, I would just have to improvise. Then I would go back to the marketplace where I left Lexon. I prayed he wouldn't be sold.

You can do this, Emi, I told myself. *You have to do this.* I hoisted myself onto the balcony railing and turned around, finding my footing below. Vines climbed up the wall to the balcony and although I couldn't trust them to hold me, they provided some comfort, just in case I couldn't find my footing with the rock. I eased myself down the wall, every muscle in my body tense and alert. I had done this dozens of times in the clinic, but I was just realizing how much closer I was to the ground from our little loft window than I was with this mansion and its vaulted ceilings. I dared to look down and tried to focus. I still had a long way to fall. I kept moving until I felt my nightgown catch on something. A thorn? Not daring to let it rip and alert the soldiers and dogs, I shifted my weight and reached down with one hand to free the skirt. Just then I lost my grip and frantically reached for whatever bearing I could get—a handful of leaves and the vine.

Its thorns tore through my skin and the nightgown, shredding both as I fell. I finally got a bearing on a sturdy bit of vine and a piece of marble that jutted out about ten feet from the ground. As

I clung to the vines, my body thumped against the wall, my head colliding into it.

I painfully dropped to the ground, vaguely aware of a dog barking in the distance. When I closed my eyes, vibrant circles of light swam inside my eyelids. I heard soldiers talking loudly while the barking got rowdier. With a shaking hand I touched my head and felt something wet against the base of my skull. Blood. Seeing it on my fingertips pricked my senses. I had to move. The barks were getting closer, the voices louder. I had to move immediately.

Flattening myself against the wall and looking ahead at the group of palms—my original intended destination—I realized that they were much further than I had estimated from the balcony—at least seventy paces. And to go around the pool as I had planned would mean putting myself in the light, directly in front of the soldiers that stood on either side of the mansion. All at once I realized what I had to do. If I went *through* the pool, not only would I stay out of the light, but I might also throw off the dogs to my scent.

I crawled to the edge of the pool, feeling my head pulse steadily, and watched as the soldiers and dogs formed a group on the east side of the mansion. Their voices were raised and alert. With them preoccupied, I silently submerged myself in the cold water. As quietly as possible, I swam, diving deep and rising only when necessary to take a deep breath at the surface. My heavy riding boots felt like iron weights on my feet, so I concentrated on my breathing, on making my muscles fluid—in sync with the pull of the water. Once I reached the edge, I turned around with my head against the rim, my body still immersed, and observed my surroundings. Two soldiers stood at the corner attempting to calm the dogs that were still barking furiously in my direction. Hidden under the shadows of the palms at this end of the pool, I was certain that they could not see me, but for how long?

The soldiers with the dogs began walking in my direction, one hand on their sword hilts, the other holding the dogs' ropes. A soldier held a lantern and yelled at the dogs, "Calm down, boys! There's nothing out here!" The dogs pulled on their leashes in my direction, and I was certain that my heart would burst, and I would drown. My feet wove in and out, pulling my body toward the bottom of the pool.

A loud crack in the distance averted the dogs' attention, and the soldiers began walking around to the other side of the house. This was my chance. Using every muscle my arms possessed, I pulled myself out to the pool's edge while the dogs were focused elsewhere. Once I was out, I ran madly to the group of palms, my boots squishing on the stone beneath me. With a thud, I sank against the back of a tree in the circle of palms to inspect my wounds.

My palms were ragged from the vines and my right arm was gashed from my wrist to my elbow. The pool seemed to help clean the cut somewhat, but it was still bleeding heavily, water mixing with the blood and dripping down onto my lap. *I'll have to have Cen stitch it when I get back to the clinic,* I thought, my eyes filling with tears. I couldn't risk taking the time to treat it here with dogs on the loose. My head was pounding, and I felt dizzy, but fortunately those were my only damages—besides the nightgown, which was completely unsalvageable at this point. It was torn almost in half, and the right side rose nearly to my upper thigh. It was inappropriate, but I could hardly think of that right now. I had to get out of this mess.

From where I stood, I could see the wall right behind me, but it was too high for me to see the top of it through the palm leaves. I walked cautiously toward the wall, determined not to make a sound, but with my wet boots and the ground littered with fronds, it was increasingly difficult. I developed a system where I took several steps, then waited behind a tree until I determined the shortest distance to the next tree. It might not have been the quickest solution, but making a sound and alerting the dogs would be a worse outcome. At last I stood with my back against the final tree. The wall was tall, and in the dark it seemed endless, curving behind the mansion and the pools we walked through. It might take me hours to reach the clinic at this rate, and how would I know once I found it?

I decided to run for it. My vision was fading, and I knew it was from loss of blood, but I couldn't quit now. I ran several hundred yards along the side of the wall, stumbling from pain, my legs shaking with each step. Then, as I began to slow, I felt two arms grab me and hurtle me to the ground. I lay dazed, making out the soldier's face briefly. I heard shouts for help and dogs barking. Then everything went black.

8

I blinked into the light. As my eyes adjusted, I found I was lying in a bright room with sheer curtains that blew gently in the breeze. The light was piercing in its purity. I sat up and felt something on my arm—a wrapped bandage. Someone had applied green kerian gum to the cuts on my other arm, and they were mostly healed. *Good to know that someone here knows what they are doing,* I thought absently. A pitcher of ice water and a glass sat on a small table by the bed and two velvet purple chairs perched across the room.

"Ah, our young patient awakes." A tall, thin man with black curly hair and a kind face entered the room, rolling up the sleeves of his tunic. "How are you feeling, dear one? You gave us quite a fright. Jolom was beside himself. He babbled on and on about harming the future queen of Deshan." He chuckled. "Poor fellow. Now," he said, looking at me, "tell me what hurts." Delicate spectacles hung from his nose and his smile was broad.

I tried to open my mouth but couldn't seem to remember how to speak. A dozen questions flooded my mind, each one an additional weight. *Where was I? How long had I been here? Was I going to be killed once I was found out? Was this the healer? Could he help me save Maddock?*

"Would you like a drink first, dear?" the kind man asked, wrinkles appearing on his forehead.

I nodded, and he poured a glass of water for me, lifting it to my lips. I drank the entire glass in one gulp and, after resurfacing for air, gestured for another with my head. He smiled and after I downed the second glass, he motioned to the pitcher, ready to offer me a third. I shook my head gratefully and sank back into the pillows.

"Let me introduce myself," he said. "You are probably very confused." I nodded again, squinting into the bright light, my eyes not yet accustomed.

"My name is Kirt and I am the royal healer. I live on the grounds and take care of the royal family and everyone else within these walls. You are in the palace clinic—a separate house similar to the one you were staying in before you . . . uh . . . fell." He looked at me inquisitively. "Now, if you are ready, I would like to ask you some questions . . . that is, only if you feel completely comfortable answering them."

Relief spread throughout my body—a better medicine than any treatment he could offer me. I had found the healer. Not in the way I expected to, but I had found him nonetheless and he seemed kind. He looked at me in the eyes, my own still adjusting to the light. I wanted to trust this man; he was a healer like Cen—like me. But he was also a Brockan who worked for the royal family. My heart pounded along with my head, and I felt my stomach surge. I was going to be sick.

"Sir," I croaked after a long pause, my voice rough, "I will answer your questions the best I know how, but the truth is, my entire experience here has been a bit of a blur."

"That is to be expected. Like I said, you sustained a rather serious head injury, as well as major blood loss." His voice was sympathetic, and he looked down at me with concern. "You should make a full recovery, of course." He smiled slightly. "First things first, dear. How long have you suffered from sleepwalking?"

"Sir?" I asked again. He thought I was sleepwalking?

"Yes. Sleepwalking. When Jolom found you, he said that your eyes were open but that you were definitely asleep. He said you kept muttering something . . . what was it? Oh—horse and rings and blood, something or other. Very disturbing," he said, shaking his head and squinting his eyes tightly. "After bringing you to me with several other soldiers, I discovered your head injury and the large gash on your arm, no doubt from falling from the balcony." He paused, rubbing his temples with his fingers on each side of his head as though he felt the pain from my "fall" in his own. "You lost a lot of blood. I'm sure that's why you lost consciousness. You are very lucky to be alive."

So this healer and the soldiers actually believed that I had been sleepwalking? That I fell from the balcony, did not wake up, swam through the water, and made it through the trees to the wall without stirring the soldiers—all while I was asleep? I almost wanted to laugh, it was so absurd, and I would have if the room weren't spinning and my head pounding.

I looked up at Kirt and stumbled through a lie. "I've been sleepwalking for years. My father usually ties me to the bed to prevent me from wandering at night," I said quickly. "I should have warned Hortense or one of the other girls, but I was embarrassed," I finished, proud of myself, albeit feeling guilty for telling such a blatant lie.

I sank against the cushions, those several sentences exhausting me. "Sir, if it is all right, could I maybe ask you a question?" He would know about the cure—two soldiers told me themselves that the royal healer administered it.

Kirt smiled at me, his eyes kind. "Of course. You can ask me anything."

I opened my mouth but felt too nervous to ask about the vox just yet. "How long have I been here?"

He nodded. "A fair question. Two days, coming in and out of

consciousness. This is the first day you've carried on a coherent conversation with me, and I must say, it has been a relief. I was ready to reach out to your family. I still can, if you'd like." Two days was an eternity for Maddock. I suppressed a sob.

I swallowed, attempting to regain my composure and then asked him my next question, as bravely as I could. "Could you take me to my family?" My voice shook with the request.

His jaw fell, and he stared at me, cocking his head to one side. "Take you? Why, that would eliminate you from the program. There's not a chance that would be allowed." Lines streaked his forehead. "You're not in your right frame of mind. Surely you would never make such a request if you were thinking clearly. This is a tremendous opportunity. You're fortunate to be involved in such a program." He stood up and paced the room. I could sense that he was nervous, although I couldn't imagine what for. I was the one who should be nervous. Then I grasped his situation. He saw me as the daughter of a nobleman, a girl who could possibly be his future queen. That realization was all I needed to speak up.

"I wouldn't dream of going home," I lied. Going home was all I could think about. "But I would like to reach out to my family. My brother at home is ill, and I want to make sure he is all right." I tried to sound ignorant, but I wasn't sure how convincing I was.

Kirt walked over to my bedside. "Your brother is ill? You came to the right person for that. Perhaps I could offer some assistance." He seemed eager to help, no doubt relieved that I wasn't going to pursue my request of going home.

"He has . . . umm . . . kiusjna?" I pretended to stumble through the pronunciation. "At least, that's what I think our town healer calls it?"

Kirt nodded, sympathy mingled with a glint in his eyes. Perhaps surprise? I could tell that the mention of kiusjna definitely sparked his attention. "Ah, kiusjna. We call it vox here. A terrible disease. How far along is your brother's?"

I swallowed. "It's getting close to his heart. He has had it for weeks, and our healer doesn't know how to help him." I felt my voice choke up when I thought about Maddock and Cen.

As Kirt watched my eyes well up with tears, his face softened. He considered this for several moments. "There's not a very accessible cure to kiusjna, or vox," he said, removing his spectacles. "The disease has not been an issue in Deshan for centuries." He paused. "Although . . . I have seen more of a resurgence as of late." Subconsciously I sat up against the pillows. "No one has come to me for treatment within the palace, of course, and they would have no reason to. But I have seen it in the marketplace at times. Usually Savian children." He knew something; I could sense it in his eyes. The question was how much he was willing to tell me.

I felt my eyes widen and I blinked, several tears escaping. "Why wouldn't there be a reason to treat it within the palace?" I asked. "And why Savian children, do you think?"

Kirt frowned and walked across the room to shut the door. I sat up tensely. "I'm sorry, sir. Perhaps I'm asking too many questions. I just want to figure out what's wrong with my brother." Kirt knew something. I was right to believe that there were secrets harbored within these walls.

Kirt ignored my frustration and perched on the edge of the bed, looking out of the window, his eyes focused. "I cannot answer all of your questions, and I do not have all of the answers. But I will tell you what I know and perhaps in my way I will be able to help your brother."

He turned to face me. "I was asked over two years ago by the late king's advisor to develop an antidote for the disease vox—or kiusjna, as you call it," he explained. "Because it is so rare, I had to venture into our surrounding countries to find it. The entire mission was funded by the crown, under royal mandate." He closed his eyes. "I met the royal healer in Sansikwa and asked him if he knew of something—anything that could cure this disease. It took loads of gold before he was willing to introduce me to another healer, a woman who lived on the top of Sansikwa's highest mountain peak."

Kirt paused, losing himself in the memory. "It took three weeks to reach the peak of the mountain. Weeks of cold, laborious hiking in the icy tundra—so different from the balmy breezes of Deshan. My men were dying one by one, but we were so close to reaching her that I refused to turn back. Each step we took brought us closer to the cure, I was convinced."

He smiled wanly. "When we finally reached her hut at the top of the mountain, we were surprised to see that the snow all around the hut was melted. Green grass was showing through! I wanted to kiss the ground, I was so happy to see anything living in the blue ice."

"How could that be?" I interrupted, "It should have been the coldest point." I was completely engrossed, and my fear was dissolving into curiosity. If only Cen and I had the freedom to go on such quests!

Kirt gave me a sad look and continued without answering me. "We approached the hut and found the healer. She called herself Levskyna." He pronounced her name with a perfect Sansikwan accent. "She let us in to her hut, which was so hot that even after weeks of cold, immediately our sweaters and coats began to feel too heavy and warm. I asked her, 'Do you have a cure for this disease?' and she smiled with a nod, but was not quick to reveal it.

"We spent weeks there, attempting to persuade her to tell us her secret, to give us the cure that our king and his advisors wanted so desperately. But she told us that we would have to wait. So wait we did." Kirt shifted slightly. "She had a room that she kept carefully guarded by two large dogs. On the night marking our fourth week on her mountain top, she invited me into the room."

"And?" I asked expectantly.

He grinned. "There was an extraordinary furnace, kept hot, she said, by the energy of the mountain. Within the furnace sat something that looked like a small stone. I laughed bitterly when she pointed to it and told me it was the secret to the cure for vox in her native tongue. But when she pulled it out, with hot tongs, I changed my mind. The stone wasn't a stone at all but some form of yeast—a bacterium kept alive by the extreme heat of her oven. She told me it was a starter for the cure. That without this vital piece, the rest of the ingredients would not function properly."

His eyes grew hazy. "My men and I spent another few months creating an oven we could carry with us to contain this starter on our journey back home. I sent word for a kiln to be built in the palace with a resting temperature of 91 units."

I coughed. "91? That's a strange number." My face began to flush. My old medicine book had been correct. It was a unit of heat! Why had Cen and I not considered that?

He nodded. "I thought so too, but it must be precise. We have tested the bacterium in several other temperatures but it dies. Using the starter she gave us, I created an inoculation of sorts. A medicine and procedure that prevents and cures vox."

"But what else is in it?" I asked.

He shrugged, "A myriad of simple ingredients. Buckweed, oirsl gel, kew butter." I nodded eagerly. All of those were familiar, relatively inexpensive ingredients. Items we used often in the clinic.

"So once you take the bacterium and add the other ingredients, does it have to be kept at the temperature?" I asked curiously. "What form of incision is used to apply it?"

Kirt looked down at me with wide eyes. "For a young lady you seem to know quite a bit about medicine." I couldn't tell if he was suspicious or impressed by my knowledge.

I gulped and offered a sweet smile. "Everything is out of concern for my brother," I explained with a wave of my hand. "I've done a lot of my own research in his behalf."

"You're a good sister."

I avoided responding. Kirt was too kind for me to invent another lie. "So what happened next? When you returned?"

Kirt stood up and again paced the floor, his hands behind his back. "I was told upon my return that under the same advisor's command I would need to protect our Brockan soldiers from the illness, since it was spreading across the borders into the villages. So for several months we have been administering it to our soldiers.

The best method is to create a roughly three-inch incision above the heart, near the collarbone, and pour the liquid into the incision. It is received into the bloodstream fastest that way and heals quickly." He smiled proudly then, putting his spectacles back on. "We have had tremendous success."

That explained the incisions and the rough explanation they gave the soldiers for why they needed to receive it. "Why has the antidote only been offered to soldiers? Why not also offer it to the Savians who are infected?" I paused, hoping not to indite myself, "Or to other Brockans? Civilian Brockans," I clarified. "Like my brother, and my family and friends?"

Kirt shrugged. "It is an expensive treatment, and its existence is supposed to remain somewhat protected. I suppose this advisor and his staff feel that it should remain a secret for now." I could tell this last point discouraged Kirt, but he did not dwell on it.

"If you could give me directions to your home, I could probably spare some time to administer the treatment to your brother. To keep you from going home and leaving the program," he added quickly, clearly trying to move on from my last question. "I'm sure the queen would not mind if we used some of the royal reserve to help a young lady in the program." Kirt had a unique way of smiling with his eyes.

"You do not know what that would mean to me," I said with all of the sincerity I could muster. "But perhaps you could just send the treatment there? Our town healer could administer it so you would not have to make the trip." Under no circumstance would Kirt believe I was a Brockan once he went to my orchard village and saw Maddock and Cen.

He shook his head. "I would prefer to do it myself. I have been asked to keep this treatment confidential. Which also means that I must ask you to keep my story and the existence of the treatment to yourself."

I nodded eagerly, reassuring him that I would keep his secret. "That's fine," I began, "We're from Canton, but my father does a lot of . . . humanitarian work in one of the east orchard villages," I explained. "Kalvos. That's where my brother is now. If you could go there, perhaps you could find them at the clinic?" I was pleased with this story. If I could get Kirt there, he could heal Maddock, and while he was gone, I could escape before he discovered that I was a Savian. I wasn't sure where I would go from there—surely they would look for me in Kalvos after I escaped, but at least Maddock would live.

"It sounds like you have a good father. And it will save me a trip all the way to Canton," he said. "Now forgive me for keeping you up with my stories! You must be exhausted. Let me get you some parchment so you can provide directions to find your father and brother. I will leave as soon as you are well." He left for a few minutes and returned with some parchment and a quill.

On the first sheet I wrote down some directions to find the clinic. Then I quickly scribbled a note to Cen on one sheet and rolled it up tightly. "For my father," I explained. I was frightened that the palace guards would censor it, so I worded it as well as I could. I needed Cen to know where I was, how I got there, and how he could communicate with me. I also needed to let him know that this was the only way I could save Maddock.

> *Dearest Father,*
>
> *First of all let me assure you that I am quite safe. The palace is a beautiful place and the group of girls with me here are all very lovely. We live in a mansion on the palace grounds, taking classes and preparing to become the future queen. It was a stroke of luck that I was able to come, since being here I have discovered that Kirt—the kind royal healer—has access to the antidote that may save my brother's life.*
>
> *We are not allowed to leave the palace gates under any circumstance, and everywhere we go, palace guards accompany us. I thought you might like to know that detail so you can be assured that we are quite safe. I pray that Kirt finds you quickly, as well as the healer in the*

village, Cen. Please keep me updated on my poor broth-
er's illness. Kiusjna is a terrible disease.

Please address me by my full name —Larken of
Canton—when you write back, to make sure the letter
gets to the correct person. I would hate for my nickname
at home, "Emi," to circulate among the ladies.

I will miss you every day until we are reunited.
Sincerely,
Larken

P.S. did you know they allow you to stall horses just
outside the marketplace? A girl here informed me that
her father stalls his horse at a southwest stall where they
charge only two finla for an entire day's feed, water, and
shelter.

Kirt smiled at me when I finished, taking the directions and the parchment gladly. "I'll be downstairs and will come back in a couple of hours to check on you again." He pulled a small porcelain bell out of the folds in his robes and set it gently on the table next to the pitcher of water. "Should you need anything at all, simply ring this bell and a servant will attend to you momentarily."

I smiled gratefully and then lay back on the bed, looking at the ceiling that seemed to spin, even when I closed my eyes. Once Maddock was healed, I had no reason left to stay. I was on the softest bed, in the finest room I had ever seen in my life, and I would trade it in an instant for my hay bale cot as long as I had Cen sleeping in the same room as me.

I came to the palace looking for answers, and I found them here. I could only hope that my own life was not the price to be paid for Maddock's.

9

I cried real tears the day I left the clinic, hugging Kirt good-bye before leaving with Hortense, who raised her eyebrows at the gesture but did not say a word. He was my savior, and literally Maddock's, since he prepared to go to Kalvos the next day to administer the cure. I hoped Maddock was still alive for him.

"Surely you are ready now?" Hortense grunted as I broke away from Kirt and his clinic staff, following her and two soldiers back to the mansion where classes were underway.

She walked slowly, her hands behind her back. "After speaking with Kirt and the royal guards, you will not have to worry about a repeated incident like that one again. The balcony will be patrolled every evening as well as all of the doors. I'm sure that will come as a relief to you." I nodded in despair. The nights were the only time I could think of to escape, and now that I could not go out the front doors or ground windows, I would have to find another way out.

Without giving me a chance to speak, Hortense continued, "You will have much catching up to do of course. The other girls have already gone through almost a week's worth of mathematics, geography, poise, fashion, and languages . . ." She blabbered on while my thoughts wandered.

The clinic was built on the other side of the castle, equidistant from the mansion. As we passed through what seemed like miles of gardens, I had a better idea of the massive size of the palace grounds. Behind the palace was a pool the size of a small lake. Fountains flowed around the grounds and groups of courtier's bathed in short white gowns and floppy hats. They turned to stare at me as I passed, and I suddenly felt self-conscious in the nightgown I was wearing. Musicians played under a cabana and servants held trays of fruits and beverages, approaching the people bathing there with their offerings. They were all Brockans. A bitter taste entered my mouth, and I swallowed, turning away so I wouldn't have to look at them any longer.

After passing the pool, we came upon a large open space where targets were set up on the far side of the field. "Where the young prince and his trusted soldiers train," Hortense offered.

"Where's the prince now?" I asked, more out of curiosity than out of an actual desire to see him.

"Never you mind that," Hortense reprimanded. "Prince Corban is kept under tight security while the girls are in the mansion. You will not cross paths until the first ball."

The stables extended beyond the open space, and I murmured under my breath at the multitude of horses that grazed beyond their fences. Large thoroughbred steeds filled the grounds, and trainers worked with several of them in a large circle. I felt tears prick my eyes at the thought of Lexon and prayed that my letter would get to Cen soon so that he could find him and bring him home.

At last we arrived back at the mansion. "Run up and change your clothes," Hortense ordered. "Your luggage never arrived, so I took the liberty of asking the royal dresser for some simple garments. Quickly dress, and then join the rest of us in the dining room for lunch."

I murmured, "Thank you" and slunk up to the room, discovering three new gowns on the bed I had claimed the first night there. The dresses were anything but simple to me. The first was a deep purple, with a laced bodice and long sleeves. The second two were blue with delicate silk skirts. On the floor at the edge of the bed rested a pair of white slippers with embroidered leaves and flowers. All of the items were finer than anything I had ever owned. Slipping out of the nightdress, I put on one of the blue gowns that, miraculously, fit me perfectly. I turned around to examine myself in the large mirror that stood against the wall at the end of the room.

I saw a girl I scarcely recognized. My hair was braided in a complicated plait—Kirt's assistants eager to play with it before I left the clinic. The dress was finer than anything I had ever seen, much less owned, and the slippers hugged my feet even better than my worn riding boots. My face looked different too. I had always kept my hair wrapped in a scarf, hiding my forehead from the sun. Now though, it was exposed completely and my blue eyes seemed to jump out from my skin like they never had before. Despite all of these changes, though, it was still me beneath— Emi from the orchard.

I sunk to my knees in front of the mirror and pressed my head against it, closing my eyes and willing my old life to return. I didn't want to be here, despite the beautiful gowns, the abundance of food, the luxurious grounds and surroundings. I wanted to be home with Cen and those I loved in the village. I wanted to see Maddock get better. I wanted to ride through the dusty orchards with Lexon.

I sat with my face against the mirror until a servant entered the room and told me that lunch was being served and Hortense requested my presence. I stood up slowly and mopped tears from my face, feigning a smile at the girl staring back at me in the mirror. I promised myself that whether I successfully escaped or died trying, I would never forget who I was—Emi of Kalvos, healer's apprentice.

I turned around and walked to go down the stairs to join the other girls, but not before turning around and looking in the mirror one last time.

* ✳ * ✦ *

The next several weeks I contemplated what to do next. I was afraid to leave and afraid to stay. I hadn't heard back from Cen and could not leave until I was certain Maddock was healed. Every time the door opened during classes or meals, I was certain it was guards sent from Kirt to take me away and try me for treason. But they never came. I attended classes and mock-balls with the other girls, struggling to fit in. I expected to be far behind those who had had formal education and private tutors, but in many ways I was right on course with them. Geography, mathematics, and languages came the easiest since I used mathematics often in the clinic, geography I studied with Cen, and foreign language terms were often used in my medical books.

I struggled enormously with other classes though, especially those involving poise, fashion, and etiquette. Not surprisingly, those were the courses that most of the girls excelled in. Cen taught me basic table manners, but I had no idea how rigid the rules of the court were. I was constantly reprimanded at meals. "Elbows *in*, Larken!" "Shoulders back!" "No, use the small fork for the salad!" "Don't slurp with your goblet!" "Napkin on your lap!"

My classmates were appalled at how poor my manners were. I once overhead Keisha say on the way upstairs after dinner, "No wonder we never saw her at any parties. Clearly her father didn't feel it best to let her out in public."

Jessra though, remained a constant friend since I returned from the clinic, sitting by my side through meals and helping me remember all of the rules. She giggled whenever Hortense reprimanded me and told me after one meal that she had more fun talking to me while she ate than she ever had at a formal state dinner. I wasn't sure I could trust her—or any of them really. But as the weeks progressed, I realized that to them, I was just another Brockan girl, someone wholly capable of becoming the next queen. I was their equal for the first time in my life.

We ate all three meals as a group to become trained in what Hortense called, "The art of eating." I was not used to having so much delicious food readily available, and I constantly had to remind myself to slow down and eat only until I was full. It pained me to see how much went to waste each night, especially when I thought of the villagers at home who saved rainwater in skeins for the nights when their water rations were low and their stomachs hollow.

Once a week we had mock-balls in the mansion's dance hall. Young servants practiced the dances with us, and they seemed thrilled with the prospect. Polite and well mannered, they were patient with me while I learned the steps. I wasn't sure if I would feel comfortable dancing at the first ball, but my hope was I wouldn't still be here to find out.

Our evenings were the only free time we had, and most of us spent it swimming in the pool behind the house, finally able to relieve ourselves of the summer heat that glued our long dresses to our sweaty skin. Jessra lent me one of her swim dresses. It hung loosely on my small frame but we cinched it with a belt and swam every evening until the other girls went inside and the soldiers told us it was time for lights out. Those precious moments were my only solace in the palace. We floated on our backs in the water underneath a sea of stars and considered our futures.

Jessra did most of the talking and I listened, worried that if I said more I would give something away, revealing myself as a healer's apprentice, an orphan—a Savian. I learned that she was from a very affluent family and had three younger sisters, educated by the best teachers in Deshan. Her voice broke every time she spoke about her sisters and she would often cry gently while I listened, understanding the pain of missing. Her mother was loving and her father firm but affectionate. She told me she did not want to leave them to come here but felt an obligation when the scout came to discuss the option with her parents. "They are so proud of me," she said more than once with a distant look. I wondered what kind of life that would be, to grow up in a big home with a mom and a dad and sisters. It sounded nice, but my heart ached to imagine a world without Cen in it.

Sometimes she asked me about myself, but it was easy to divert the attention back to her. I told her as little as possible—that my mother died in childbirth but I had a loving father. That bit wasn't too far from the truth. I did have Cen, even though I had no idea who my real father was.

One evening she asked me if I had ever been in love. That night, clouds hid the moon and a cool breeze rustled through the palms surrounding the pool. I floated on my back, my legs waving in and out rhythmically. When she asked, I submerged myself in the water to think before I responded too quickly. I stayed there until I couldn't possibly hold my breath any longer.

"Maybe I shouldn't have asked?" she said to me with a smile when I resurfaced. "Who is he?"

"You first," I told her with a smirk, hoping that I could divert the attention back to her like I usually could.

She looked me in the eyes and shook her head solemnly. "I've never been in love. Part of the reason I was hesitant to come here is because I am so afraid of loving a man who doesn't choose to love me back. Say I fall in love with the prince, but he falls in love with someone else. Then what? I don't want to return home with a broken heart instead of a crown."

I nodded in response. "There are a lot of beautiful girls here. I can understand that. But how do you know how bad heartbreak really is? Maybe it won't hurt as much as you think."

She smiled, her seriousness gone. "You didn't answer me, Larken of Canton. Tell me! Have you ever been in love?"

I released my feet and resumed floating on my back, waiting a long time before finally replying. "No." And that was the truth. Not only had I never been in love, but I had never even *considered* the idea of love. There was always too much work to do, too many patients to see, too many books to read, another cure, another treatment. I wasn't even sure if I ever planned on marrying. All I saw in my future was becoming the best healer possible for the people in my village.

My stomach dropped as I thought of healing. It had been weeks since I left home—weeks of fear and sleepless nights and heart-ache for leaving Cen and Maddock behind. I wondered if it would ever get better. Yet I couldn't leave; I couldn't attempt an escape without knowing that Maddock had been treated. Kirt had not contacted me at all since I left the clinic, and I knew that if I left, I would never have such close proximity to the antidote again. After all, Maddock's whole village contracted the disease. There had to be a way I could help them too.

Jessra nodded in consent, accepting my answer and we floated in silence, both consumed with our own thoughts until the clouds moved from behind the moon and the soldiers told us it was time to get inside.

*   *   *   *   *

Two weeks before the first ball, Hortense lined us up and led us to the tailor's, a house near the clinic.

The flurry of excitement was tangible. Keisha and another girl, Nadia, held hands tightly, beaming at one another; other girls cheered aloud until Hortense silenced them. I walked with heavy feet. A ball meant facing hundreds of Brockans—all of them ana-lyzing me, trying to determine how I fit with the rest of the girls here. I hoped to be gone long before this ball, but as the days passed without any word from Cen or Kirt, it looked like I would be attending with the rest of them.

Eight soldiers surrounded our group as we walked, and Jessra and I held up the back, admiring the beautiful grounds. The trees seemed much fuller than they did when I took my walk back from the clinic almost two months before.

We passed the stables, the prince's training grounds, the gar-dens and the enormous pool, which was unoccupied today, until we reached a tall white house behind the clinic, near the back wall. As we approached, a thin woman with unruly dark hair and dressed in a fitted white gown stood to greet us. She smiled warmly and motioned for us to join her inside. When she turned her back to us, she revealed a crimson stripe that ran the length of the dress. The inside of the house was cramped with all of us shuffling in. Enormous spools of thread hung above our heads, and along the walls ran shelves of fabric with every print, color, and design I could ever dream up. White stools formed a semicircle, and we each took a seat around the woman.

Once seated, she spoke, "I'm Veda. It's so wonderful to meet all of you!" She never stopped smiling, revealing a charming gap in her front teeth. "I'm the queen's personal dresser and also run the tailor house, where you are now. As you know, the queen sets the trends and styles of her subjects, which is why it is such an important part of your education this year. To help you, each of you will be paired with one of our most promising tailors. They will be creating your gowns and working with you on your designs." Most of the girls craned their necks to see whom they were partnered with, but I was too embarrassed to turn around. I was raised a slave and had never had more than one pair of pants or boots in my life. I had not even considered what I might wear to the ball, expecting to sport one of the dresses Hortense had made for me.

Veda smiled at those of us who hesitated. "Go ahead then—turn around and meet your partners."

I swiveled around on the stool and met the eyes of a short, ruddy young man with blue eyes and a wide smile. "A pleasure to meet you miss," he said, offering a bow that made me cringe. "My name is Ruldet."

I stammered nervously, unsure of whether I should curtsy to him. What did Hortense tell us about curtsying to someone at a lower status? Since I was uncertain, I stood and curtsied to him anyway—just in case. "My name is Larken of Canton. A pleasure to meet you, Ruldet." His eyes widened when I curtsied and I looked across the room and saw Hortense frown at me. Wrong guess.

"Well, Larken of Canton," Ruldet said finally, overcoming his embarrassment. "What do you have in mind for your dress?"

I shrugged. I was not as interested in fashion as I was about staying out of the spotlight. "I . . . was actually hoping to leave my dress up to you," I said with a smile. "Fashion is my worst subject. I am so sorry that you are stuck with me."

"Nonsense," Ruldet replied. "I'm sure you must have some ideas—things you've seen at past balls perhaps? In books?"

I shook my head. "Honestly, I don't have the slightest idea about fashion. I couldn't begin to tell you what I might like."

He frowned. "Are you certain you want to leave it entirely up to me?" I couldn't tell if he was disappointed or excited to have more freedom.

I looked around the room. All of the girls were giving critiques and opinions to their tailors. I saw Nadia dramatically flail her hands in the air, demonstrating how she wanted it to fit. Younda's tailor was almost in tears as she hammered the details of her gown into her. Jessra was holding a pencil and sketching on her tailor's papers.

I turned back around to face Ruldet. "I am absolutely certain that I want to leave it entirely up to you. My only request is that you not make it too . . . flamboyant." I was thinking of the court when I said that last bit. It would be difficult enough not to stand out as a Savian in a Brockan ball, and the last thing I needed was a showy gown that drew unnecessary attention—especially if I was going to disappear soon.

Ruldet bowed again, his face flushing. "Thank you for your confidence, Miss Larken."

I liked Ruldet already. He took my measurements quickly and scribbled them on a parchment.

Hortense clapped her hands twice, and the bustling room died down. "Time for lunch, ladies," she announced. "Thank your tailors. We will return a few days before the ball to witness the outcome of your styles."

"It was a pleasure to meet you, Miss Larken," Ruldet said with a smile.

"No, the pleasure is mine. And please call me Larken. The 'miss' is unnecessary." He nodded curtly at me, holding my gaze longer than necessary. On our way back to the mansion I was quiet. It wasn't that I hated the idea of a pretty dress and a ball. I thought of the other girls in my village at home. This opportunity would be the highlight of their entire lives. But to me, it made all of this— my experience here, my distance from home, my time away from Cen—feel permanent.

*　*　*　*　*

A week later, during our politics class, Hortense received a letter from a messenger. She stopped the class and read it, then turned to me. "Kirt requests you at the clinic. He says he has something for you. Since you can't go alone, I will send two soldiers with you to get you there and back safely." She paused, scrunching her eyebrows together. "And if you are late for dinner, Larken of Canton, you will not have free time for three full days. That includes swimming at night," she said with a sneer, glancing at Jessra. "Instead you will rehearse poise with me."

My heart pounded on my walk to the clinic. Finally some answers. I sauntered quietly ahead of the two guards, almost turning to ask if they could hear my heartbeat because it was so loud. But then I remembered that we were not to talk to the soldiers at all, since the royal family did not converse with them. "Guards are to be silent protectors," Hortense had said. "The minute one gets attached to a guard, one is at risk of becoming vulnerable, and thus unprotected. The guards hear all of the secrets of the palace. Give them as little information as possible." I thought briefly of the soldiers in the orchard those many months ago—crude, mean, demanding. At home I was the one who was looked down on. I always thought it would feel different—better—to be the one at the top, but I was wrong. Both hurt.

As I entered the clinic, Natty, Kirt's assistant, curtsied deeply. "Wait here, Miss Larken. I will let Kirt know you have come."

I sat on one of the purple chairs that flanked the entrance until I heard Kirt's voice echoing down the hallway. "Ahh, my dear Larken. How good it is to see you again." Kirt bowed deeply, and I resisted the urge to throw my arms around him, curtsying in response.

Even if Maddock was not saved, Kirt had already helped me more than I imagined he would by offering to give him the antidote. I inhaled deeply. I missed the clinic. The familiar herbal smell, the clean racks of dressings, and the instruments that filled cabinets against the walls in every room—this place was the closest I could get to home. To Cen.

As I rose from my curtsy I looked into his eyes that seemed heavy. Sad, even. "Is my brother all right?" I asked nervously, instinctively reaching for my neck to check my pulse.

His face was solemn. "As much as I wish this was a quick and simple visit, I do have much to tell you." I felt my stomach drop. Something was wrong.

"Please, dear one, come into my office." I followed him in while the soldiers stayed outside and perched myself breathlessly on the edge of the chair that faced his large desk. He shut the door tightly and drew the curtains on the window adjacent to his desk.

"What is it, Kirt? Is my brother well? You have me worried," I tried unsuccessfully to mask the fear rising in my chest. *What would a queen say?* I kept thinking. *I must deny any accusations. I must not reveal my identity for any reason.*

"Larken, I was able to locate your brother." Kirt's dark eyebrows raised keenly and I gazed at my hands, certain that he had discovered my secret.

"The antidote is valuable and difficult to transport, and I wanted to make sure it did not fall into the wrong hands. I asked Natty to watch over the clinic for the day while I ventured out to the village you spoke of. Using your directions, I found my way to a Savian clinic, greeted there by a large group of Brockan soldiers who seemed to have occupied it. They were surprised to see me so far out and told me that there was only one healer there and he was Savian. 'The best' they told me, which is why they attended that clinic instead of visiting with their assigned barrack healer. I asked about your father, but they told me that there was no one from Canton there."

I drew in a sharp breath, keeping my eyes focused on the ground.

"I waited until evening before introducing myself to the healer," Kirt continued, "a kind, elderly man who introduced himself as Cen."

I choked at his statement, immediately regretting my foolishness at sending the letter, but it was the only way I knew to tell him that I was alive. *Please don't let him be hurt,* I prayed. *Please let him be all right.* I felt my face flush, and prickles of fear scattered across my arms and legs.

"May I continue, dear one?" Kirt asked, obviously noticing my reaction to his mention of Cen's name. "Let me get you a glass of water. I can see that you are upset." Kirt poured me water from a pitcher that rested on his desk, and I quickly gulped down the cold drink, two hands on the glass until I felt ready to listen again.

"There was no sign of your father, but Cen gave me a tour of his clinic after I told him I was the royal healer. He even closed the clinic for the evening, asking me if I wanted a pot of tea. He was quite gracious. I told him there was a girl in our program who told me about her little brother in desperate need of a cure for vox. I asked if he knew of the boy, and he told me that indeed he did. Further, he was very interested in learning more about you, so I continued to tell him about where you are living, what happened with your balcony accident—everything I knew before giving him your letter and asking him to pass it on to your father, whom he said was out of the village at the moment, searching for a cure for the boy.

"That evening, he asked me to wait outside while he located your brother and brought him to the clinic. I took a walk around the village, observing the people and speaking to several soldiers before I returned." His face was serious. "When I returned, Cen had your brother downstairs on the clinic bed, and I showed him how to administer the antidote, telling him the same story I told you. His disease was advanced; it is good I arrived there when I did." A tear of gratitude fell down my face. Maddock would get better.

Kirt paused. "I left that evening, but not before telling Cen and your brother that they could count on me to relay any messages they had"—he frowned—"as well as your father. Cen hastily wrote me a reply, which I have for you here." Kirt pointed to a drawer in his desk.

"It was an odd experience, although I greatly enjoyed Cen's company." Kirt's forehead wrinkled as he pulled his spectacles off. "Larken, is there . . . anything you would like to tell me?" His long spindly fingers tangled around each other, pressed against his heart.

Hot tears pooled in my eyes. Kirt was definitely suspicious, and why shouldn't he be? Perhaps in saving Maddock's life I sentenced my own. I felt my breath become inconsistent, and my head grew dizzy from what I had done. I could leave now. I could leave and I would never see Kirt again or Hortense—or anyone in this palace. When I was finally ready to respond to him, I forced out a broken, "No, sir. Nothing."

He held my gaze for several moments longer before standing. "You're sure?"

I looked up at him and felt myself nod. "Yes, I'm sure. Nothing I need to tell you, but thank you," I murmured. "For saving my brother's life."

He stood up, his eyes wide as he studied my face—perhaps analyzing my features, matching them to Maddock's so obviously Savian traits. He twisted his lips to one side and scratched the side of his head, his fingers lingering there as he exhaled deeply. "All right," he said slowly. He didn't believe me, but it didn't matter since I would be leaving soon. Shame overcame me as I realized that my lies were the thanks I gave him for saving Maddock's life.

"I almost forgot," he said, abandoning his suspicion for the time being. He rummaged around in the desk's drawers. "Your letter from Cen. I assume your father's letter will follow up after he returns."

He handed me the letter. Scrawled across the top in Cen's familiar hand was the name, "Larken of Canton."

I tore the letter open.

Dearest Larken,

The royal healer is relaying this message. I pray it remains private until you receive it. I am not sure how you have gotten into the position you are in, but I thank the heavens above that you are alive. You cannot imagine how I have mourned for you. Thanks to you though, Maddock received his treatment. He will live, all because of you.

In my old age I am afraid I cannot help you escape. If anything, an attempt to see you may be more dangerous for you than staying where you are. So until we figure out an exit plan, you must do everything you can do to remain safe.

Things are only getting worse in our village. They have started to build the tall gates Maddock described from his village—beginning on the north side. Our prisons are full. Perhaps you are safer there than you are here, but a deeper part of me feels that maybe you are there at this time because there is something you can do to save us all. Consider that for me, if you will.

I love you, Larken of Canton.

Cen

P.S. I was not aware that they housed horses in that particular place in the market. They are tough bargainers, but I know a good horse when I see one.

I exhaled a sigh of relief after finishing the letter. Not only would Maddock get better, but Cen also knew I was alive and had already located Lexon in the square.

Kirt studied me while I read. "Larken," he said after I finished.

"Yes?" I replied, folding up the letter with shaking hands. I was so lost in the letter that I almost forgot that I was still here in the palace, in great danger if Kirt were to uncover my secret. Perhaps he already had.

He studied me for several minutes and then shook his head.

"Nothing. Be careful on your walk back. When you are ready to send another letter to the clinic in hopes it will reach your father faster, please let me know. I am at your service." He bowed deeply, his face serious but his voice rife with doubt.

I nodded to him. "Thank you, Kirt. For everything."

I exited the room, a sigh of relief washing through me. I did it. I'd saved Maddock's life. The beauty of the grounds blurred from the tears in my eyes. How soon until he would be able to return to his village? And what would he find there when he did? More death? Or would his return bring his village hope? Could he even return, after escaping the way he did?

Whatever his decision, Maddock would be leaving Cen soon and I had been gone long enough. It was time to go home.

It was time for me to escape.

10

The doors and windows were locked each evening. "Barricading us from intruders," or so Hortense said. But I knew they weren't just locked to keep intruders out. They were locked to keep us in, and not just from sleepwalking. For days I tried to find another way—a moment of solitude on the grounds, an unlocked window left unnoticed by the guards. It seemed that my attempt to leave the first night sparked a new fervor of security. We were trapped here: prisoners as much as princesses.

The morning of the first ball our dresses were delivered. Most of the other girls chose the royal white for their gowns with touches of blue or orange that they all hoped were the on-trend colors of the season.

My dress, however, was a soft gray, pleated all the way around. It hung in a straight fit, with small sleeves that rippled off my shoulders. Ruldet beaded the bodice with sparkling silver stones, giving the top the impression of being made of ice. It flowed so gracefully it almost seemed liquid.

Hortense, wearing a matronly peach chiffon dress that was

as unflattering as the frown that began right where her nose ended, gathered us at the top of the palace's staircase to introduce us formally to the royal family and the court.

As usual, Jessra and I hovered at the back of the group, and when it was finally our turn to step around the curtains and enter the ball, I motioned for Jessra to go first, so I could be the last. Surely the court was bored by this point and would not recognize a simple girl like me. If no one noticed me, no one would miss me when I left. My stomach churned as the caller asked me for my name and then announced loudly, "Our final young lady to be presented to the court is Larken of Canton."

I stepped through the curtains into the ballroom and immediately felt showered by a sea of stars. Chandeliers as big as carriages hung from the ceiling, their candles glittering the air with light that illuminated the ballroom. "Curtsy!" I heard Hortense hiss behind me, and obediently, I lifted my skirts. My curtsy was received by applause by the crowds below. I managed to walk down the staircase without tripping and considered that a success.

A small orchestra in the far corner of the room began playing, and I watched from the staircase as men and women formed lines and danced the same dances we had been taught in practice. A handsome young man with a purple suit climbed up the stairs and asked Jessra if she would like to dance, his face eager. Several other girls looked crestfallen that she was the first to be asked. She looked at me and I nodded, grinning widely at her. She giggled and moved to join him on the floor. Now that she was taken care of, I looked around for an exit. The dress that I thought would allow me to stay out of the spotlight seemed to spark a lot of attention. I hoped that people would be so interested in the dress they would forget to talk to me about my past, my family, or my hopes to become queen.

Unfortunately, that was not the case. Courtiers bombarded me since I was one of the few girls not asked to dance. *Where was I from? Canton? The scouts ventured that far from the capital for participants? Interesting. Why did I want to become queen? What would I change in the kingdom? Why not a white dress like the other girls? How old was I?*

88

I was courteous but did not offer any more information than necessary, and when I finally had a spare moment I headed for the back entrance, attempting to imprint the beauty of this experience on my mind before I returned to my village. There were hundreds of courtiers, their dresses and suits colorful and elaborate, layers of silk and taffeta, velvet and feathers.

My eyes strained with the colors until the light shifted and I was met with the eyes of a young man, not much older than me. He was dancing with a girl from the mansion, though I couldn't tell who since her back was turned. She wore a white dress, like most of the other girls, with purple straps that crisscrossed gracefully across her back. He held my gaze for several moments before turning to give his partner his full attention.

"He's dreamy, right?" one of the girls, Olia said, stepping around a courtier between us. "I don't understand why anyone would keep him inside the gates. It doesn't seem fair."

I laughed a little, nodding in agreement before turning back to look at him again, unable to move. Olia was swept up for the next dance.

Jessra and I speculated before about what the prince might look like, but we couldn't have been more wrong. Since he did not ventured out in public, we joked that he was probably a childish boy with a sour disposition from being spoiled all of his life. Fat from the fine foods available to him, and perhaps short or disfigured in some way. I definitely wasn't expecting the bronzed man that smiled at me. He was tall, with a strong frame, and thick brown curls outlined his face. He did not wear a crown but rather a silver suit, his royal sword hung decoratively at his waist. His eyes looked kind, even from here.

When I no longer felt right about staring at him and his partner, I rounded the corner to exit the ballroom. I had to take my chance while the courtiers and guards were preoccupied, as hard as it was to take my eyes off of the prince and his smile. I could have watched him all night.

The guards standing watch at the door merely nodded at me as I exited the ballroom and entered a dimly lit hallway. Marble floors reached almost endlessly in three directions. I bit my lip as I studied the halls. Which one would take me out of the main palace? I started down the hall furthest from me, walking briskly and passing several courtiers who were too drunk to acknowledge my presence.

When I reached the end of the first hall, I was faced again with another. I turned quickly, almost colliding with a tall bald man in a bright red suit. His face was narrow, and his eyes oddly close together in the dim candlelight. "Leaving, are we?" he asked with a smirk, crossing his arms. "But we haven't even met yet."

Startled, I replied quickly, "I'm sorry, sir. How rude of me. My name is Larken of Canton." I heard the uncertainty in my own voice, the awkwardness of my rushed curtsy. Upon closer look I could see long hairs protruding out of his nose. He reeked of smelling salts and sweat.

"Canton, you say? Very interesting. I'm Marley. Personal advisor to the late king—and, of course, the future king," he bragged. "I sit at the head of Deshan's chief counsel while you young women are in the program. Once one of you is crowned, I will return to my position as personal advisor, but for the next year, I am the law." He said the last sentence with a little chuckle. It obviously gave him great pleasure to announce his title.

"Ah," I replied, wondering where I had heard his name before. "It seems that you have a very important position in the kingdom, Marley." *Now please go back inside the ball so I can leave,* I thought urgently.

"Yes," he replied, adjusting the lapel of his suit. "The most important in fact, next to the king himself. I also carry quite a bit of sway with the young prince and will assist him in choosing his bride. I thought you might be interested to know that. The other girls were." He motioned in the direction of the ballroom, scratching his chin absently. He stared down the long hallway behind me. "So you could say that it's important to be on my good side."

"I see," I said, my words failing me.

He clicked his tongue and looked down the hallway again, uneasily. "What did you say your name was again?"

"Larken of Canton."

He shook his head, suddenly interested. "That's not possible. We did not even venture to Canton—we never do. That is the land of hills and goats!" He chuckled a little, while I felt my jaw tense, petrified that he would prod more. "Now, what is your father's name?"

Before I could answer him, two guards raced down the hallway, their white coats glowing in the candlelight. "Ahh, miss!" one of them said to me with a bow, his breath uneven. "How fortunate we are to have found you!" I stared at them open mouthed. Just moments ago I walked right past them and they did nothing to stop me. Why the urgency in returning me to the ball now?

The other soldier noticed Marley and bowed, his face red. "Your grace," he said nervously, casting a glance at his partner. "I apologize. I did not recognize you there."

Marley nodded to them briefly. "You men need to keep a better eye on our participants," he scolded. "You can never lose count. Can never allow distractions to keep you from your task. Do you understand?"

The guards hung their heads. "Yes, sir," they said in unison.

"Very good. Now if you can ensure that you will not let it happen again, I will not report it to your supervisor." Retrieving a pocket watch from his jacket, Marley leaned in to inspect the time.

"I must be on my way. It was nice to have met you, Larken. You would be wise not to wander off again. It is not safe." He pronounced each word thoroughly, his voice hollow, but his eyes searched mine indignantly until I looked down at the marble floors, unable to hold his gaze any longer.

"It is lovely to have met you, Marley," I lied, offering a deep curtsy. He was gone before I rose, disappearing into the dark halls.

The soldiers escorted me back to the ball silently, closing the doors securely behind them once there. The hustle and music of the ball once again overwhelmed me. *It was my first chance to return to Cen*, I thought desperately, tears pooling in my eyes. I found a quiet corner to sit. *And it may have been my last.*

* * * * *

Hortense was waiting for us as we entered class the next day. "Ladies, did you all enjoy yourselves yesterday evening?"

A chorus of cheery yeses oscillated across the room. I dug my nails into my palms miserably, clenching my fists as I reviewed the frustrating evening I'd had.

"I'm so glad. Thank you for presenting yourself in an appropriate manner. I do have to say, though, that I am disappointed that not all of you had the chance to dance with the prince."

Whispers ensued, as the girls turned to each other. "Did you dance with him?" "Who didn't dance with the prince?"

Jessra looked over, her mouth wide. "Larken?" she whispered.

I shrugged in response, glumly studying the white sheen of my desk in an attempt not to cry.

I felt Hortense look at me, though I didn't raise my eyes to meet hers. "I receive a tally after every ball. We want every young lady to have her fair chance. So in order to help you feel extra confident for the next ball, we will be having daily dance practice in addition to your other studies. Also, I feel I must remind you that it is important for all of you to remain with the group at all times. I had a bit of a scare yesterday when I only counted twenty of you in the ballroom instead of twenty-one." Her eyes rested on me again. "Please do not allow yourselves to wander off."

So it was Hortense who alerted the guards last night. They must have thought I was just another courtier since I did not wear white like the other girls.

I rested my face on my hand. Hortense would definitely be watching me closely now.

The next few weeks were a blur of classes. We practiced so much that I was certain I could perform the dances in my sleep. When I told that to Jessra, she joked that she would have to tie my hands up along with my arms, so I didn't "sleep dance" off the balcony. It made me laugh that she still believed that story.

The mundane classes were unbearable. I looked for every opportunity to run—but none came. The security had been heightened even more, and soldiers walked us from our classroom to our bedroom and occasionally locked us in before meals. The highlight of those weeks was receiving another letter from Cen. Kirt sent a messenger from the clinic to deliver it.

> *Dear Larken of Canton,*
>
> *I have good news. Your brother has made a complete recovery. It took a few weeks for the swelling to go down in his feet, but just yesterday he pronounced that he has "never felt better." He left to find Levi. The rings were just inches from his heart the day they began the treatment. One day longer and we may have been too late.*
>
> *You saved him. You discovered the cure, and you found a way to deliver it to him. Words cannot express my pride for you, although pride is a feeling I am all-too familiar with, having you as a daughter.*
>
> *I miss you every day, and so do many of our patients. I've convinced them that you have taken a rather long holiday to Canton. I'm not sure they believe me, but I thought that might give you a laugh.*
>
> *I love you, Larken. Be strong.*
>
> *Father*

I tucked his letter in my gown so I would always carry a piece of Cen with me. Maddock was healed; he was better now. The joy I felt with that knowledge surpassed any other. It also reminded me that as safe as I was beginning to feel in the palace among the other girls, I was still a Savian. I would be imprisoned instantly if my identity were revealed at any point, and most likely publicly executed if I could not find an escape soon. I could pretend to be someone else, but in reality, I was still an impostor. A terribly defenseless impostor.

11

Weeks passed without any other word from Cen. I went through the motions as a girl in the program, attending all of my classes, eating meals with the group, and swimming after dark. I looked for any chance to escape, but none came. I felt all hope was lost—until one day, about three weeks before the next ball, when a dark-haired gentleman interrupted our language class.

Instead of angrily asking what he was doing there like she did with most interruptions, Hortense giggled and her face flushed from pasty white to bright red. "Young ladies, we have a special visitor today." She paused. "*Very* special. And I expect you to give him your full attention." She turned to the man with a look of admiration on her face and attempted to perch delicately on a chair at the front of the classroom, where she often lectured. But instead it wobbled, and she had to catch herself brusquely from falling to the floor. She looked around embarrassed, as if to make sure no one saw. I stifled a giggle and Jessra turned red from trying to hold in a laugh.

"Ladies, I have a bit of a surprise for you," the dark-haired man said. Every eye in the room fixated on him. He was handsome, with tanned skin and bright green eyes; his groomed mustache and beard trailing down to a broad smile. I could see why Hortense didn't argue when he interrupted.

"My name is Hendrik. I am in charge of the royal stables and weaponry training facilities here at the palace. Before I go on, let me say that the prince enjoyed himself immensely at the last ball."

Instantly a murmur of voices rose, and the girls whispered excitedly to each other. Any news from the prince was gold to these girls. I didn't join in, but inside I wondered how a stable master knew that the prince enjoyed himself. *He must spend a lot of time with the prince for him to know that.*

Hendrik waited at the front, embarrassed by the reaction in the room, and when we finally settled down he spoke again. "I regret to tell you however, that Prince Corban has decided to cancel the next ball."

An angry chorus of voices rose, directed at Hendrik. Two girls, Tulia and Petra, burst into tears, shaking their heads in disbelief. Keisha, the girl who always lectured me for eating too much, looked down at her waistline and began to weep as well. Younda hissed, "I'm going to have to tell my father about this, and he will not be happy. We were promised *six* supervised balls." I was probably the only girl in the room who felt relief at his announcement. The more exposure I had to the court the more dangerous my position here became. Instead of blushing at our sudden anger though, Hendrik smiled until we calmed down enough for him to speak again.

"The ball may be cancelled, but the prince has something entirely different planned for you ladies." Now he had our interest. "Every year in the late summer, Prince Corban takes a hunting trip a few hours south of the capital. And this trip, he would like to take you girls with him." A flood of voices rose in response.

A hunting trip? I felt a smile form on my face. *That would mean leaving the palace gates. On horses. This could be my chance.*

"I became aware recently that many of you girls are not familiar with horses, so during your usual dance class time we will now be riding and getting you ready for the hunt." The girls seemed to accept this answer, and a dozen hands rose in the air to ask Hendrik for more details about the excursion.

I daydreamed about taking off on a horse and jumping the wall, heading straight for my orchard village. Back to Cen. Back to my old life. It was just a daydream, but in that moment, it gave me some hope.

* * * * *

We began training the next day, waking up to a pair of black leather riding pants and a black tunic on the end of our beds. Tall tan boots sat next to the bed, along with long socks to wear under them. Most of the girls looked glumly at the offering compared to their bureaus full of dresses, but I squealed with delight and jumped out of bed to pick them up and try them on. The fit was perfect. They were worlds away from the riding pants and boots I wore at home. I reminded myself to thank Ruldet later for doing such a fine job.

Hendrik led us to the stables, which were even grander up close. We stood in the door of the entrance, the morning light breaking and filling the castle grounds in a way I had never seen before. For a moment I was reminded of home, the way the light would come over the orchards and spread like a vein throughout the village. I shook my homesickness off as Hendrik began to speak. He stood at the front, lecturing about basic riding skills and stable rules.

After explaining the basics, Hendrik led us into an open field where there was a saddle for each of us placed atop hay bales. I rolled my eyes at how basic it felt to be sitting on a stationary saddle, but from looking around I saw that many of the girls had never ridden a horse before. Keisha and Nadia sat up proudly, clearly having been taught proper riding, but others struggled with their balance. Jessra, especially, struggled to even stay on the hay bale saddle.

"How are you doing this?" she hissed at me. I laughed at her and got off my saddle to show her the best placement for her feet and how to shift her weight.

"If you sit up straight and keep your hips even, it is easier to keep your balance," I explained, tucking her feet into the hanging stirrups.

Hendrik came over to observe. "Well, that's one way to stay on the saddle," he said to me with a half smile. "Who taught you to ride?"

"My father," I told him shyly, holding up my hand to block the sun.

"It seems he did a fine job, although your form is not exactly royal. Do you ride well?" he asked. "What kind of horses did your father stable?"

I avoided his second question. "Yes," I replied confidently, "I ride very well." It was true after all. I couldn't say that I was good at poise or fashion or dancing, but riding was one thing I could claim. "As for my form, I was taught rather . . . untraditionally."

Jessra grunted in frustration and offered, "She's from Canton."

For some reason, the mention of Canton sparked Hendrik's interest. His eyes grew wide and he cocked his head to the side. "Canton, you say? I hear their horses are excellent."

I thought of Lexon and how loyal he was. "They are the best horses in the world, sir," I spoke assertively. "I am so eager to get riding. When can I get on, umm, a real horse?"

He laughed, revealing a mouthful of white teeth. "While the other girls are saddling up and practicing with my aids, why don't you help me bring the horses around?"

I curtsied in my tall boots. "I would be honored," I said, making him laugh again.

He walked over to tell Hortense he was enlisting my help. She seemed more than willing to please and batted her eyelashes wildly. Before he walked away, she touched his nose with her pointer finger, which explained the red face he sported as he walked back toward me.

Silently, he led me around the side of the stables and began opening the stalls. "I neglected to ask for your name earlier, my apologies. Miss . . . Miss . . ."

"Larken," I offered.

"Ah," Hendrik said with a strange smile. "From Canton you say?" He paused for several moments as I stood uncomfortably, waiting for some direction. Finally, he cleared his throat. "My aides have already saddled and groomed the horses and so they are ready to ride. There is nowhere for them to run but out into the circle fence." He motioned to the grassy field connected to the stables. "Your job can be ushering them out there. Why don't you take care of this row, and I'll do that one?"

As I opened the stalls, the horses grunted, eager to be let out into the fields for some exercise. I led them one by one into the circle, where some of them ran around and others snorted and waited expectantly, their whinnies echoing across the yard.

When the last horse from my row was led into the circle, I ran into the stables again, expecting to see Hendrik leading the final horse into the yard. As I turned the corner at full speed, however, I crashed headlong into a tall boy, causing him to fall backward onto a pile of hay bales. His brown curls fell over his eyes, and I clutched my side, feeling for the bruise that would inevitably appear there.

"My apologies! I was just coming to tell Hendrik the horses were all taken outside. I should have slowed down!" I reached forward to lift him up, and he accepted my help. After he brushed himself off and shook his hair back, I realized that it wasn't one of Hendrik's aides at all.

It was Prince Corban.

"Lady!" he uttered, clearly surprised to see a girl from the mansion there. "I was not expecting you. Why are you not with the rest of the group? I was told it was safe to come here, since you were working out exercises in the south yard. I am terribly, terribly sorry, although glad to be able to meet you. I did not get a chance to dance with you at the last ball, did I?"

His voice was deeper than I expected, and kind. Standing so close to him, I saw his features for the first time up close. All at once I understood the fuss the girls made about him. His eyes were a deep brown and seemed bottomless, with flecks of light dancing inside. His jaw line and cheeks were chiseled and his hair honeyed. It was his smile most of all that I reacted to, though—it lit up his entire face.

I stammered, struggling to explain what I was doing there, when Hendrik came up behind Corban and interjected for me.

"Corban, I should have warned you. Miss Larken is further along on her riding skills than the other girls, and graciously offered to help me bring them into the circle. I was not expecting you this morning, otherwise I would not have invited her to join me."

Prince Corban nodded to Hendrik and then turned back to face me, his hands brushing off the excess hay that had stuck to the back of his legs. "It is no trouble, really. Were you ill at the ball? I just saw you one moment. Please forgive me for my unkindness in not searching you out." I looked at Hendrik, wondering if the prince was joking, but they both had serious faces. The prince was being sincere. The *prince* was apologizing for not dancing with *me*—a Savian girl.

I forced myself to reply. "Please do not apologize. You were fortunate to have missed out on a dance with me. I'm afraid my dancing skills are . . . not quite where they should be." I smiled at him as I said the last sentence, eager to make him feel comfortable around me. The last thing I wanted was for him to ask me to dance at the next ball out of pity.

"I'm sure you are quite a fine dancer," he responded. "Although it sounds like maybe riding is a stronger point for you. How long have you been riding?"

Hendrik laughed. "She's from Canton, Corban. She's probably been riding since she could walk. Certainly as long as you have. My guess is that she could be a good rival for you in a race. I've never seen riders like those out of Canton." Corban rested his hands in his back pockets jovially, nodding in response to Hendrik's charge and shooting a glance at me to gauge my reaction.

I stepped closer to Corban, about to respond, when Hortense's shrill voice surprised me from behind. "Your HIGHNESS!" she screamed, stepping in between us so that her body blocked my view of Prince Corban and Hendrik. "So wonderful to see you." She offered a deep, prolonged curtsy and I saw Hendrik fight a grin as she came up. "I did not think we would be so blessed to be graced by your presence. However, you understand that I simply cannot leave Miss Larken here with you. It is against the rules to spend time alone, as Miss Larken should know." She turned around and shot me an angry look, before turning back to face Hendrik and Prince Corban. Her large teeth rested on her lip gawkily.

"The ladies are waiting round the circle for your instruction, Sir Hendrik. Perhaps I should let them know the prince will be joining us as well? All of us?"

Prince Corban smiled at her before replying. "You are kind, madame. I was merely coming to saddle up my horse for a ride and happened to run into Miss Larken here while she was helping Hendrik. It was entirely my fault, and Miss Larken is not to be punished for it." I lifted my eyes to look at him gratefully, only to see that his were resting on mine. "I regret that I will not be able to join you and the rest of the ladies," he said, "but I look forward to seeing all of you on the hunting trip." He bowed politely and stepped around Hortense until he was just inches away from me.

"It was a pleasure, Miss Larken," he whispered. "I look forward to racing you at the hunt, if you are up for the task?" His brown eyes danced as he said the word *racing*, and I grinned back at him, nodding and offering a slight curtsy.

"Our horses in Canton are quite fast, Prince. I accept your challenge."

"I look forward to it," he replied, his eyebrows raised in surprise at my candor. I was surprised that words came out of my mouth at all. "Now if you will excuse my rudeness, I have a ride to get to and a very eager horse. Thank you, Hendrik. Very nice to see you again, Madame Hortense."

Hendrik cleared his throat after Prince Corban excused himself. "Well, Miss Larken? Should we go teach these ladies a thing or two about riding a horse?"

"It would be my pleasure," I said back to him. I glanced behind me to see Prince Corban leading a tall black mare out of the other end of the stables, her long tail swishing back and forth with each step. I hoped he would look back at me right then, but he continued on through the stables and into the field.

We entered the circled fence and I spent the rest of the day helping nervous girls and their horses trot in a circle around the stable yard. Mercilessly, the sun beat down on us through the palms, and all of us strained our eyes in the bright light. I didn't mind too much though, because every time I blinked I saw a pair of brown eyes dance inside of mine.

12

The day of the hunt, I woke early out of either nervousness or excitement—it was hard to distinguish the two these days. This was my chance to return to Cen, and I had to take it. I dressed quickly in my black tunic and riding pants, tucking them carefully into the tan riding boots we were each provided. Jessra braided my hair, twisting one side so that a small braid trailed around the long braid that hung down my back. "Don't leave me all alone on the hunt like you did at the practices," she teased, "I don't want to be stuck in the back with Hortense and the rest of the primeval courtiers."

"Of course not. I'll stay with you the whole time," I assured her. I hadn't told anyone about meeting Prince Corban in the stables that day, and I felt guilty for withholding such an important detail from Jessra. Still, the last thing I needed was to draw more attention to myself and any mention of a private encounter would automatically cause the other girls and courtiers to focus more on me. Besides, staying in the back might make for the best escape route. I could slip off without anyone noticing.

We ate a quick breakfast of oatmeal with strawberries and cream before making our walk to the stables, soldiers surrounding us. Extra reinforcements were sent for the hunt to ensure our "safety." Once we arrived at the stables and saddled up, Hendrik led us to an open field on the far end of the palace gardens where Prince Corban, the queen, and their royal entourage waited. I spotted Marley at the queen's right. Behind them stood Kirt and a few members of his staff dressed in their healer's robes with large sacks of what I assumed was medicine hanging on their horses. I wondered if they brought any of the vox cure with them, but then remembered that a portable furnace would be required for that.

Hendrik dismounted and bowed deeply before the queen, and each of us followed suit. I was in the back of the crowd and could not see Prince Corban's face, but looking around me I saw that each girl was casting eager, hopeful glances in his direction. After a brief ceremony involving a flag folding, we mounted our horses again and a trumpet was sounded. The hunt began.

We exited behind a heavily armored gate at the rear of the palace and started for the steep mountains of Deshan. Making our way south, we soon reached a large grassy bank—the outskirts of the capital. For the first few hours of the ride, I stayed in the back of the group with Jessra. Soon enough we lost sight of the royal party and the group of girls who rode fast enough to keep up with them. Jessra's horse, named "Largo," was slow and stubborn, and she had difficulty guiding him to where she wanted to go. My horse, Kinglo, was fine and attentive, but nothing compared to Lexon, who could read my movements from the way I shifted my weight or stroked his hairs.

"Petra is the prince's favorite, I think," Jessra remarked as we rode. "Rumor has it she grew up near the palace and is childhood friends with the prince." I nodded aimlessly. Petra was nice enough, even if she was a good friend of Younda's.

"It seems unfair that they would allow someone who already knows Prince Corban to enter the program," she continued, gauging my reaction.

"Yes," I replied distracted. "Although if she is eligible, why should she be punished for a previous friendship?"

She grunted back something inaudible.

We rode all morning and into the afternoon and I still had not found an opportunity to ride off, with guards trailing behind the last of us. While we rode I could not get Corban's brown eyes and challenge to race out of my mind. *Has he forgotten me?* I carried on an internal battle between hoping he would race me and hoping he would ignore me completely, which would keep me safe from the scrutiny of the other girls and royal party. We ate a quiet lunch of ham and warm bread under the trees before continuing our ride.

The heat made everyone miserable; sweat cascaded down our faces and the sides of our horses. Jessra helped pass the time after lunch by telling me a lengthy story about a tutor she once had. Her impressions made me double over with laughter, and since Hortense rode several yards behind us by then, I felt that I could laugh freely for the first time since I arrived. I didn't even mind the heat. This summer afternoon was the closest to home I could get: on the back of a horse, the blue sky welcoming, and familiar boots and riding pants instead of tight dresses. It almost made me want to stay. Almost.

Just as Jessra was describing a particularly hilarious encounter wherein she and her sisters dressed as servants and spied on the tutor, we topped a tall hill, squinting into the sunlight. Beneath us the entire hunting party waited, horses stomping and snorting, women in large black, floppy hats and men with their glistening arrows resting on their backs. Behind them were endless rows of white tents, a great tent resting in the center. On the top of the center tent, the Deshan flag waved in the wind, the purple stars on the white background beckoning us. The servants must have come a few days before to arrange our camp.

"How kind of them to wait for us," Hortense murmured from behind, evidently touched. I urged Kinglo to a canter, and the last of the group followed me down the hill. Scanning the crowd, I saw that several girls had circled their horses around Prince Corban, each attempting to move her horse closer to his. He looked completely overwhelmed by the conversations he was carrying on with multiple girls. The horses stomped angrily, trying to pull out of the circle despite their rider's urging. Jessra was right—Petra was among the group at the front, as well as Younda and Nadia. I pulled the brim of my hat down further to mask my face.

Marley cleared his throat so loudly that the entire party ceased their chatter and looked at him expectantly. "We will rest here tonight. Tomorrow we will venture further south and spend one more night before returning home. But, first, a ball!" he exclaimed, his black eyes small against his large forehead and cheeks. A chorus of cheers came from every girl in the group. The courtiers laughed politely while Marley grinned, glad to be the bearer of such good news. "Yes, yes. A hunt and a ball. You girls are a lucky group."

That evening we all dressed in the gowns that waited for us inside our individual tents. "Your tailors were given full creativity this evening, as is customary," explained Hortense. "It is tradition to have a masked ball the first night of the hunt. We wanted it to be a surprise for you all!"

My gown was made of fine black velvet, perfect for slinking off into the dark night. And with a mask—no one would be able to tell who I was. I couldn't have planned it better myself.

Ruldet outdid himself on the gown. Each sleeve was detailed with gold lace almost concealed beneath the velvet. The inside of the dress was lined with gold silk, which peeked out of the bottom of the dress. The same gold silk rippled across the back as though tied in knots in the center. It was impeccably made. A matching velvet mask lay next to the gown, and on its inside, Ruldet had embroidered a hunting scene. He had even stitched me on a white horse wearing the black dress. I was wearing the mask, and Prince Corban stood behind me.

A feast was held in the large white tent, where black lanterns hung dramatically throughout, dimly lighting the interior. We ate large bowls of wild rice soup with enormous plum-colored tomatoes and hot flatbread sizzling with garlic. The main course was a roasted pig, served with clusters of sour green apples and sharp goat cheese. Dessert was sparkling, white jellied custard with sugared berries and frosted almonds. I ate until I was sick. Although our meals in the palace were excellent, we had never feasted like this before.

Jessra sat next to me, wearing a midnight blue gown with a large silver bow. Her mask was silver and she made all of the guests around us laugh loudly with her stories of trying to get Largo to move faster on the ride. Just as she was imitating his aimless wandering into a small creek bed, Marley stood and clapped twice. Instantly the servants began clearing the tables, making room for the ball. A chorus of strings followed, and the ball began. I looked around eagerly, hoping to blend into the outskirts of the ball and from there, formulate an escape route.

Already, some of the girls had removed their masks, revealing their beautiful faces, tanned from the long day of riding. I retreated to a corner of the tent. From here I could see all of the exits, each heavily guarded. It would take a miracle to escape this tent prison, even in such a dark gown. I sat in the corner for most of the night, resting my head in my hands, formulating a plan for tomorrow. If I could distract Jessra, no one else would really miss me. It made me sad to think of leaving her like that, but my worries for Cen exceeded my loyalty to Jessra. Thankfully no one seemed eager to talk to the masked girl in the corner, so I occupied my time alone, enjoying my last night in this world—the music and the colors of the spinning light, even more beautiful when muted by the lantern-lit interior. Glancing around, I was so caught up that I did not see Prince Corban standing in front of me, unmasked and smiling broadly.

"Miss Larken?" he asked politely. "Is that you?"

"Yes, Your Highness!" I murmured quickly, coming out of my daze and rising hastily to curtsy.

"I told you in the stables that I hoped to dance with you. All of the other girls have removed their masks by now," he explained, gesturing around the room. "I wanted to find you, but in my search I embarrassed myself more than once by asking other masked women to dance," he said with a laugh. "One of them was my great-aunt Kiko. It was hard to see in the dark, but it turns out, she wasn't wearing a mask." His laugh was unfeigned and loud.

I removed my mask, feeling pleasantly unobstructed without it. I could finally see everything, and just as the prince said, all of the other girls had removed their masks and most of them were looking impatiently at Prince Corban and me in the corner.

"I apologize for the search, Your Highness. Although, I am flattered that you find me a more suitable dance partner than your great-aunt Kiko," I replied with a smile that was annoyingly persistent. I did not want to like him this much.

"Oh, the dance was fine. It was after the dance that was difficult. She seemed to believe I was her late husband Alver and refused to let go of me. Rather awkward." He chuckled. "Now that I have found you, Miss Larken, may I have the pleasure of this dance?" He held his hand out to me, and I timidly took his arm. Jessra's eye caught mine as he led me to the center of the dance floor, and she raised her eyebrows and licked her lips, making me giggle as a slow, almost stationary dance began. Fortunately, this was an easy dance to remember, and I did not need to concentrate too much.

"Did you enjoy yourself today, Miss Larken?" Prince Corban asked, his brown eyes as deep as I remembered.

"It was the best day I have had since arriving here, my lord," I replied honestly.

"Oh please—call me Corban" he interjected. " 'My lord' is what my father was called, and, well, it doesn't quite suit me." His expression fell when he mentioned his father. It stung me too, making me think of the conversation I had heard in the orchard months before. It was so easy to forget that Prince Corban had problems too. His father had been killed—and I doubted he even knew it. He probably believed that it was a "fever" like everyone else. The program started so soon after the king's death, that he hardly even had a chance to mourn.

I nodded in understanding. "Corban," I said, trying it out. "A hunt is a welcome substitution to a ball," I offered, watching his eyes carefully.

"Agreed. There is nothing like a hunt. But I believe most of the girls prefer a ball, which is why we threw a ball as well," he explained. "It was Marley's suggestion. The hunt is a yearly tradition, and there is always a masked ball the first night, but the girls from the program have never been invited before. I thought it was a good idea myself. He believes that the young ladies in the house should have as much interaction with the royal court as possible."

"I agree," I replied. "How else will you be able to reach a decision without spending time with each of the girls in the house?" I regretted those words as soon as they left my mouth.

Corban frowned. "Oh yes. The decision. I would rather talk about the hunt," he suggested graciously. "If you don't mind?"

I smiled widely. The way he diverted questions reminded me of how I was with Jessra. "I would love nothing more."

We chatted easily about the hunt, and I told him all about Lexon, how he could read my subtle movements and all about our long rides together. He told me about his favorite horse and the afternoons when his father would take him for long rides through the palace grounds. He also told me about his father's horse, a strong white mare that loved his father dearly. "She used to begin snorting before he even entered her stall," Corban told me with glazed eyes. "She recognized his scent." He continued telling me stories about his father until I received a heavy tap on the shoulder, interrupting our dance and conversation.

I turned around to meet the black, beady eyes of Marley, his forehead shiny with the lantern light. "Prince Corban, I believe you are neglecting your other guests," he reprimanded, motioning to the clustered group of girls, all shooting looks of disgust in my direction.

"Oh, right," Corban said, looking around sheepishly. "How many songs has it been?"

"Your Highness has danced for more than five dances with the girl from Canton," Marley said, pointing an accusing finger in my direction.

I curtsied, feeling my face blush at his condescending tone toward me. "Of course. Thank you so much for the dance, Your Highness," I managed to murmur out.

"Wait," Corban spoke loudly. Brushing past Marley, he touched my arm lightly, pulling me closer to him. "I look forward to our race tomorrow, Larken. Don't be hiding out in the back of the party like you did today, because I will find you." He laughed playfully, before walking off with Marley in the direction of the other girls. I did not dance with him again for the rest of the evening. My heart fell, but I couldn't be sure if it was because his attention would make my escape difficult tomorrow or if it was because I was no longer in his arms.

Jessra dragged me to the corner and insisted I tell her everything he said. As I rehearsed his stories about his father, I wondered vaguely how he knew I was riding in the back of the group when I didn't remember telling him that.

13

The second day of the hunt was overcast, which was a welcome change for all of us. Our horses were still sweaty but seemed to move much faster than the day before. I stayed in the back of the group for the first few hours of the hunt as the men ran ahead with their bows and arrows outstretched, eager to catch whatever it was they were hunting. A dozen soldiers held up the rear, circling the group protectively like sheep dogs. There was not one opportunity for me to lead my horse away. Instead of escaping like I planned, I let Jessra tell me all of the gossip from the night before. How the prince told Petra she looked beautiful in her crimson silk. How he danced three times in a row with Keisha, her braid bouncing against her knees. More than anything though, she told me that everyone wondered what he said to me that night. Five dances in a row was the most time he spent with anyone the entire evening, and several girls were jealous. I attempted to divert her attention to no avail. We talked about the ball, the gowns, and the food for most of the morning.

After a lunch of olive salad and hot cheese bread, the men returned and joined us on our venture south. Prince Corban, along with Hendrik and several soldiers, shepherded the group. In the middle of one of Jessra's impressions of Younda droning on to the queen and her friends about who her father was, I lifted my eyes and saw Corban riding against the flow toward us. The girls near the back looked at him expectantly, smoothing back their hair and smiling sweetly as he approached.

I kept my eyes down. I wanted that race with him more than anything, but I could not risk drawing more attention to myself. Not now, when the soldiers were beginning to drift past our group of courtiers, bored with their pace. He steadied his horse as he came near us. "I told you, Miss Larken, that I would come to claim my race. Fortunately I knew just where to find you. Shall we just admit that the outcome of the race is decided?"

I looked at Jessra, whose eyes were opened wide in surprise. Several other girls looked at each other in disgust at my singled out attention while others pouted or gazed longingly at Corban. Jessra, however, was grinning widely now, waving me to go ahead. Grateful, I turned Kinglo toward Corban's horse, ready to race.

"Well, I was going to say that a lady would never race, but when you put it like that . . . let's see if you can keep up with a Canton rider." I gave him a competitive smile and then spurred Kinglo forward, tearing ahead of the group. The prince's horse galloped close behind mine as I steered toward the grass and around the large hunting group. No one attempted to stop us. The wind blew off my hat as we neared the front. I turned around to see how close Corban was and was passed by a black blur.

I rode freely, the way I had ridden Lexon through the orchard only months before. I followed Corban and his horse closely, and we rounded a corner of the trail that led into a shallow forest hanging delicately on the edge of a rocky cliff. The air was fresher up here and cooler already. Our horses climbed noisily, their thundering hooves rattling against the stony ground. Once we reached the top I dared to look around, expecting to see soldiers following us, and instead discovered that the rest of the group was not even in sight. If I could distract Corban, this could be my chance to escape.

We rode for so long that my legs began to cramp and Kinglo started to slow down, wheezing as he inhaled. Corban wove in and out of the trees, his horse much stronger, until he saw that I was slowing. He lifted his eyes to shade his face from the sunlight that filtered in between the leaves. "Let me guess, Miss Larken," he said out of breath. "The horses in Canton are not as fast as those in the palace?"

I smiled. "Well, this horse is not, but my horse at home could challenge yours any day."

He laughed. "Maybe so. I look forward to meeting Lexon someday, if you would allow me to. What do you say we get these horses some water and a break?"

"They've earned it," I said to Kinglo, rubbing his ears affectionately. We had both slowed to a trot and were approaching a small pond just beyond the trail, surrounded by trees on every side.

Corban inhaled deeply. "What a beautiful day. I can think of nothing more I would rather do."

"It's perfect out here." We became quiet as we approached the water. The foliage grew denser the closer to the pond we got.

"Oof!" he exclaimed suddenly, looking toward his right arm.

"Is everything all right, Prince Corban?" I asked anxiously. "What is it?"

"It's nothing," he said with a smile, shaking his head, embarrassed. "It's just that we've reached the pond!" He gestured but continued to hold his arm strangely. "Let's give the horses some rest." We both dismounted, him with considerable difficulty since he used only one arm. We sat together on the edge of the pond, allowing several feet between us.

As our horses drank, Corban rolled back his sleeve, examining his arm.

"Is something the matter, Prince Corban?" I asked as he clutched his arm in pain. "What is wrong with your arm?"

"I think . . . ," he murmured—but before he could finish, he fell to the ground, convulsing. He shook wildly and his eyes rolled back, showing only the whites. Screaming for help, I cleared the space around his head and rolled up his sleeve to get a better look. My heart surged with the same familiar energy that came to me a hundred times before in the clinic. It had been so long since I felt it. Exhaling, I realized his arm sported a large red circle surrounded with an ashy gray halo.

"Floittles," I spat angrily. Floittles were flying insects with razor-sharp stingers. Although not common in Deshan, they were occasionally found in the woods and the orchards. Sometimes we treated floittles stings in the clinic, although they were rare. If untreated for longer than fifteen minutes, the ashy gray ring expands and eventually cuts off the blood supply. The antidote is the kijung leaf, which is common in wooded areas, but I was unfamiliar with these woods and not certain if I could find them. I was sure Kirt would have an antidote, but he and the rest of the party were nowhere in sight.

I glanced down at Corban as he convulsed, then glanced fleetingly at the open forest behind me. I would never have such a clear opportunity to escape again. I could steal Kinglo and escape into the forest, making my way back to Kalvos. It was a foolish feeling, though. I knew I could never return to Cen—could never live with myself if I left at that moment.

Continuing to yell for help, I ran toward the forest, rummaging through the nearby bushes looking for the kijung—a large, bay-like leafy tree. As I got closer to the pond I thought I saw one on the other side. I couldn't be sure, but it looked close enough from here. There wasn't time for to run around the pond, so I dove into the water and swam violently toward the other end. The water was murky and filled with plants and sticks. As I neared the edge of the pond, I caught my arm on a sharp hanging branch and felt it rip through my tunic. Blood was seeping through the fabric already, and pain radiated down my arm. The kijung leaves hung low. I tore off a whole branch and began my swim back. It was much slower this time because of my bad arm, and more than once I felt something slither around my ankle, but I kicked wildly, willing myself to the other side.

When I got back to Corban, his face was completely gray; the halo surrounding the sting had expanded rapidly. I couldn't tell if he was still breathing. Frantically, I tore off a leaf from the branch and began to chew it. In the clinic we would mash it in a bowl with some water, but I didn't have that luxury here. When a bitter mush of leaves had clotted in my mouth, I pulled it out in a clump. Desperately, I rubbed the pulp on Corban's sting.

"Come on, Corban, breathe. Breathe!" I pleaded. I chewed up more leaves, while continuing to rub the pulp into his sting. "Wake up, Corban. Wake up. Please wake up." Fear swarmed my senses. It wasn't just Corban's life that was in danger, I realized as I chewed. If anything happened to Corban, my background would be checked, and my secret would be discovered. And Corban . . . I didn't even want to think about it.

For a brief but potent moment of weakness, I considered again mounting Kinglo and riding far away into the forest. I had done what I could for Corban—the rest was up to him. From there I could go back to the orchard village and resume my normal life.

I looked down at Corban, his face still gray and his body still. I barely knew him, but I knew I could never leave him. Not now, not when his life was still in danger. Even if he was the ruler of the Brockans. Even if he would soon be the king, the one to continue to keep my people as his slaves. I heard Cen's voice in my ear: "We're healers, Emi." I continued to chew the leaves.

The rest of the party neared the pond, horses clanking up the rocky mountainside with each step, courtiers chatting and whistling. I brushed Corban's sweaty hair away from his face, willing him to wake up, praying with everything in my soul—and just as the others rounded the corner, he began to cough. I let go of his head as he sat up and continued to cough wildly, his face still completely white.

"Over here!" I called. "Please help!" The riders steered their horses to me, following my voice. Hendrik was the first to reach us.

"What happened?" Dropping from his horse, he ran to Corban's side, followed quickly by several men. "Call for Kirt!" Hendrik yelled in the direction of the group.

He took one look at me in my soaked, torn tunic and the blood dripping from my wet sleeve, before wrapping me in his arms. "Oh Larken, what happened?"

I opened my mouth to reply right as the girls from the mansion approached the scene. "Is the prince wounded?" I heard Keisha exclaim, causing an influx of girls to surround Corban, eager to hear about his bravery and console him. Hendrik left me to supervise them while several girls screamed and others began to cry. I never understood how so many of them could cry on demand. I sat trembling on the outskirts of the group, too shocked to look down at my own arm. Kirt was led through the crowd to examine Corban, motioning for the girls to give him some space. For several minutes I sat watching from a distance as Corban was given bread and water. His mother knelt at his feet, touching his face as he smiled at her and nodded, reaching to clasp her hand. The other girls in the program formed a circle around the two of them, several of them with tears in their eyes, casting hopeful glances at him, though his eyes were focused on his mother.

"Larken is hurt too," Hendrik informed Kirt, who ran to my side with his kit when he was finally confident in Corban's well-being. I showed him my torn sleeve, which was drenched in blood. I was beginning to feel light-headed from the loss of blood, and the loud noises of the group did not help the throbbing pain emanating from my arm and head. Not to mention the bitter taste in my mouth left from the leaves. Before asking what happened, Kirt tore my entire tunic sleeve off, revealing a sharp gash in my arm. A piece of wood was still lodged there, and I bit my fist as Kirt pulled it out in one painful motion. Several splinters from the wood were left behind, and he slowly retrieved them with his tools. looked away, focusing on the ground as he pulled them out. The sounds of the courtiers became a dull hum in my head. Once the splinters were removed, Kirt cleaned the wound with some blue ointment and stitched it up.

As he was sewing, he bent his head close to mine. "Kijung leaves?" he whispered, too low for the others around us to hear.

"You saved his life, you know." I was beginning to feel a release from the shock and craned my neck to see the girls crowded around Prince Corban, his mother stepping back, tears still streaking her face. He was smiling, his hands motioning downward as if to assure them that he was fine. Before I knew him I might have thought that he would act like a hero, relishing in the attention they gave him. Instead, I noticed his disinterest, scanning the crowd as though he were looking for someone.

Kirt wrapped my stitches in a bandage as I asked, "Is the prince all right?"

Kirt smiled. "What do you think?" He gestured to the group of admirers. "I'd say he's more than all right." He pulled me close and in a low voice asked, "Larken, how did you know it was floittles? And even more, that a kijung would treat it?"

My pulse returned. How long would I have to lie to Kirt? I shrugged, my eyes wide. "I think I read it somewhere once." He nodded, but the look on his face said that he didn't believe me.

"Her treatment is complete," he said to Hendrik, standing up and smoothing down his robes.

Hendrik offered me a hand up with my good arm. "You'll ride ahead of the rest of the group with me, Larken. We want to get you to a safe place where you can rest. I'm sure you could use it." I smiled gratefully and allowed him to help me onto his horse, which would now carry two riders. My heart sunk in my chest. Gone were my hopes of escaping on the hunt. After what happened, I would never be left alone again. Kirt climbed on his horse as well, and the three of us rode through the forest, Hendrik cutting down branches in our path, and Kirt following closely behind.

Once we arrived at the rows of tents, a servant showed me to a private one, where I fell into a strange, disturbed slumber. As the sun blared down through the white canvas, I had the same dream repeatedly. I was in a black sand desert, the sky a brilliant forest green with multiple moons dotting it like stars. Corban convulsed face down, his arms thrashing in the sand as though they were liquid—the waves of the ocean. I waded through waist-high sand to reach him. But when I went to turn him around, it was Cen's face, motionless, looking up at me instead.

✳ ✳ ✳ ✳

When Hortense woke me, it was dark. "Are you feeling quite all right, Miss Larken?" she asked, holding a candle close to my face.

"My arm hurts," I answered honestly. "How is Prince Corban doing? Is he feeling better?"

She scratched her face with two fingers. "Oh yes. His Excellency is feeling quite well, and I understand it was all thanks to you." She gave me a toothy smile. "Trouble seems to follow you wherever you go, Miss Larken, but I'm glad that you were there when this trouble arose. Sir Kirt told me that you knew just what to give the prince to save his life. And Sir Hendrik had nothing but good things to say. Of course I told him that we discussed some healing in our classes, and he was rather impressed by my teaching skills." She fluffed her hair with her hands.

We had never discussed healing in any one of our classes, and I doubted whether Hortense even knew what floittles were, much less the cure, but I bit my lip and smiled up at her, not feeling well enough for an argument. "I owe it all to you," I said with a grimace. "I was hoping that I could continue to sleep. Although I am rather hungry," I admitted. "Perhaps a meal could be brought to my tent?"

She wrinkled her nose. "Oh no, the queen herself asked me to make sure you are in attendance this evening. There will not be a ball, but there will be a feast!" She clapped her hands together. "I brought your gown. Please be punctual; it will begin shortly. The soldiers outside of your tent will escort you to the feast when you are ready." She laid a white dress and a neatly folded emerald sash on the edge of my cot. "I will see you soon, Larken. Don't be late." Right before exiting she turned around to poke her head back in the tent. "And brush your hair!"

With one hand I attempted to brush out the leaves and sticks that were caught in my hair from the pond, braiding it with difficulty. *Where is Jessra when I need her?* Putting on my gown was even more difficult, and tying my sash was ridiculous. Two soldiers followed me on the long walk to the main tent.

The rest of the girls were seated before I came in, all wearing the same white dress I sported with a different colored sash. Jessra eagerly motioned for me to join her. The rest just stared at me and turned to each other to whisper—no doubt about the state of my hair and sash. Before I could ask, Jessra stood up and braided my hair, retying my sash while glaring at the other girls. "Thank you," I whispered to her, once again surprised by her kindness, but she just smiled in response, rubbing my back lightly with her hand.

The food was as elaborate as the night before, but for the first time since arriving at the castle, I barely touched it, still feeling ill about what happened on the hunt. Jessra begged me in a whisper to tell her about the race and Corban's injury, but when I opened my mouth to tell her, every girl in the program leaned in close, hoping to get some details as well. With a shrug I closed my mouth. "I'll tell you later," I murmured. I kept looking at Corban, a few tables over, hoping he would catch my eye, but he never even glanced over at us. Instead he chatted with the courtiers near him, including Marley, who sat at his left.

After the feast, Marley stood up and clapped his hands. The entire tent hushed, looking to Marley expectantly. "Her Majesty the queen has something she would like to say," he shouted, offering his hand to help her up from the chair. We had not heard from the queen since our first day at the castle and all of us sat up attentively. Her kind eyes smiled at our group, resting finally on me.

"First of all, please let me say what a joy it has been to have you young ladies along with us on the hunt this year." She smiled graciously. "The hunt has been a tradition for my family for many years. Since the death of my husband, King Jairus, we have not had much happiness in our home at the palace. This hunt has restored so much joy to me, as well as to my son, Prince Corban." She looked down at Corban tenderly. His arm was resting in a sling at his side, the black blending in with his suit. "However, there was an incident this afternoon that could have turned out very badly. Thanks to one young lady who showed tremendous resourcefulness, it did not." She paused, and immediately the girls sat up straighter, flashing white, toothy smiles at the queen. "The lady I wish to thank is Miss Larken of Canton."

I reached up to touch my face, flushing with embarrassment. I had never had so many people look at me with such interest in my life. My plan to avoid attention was not working.

"Prince Corban was wounded on the hunt," she expounded. A collective gasp echoed throughout the tent, even though I was sure everyone had already heard. "Miss Larken, I am told by our chief healer, knew just what to do when my son sustained a life-threatening insect sting. She cut her arm badly during the process of retrieving the only leaf that could heal it. My chief healer told me that without her knowledge and persistence, Prince Corban might not have made it." Several of the girls around me were either crying, or pretending to cry about his nonexistent death as the queen continued. Some of them held white handkerchiefs to their faces dramatically, and if I weren't so embarrassed by the public attention, I would have had difficulty controlling my laughter. "My sincerest gratitude is yours today, Larken. Thank you for your ingenuity and courage."

Silence settled through the tent when she finished until Jessra began to applaud, and although reluctantly, the rest of the girls set their handkerchiefs on their laps and joined her. Soon the entire tent was clapping. I looked toward the open door of the tent and saw Hendrik and Kirt standing near each other, also clapping on my behalf. I dared to peek at Corban and for a moment his eyes locked with mine. He smiled widely, attempting feebly to clap along with the group and mouthed the words, "Thank you," before being pulled aside by the courtiers sitting next to him, each eager to hear his story.

When the excitement died down, Marley stood. "Thank you, dear queen. Dessert is still coming. Please enjoy the final night of the hunt."

Midway through my dessert of pineapple-pear cake and candied lentils, I felt a tap on my shoulder.

"Marley requests your presence in his tent, Miss Larken of Canton," a soldier said mechanically, his eyes staring straight ahead instead of meeting mine.

Jessra shot me a concerned look, and I wiped my face with my napkin before standing. "Please show me the way," I replied, grateful that the long white skirts covered my legs, shaking uncontrollably in fear.

14

Two guards escorted me to Marley's tent in silence, drawing their weapons after I lifted the flap to step inside. The interior of the tent was lined in black silk. A large black metal bed stood in the direct center of the room, with enormous fuchsia and gold patterned pillows littering the floor. Incense burned nearby, the scent sickly sweet, a thin veil of smoke filling the black cavern. Marley stood near the rear of the tent with his hands clasped behind his back.

I cleared my throat. "Sir? I was told you wanted to speak with me?"

He waited for several moments before turning around, as though the black silk walls of the tent were more significant than any human. "Yes, please sit," he purred, gesturing toward a circle of large pillows that surrounded a black marble table.

I perched on the edge of a pillow delicately, my sash falling across the silky floor. "Did you want to talk about the hunt?"

"Yes, of course, among other things," Marley said, crossing the room to sit on the pillow directly across from me. The marble table was the only thing resting between us. He looked up at me. "Did you enjoy yourself today?"

"Immensely," I replied, my lower lip quivering. I tried to smile so he wouldn't notice.

"Excellent. You showed bravery in the forest, although I am uncertain why you were alone with Prince Corban in the first place. It is against the rules, as I am sure you are aware."

I released a sigh. He called me here to reprimand me about following the rules and nothing else. "Yes, sir. It was not my suggestion."

"You dare blame the misconduct on the prince?" he exclaimed, rubbing his chin with his long fingers. There were rings on each finger and two on his pinky, each of them with a different colored gemstone on a gold setting. "Interesting."

"N-n-no, sir," I stammered, tearing my eyes from his jeweled hands. "I take responsibility for the misconduct. I was only stating, rather, that the race itself was Prince Corban's idea."

"Same thing." He waved with a brush of his hand. "Despite your wrongdoing, the queen determined that you should be given another chance. Her decision, not mine. Since you are going to be around for a little longer, thanks to her mercy, I have made it my personal responsibility to get to know you better."

I groaned inwardly. "I would like that," I offered with a hoarse whisper.

"Tell me about yourself, Larken. I must admit that you are a bit of a mystery to me. My scouts interviewed every other girl personally and I myself attended several interviews. I have met the parents of all of the other participants and I am personally familiar with most of them." His eyes focused on the tent wall behind me. "Many of them were raised as courtiers or otherwise have connections to the throne . . . then there's you.

"You come from Canton, they say—although you look nothing like a Cantonian." If I were not so afraid, I would have taken that as a compliment. Marley continued, "We rarely venture that far from the capital to select participants in the program, but a scout informed me that they did venture into your region, albeit briefly. I assume your father met with one of them?"

I gulped. "Yes," I replied. *This is where I get found out. Marley will kill me.*

"Then you won't mind if I send another scout there to verify that he did, indeed, meet with your father?"

My heart raced as he asked, but I did my best to remain confident. Perhaps he was bluffing. "Of course not, sir. My father would be happy to receive one of your men."

He snorted, clearly not expecting that answer, before changing the subject again. "Hortense has given me a full report on you, per my request. You know nothing of courtly table manners, you speak out of turn, and you struggle with your poise, conversation and fashion. Yet you are excellent at foreign languages, you ride a horse better than the prince himself, and miraculously you knew *just* which leaf would save Prince Corban's life. What can you tell me of that, Larken of Canton?" He practically spit out my name, unable to refrain from his obvious frustration at knowing so little about me.

He lifted his eyes until they rested evenly with mine—piercing and thorough, as though attempting to extract every truth contained within me. "You also behave rather like a . . . Oh never mind. Not possible," he muttered.

Like a Savian? "Excuse me, sir? I don't understand." I feigned ignorance, trying to sing the song that comforted me in my mind but the terror of my thoughts wouldn't let me. *Ring out the Bells . . . This is it. I am found out . . . Pull up your boots . . . I will be publicly killed. They will kill Cen—they will lash out against my people because of my treason.*

"And what is it that you do not understand?" Marley's voice boomed.

I struggled to find the right words, carefully omitting any mention of my identity. "I admit that my training has been less than traditional. I know also, that many of my weaknesses are strengths of the other girls, and that my strengths, in turn, are their weaknesses,"

I confessed. "Perhaps we are just different? Although I believe that I can compensate for those weaknesses. I am learning so much from Hortense."

Fortunately, this statement shifted his attention. "What are you learning about that appeals to you most?" he asked, watching my eyes carefully.

I looked at him without flinching, his tiny, beady eyes my new focal point. "Geography and foreign policy are my favorite," I replied. "As well as foreign languages."

"Ah," he responded. "What of government?"

"I enjoy my classes in government as well. In particular, the history of government is a special interest of mine."

"Hmm. History," he muttered, stroking his beard. "Tell me then, Miss Larken of Canton—are you aware of the infestation of Savians in our Deshan borders? The history books are rampant with those old tales of wars, skirmishes, sedition. Why, you cannot read a history about the Brockans without extensive coverage of the Savians as well. A bit unfair, actually, for those of us who would like to forget that hopeless race." He laughed, looking at me for a reaction, seeming disappointed when he didn't get one.

"I am aware that there are many Savians in Deshan," I replied, hopeful he would not catch the emotion in my voice.

"Yes. A rather worthless people," he spat. "What is your opinion on them as a whole? Should we continue as a nation to support their habits? Their 'way of life?' Why, right now most of our military force is spent on those creatures. Making sure they work, making sure they pay their necessary tributes, making sure they don't break off and run away. Why, without them this nation could really rise. With our soldiers focused on expansion, we could multiply Deshan, carrying our fine lifestyle and culture into all walks of life beyond the boundaries here. Perhaps even those in Canton could participate," he said with a wink.

"Where do you suggest the Savians go?" I whispered roughly, stunned that he would share his plans with a mere hopeful—a young woman residing within the palace walls, a young woman he knew little to nothing about.

"I don't much care where they go!" he boomed, before laughing hysterically, his hands grasping his sides. "As long as it is out of my way and the way of this great country. Of course I would have to convince Prince Corban—I still have to show him what his nation could really be without them. He could be heralded as the greatest king in history! Completely legendary—with me at his right hand."

He stared at me as though memorizing my face, my features. "It would be helpful to have a girl Corban fancies on my side. If you could convince him somehow that my plan is the best for the king-dom, why, this country could really go somewhere. And if you were to become the queen . . . well, you would have more power than you can even comprehend now."

When I didn't respond right away, he prodded me, "Well? Will you help me or not? By doing so, of course, you would only be helping yourself. Granting yourself more power." He formed a wry smile. "And believe me when I say that I am someone you want as an ally."

"What exactly is your plan, sir?" I asked, trying as hard as I could to not let the tears welling up in my eyes from falling. His eyes narrowed, so I hurried to explain myself. "I couldn't very well convince him of a plan I knew nothing about," I added.

He frowned and stood up, turning to face the dark wall again. "All you need to know is that there is a plan. One that will rid this country of the vile Savians for good. It has already started actually— a few orchard villages have already been experimented on and it has proven to be quite successful. It has the potential to destroy their race forever." His voice was solemn but proud. I hated it.

My voice caught in my throat and all at once, I knew exactly who Marley was. The night in the orchard, one of the soldiers had spoken his name: *"Marley has made it clear to me and the rest of his loyal followers that he wants the Savians gone."* I gasped at the real-ization. I was trapped in a tent with a man that sought to destroy my entire race. Not only did he want to destroy them, but he also wanted me to help him. I covered my mouth, feeling like I might be sick.

"Something the matter?" Marley asked, clearly sensing the urgency in my face and sudden change in behavior.

"No sir, nothing at all. I just don't feel well all of a sudden," I mustered out, knowing I would not be able to contain my anger much longer.

"Too hard of a ride for you?" he asked rudely. "Most women feel the same after a long ride. They are much weaker than men, you see. Very well then. Thank you for coming to my tent, Larken of Canton. I feel that we are friends now. That we have an understanding." His tongue flicked the word *friends* to me, but his dark eyes conveyed that he definitely did not consider me a friend.

"Of course, Your Excellency," I offered, with a deep curtsy. "I appreciate your interest in me."

"You would be wise to consider the plan," he affirmed, unflinching. "You are evidently one of Prince Corban's favorites, or I would not have asked. I will not forget this conversation."

I could not bring myself to smile at him. I could not agree or even feign acceptance. So I left with only a curtsy. "Get her back to her tent, boys," Marley ordered the soldiers, who saluted and stood on either side of me on the long walk through the rows of tents until we finally reached mine.

I clambered into the bed that was rolled out for me, not even bothering to take off the white dress, and buried my face into my pillow. Then I screamed until my voice was hoarse and no more tears could fall from my eyes.

15

When we arrived back at the palace, I had a letter waiting for me. On top was a note from Kirt's assistant Natty, stating that it arrived to the clinic. I tore it open as soon as I received it, while the other girls took off their riding clothes and changed into dinner attire. Amid all of the chatting and giggling about the hunt and its events, I read.

Emi,

> *I don't know if this is safe, but Cen told me he would send this to you. I am alive. I hope I can repay you someday.*
>
> *I went to my village to find my brother, but it was too late. Most of my village is dead—mass graves were dug to bury them.*
>
> *The soldiers at our village don't have the disease. Less of them are needed now. They are ransacking homes. We are so hungry. Many have vox, but some have avoided it. I wish I knew more about the disease. I wish*

*I knew how to give them the same antidote your friend
Kirt gave me, but he only brought enough for one.*

*I know there is nothing you can do from there, but I
wanted you to know what is really happening outside the
palace gates. And I also wanted to say thank you again,
in case I don't get another chance. You'll never know
what your sacrifice means to me.*

Maddock

I looked up from my bed and could tell Jessra sensed the
urgency in my face. "Bad news from home?" she asked timidly, her
eyebrows raised.

I nodded. My face must have reiterated how serious this was,
because Jessra didn't ask any more questions.

She reached out her hand to mine and gave it a squeeze. "It's
about time for dinner. Why don't you come down when you're ready
and I'll save you a seat? I'll tell Hortense you needed to lie down."

I nodded gratefully. "You're a good friend, Jess," I called out as
the other girls filtered out of the room.

As soon as they were all gone, I lay on my back, staring at the
vaulted ceiling above me. It seemed strange that I would receive this
letter so soon after Marley spoke to me. I knew there were many
from Maddock's village infected by vox, but not as many as his
letter made it sound like. I knew why the soldiers were unaffected—
they had already received an antidote—but how could it spread so
quickly among the villagers? And how did King Jairus know it was
coming? Or was it Marley who asked Kirt to discover a cure? Being
here, being trapped in this palace, made me forget momentarily
that there were so many lives in danger besides my own.

I closed my eyes and sang the Savian hymn softly, in honor of
Maddock's brother and so many of my people who lost their lives
to the disease and at the hands of the Brockans. "*Ring out the bells,
Pull up your boots . . .*" After several repetitions, and with swollen
eyes, I ventured downstairs for dinner.

Unfortunately, the other girls had not forgotten the hunt or the attention I received from Corban and the queen. I received a roomful of cold, angry eyes in my direction. More than once I asked a question of another girl, only to receive a sneer instead of a reply.

I tried to focus on my meal—cool cucumber walnut soup with crusty bread—and later swam with Jessra until the stars came out and we were told to go inside. Even after my exhaustion from the hunt, I lay awake in bed while Maddock's words danced on the dark ceiling above me. Sleep finally came, but in the morning I awoke with images of starving old women and infants, rings on their feet, crying into a darkness where no one heard them.

* * * *

A week or so after the hunt, Kirt called me back to the clinic. "He told me he needs to examine the arm you injured during your heroic rescue of the prince," Hortense said in front of the entire class with a sweet smile. She, unlike the girls, had been kinder to me since the hunt. "Of course I told him we could spare you for just a few minutes for something so important." I felt the heat of anger coming from the other girls and avoided looking at them. My arm was completely healed; Kirt's stitches had formed perfectly and he knew it. It had to be something else. The soldiers struggled to keep up with me as I ran to the clinic.

Kirt greeted me with an embrace, his regular black robes replaced with gray ones today. He led me to his office and shut the door purposefully behind him, standing against it while I took a seat.

"Is it another letter?" I asked him, my voice shaking as I looked up. "Natty delivered one to my room after the hunt. That was kind." It had been several weeks since I heard from Cen, and since Maddock's letter was less than positive, I wanted to hear that Cen was doing well despite the worsening oppression. More than ever, I needed some encouragement.

Kirt shook his head. "Not this time. There is something else I would like to discuss with you, but first let me examine your arm."

I nodded, rolling back the sleeve of my dress while he inspected my stitches. "Perfect," he murmured, patting my arm gently to let me know he was finished.

"What is it then?" I asked, "Is it about Corban? Has he recovered?"

Kirt smiled at the mention of his name. "Corban is completely fine. Better than ever, actually—all thanks to you. However, that is partly what I wanted to speak to you about today." He looked at me for permission to begin and I nodded, eager to hear what he was going to say. I hated to admit that news of Corban was almost as golden as news from Cen.

"Larken," he began, then walked to his chair and sat across from me, looking over his desk now. "Larken, if I had been there while Corban received his sting, I would have been able to save him." Kirt paused. "But I would have done it by applying beech root shavings, instead of the kijung leaf. It is cleaner, for one, and also slightly more effective."

I nodded. I'd read that beech root was better, but we never had access to it. Since kijung grew freely, it was always our course of treatment. "I didn't have a beech root," I replied. "Much less a tool to shave it with."

He looked down at his desk, removing his glasses. "Yes, I understand that. You did what you could. What concerns me, however, is that the kijung route is historically acknowledged as the Savian course of treatment." He spoke faster, avoiding my eyes, which would give everything away. "I will admit, I had my suspicions about you before, but the fact that you applied the kijung, and with the healer at the clinic and your brother looking the way he did . . . I had to bring you here so I could ask you myself."

My palms began to sweat. "I'm sorry, Kirt. What are you implying exactly?"

He sighed and rubbed his eyes before turning to meet mine. "When I met Cen from the orchard village, he called you his daughter *until* I told him that the girl I knew had a noble father from Canton. He quickly corrected himself, but I still found it odd. I did not ask him about your race. I knew he was Savian and I admit, I was rather curious about you because of some of your mannerisms, but there is enough light in your eyes that you looked Brockan enough, so I ignored them initially." I was startled at his revelation. My entire life I was told that I could pass for a Brockan, so despite the danger those traits poised to me in the palace, I felt proud that he recognized some Savian mannerisms in me.

"Larken, I simply cannot ignore the signs any longer. There is too much danger in your position here for me to ignore them."

I looked up at him, my body growing hot, searching his expression for signs of malice but all I saw was Kirt's simple face. He looked understanding, not angry—his eyes full of kindness. Tears hung, ready to pour from my eyes, as I contemplated what it would mean to tell him the full truth.

"Larken, are you a Savian?" Kirt's voice was completely flat. "You don't have to say anything. You can merely nod your head yes or no." His long spindly fingers tangled around each other like always, his eyes squinted. *This is where you lie, Emi*, I told myself. *This is where you tell him that his accusation is offensive and a complete lie. This is where you deny everything.*

Before I could stop them though, hot tears began to stream down my face. I didn't know how to respond to such a bold, life altering question but somehow I did subconsciously, my voice forcing out a broken, "Y-yes." I couldn't do it. I could not deny Cen and my mother—I could not reject my people. Even if this was the end for me, I knew I couldn't lie to Kirt.

Instead of getting angry or accosting me further, Kirt walked around his desk and knelt beside the chair I sat in, his arms wrapping around me tightly. "Oh dear one, you are in a difficult spot indeed." He held me as I cried out of fear for my own life, for Cen, for my village, for everyone I loved. I had put them all in a grim situation by being here, and I knew it was possible that were I to be found out, the punishment for my intrusion would be lashed out on to my people as well as to me. How could it be otherwise with Marley at the head of the council? I tried to stop, but it felt as if all of these months I had built up fears and feelings that were finally being released. It was scary, but it was necessary too. I heard myself sob, "I just wanted to save Maddock. I couldn't watch him die, Kirt. I couldn't watch it."

When I finally calmed down, Kirt spoke again. "Tell me everything, Larken."

I told him all. How I had a Savian mother who was killed. How Cen had raised me in the attic above the clinic, trained me to be the healer for my village. I told him about Maddock coming to our clinic that fateful night, ready to die if he did not receive treatment, and how I forced myself into the group in the marketplace, hoping I could get him the medicine he needed to recover. How I tried to escape that first night. I admitted that I had never slept-walked in my life, but I was trying to get to the clinic to find him. He nodded knowingly when I revealed this bit—clearly he had already put those pieces together on his own. I told him that every day since I had been gone, I lived in fear that my identity would be realized. Finally I told him how I missed Cen so badly that I felt at times that the missing would suffocate me.

At the end of my story, Kirt's eyes were wet. "You know what your secret means for me, Larken. Harboring it could mean death for treason." I nodded solemnly, my eyes too sore to cry anymore. I felt terrible about the situation I had placed Kirt in. The last thing I wanted was to cause him trouble because of me. "But do you also know, dear one, what it means for you?"

I shook my head "I don't know. Death. Worse than death."

He nodded. "You are right, as much as it pains me to admit that. You might be tried as a spy if you are found out, especially in these times. They will make a spectacle of you to the other Savians, affirming that the royal kingdom will not be mocked." I shuddered at the thought. I had never considered that they might think I was a spy. Kirt also confirmed my prior suspicions—that I would be made an example to the rest of my people. That my involvement here would affect far more than just me.

"So help me leave, Kirt!" I pleaded, a dry sob forming, "With your help I can escape. I can leave forever—return to my village.

Please. Every day I live here I risk someone discovering my secret. Please help me escape." I rubbed my face as I spoke, attempting to level my voice to no avail.

He waited several moments before he replied, each sentence he spoke very deliberate. "Larken, I have thought incessantly about you since my meeting with Cen. Of course part of that time was wondering if you were who I suspected, but that treatment on the hunt confirmed it for me." He pushed his clasped hands to his chest. "I thought briefly about turning you in, but I quickly determined that I could never do such a thing and live with myself."

My heart swelled in gratitude for Kirt at that moment. "Thank you," I whispered desperately.

"Dear one, I cannot help you escape. At this point, that is not an option. You have already, unwillingly perhaps, attracted Prince Corban's affections. He and the queen and Advisor Marley are carefully watching you since the hunt. Everyone in the palace is aware of it. Were you to leave, they would track you down. They would bring you back. Not to mention, your security is being tightened as we speak because you are in favor with the Prince." I rested my head in my hands, blocking the light emanating from his window. How could this happen? Why had I allowed myself to be alone with Corban?

Kirt continued, "Which means there is only one thing you can do. Stay here. Pretend. In eight months a queen will be chosen and you will be released. But you cannot leave, and you cannot try to escape. You can only do your best to blend in, as difficult as that may be for a bright ray of sun like you. As I said, you have already captured Prince Corban's attention. You must do all within your power to divert that attention. The closer you get to him, the more intensely you will be analyzed and the more likely your past will be uncovered. Stay out of his way, stay out of Hortense's way, and make yourself as plain and as insignificant as possible. That is what you must do if you want to survive."

I nodded in reply. He was right. It was the only thing that could be done. If I ever wanted to see Cen and those in my village again,

I would have to be released officially from the palace. I could do it. I could keep my secret for a little longer. I could avoid Corban; I could present other girls in a better light. And I would, even though the thought of him with another girl from the program tied my stomach in knots. How could I care so much about him at a time like this?

"You'd better go," Kirt said, looking at the sunlight narrowing through the tree behind his window. "I don't want Hortense to be angry with you. In the future it would be best not to attract too much suspicion from her."

I wished I knew how to express my gratitude to him for harboring my secret but I didn't, so I stood to obediently to go. At the door I hesitated, then turned back to him once more before opening the door.

"Kirt," I asked, "why are you doing this? Why risk your own life for a Savian girl you barely know?"

He put his spectacles back on and stood from his desk. "Because I don't believe we are as different as they tell us we are."

I waited for him to elaborate, but when he didn't, I realized that was his whole answer. It reminded me of my mother's letter. Maybe it was time for me to start behaving a little more like Kirt. This time I didn't run home to the mansion. I walked methodically, analyzing each stone on the path before me—each step, each rivet in the rock. Despite the fear still within me and the dread I felt at having to let Corban go, I hadn't thought it would feel this good to share my secret.

16

Weeks of silence went by. No new letters came from Cen or Maddock, although Kirt assisted me in delivering several to them. A veil of anxiety seemed to settle around me. I was constantly afraid I would receive a letter only to find that someone I loved had been imprisoned—or worse. The anxiety was made worse as my conversation with Marley resurfaced in my mind—over and over I heard his words, saw the shiny crease of his forehead as he formed the words *creatures* and *vile*.

Classes became increasingly difficult, and we were required to speak only in foreign languages during meals. For breakfast we spoke to each other in Kuhndan, lunch was Orplesh, and dinner was Sansikwan. It was so difficult that most of the time we did not speak at all. Instead, we ate our meals in silence—not that I was unaccustomed to silence. None of the girls had said a word to me since the hunt besides Jessra, although I heard them talk about me plenty.

A few weeks before the next ball, Hortense lined us up and directed us toward the tailor shop. I heard Younda and Nadia talking loudly about me on the walk there. While I was used to the other girls talking about me as though I weren't there, this time was different. It seemed more personal, spurred by something stronger than jealousy. "What I find strange," Younda said with a haughty tone, "is that Larken was never seen before coming to the mansion. The rest of us all knew each other before. Right, Nadia? She came out of nowhere."

Jessra turned around to say something, but I pulled her arm and told her to ignore them. "If you get mad, she wins," I said softly and Jessra shook her head, her face fuming in anger. I was lucky to have such a good friend. She had told the other girls off more than once for being rude to me, but until then, she had managed to maintain her composure.

"Shut it, Younda," Jessra whispered under her breath. Younda overheard her though, and it fueled her to keep going.

"We all can agree that it's curious that Prince Corban likes her at all," Younda continued. "Really, he must be blind. All of the girls here are more beautiful than Larken, and at least look their age. She is so scrawny and small, I think we all know why he has showed her some extra attention." She paused for dramatic effect as Nadia and some other girls giggled. "He clearly feels sorry for her. There can be no emotion other than pity." I felt Jessra's fist stiffen beside me, so I reached for her hand. The last thing we needed was to cause a scene when I was already being watched so carefully. Still, more than anything I wanted to form a fist myself and punch Younda in the face.

But Younda didn't stop there. "She can ride a horse, she knows medicinal treatments, and she lacks poise and table manners. Why, if I didn't know that the royal family would never allow it, I'd go so far as to say that she is completely Savian." Nadia gasped, and Jessra broke away from me with her fists drawn.

"That's enough!" Jessra yelled, rushing toward Younda with her arms outstretched. Before I could stop her, Jessra had pushed Younda to the ground and they were rolling around, wrestling each other. Jessra pulled Younda's long braid and Younda cried out, struggling to get free and kicking and punching Jessra wildly. They rolled off the path onto the grass, both huffing and screaming.

"Leave her alone!" Jessra yelled. "She never did anything to you!" I rushed over to pull Jessra off, and she slapped me out of the way. "No!" she screamed, "Let me do this!" I stood back with my hand on my face, stung by her ferocity. Frustrated, I looked back at the rest of the girls for some help, but they just watched helplessly, a couple of them pulling out their handkerchiefs and bursting into tears. Right on cue. Most of them, though, were smiling. This fight was the most exciting thing to happen to any of us since the hunt.

Hortense was behind us then, lifting her skirts and whistling for the soldiers to break up the fight. They stood watching, clearly unsure where this fit into their typical protocol. As they pulled the girls apart, I saw that Jessra's dress was torn on the sleeve and Younda's face was covered in dirt. Both girls snarled at each other and struggled against the soldiers, eager to get back to the fight. "What is the meaning of this?" Hortense yelled. "The future queen of Deshan would never react in such a way! Now tell me what happened, before I send both of you home."

Younda opened her mouth to speak and Hortense cut her off. "No, not you, Younda. I don't want to hear about who your father is or what he would say about this. I want to hear the *truth* about what happened." Younda clamped her mouth shut sheepishly, concentrating on the ground, clearly about to remark about who her father was. If I weren't so concerned about Jessra, I might have laughed. A wave of affection for Hortense filled me, albeit briefly.

Jessra piped up, her teeth clenched. "Younda was saying some nasty things about Larken, and well . . . well, no one would stop her, so I did!" Large tears streamed down her face, filling the gaps between her freckles. My eyes were wet too, seeing her so defensive of me.

"So you are admitting to starting the fight, Miss Jessra of Roding?" Hortense remarked, tapping her foot and folding her arms expectantly. "You said yourself that you had to stop her. Is that what happened, Younda?"

Younda nodded her head pitifully. "I didn't mean to cause any trouble." She conveniently stroked her arm as if there was some injury to it. "She just attacked me for no reason."

Hortense shook her head. "That I do not believe for a minute." Turning to the soldiers, she ordered, "Take the other girls back to the mansion. Make sure not one of them leaves the house until I get back." They nodded in response, and the other girls began to form a line.

"Now you two. Come with me," she ordered, gesturing to Jessra and Younda. "Oh and Miss Larken?" she asked, turning around, "You come along as well."

Hortense took us to the infirmary first. Kirt examined Younda and Jessra individually. Younda had a few bruises forming on her arm, and Jessra had some scratches on her neck, but besides that, Kirt exclaimed that they were no worse for wear, reassuring Hortense that there would be no lasting damage whatsoever from their little scuffle. He turned to examine me next, reaching for some swabs from his kit.

"Don't touch her. She's fine!" Hortense snapped. "If there's nothing more to do, let's get on our way."

Kirt looked at me with nervous eyes, and I shrugged in response. There was nothing I could do now.

Without saying another word to the three of us, Hortense led us on a walk. "Where are we going, madame?" Younda questioned, but one look from Hortense told her that speaking would not be tolerated. She led us to the main palace, a place we had not entered since the first ball. I hoped the queen would not discipline us. Even though Younda was the only person to suspect I was Savian, I felt that explaining that the reason for the fight to the queen would prompt deeper questioning of my race. She may even command Marley to seek out the scout that supposedly found me in Canton— if he hadn't already done it.

Once we entered the palace, Hortense turned only a few corridors before leading us into a hallway facing a large black door. The guard at the door looked at us curiously, while Hortense whispered something to him, at which he stood aside and allowed us to enter. We stepped into a tall library with black bookshelves that reached from the floor to ceiling. I gasped at the enormity of the room and the thousands of books lining the shelves. If it weren't so dark, it would have been the most beautiful sight in the world to me. The room was rounded on the far side, where windows stretched from floor to ceiling instead of shelves. Purple velvet curtains fell to the floor and four dark leather chairs faced a large, rounded desk. Behind the desk was an overstuffed black chair, studded with gold spikes around the edges. It was exceptionally cold, although it was the hottest day we'd had all week outside. "Wait here. Don't touch anything," Hortense ordered as we each sat down in one of the chairs. "I'll be right back."

Gold accented the entire room from the rounded desk to the studs on the chair. Even the black carpet we walked on was flecked with specks of gold. The workmanship of the shelves was unlike anything I had seen before, with intricate details and rounded edges. Creatures were carved into the wood too: snakes with two heads, ferocious-looking beasts that walked on their feet like a man, elephants with tusks bordered with jagged teeth.

Jessra and Younda both burst into tears the moment Hortense left, but I was too afraid to cry. I knew the moment I walked into that room that the person coming to discipline us was Marley.

* ✳ * ✳ *

We waited for almost an hour before Marley arrived, and by that point Jessra and Younda stopped crying. Jessra sat stunned, sullen, and silent. Younda kept whimpering like an injured puppy, huffing and whispering remarks about her father and the court. While they sat on the chairs waiting, I explored. I wanted to know everything there was to know about Marley, just like he wanted to know everything there was to know about me.

First I examined his shelves of trinkets. They were not the typical shells, stones, and statues I had seen all over the palace. Instead, his ebony shelves held vials. Some were filled with what looked like blood, and others held brightly colored fluids. The jaw of a small alligator was placed on the shelf in a glass case, the word *Token* engraved on it. He collected chess sets too, though these were not ordinary sets. They were made of rare stones—malachite, amethyst, and ruby. But the medium was not the only defining feature. Each set had one thing in common. All of the figures on one side were large and dominating while the other side had small, hunched-over figures. There were also no queens in any of the sets.

A chill crept up my neck as I analyzed his books. There were thousands of them, most of which were historical. *Deshan through the Ages*, *A History of Conflict*, and several copies of the popular history book that I had read dozens of times—*Brother Nations*. It detailed the history of the Savians and the Brockans and their ancient beginnings. Beyond the history books, Marley kept more unique titles. *Violence and Victors, Blood King*, and one book titled simply, *To Destroy a Race*. I did not know so many books existed beyond those I had been exposed to of history, medicine, and tales, but if there was a book about violence or war, I was certain that Marley owned it. I wouldn't be surprised if he had authored one.

"You really shouldn't be touching anything." Younda startled me, lifting her face up to reveal blotchy cheeks. "Hortense will be back any moment."

"Leave her alone!" Jessra snarled. "She can take care of herself."

Younda quieted down as soon as Jessra opened her mouth, retreating back to her whimpers.

I ignored both of them and wandered around to his desk. They began to bicker and I took my chance, cracking open the top drawer of the desk. Loose papers fluttered, and I saw a jewel studded gold knife. I examined the papers—nothing too interesting there. Some scrawls about meetings, the occasional list of things to do. But nestled in the back corner was a strange book. It was leather bound, and the top cover had a design of a circle with an arrow running through the middle of it. Curiously, I cracked it open to the front cover. There was a note scrawled in it that read "Project 11."

Timidly, I began to leaf through the pages, all of them filled with a scribbled, handwritten script. Some of them contained battle plans, outlining routes and troop numbers. Others had lists just like the ones that fluttered from his desk drawer, but there were names, instead of tasks to complete. Once I sorted past these, the book fell easily to a page in the center, where the binding was creased from use.

The page was held open by a map of Deshan with red circles scattered across it. Within each of the red circles was at least one green dot. In that same, familiar scrawl, several small details were written, but I couldn't quite decipher them.

Footsteps sounded on the cold marble tile outside the door, and I put the book back and quickly slammed the drawer shut, pocketing the map before I did. Madly I ran to sit next to Jessra just as Marley made his entrance. He wore a long dark robe that trailed the floor behind him. It had a cuff on the collar that rose upward almost touching his face. His bald head was shiny in this light.

"Ah, pets, I heard that there was a bit of a scrap this afternoon?" He sat across from us at the enormous desk, smiling down as though we were small children. "I was hoping not to have to see any of you until the next ball, but Madame Hortense let me know it was a matter she wished for me to address." He pretended to pout. "Not my favorite thing to do, but, well now, tell me everything. What happened, who said what? I promise I will lend a listening ear." He smiled, revealing glints of gold in his mouth. I imagined for a moment that if he stuck out his tongue it would be forked like a snake's.

Younda thrust an angry finger at Jessra. "This girl attacked me this afternoon and pushed me to the ground for no reason whatsoever! I am humiliated to even be sitting here in front of you. Truly, wait until my father hears about it." She huffed, all of the sadness and pity she expressed earlier clearly gone from her face. Now it was pure anger. "I expect you to punish her accordingly. She no longer belongs in the program."

Marley considered Younda's testament for several moments

before turning to Jessra, whose face was completely crumpled in fear. "And is this true, Jessra of Roding? Why, I hardly expected this kind of behavior from you, being from such a fine family." Marley gave her a twisted grin. "Tell me, did you really attack Miss Younda?"

Jessra's face blushed at the mention of her family. "Sir, she was saying horrible things about Larken, and I couldn't bear to hear them any longer. I had to stop her." She hung her head, defeated.

"Ah," Marley said, tapping his fingers together in front of his face. He wore different rings today, each finger featuring a large, sparkling black stone with jagged edges. "Now the truth comes out. Tell me, Miss Jessra of Roding—what sort of things was she saying about Miss Larken of Canton?" He looked at me for the first time since entering the room, offering a smug facial expression. I knew he was angry with me for my ambiguous response to join Corban to his plan. I sensed it in his voice.

Younda attempted to protest but was silenced by Marley's hand. "We'll talk to you in a moment, pet," he murmured with a grin. "Right now I want to hear what was said that was so awful about Larken that made a lady lose her temper."

I shook my head at Jessra, but she ignored me, her eyes red from her tears earlier. "She said that she didn't deserve to be here. That she was small and ugly." Her eyes filled with tears again and she shook her head in frustration. "Then she said that if she didn't know any better, she would say that Larken was . . . was . . . a Savian." She gushed out the last words, sobbing into her hands, while Marley looked on at her, amused.

"Ah, a Savian?" He looked at me. "That is an insult, indeed, Miss Younda. I would never have expected one like that from your mouth. Indeed, their kind is the vilest of any, although I do not know if even that insult should have merited a fight. After all, if one of you were fortunate enough to become the queen of Deshan you would have to deal with their lot on a daily basis. But hopefully not for long." He winked at me, and I bit my tongue to keep from crying out.

Jessra whimpered, her face humble. I knew she was worried about what her parents would say if they heard about this, how it might affect their standing with the court, but I wondered if she considered what Marley said at all. If the fate of the Savian race was any concern to her.

Marley sat up straight in his chair. "The truth is, I am pleased that this is what the fight was about. Younda," he said, motioning to her, "you felt it the biggest insult of all to call Miss Larken a Savian. And Jessra"—he motioned to her—"you were insulted for your friend and reacted to the accusation." He stopped then and stared directly at me, until I felt that he could see all of me—through my skin and bones and organs and straight to my soul. "That leaves only you, Miss Larken of Canton. Did you not feel that such a name merited a reaction? Did you not feel the need to join your friend Jessra of Roding in the attack?" He leaned over the desk until his face was close to mine before spitting out, "Do you not agree that being called a Savian is the worst name you could be called?"

I stared at him, unflinching. "I have been called worse," I said aloud, annunciating each word carefully. Jessra jerked her head to look at me, her eyes wide in astonishment. Younda cupped a hand over her mouth, horrified by my response. But Marley just stared at me, his expression unmoving. He leaned back in his chair and nodded his head twice before speaking.

"I see." He paused. "Miss Larken, it is too bad that you do not feel as your friends here do. You could have been a very valuable asset to the Brockan people." He sniffed before continuing, and I knew he interpreted my response as a blatant refusal to cooperate with him in any way. "Seeing as how you did nothing wrong, you are dismissed. I see no reason for you to receive any form of punishment, just because you were being teased and called ugly names." He waved his hand in disdain. "But before you go, I want to remind you that you have been close to being dishonorably released from the program before for breaking rules. If there is even so much as a whisper that trouble might be coming from you, I assure you, I will go directly to the queen herself and make certain that she disciplines you and involves your family in *Canton*." Already he was standing and gesturing to the door for me to leave.

I felt my breath quicken but stood to go. "Thank you for your time, sir. And thanks, Jessra," I whispered sincerely, her eyes swollen from the tears. "For sticking up for me."

She looked back at me gratefully, her shoulders relaxing a little. "Of course," she whispered back, offering me a feeble smile. "You're my best friend."

Before I even left I heard Marley ring a bell, calling for a servant to come. "Now that she is gone, I wanted to take this time to get to know you both a little better. Who is in the mood for some cookies and tea?"

I shut the door behind me, taking deep breaths to control my rage. I walked down the hall away from Marley's study, thinking that the soldier standing at the door would follow me and escort me to the mansion. But when I turned the corner and saw that he was not accompanying me, I began walking faster until I was running through the empty palace halls. Angry and alone for the first time since entering the program, I felt invincible.

And I had the map from Marley's book with me.

17

The palace was silent; the only audible sounds were my own footsteps clicking on the white marble. I needed to find Kirt. He would know what to do about the map and would be able to deliver a letter to Cen for me. And now that I had this map, rolled tightly and tucked into the bodice of my dress, I might be able to do something to help my people . . . if I could only determine what it meant to do that. It was clear Marley was trying to get rid of us—possibly kill us all.

By now I was completely lost—I couldn't remember how many turns I had made since Marley's office, and I only vaguely remembered the way Hortense took us through the palace to get there in the first place. I figured Marley would drink tea for an hour or so with Jessra and Younda, maybe less, and there was no way I could show up later than them to the mansion where Hortense would be waiting for us, expecting a full report.

It had been ten minutes since I saw the guard outside Marley's office. I kept walking, the maze of the castle continuing in a white, blank circle. There were no landmarks. No chairs in the hall, no portraits on the walls. Just white marble stretching out before me and white walls stretching out around me. This palace was built defensively. Any intruder would get lost and trapped inside before they found their way out. It was brilliant, sure, but terrifying at the same time. I wondered if Corban knew his way around after living here his entire life, but quickly pushed Corban out of my mind. The less I thought about him the better.

I kept walking until finally I saw a light around a corner. I approached timidly, hoping it would lead me outside. I knew the grounds better than the castle and could make my way to the clinic from the outside. As I came around the corner, I sucked in my breath at the beauty of this hallway. From the floor to the ceiling, mirrors stretched as far as I could see up. The entire hallway was hung with crystal chandeliers at varying lengths. Reflected against the mirrored surface, all there was to see was light. Light sparkling against the walls, the shiny white floors, the chandeliers themselves. It seemed to multiply until light was causing more light. I heard the tinkling of bells and looked up to see that some of the chandeliers also had chimes, which blew against each other, causing a ripple across the hallway. I stood, stunned in complete awe at the beauty of it—so amazed that I did not hear someone come up behind me.

"Beautiful, isn't it?" a voice spoke, breaking my concentration. I saw who it was through the mirror without even turning around.

"I remember the first time I saw this hall. I had just married King Jairus, and they walked me through this hall to my chambers." She smiled sadly, looking down at the ground. "Jairus brought me back here many times and asked me to stand against one side of the mirror. Our reflections continued on forever. He said that it represented the two of us living and ruling forever together—and I believed him."

I turned around, sinking to my knees. "Your Highness," I whispered, "I am so sorry to have disrupted you in your quiet place." As frightened as I was to see the queen, I also felt relief. Surely she could point me in the right direction to find Kirt. But being here at all was a violation of so many different rules I was certain Marley would convince her that I did not deserve a second chance.

Instead of looking angry with me, she smiled. "I'm sure you will get a chance to explain yourself, Larken of Canton." I looked at her in surprise when she said my name. She laughed a little at my surprise. "Of course I remember you," she said as though reading my thoughts. "One could never forget the brave girl who saved my son." She gestured to the mirrored wall next to us. "I wonder if you would be so kind as to join me for tea? I rarely have guests in my chambers, but I would love to get to know you better."

I nodded, surprised again. "I would love that."

Her kind eyes looked heavier than they had the first day of the program, dark crescents hanging beneath her lashes. Delicately, she reached around her neck and retrieved a necklace with a key attached, pressing it into a hole in a mirror. I watched her, waiting for her to move or push the door open but before she could, the chandeliers above us began to rearrange. The beautiful shapes turned in a pattern across the ceiling, crystal clinking together but not breaking. When they finished moving completely, a panel of the mirror began to slide sideways, allowing an entryway into the queen's chambers. She smiled at my surprise. "Beautiful, isn't it? Almost like magic. I'll never get used to it. Brilliant engineering." Waiting patiently for the door to open, she lifted her skirts and stepped in gracefully, motioning for me to join her.

I turned around to see if anyone was following us and felt for Marley's map against my chest before stepping in behind her.

* * * * *

Her room was much larger than I expected it to be from such a small entryway. In the center stood her bed, a massive structure that was made of what looked like tiny pieces of glass, all fused together. A large, blue glass chandelier hung overhead, reflecting off the bed and casting blue rays of light all over the room. There was a large sitting area as well, surrounding a fireplace that glowed icy blue and green instead of red and yellow flames. Heat did not emanate from them, but cool air blew, almost like a hand fan. I couldn't take my eyes off the flames.

She perched gracefully on the edge of one of the seats and pulled a bell out from the inside of one of the footstools, ringing it loudly with a flick of her wrist before turning to speak to me.

"Larken, I am so happy to have you here with me, but I must ask what you were doing in this part of the castle unaccompanied. Surely you did not come here on purpose. I myself get lost in these halls on occasion, and I have lived here for many years. Did someone guide you here?"

"Your Majesty," I stammered, "it's a long story."

She smiled, her lips pursed together but nodded in understanding. "Well, we have time. Why don't you start at the beginning?"

I told her *almost* everything, beginning with how the other girls had treated me since the attention I received at the hunt. She listened intently and kept a solemn face when I told her next about the fight and how Jessra stood up for me. I told her that Marley dismissed me but kept the other girls there and that I got lost in the castle, unaccompanied by a guard. What I didn't tell her was that Younda called me a Savian and that I stole Marley's map. When I finished I sank back in the chair, feeling anxious about what her response might be.

While I was speaking, a servant brought in lavender tea along with lemon tarts encrusted with toasted coconut. The Queen waited for several moments after I finished before asking, "Tell me—what do you feel you could learn from that experience?"

I did not expect this question. She did not press for further details, nor did she pressure me to reveal more about myself. I looked up at her eyes. They were the same as Prince Corban's. Deep, brown, and thoughtful. It seemed strange that brown eyes were considered a Savian trait, when the prince and queen of Deshan had them.

"I suppose I learned who a true friend was?" I stammered, and she nodded.

"Yes, very good. But what else did you learn? You see, as a queen you are constantly attacked for your actions. You might think it is an easy position, one of glamour at all times, but that could not be further from the truth." She placed her teacup on the tray and sat back in her chair, her ivory crepe dress almost blending in with the chair she sat on. "Inevitably, there are those that will oppose you. It is not a question of if—it is a matter of when. And when they come, you can either ignore them or you can fight them, but you must always learn from them." She rubbed her eye gently.

"So how do you know what to do when the time comes? To react or ignore?" I asked.

"I suppose you must realize what the cost is. If I ignore, how many will be affected? If I react, how many will be affected? Being a leader is not always about being popular. Often, being a leader means doing what you know is right even when others may disagree or be angry at you for doing so."

She stopped and I took the opportunity to speak up. "My lady, may I ask you a question?" I then added, "You may not like it."

She laughed softly. "Those are the best kinds."

"How do you feel about the Savians?"

She looked at me straight on, her dark eyes piercing. "How do I feel about their race as a whole?"

I sat up straight. "They are your subjects, are they not? I understand they are not at the forefront of your mind, but they are still your subjects. Do you feel any obligation to take care of them? To protect them? I have always wondered."

She cocked her head to the side thoughtfully. "I admit that I have not personally met many Savians in my time as queen. Most of those I have been acquainted with are servants whom I rarely if ever see, or criminals whom I must discipline. While they are my subjects, they are not free subjects. They do contribute much to the nation's food supply; however, the ranks it takes to guard them is an expense that many do not feel necessary." *Marley*, I thought. *An expense Marley does not feel is necessary.*

"Have you considered freeing them? That would eliminate the expense, would it not?"

She laughed lightly. "Oh, I couldn't possibly do that. If you have studied your history books, you know that our two people have a long history of conflict. We would be at risk for an uprising—the entire monarchy could be overthrown. No, sadly that is not an option." She was wrong. The threat of an uprising was an idea Marley gave her. It had to be. She paused. "Why the interest in the Savians? Most of the young ladies of the court seem more interested in my wardrobe than in my political opinions."

I gulped. I may have just convicted myself by speaking so boldly. "I just feel that as a potential queen, I need to be completely aware of all political situations at hand, and this issue is a pertinent one." I attempted to say this confidently, but I could hear my own voice waver. "I apologize for not asking you to see the contents of your closet. I'm sure it is lovely."

She laughed, genuinely this time. "No apologies necessary. I am so tired of giving guests tours of my closet. You won't believe how many questions I am asked that I have no idea how to answer. When it was made, how it fits . . . it is refreshing to meet a girl who is more interested in the responsibilities and not only the allure of being a queen."

I twisted uncomfortably in my seat. The idea of becoming queen *was* intriguing to me—despite what Kirt told me about dissuading Prince Corban's affections. It wasn't the power or the wardrobe that I wanted though, it was the possibility of making real changes—positive changes for my people. The ability to stop people like Marley. And, if I was being completely honest, spending my life with Corban sounded nice too.

"It is true that I am not as interested in the glamorous parts of being the queen. It is people that I care about, which is why I brought up the Savians to you." It might have been a bad move on my part to bring up my people again but I might not have another chance to talk to her about it and I had to know where she stood, if she knew about Marley's plans to destroy us all.

She paused for several moments. "You are a smart girl, Larken," she said. "I have no doubt that you would make a wonderful queen.

However, I would advise you to keep your opinions on the Savian populace at a minimum. It is a controversial subject right now. Why, my advisors . . ." She stopped and shook her head, gazing down at her teacup. "Well, never mind. I am sure Hortense is worried sick about you. I must find you an escort to help you find your way out of this maze." She rang her bell again, and several moments later a servant appeared from behind her dressing screen. "Irla, please lead Miss Larken to the outer staircase. A guard will be there waiting to take her back to the mansion."

She reached over the chair and squeezed my hand. "Larken, it was a pleasure. You are a beautiful girl and my son definitely has a difficult decision to make."

"It was a delight to speak with you. I will remember it for the rest of my life" I said.

"And I as well," she replied kindly, turning to leave me. "I would love the opportunity to meet with you again. Oh, and Miss Larken? Please do not tell anyone about our meeting. I will make sure Hortense knows so that you will be excused but I would hate for the other girls to have another reason to be unkind to you."

I curtsied deeply. "You have my word."

Irla led me to the mirror and pressed a key into a slot just outside the queen's door. We stepped through the queen's quarters into the chandeliered hallway, and she led me through the winding passageways until we met the guard who led me back to the mansion.

✳ ✳ ✳ ✳

"Where were you?" Jessra hissed when I arrived at the mansion. "Marley dismissed us almost an hour ago! Younda and I wondered if you'd gotten lost."

"I . . . stopped by the infirmary for awhile," I lied. There was no way I could tell even Jessra about my meeting with the queen. "I didn't feel well. Heat exhaustion, according to Kirt—I need to drink more water." I raised my hand to my mouth in a drinking gesture. She seemed to believe this explanation. "How did the rest of the meeting go? With Marley?"

She rolled her eyes. "Well, he brought out some tea and cakes and then proceeded to talk to us about politics for half an hour. I really should have paid more attention in government class but I can't help it. All of the affairs of the state, the subjects, warfare . . . It's so boring to me. Then he gave us a pat on the back and told us not to fight with each other anymore. That it isn't 'becoming to the future queen of Deshan.' Something like that. I'm still so mad at Younda though. If I get the chance to hit her again, I'll take it. I mean it."

"What did he say about subjects?" I asked, ignoring her gritted teeth. "Any mention of Savians? That situation?"

"Why do you ask? You were the one who didn't seem to care when Younda called you that. But, yes, some talk of them. Mostly about how he has an experiment planned to restructure the orchards and the farm boundaries or something or other."

That pricked my interest. "Wait, what? Tell me what he said exactly. Please, Jessra—you have to remember." Unfortunately, by now some of the other girls had congregated and were listening in. It must have been the intensity of my voice as I said it, but the last thing I needed was a crowd.

She looked around, uncomfortable. "I don't remember honestly, just something about the villages and some experiment. That it's going well in the villages he's tested already. It will probably come up in politics class eventually. Besides, why do you care so much? You've been so strange lately." She rolled the blankets on her bed down and climbed into it. "Do you have some Savian friends or something?"

I shrugged as if I didn't care either. Clearly Jessra had no more information to give me. "No, of course not," I said aloud, feeling my stomach churn as I said it. "I was just . . . curious, that's all. I know it's a controversial subject right now and I want to know as much as I can about it." She and the other girls seemed to accept my explanation and resumed climbing into bed and chatting about the course of the day and the next ball that was coming up.

But even after all of the candles had been snuffed out and the talking subsided, I couldn't fall asleep. I turned on my side to face the wall and thought about my mother, how she would handle this situation, what she would do.

Cen told me that before she came to the clinic, she was being held for treason against the crown, but what could that possibly mean? I wondered if she had ever been this afraid, if she ever had to hide who she was. Hide her race and her true identity out of fear. I decided that my mother never would have lied about her heritage like I just had. She would have been honest. She would have been honest despite the terrible things people said. She would have held her head high.

Usually, thinking about her brought me comfort. Tonight, it brought me shame. I lay on my back hoping for sleep to come but it didn't. I tried every breathing exercise and solution I could think of, and even sang the song that always brought me comfort in my mind, *Ring out the bells, steady and true . . .*

When that didn't work, I lit a candle and walked to the staircase that led downstairs. I would have gone to the balcony but it was locked just like every other night. Once I was sure I was alone, I pulled out the map I stole from Marley, spreading it out across the marble floor. Awkwardly, I positioned myself so I was lying on my stomach with the map spread out beneath me, the candle resting at the top center to illuminate the details of the page.

The red circles were almost innumerable, getting denser the further away from the capital. Small words like "Armed," and "Experiment group," were scrawled in, but they seemed to be assigned randomly. I searched the map for any piece of meaning until my eyes grew heavy and the candle melted into a puddle of wax across the floor. I rolled up the map until it was as small as possible, and tucked it inside my nightgown. From then on, I would never take it off my person. It seemed like the only thing I, a Savian girl, possibly had to use against the most powerful man in Deshan.

18

The day of the third ball, I dressed solemnly. No word from Maddock or Cen—and after what Jessra had told me about the village experiment, my mind raced with all the possible reasons for their prolonged silence. Even as I dressed in the open and spacious room, I felt backed into a corner. Trapped. I had only one way out. One way to find the truth.

I had to talk to Marley.

Talking to Marley was like waking a snake—it would only be a matter of time until he attacked. But I knew that he had already declared war against my people, ensuring that he would win. He made sure that we were completely defenseless. After poring over the map every night for two weeks and having the kitchen maid wonder why I was using up so many candles, but never getting any closer to finding what I needed, I knew that tonight it was time to face him. To figure out what he had planned against my people. The people that I loved.

I lurched a moment, my hands fumbling at the buttons on my dress as I thought of the word *love*. Suddenly I saw myself with Corban in a palace, far away from these people but very much like this place. It clashed horribly with the longing in my heart to just be home with Cen . . . and with Maddock. But again, Corban was there, waiting for me just outside of my imagination and just outside of my reach. *Stop it!* I scolded myself. *Maddock and Cen need you.* I could never have Corban and them too—or could I? If I were to become queen, could I have them both? I allowed myself to dream about that arrangement before remembering Kirt's warning to me before. I knew he was right. I had to divert Corban's affections—under no circumstances could I allow myself to be chosen.

The gown Ruldet created was my favorite yet. It was fitted at the waist and opened like a petal, revealing layers of navy silk at the bottom of the dress. The sleeves hung off my shoulders, and he had hammered tiny silver studs onto them, giving the dress a dull shine. Jessra styled my hair in a loose knot and lent me a pair of her silver slippers. She wore a yellow gown, fitted on top and voluminous beneath. It was the happiest gown I'd ever seen, perfect for Jessra.

I entered the ball with determination. *Avoid Corban; seek out Marley* I rehearsed as we stepped inside. What I didn't realize was that news spread fast about the hunt, and every courtier at the ball seemed to want to talk to "the girl who saved Prince Corban's life." From the moment I entered the ballroom I was bombarded with their questions. Most of the courtiers did not attend the hunt, and they wanted every detail of the incident. "How did you know which leaf to use?" "Had you ever been stung by floittles?" "Did Prince Corban cry?" I answered the questions briefly and politely, eager to discuss other matters, but to no avail. Jessra bored quickly and ran off with the boy in the purple suit, who was wearing a blue suit tonight.

The ball was almost halfway over and still I had not spoken with Marley or danced with Corban. I caught Corban's eye on more than one occasion while he danced with the other girls from the program, and each time it sent a surge through my body that I welcomed as much as I resented. I could not allow myself to develop

feelings for him—it would only complicate this already complicated situation. The harder I tried though, the more I realized that
my feelings for him were beyond my control.

I was talking to a courtier whose son was once *almost* stung by
a horse nettle when I saw Corban walking toward me. All I wanted
was to spend just one dance in Corban's arms, but I reminded
myself what was at stake if I were to get even closer to him. I curtsied politely to the courtier who had one eyebrow instead of two
and made an excuse about needing to sit down. She nodded and
intercepted the prince while I ran out of the main ballroom toward
the powder room.

On my way there, I rounded the corner to see Marley standing with two men, deep in discussion. They looked extremely concerned about something, but I couldn't gather what it was from
here. I stood at the corner where the walls intercepted and did my
best to listen. They repeated the words *rebellion* and *warfare* and
at one point Marley said, "We have got to keep their communication minimal. No letters." I had difficulty picking much else out
through the sounds of the orchestra swelling through the doorway.
A maid came up behind me and asked rather loudly if I was lost.
Flustered at the noise she made, I shook my head "no" and turned
the other way down a small, dark hallway—unlit by the multitude
of candles in the ballroom.

"Wait there!" I heard someone call behind me.

"Yes?" I turned around, trying to look innocent. Instinctively,
I sunk into a deep curtsy. "It is good to see you again, Advisor
Marley."

"Ah yes. Larken of Canton. These circumstances are much better
than the last time we spoke. Where are your little friends? The ones
who fought?" He chuckled. "Darling girls. How long have you been
standing there? And where might you be going? The ball is that
way." He pointed toward the ballroom and ran his palm across his
shiny head. "You wouldn't dream of breaking any other rules or
running off again, now would you?"

"Running off?" I asked as he studied my face.

"Like you did at the hunt, of course!" he bellowed. "And the first ball . . . always somewhere you shouldn't be."

"Oh . . . no, of course not," I replied, my voice shaking. "I was . . . I was just looking for a quiet place to sit down."

"Aha," he said, looking down with me in complete disdain. "Well, in that case—"

"But I was actually hoping to run into you!" I exclaimed. I had to hold his interest before I lost my chance. "You see I had a question of sorts . . . I heard something mentioned briefly in a class, and Hortense didn't have the answer. I thought since you are the expert in political affairs, you could explain it to me?"

His mustache twitched, and he formed a sly grin. "I am the expert. Now, what is it you were wondering? I don't have much time."

"Well, my friend Jessra was telling me that after I was dismissed from the meeting the other day, you discussed some restructuring experiment with the orchards and farms in the outer provinces?"

He nodded a little nervously, his face twisted up in a scowl. Why did he tell Younda and Jessra about this experiment, when he obviously was uncomfortable with me knowing about it? "Yes? What does that have to do with your question?"

"Well," I said, my voice shaking slightly. "I just wondered what the practical objective is behind the restructuring. If it is based off the boundaries or the workload or the expanding orchards . . . Hortense was not certain, but she said that you would know." I paused, my pulse racing. Maybe I had pushed the issue too far.

He examined my eyes for a moment, his lips twitching. "The restructuring is based off the fact that there are too many Savians occupying the orchard and village farms. It costs more to feed them than they are worth. In the villages we have tested, the project I put together has been phenomenally successful. We plan to continue it throughout, mainly because another route may encourage an uprising. More details will be forthcoming, although most are reserved for only specific military personnel. You already know far more about this project than you should." He clicked his tongue rudely. "Any more questions?" He clearly was not willing to answer

157

any more questions. But something about the way he said the word *project* sparked something inside of me. *Project 11,* I thought. *The map I had in my pocket right now was labeled Project 11—is that what he was referring to? Did I have a map of all of the Savian villages tucked in my dress at this very moment?*

"No, no, sir. That helps," I replied.

He nodded brusquely. "Well, I have a question of my own."

"Yes, anything." I felt heat rise to my face. He hadn't even asked me his question and already I was blushing in apprehension.

"Am I right to believe that you refused my offer to help me persuade Prince Corban? That is the conclusion I have reached due to your indifference, which is unfortunate for you. Not for me, because you see, I have twenty other girls whom I can offer it to now." His eyes narrowed, "You will not work with me, so I cannot work with you. You will be lucky to get close to Corban in the future. I will see to it that the two of you are apart as often as possible. He will forget your presence entirely." I opened my mouth to respond, but he continued before I could speak. "You will stay out of his way, or you and your family in Canton will suffer the consequences. Is that clear?" He stared at me piercingly, his expression fierce.

"Yes, sir," I replied, with anger burning in my eyes. Right then I wasn't afraid of what he would do to me—I was already planning on staying away from Prince Corban. No, I was afraid of what he would do to Corban. What he was already doing to Corban. Controlling him like this. How long had it gone on?

"Excellent. I'm glad that we understand each other," Marley sneered, stepping past me rudely and entering the ball. I could hear him once he got inside, calling out to the courtiers as though nothing had happened.

I slunk down the dark hall quietly. There was a door midway through, and after looking around to make sure no one was following me, I tiptoed in. It was a closet stocked with linens, towels, and pillows on shelves that ran on either side of the room. Small, but still the perfect place to hide for a couple of hours from Marley and Corban until the ball finished.

I sighed with relief, sitting on the ground with my back against the shelves. Several minutes passed, close to thirty I'd guess. I passed my time thinking about my conversation with Marley and the conversation I overheard between him and the courtiers. How did they piece together? Was I holding the map for his village restructuring? And what did that have to do with vox? From where I sat in the closet I could hear the chatter of the ball in the distance, the orchestra playing a lively piece, the clink of glasses. My eyes grew heavy as I propped my head against a stack of towels. Then I heard footsteps nearing the closet. They stopped in front of the door where I hid, blocking any light that was coming in before.

The handle twisted and I stood up, frantically looking around me, but there was no place to hide.

"Larken, is that you?" Corban whispered, letting himself inside the closet. "I thought I saw you steal away and tried to follow you, but Marley blocked me on my way over. I convinced him that I needed to get some fresh air just a few moments ago, so he finally left me alone." He closed the door tightly behind him, a candlestick with a single flame in his hand. "Although I must admit, this is quite the opposite of fresh air. What are you doing in here? I was hoping to dance with you."

I exhaled slowly, "Prince Corban—I'm—I'm sorry. I wanted to dance with you, I did—"

"You did? As in, you don't anymore?" He smiled sadly at me. "Why are you hiding out in the linen closet? If you did not want to dance with me, you need only tell me no," he said gently. "I can leave you." He bowed politely, reaching for the door handle.

"No! Wait!" I exclaimed. "Please let me explain." *Stop it, Emi, I told myself. Kirt told you to divert his attention. Let him go.*

He smiled, looking relieved. "Of course, but can we sit? My legs are tired from so much dancing."

"Yes, let's sit." I sat down first, my back against the shelf like I had it before. He set the candlestick on an empty shelf above us and sat as well, his posture more relaxed than I expected for a prince. "Please let me explain," I said.

"Does this have to do with the hunt?" he asked, turning his head to look directly at me. "I apologize if what my mother said at the feast has affected you in the house. The thought of losing me frightened her, and I think she only said it because she was so relieved and wanted someone to thank. And let me just say, since this is my first chance—thank you. Thank you for saving my life. Even if we never speak again and you refuse every dance, I'll never forget what you did for me." He shook his head. "Those minutes were among the most frightening of my life and I have not been able to stop thinking about them since. I feel so grateful to have had you there with me. Truly," he said, blinking with his perfect, wide eyes. "I'll never forget it."

I felt my face flush. "Please. I don't want you to feel like you owe me anything."

"Owe you anything? I owe you my life, Larken. If it weren't against the rules I would have come to you sooner. I tried to send a letter or a note but Marley forbade it, saying it was showing favoritism and would be rude. That's why I hoped for even one dance with you tonight. I wanted to thank you myself. In person." His eyes drifted up and he gazed at the dark ceiling above us, the glow of the candle flickering. "I guess this linen closet will have to do. It's a little quieter here than in the ballroom anyway." A faint smile crossed his lips.

"I came to this closet not because I was avoiding a dance," I assured him. This whole diverting his attention was not working so far. "I came here to hide because of all of the questions as a result of the hunt. Word travels quickly in the palace, and everyone wanted to meet the girl who swam through the pond to save you from the sting." I laughed a little. "I mean, who could blame them?"

He chuckled. "Is that it? I wish I could say that it gets better, but sadly it doesn't. The courtiers will ask the most outlandish questions for an original piece of news. One courtier asked me when I was younger, how I liked my eggs and then offered to cook some for me right then and there in the middle of a party. Another asked if she could paint me for her personal collection. Others have offered to interpret my dreams. If that's all it was, then maybe a dance would help, if only momentarily, to stop the questions?" His voice was eager in the best way.

I blushed, flattered at his persistence. "Your Highness—"

"Corban," he interrupted, turning to look at me. "Please, Larken, call me Corban."

"Corban," I began again, "you were right about your mother's speech affecting the way I am treated by the other girls in the program. That's another reason why I have been hiding from you. They aren't just jealous that the queen publicly thanked me; they are jealous of the time alone we had at the hunt. I thought that by sitting out one ball, their attention might be diverted." It was exhausting trying not to like him as much as I did.

"Understandable as well," he said with his eyes focused on the light from the candle flickering on the wall. "I have done some research on floittles since our incident at the hunt. Kirt the royal healer lent me a book on them. Can you believe that? An entire book on floittles."

I looked at him, genuinely interested. We never had access to such specific books in the clinic. "Oh? What did you learn? They are funny little creatures. Almost cute, if they weren't so deadly."

"That's exactly what I thought!" he exclaimed, his face lighting up. "Did you know that they are reborn three times? After they die, their body hardens into a shell and they are reborn as new creatures just a few weeks later?"

I nodded eagerly. "Yes, and you can hear them approach if you are careful. Their wings expand when they are nearing human blood and their flaps become as loud as a bird."

He laughed. "They travel in packs, but only one in the pack will sting a human as a sacrifice to protect the others. That is why they are always spoken of in the plural. 'Floittles' instead of 'floittle.' They are amazing! I decided I owed it to them to learn a little more after one of their own nearly killed me." He chuckled. "I had no idea you were interested in insects!"

"Oh no, it's not insects I'm interested in. It's more medicine. I just know about them because . . ." I caught myself before talking about Cen and the clinic at home. It was easy to feel comfortable with Corban. "I just think medicine is interesting," I said, choosing my words carefully. "That healing is an art."

Corban nodded enthusiastically. "Then you would get along well with Kirt. No wonder he speaks so highly of you whenever I see him." He smiled. "I feel so grateful that you have such a useful interest. And I know you are ready to move on from it, but you really saved my life, and that is the last time I will mention it," he said with a laugh.

I joined him, laughing freely in this small closet. "And I am grateful for that."

We both sat in silence for several moments before Corban spoke again. "Can I ask you something, Larken?" he said with a serious expression.

I nodded in assent. "You can ask me anything."

"Can we meet here again? Next ball? I don't care if I ever dance with you again, as long as I can just hear your voice and see you smile—but mostly hear your laugh. That is all I need."

My heart raced, and not the way it did in the orchard when I overheard the soldiers, and not the way it did when I tried to escape from the castle.

He reached over and took my hand, holding it tightly in his. We sat in the quiet closet as the orchestra swelled from the ball. He rubbed my hand with his thumb and squeezed it tightly one last time before he stood to go, reaching for the candle on the shelf behind us.

"You are a rare one, Larken," he whispered, before stepping out into the dimly lit hall and shutting the door to the closet.

Cen told me once that true happiness was best found in nature because it had room to spread out and breathe. But I knew that couldn't possibly be true, because just for a minute in that tiny linen closet, I felt that if I could step outside of my body, I would break out in blossom.

19

The night of that last ball played through my mind daily, particularly the confirmation of Marley's plan. Kirt assisted me in delivering several letters to Cen, and in each one I tried to warn him so he could counsel the others in my village, but received no response. What else could I do?

I daydreamed about Corban whenever I wasn't worrying about Cen. I tried so hard to forget the ball and our time together so I could focus on my own safety and his, but even the thought of his hand in mine sent spirals of chills down my body. The other girls in the program expressed similar feelings but had the luxury of embracing it wholeheartedly. I secretly envied their freedom to choose him back. Kirt was right: I had to divert his affections, but that didn't mean it was easy.

A week later Hendrik interrupted our class. He was an unexpected visitor but a welcome one, since Hortense had been droning on about a historic battle between Deshan and Irngia, our neighbor to the west. She stopped the class and introduced Hendrik for the second time, swooning with each word. "Ladies . . . we have a most important visitor. Perhaps the most important visitor we will have in this program, save for the queen or another royal messenger, a visitor who is vital to our understanding of the crown from on high and throughout. He comes with words and announcements that will benefit us all I'm sure, and if you keep your lips shut and your . . . smiles handy, he will deliver his message without regrets."

Jessra leaned over to me and whispered, "Did you understand anything she just said?"

I stifled a giggle. "No."

Hendrik looked curiously at Hortense while she spoke and then turned to us with a smile. In return he received smiles from every girl in the room, including myself. I hadn't seen Hendrik since the hunt, and I hoped that he was here to announce another.

He scanned the room and cleared his throat. "Ladies, it is such a delight to see you all. My apologies, Madame Hortense, for interrupting your class yet again!" When he winked at Hortense, she almost fell out of her chair. She waved her hand as if to dismiss his apology, her underarms soaked in sweat.

"As you know, you are officially halfway through the program. The last ball marked the midway point and before you know it, the prince will be choosing a queen and the program will end. Before that, though, you will be given the opportunity to receive more in-depth training on the subjects you are most interested in. You will still have classes in the mornings, but your afternoons will be free to spend as you choose as long as they are spent participating in an approved activity. Later today you will hear from the other instructors, but as you may know, I represent the stables as well as the royal armory. If you are interested in learning more about riding or basic defense, I will be teaching those classes in the afternoon. Any questions?"

A dozen hands shot up, making Hendrik laugh. "Wow, a lot of interest in riding. You first," he said, pointing to Olia. I was surprised she was interested since she had considerable difficulty riding at the hunt. "Will the prince be present at any of the lessons?" The class erupted in laughter, and Hortense shook her head in disapproval at Olia.

Hendrik chuckled. "No, the rules will not change. The prince will be riding and training in the mornings, so he will not be present at the classes. Just me. Sorry to disappoint you."

Hortense batted her lashes at Hendrik and piped up, "Oh, I'm sure that is hardly a disappointment, Sir Hendrik . . . to me, or to any girls present." She waved her hands wildly as she spoke, awkwardly avoiding Hendrik's eye.

I turned to Jessra and raised my eyebrows.

"Any other questions?" Hendrik asked, turning back to the class. Not a hand rose in the air. "I see, I suppose you all had the same question as Miss Olia. In that case—"

Younda raised her hand abruptly. "Sir Hendrik? What other courses are being offered?"

Hendrik looked at Hortense for help. "I'm not sure. I am only in charge of this course. Madame Hortense? Do you have any insight?"

She smoldered at Hendrik and replied in a high squeaky voice. "Yes, Younda. There will be fashion design, poise, foreign language, needlework, community relations, and many others. Like Sir Hendrik said at the beginning, we will have the other instructors come to us later today to provide more details. Although I know you will all be missing your dear, sweet Hortense in the afternoons." She giggled, her voice annoyingly sweet. I half expected her to walk across the room and pat Younda on the head like a puppy.

Hendrik raised his eyebrows and nodded, eager to get back to the stables. "No more questions?" He made eye contact with me for some reason, cocking his head slightly to the side. "None at all? No questions?"

I coughed, raising my hand. "What weapons will be taught?" The other girls looked at me in disgust. I think for most of them, the thought of wielding a weapon was revolting, but it was illegal for Savians to own or use any sort of weapon. I couldn't pretend the thought of learning to fight wasn't intriguing.

"Bow and arrow, sling, and sword for starters," Hendrik said without hesitation. "Although we will primarily be focused on riding. Can we expect to see you there?"

I gave him a knowing smile. "I will definitely be there."

"Excellent. I look forward to it. Good day, ladies. Thanks again Miss Hortense for allowing me to interrupt your class." Hendrik gave a slight bow.

Hortense wiggled her hips as she stood up and offered Hendrik an embarrassing wave with her fingers, which he did not return.

"Classes will begin tomorrow, ladies," she said as soon as he left, returning to her regular gruff voice. "Now open your books to page 163."

* * * * *

Fourteen of the twenty girls attended fashion design the next afternoon, including Jessra. Veda from the tailor house offered a compelling proposal on how important it is for a queen to dress well in order to send the correct message to her subjects. Three girls attended needlework, two irrational girls attended poise (which Hortense taught), and two of us went to the stables—me and Younda.

Hendrik seemed surprised when only two of us showed up. "Where are the others?" he asked in disappointment.

"Where else?" I replied with a laugh. "Fashion design."

Hendrik smiled. "Madame Veda can be quite convincing. Tell me then, what are your plans? Are you going to attend my class every day, or are there others you would like to visit occasionally?"

Younda piped up before I could, her voice pitched much higher than usual. "I plan on attending fashion design twice a week and needlework once a week, so try to teach me as much as you can when I am here. I am primarily interested in lady riding. I have no interest in 'horse tricks' or battle strategies whatsoever." She batted her eyes at Hendrik, who grimaced when she said "horse tricks."

He cleared his throat and then turned to me, clapping his hands. "And you, Miss Larken? What is it you hope to gain from this class, and will you be attending others?"

I swallowed. "I would like to attend foreign language once a week. Otherwise I will be here every day."

He rubbed his hands together and nodded in approval. "Excellent. Today we are not going to ride. It's a little hot out for the horses, and Prince Corban and the rest of the entourage have already tired them out from this morning's group ride." Younda's eyebrows raised in delight at the mention of Corban's name. "I was thinking that we might start with some basic archery skills. A lady should be able to shoot, although she will rarely be asked to do so. With that, please follow me behind the stables where we will begin our practice."

"I am already a very skilled 'archist,'" Younda bragged as we followed Hendrik. "Father taught me how to use the bow and arrows."

I smiled at her word choice. "Well, I'm sure you will have so much to teach me. I've never picked up either in my life."

She sneered. "Good. It would be dangerous for someone like you to have access to such deadly weapons. Who knows what you might do with them."

"What do you mean by that?" I asked her, genuinely curious. It wasn't a secret that she disliked me but to suggest that I was dangerous was absurd.

"Your people . . . They are different from us. Father told me that those in Canton might as well be Savians, they are so barbaric."

I gritted my teeth, deciding whether I should retaliate or ignore her, but fortunately Hendrik made that decision for me. He turned around abruptly. "Miss Younda, I will ask you once and only once never to speak rudely to anyone in my presence. I would also advise you to steer clear of speaking that way around Prince Corban if it is indeed his affections you are after. Are we clear?" His eyes locked with hers until she turned away in shame. I opened my mouth in surprise at his honesty with her. Most of the adults we interacted with in the program were careful about what they said to us, probably out of fear that one of us would become queen and remember whatever it is they said.

"But my father . . . ," she murmured before stopping herself. I caught Hendrik's eye and smiled. I felt safe being here with him.

Hendrik explained some basics to us before we started. How to hold the bow, where your eyes should focus, which fingers to use to pull back the arrow, and where the feather fletching should line up.

It was all new to me. I saw swords and bows all the time, but only soldiers carried them. It felt strange to hold one.

"All right then, I'm going to bring around some targets and let you two get started," Hendrik called out, carrying a large target and setting it about thirty yards away from us.

"Oh really, Hendrik," Younda said, giggling, "you needn't go so easy." She pushed her long braid behind her and picked up an arrow, releasing it haphazardly toward the target. It flew ten yards or so and bounced off the ground. "Just a warm up," she sang in an embarrassed voice, before picking up another. "Father was busy the weeks before I came here and I haven't had as much time as I'd like to practice . . . So many social events." She released arrow after arrow, none of which came close to hitting the target, stomping in anger as each one skidded across the grassy field.

Hendrik raised his eyebrows in amusement. "Well, you try!" she yelled to me angrily, folding her arms across her chest.

I fought my smile to no avail. "I'll try, but I probably won't be any good." I picked up an arrow, lined it up like Hendrik demonstrated, and then released it. It hit the dirt just like hers did.

"Let's keep practicing," Hendrik said, his eyes hopeful.

Younda and I released arrow after arrow in the afternoon heat. Sweat was racing down my hairline, and my hands were sore from gripping the bow so tight but by the end of the session we could hit the target at thirty feet, although neither of us was close to the center.

On our walk back to the mansion, she proclaimed that she would not be attending the stables again for afternoon classes. "I'll leave the riding and weaponry to you. Since you'll never become queen, what use do you have for beautiful clothing and needlework?"

I couldn't agree with her more.

*　*　*　*

I lived for my afternoons with Hendrik. They were the best distraction I had for my worrying about Cen and Maddock and those at home in my village. Occasionally another girl from the program would accompany me to the stables, and on those days we would ride horses in a circle in the pasture or discuss self-defense tactics. Fortunately most days it was just Hendrik and I, and those days were the best because he was able to teach me one-on-one.

I didn't need much help with my riding skills, but that didn't stop Hendrik from teaching me small details—how to ride and shoot an arrow, how to communicate more effectively with my horse, and how to hold a shield while I rode. It was a dream to sit through classes in the morning and then have my afternoons to ride. While we started with my horse skills, that quickly evolved into weaponry. "A queen should be able to defend herself as well as her nation if need be," he said, after suggesting that we begin weaponry classes.

After archery, Hendrik taught me to use a sling. He explained how to position a stone in the sling, the best time to use a sling versus a sword or a bow, and how to determine distance. "Slings are the most ancient weapons and the most discreet," he explained. We discussed which stones were best—smooth or jagged, where to aim to knock someone out without causing death, and how to quickly load and fire. Mastering the sling took only a matter of days, and by the end of the week I could hit a moving target from my horse. The sword was a completely different story.

We started out by using very dull swords with the points covered in fabric. "It's important to train with the real weight of the sword," Hendrik explained. "Too often soldiers are trained with wooden swords and their muscles do not properly develop for real battle." As soon as I picked up the sword I knew what he meant. My forearms were weak and I could barely lift the sword above my head.

"Is this a man's sword? Can't I get something a little lighter?" I complained, after struggling to even hold it straight in front of me.

He smiled. "I'll see what I can do about that, but for now this is all we have. Your strength will increase faster than you think."

At first we practiced fencing on the ground. He showed me how to position my feet and which steps to take to circle my enemy from behind, how to deflect a blow from above and how to cross over the hilt to attack from beneath. We fenced every day for weeks, all throughout the afternoon until we were both drenched with our own sweat. My muscles ached for days after particularly intense sessions, and more than once I visited Kirt in the clinic for liuli herbs to repair my sore muscles. "You need to take it easy, Larken," he warned me. But training with Hendrik at the stables was like an addiction for me now—the only thing that kept me from my fear for Cen and my people. I couldn't stop.

I slept deeply every night from total exhaustion, and more than once fell asleep in morning classes, much to Hortense's chagrin. I also ate more than I ever had, guzzling large amounts of water at each meal and finishing everything on my plate as well as whatever Jessra left on hers. "You're a bottomless pit these days, Larken," she teased me. "What is Hendrik having you do? You might need to take a break from the stables and come to fashion class one day. Give your body a chance to recover."

But every day I spent in the stables I was getting better. Hendrik was right—my muscles grew stronger faster than I expected. I could keep up with him now without completely losing my breath, and the sword no longer felt so heavy. Eventually he removed the fabric from the points so that I could experience the real sounds and pressures of the fight. He was still impossible for me to beat, but every time he cornered or trapped me, he taught me what to do to avoid that position next time, and I learned.

He also set up a training regimen that had nothing to do with weapons or horses and everything to do with strength. "Your body is not as important as your mind when it comes to weapons, but it might help if you had some strength on your side. Pair a little strength with your wit and courage, and you can keep up with any opponent, regardless of size." I raced the horses around the pasture circle, my arms pumping and my legs lengthening to keep up with them. I was one of the fastest runners in the village at home, but Hendrik made me feel like I still had a long way to go.

He mounted a bar for me in the stables and told me he expected me to be able to pull myself above the bar fifty times in a row by the end of the month. At first I struggled to even do one, but every day

I was able to add one or two more, so by the end of the month, he was right. I was much stronger than before. I learned how to hold my own weight, while focusing on the specific muscles in my arms.

Horse training was my favorite of all, though. Hendrik provided me one of the most beautiful horses for my training. She was a petite thoroughbred with sandy blonde hair, named Riushka, the Sansikwan word for "goddess." I practiced shooting arrows and slinging stones from her back for hours, until her hair became so laced with sweat that I slid off her back. I still missed Lexon and his familiarity, but Riushka and I had a rhythm that reminded me of riding Lexon. She seemed to listen to the weight of my body.

"She's a trained warhorse," Hendrik explained to me after my first session with her. "One of our finest. A favorite of the queen's." I could see why. Although I would never be allowed to really ride her outside of the palace walls, I already knew she had the strength to ride for hours.

One afternoon Hendrik told me he was going to teach me how to mount a moving horse. I almost laughed until I realized that he was completely serious. If Cen were there, he would cringe at the possibility of broken bones and torn muscles. The first several times I tried, I fell—hard. On my fifth or sixth attempt, I tried to listen to Riushka's body. I ran fast, keeping my pace steady at her side, but when I leapt for her mane I closed my eyes out of fear. After a few moments I realized, with my eyes still closed, that I was riding her, my feet both balanced on one stirrup. She slowed down to let me mount, and every time after that it seemed more seamless than the last. I never fell again. She knew when I would jump, where I would land, and where my weight would rest. Our chemistry was beautiful.

At night I dreamed about riding, and whenever I was somewhere besides the stables for the day, the horses and my time there was never far from my mind. The stables were the best distraction I had from worrying about Cen or fearing for my own life as an impostor in the program.

"You are a born warrior," Hendrik remarked to me one afternoon after a particularly trying day. It was strange. Months ago, even weeks ago, I never would have believed him when he said that. But I felt myself grow stronger with every class we had, and I was beginning to think he was right.

* * * *

One day I arrived at the stables ready to train and found Hendrik in his office above the stables writing a letter at his desk. He gestured to me with his hand as though to tell me to wait a moment while he finished.

"I can wait." I sunk into one of the enormous armchairs he had in his office. "Believe me, my arms will thank me for a little break." I said it with a laugh, but I meant it with all sincerity. I was exhausted.

"No, we can't waste any time," he told me, finishing up his writing and rolling the scroll. "Thank you for coming up here instead of waiting for me downstairs, because I have something for you." He placed the scroll in a drawer in his desk and locked it, placing the key around his neck and tucking it underneath his shirt.

"What is it? A letter?" I asked eagerly. For a moment I wondered if he could have a letter for me from Cen, then I shook my head. He had no idea who I really was.

He shook his head in confusion. "A letter? From whom?" I swallowed, but he continued. "No, not a letter. Something even better."

"What is it?" I asked eagerly.

"You'll see," he told me with a laugh. "Now sit there and close your eyes. No peeking!"

I nodded obediently and closed both eyes as he rummaged around behind his desk for several minutes. Outside his office window I heard horses grunting, and several aides whistling and calling at each other. The weather was beginning to change slightly—the air was less muggy and hot. A warm breeze blew through the open window while I waited for Hendrik.

"I have been waiting to give you this," he said, "but your hard work these past few weeks has proved to me that you've earned it. You can open your eyes now."

As I opened my eyes, Hendrik placed a sword in my hands, wrapped in black velvet and tied at the top with a black leather cord. "What—" I stammered. "Is this is for me?"

Hendrik nodded. "Unwrap it." He could barely contain his excitement. His eyes lit up as I slowly unraveled the cord and removed the fabric, revealing a shiny silver blade. The sword itself was much lighter than the others I fenced with, yet the blade was the same size as the others. The hilt was smaller and easier for me to grip and beautifully designed, with carved rivers that ran down the sides and interlaced with each other so I could not find where they began and where they ended.

"This is mine?" I breathed. "I don't know what to say." I held the sword up to my face. The blade was so shiny I could see my reflection in it.

"You'll have to keep it here of course," Hendrik said, "but it is your sword. You may take it home with you at the end of the program if you are not chosen to be queen."

I nodded, the reality of his words sinking in. I would have to hide it, of course, but I would have it. And more than that, I knew how to use it. He allowed me to admire the sword a little longer, smiling as I ran my finger across the blade delicately. I surprised myself when my eyes filled with tears. I had never been given a gift like this before. Something that I could really use to protect myself. To protect Cen and my people. "I am honored," I murmured. "Thank you, Hendrik. Who made this for me?"

He smiled. "A friend of mine who works in the forge. I explained to him how hard you have been working and he thought he would offer it as a gift." He eyed the sword affectionately. "Are you ready to practice with it?"

It was so much easier to work with than the practice swords. My arms moved gracefully as we fenced in the side yard, each clang of the swords spurring me forward. My feet moved faster as I pushed Hendrik deeper into the fields. More than once he almost trapped me, but this new sword seemed to give me strength I didn't have before. Sweat dripped from my forehead. This was the longest we had ever sparred without him trapping me, and the length of the fight was motivating. Each time our swords connected, I felt my muscles surge with more energy. Hendrik darted forward to tap me on the shoulder and finish the fight. I twisted his arm around my back and held him there, pinned with my sword against his chest.

"All right! All right!" he laughed, and pulled away from me. "You win. It looks like somebody likes their new sword." He sheathed his sword and rolled his shoulders back, a smile plastered beneath his beard.

I raised the sword in the air as a sign of my victory, bowing to an invisible crowd. That is, until I heard clapping behind me. Hendrik looked up but immediately bowed, a serious look on his face. "It looks like we have an audience, Miss Larken."

I turned around anxiously and saw Prince Corban on his horse, clapping with reins in his hands as he trotted toward us.

"Miss Larken, dare I say that you have outfought Hendrik for the first time in his life? Brilliant!" I hurried to mop up the sweat that trickled down my face with my tunic sleeve. I wasn't sure whether I should be delighted or mortified that he was there.

"Prince Corban! How long have you been watching us?" I attempted a curtsy, but it was awkward since my sword was still in one hand.

"Unfortunately, I didn't get to watch for too long," he said, dismounting. "I saw two fencing specks in the field and came over to see who it was. I recognized Hendrik, of course—I have been fencing with him since I could walk—but his opponent looked so small that it sparked my curiosity." I swallowed and opened my mouth to reply but Corban went on. "So you ride, you can miraculously cure perilous bites, and you can fight? Is there anything you cannot do, Miss Larken of Canton?" His eyes were wide as he gripped the reins, leading his horse closer to us.

Hendrik coughed. "Allow me to take Jursky in for you, Corban. It will give you two a chance to talk on the walk back, and I have to admit, Larken, that match completely wore me out. I could use a ride back."

"Thank you, Hendrik. I appreciate that." Corban smiled broadly at him, removed his riding gloves, and handed over the reins.

"I think we're done for today, Larken," Hendrik said. "I'll take your sword, if you don't mind, and will call a soldier to escort you back. Excellent, excellent work. I haven't been cornered like that since . . . well, ever." I grinned at him. He definitely allowed me to win, but it still felt good. I handed over the sword reluctantly. Then Hendrik mounted and thundered through the field on Jursky, leaving Corban and I alone for the first time since the linen closet.

I coughed uncomfortably, looking around. "Are we going to be in trouble for being alone?" I asked immediately, thinking about Marley's angry meeting in the tent where he chastised me for being alone with Corban at the hunt.

"No," Corban said, shaking his head. "The rules are more relaxed than they let on. My mother told me that she saw my father alone on a weekly basis the last few months before the program ended. They would meet for a few hours near the healer's clinic in a private grove. I suppose they have become stricter about soldier escorts, but we won't be in trouble. And if we are, I promise to tell Hortense and mother that it was my idea."

I smiled, worried more about Marley than the queen or Hortense.

Corban chuckled. "I have to confess that I lied earlier. When I said that I saw a small figure fencing with Hendrik. I knew it was you. I ride every afternoon I can and sneak in the back stable door. I've seen you here every day and for the most part, you're here without any of the other girls. I can never watch for long but your weaponry and riding skills are incredible. Truly, Larken, I'm afraid I might not be able to beat you in a fencing match, and I know without a doubt that you're a better rider than I am."

I shrugged. "You beat me on the hunt. And I'm not as good as I look. But I love it outside, training and riding. Some feel that this training is not practical for a queen, but after really doing it, I disagree. I think it is the most practical skill we are offered here. There is not a class I would rather attend."

Corban turned to me, his eyebrows furrowed. "What makes you say that? Not that I disagree, but I am curious to know why you feel so strongly that a queen should know how to ride and fence so masterfully?"

My arms fell limply at my sides as I contemplated my response. I could never really tell him what it meant to me—the power to defend myself for the first time in my life. Being here and learning to fight with Hendrik made me feel strong, not weak and victimized as I had felt every day at my village. Telling Corban that would reveal my identity—but it was the truth. Besides, it wasn't as if I could be queen. I hadn't forgotten what Kirt told me in the clinic. But sometimes I wondered if I could make more changes for my people from behind these walls than outside them. "Let me respond to that question by asking *you* a question, if you don't mind," I said.

"Trying to get out of it I see," he replied jovially. "Very diplomatic. Of course. I'll tell you anything."

"In your mind," I began, "what is the purpose of a queen? Is she merely a figurehead or is she more to her people? How many political affairs meetings does she sit in on? How many strategy sessions? How many wars does she fight in for her people?" I spoke slowly, careful not to scare Corban off. The last thing I wanted was to make him angry, especially since we had such limited time together.

Corban stopped for a moment and rubbed his eyes. "Larken, a queen cannot fight in battle. Her position is too vital to the state. There's a reason we have paid soldiers. If kidnapped in battle, she could become a valuable ransom. It's too risky."

"Suppose she wants to," I offered. "Suppose she does not want to be a mere figurehead. What then?" Without meaning to, I felt my voice rise. "I've done my research. Queens used to fight anciently for their people. They used to lead the army at the very front." I was right too. Hortense passed over it briefly in our history class. Though it was a small detail, I had not forgotten it. It felt important to me that I focus on the queens of the past. Sweat trickled down the side of my face, and I quickly rubbed it away with my sleeve.

Corban stopped walking and turned to face me, considering what I said. "You're right. I've learned about the ancient queens and their place in a battle. But that was a long time ago, when our land was less civilized. Things have changed since then. Now the queen stays behind the gates like the rest of the royal family."

I took a deep breath. "I just feel that if the queen is the mother, the protector of her people, she should be the one doing the protecting." I shrugged as though it didn't matter to me at all, while in reality it mattered. It really mattered.

He shielded his eyes with his hand. "That's one thing I admire about you, Larken. It's easy to see your passion for serving and not merely being served."

I looked up to meet his gaze. "That attitude is not as unique as you think." I had to divert his attention to the other girls. "Most of the other girls in the program are extremely passionate about serving."

"You're so different though," he disagreed. "You prefer riding boots and a tunic to any of your dresses." He gestured to my ensemble. "You avoid the courtiers instead of entertaining their silly questions because you're not interested in attention or fame or praise." He smiled at me, his hair glowing in the sunset behind him. "Am I right?"

"You admitted to hating the courtier questions yourself. And besides, I only own three dresses," I confessed sheepishly. "Which is probably why I prefer a tunic and boots."

"Who cares?" Corban cut in, embarrassed. "I know about your classes too. They send me your scores, you know." He shook his head shyly. "I see all of your marks and reports. They think that it will help me choose more easily. I have read all the reports—the important ones anyway. Which is how I know that you have the highest marks in language, history, and foreign affairs. Hortense wrote on one of your reports that you are 'emblazoned with passion for learning.'"

I blushed and turned my head, but he reached toward me, gently pulling my chin toward him until I finally met his eyes.

"You are the only girl who trains for battle. You can ride a horse better than anyone I've met . . ." His voice softened. "Who are you, Larken of Canton? What can't you do?"

Choose you back, I thought desperately. *Become the queen.* But instead I said, "Hold my teacup properly and dance without stepping on toes. Surely you haven't ignored those scores. I know I have not scored well with the balancing-books-on-head trick.'"

He laughed softly. "An important skill." He paused and his voice became more serious again. "There is something I want to ask you. If your answer is no I understand, but I hope that you will consider it." The sun sifted through the trees above us, lighting up the field of wheat we stood in until it looked as though we were standing in a sea of gold. I looked to my right and saw four soldiers marching toward us, clearly given orders to deliver the two of us to our separate quarters.

I turned back to him instead though, ignoring their imminent presence. "Of course."

He leaned his head in close to mine and took my hand, rubbing it softly with his thumb like he did in the linen closet. "Meet me at the grove of trees by the clinic in two nights at sunset? Waiting three more weeks for a ball to see you is far too long."

He held my gaze for several moments, searching my eyes with his. I could barely choke out a yes or no, my head commanding me to stop this relationship, and my heart aching with permission to choose him.

"Yes," I whispered finally. He turned and walked toward the soldiers that waited for us at the end of the field, his smile revealing everything he felt. I stepped quickly to catch up with him—and when he reached for my hand beneath the tall sheaves of wheat, I didn't pull away.

20

The next day at the stables, Hendrik asked me if I would like to see all of the palace grounds. "They're enormous. So big that it would take us every minute we have until dinner to really see them."

"Really that long?" I asked incredulously. "I feel like I've seen so much of them already." The mansion, the main palace, the clinic, stables, tailor house . . . "Wouldn't it be a better use of our time to train here?" After yesterday's fencing match, I was eager for more, ready to see if beating him was just lucky.

"We can't take the horses too fast inside the grounds, which is why it will take awhile," he pushed, his eyes persuasive. "But I think it might interest you." There was a fleck of something in his voice—a specific reason why he suggested we do this.

I shrugged, reaching for Riushka's saddle. "That's fine then. I'd love to take an official tour."

He smiled broadly, his beard glinting in the sun. "I hoped you would say that." He lifted his saddle on his horse—a chocolate brown warhorse—and we began our ride, starting at the north of the palace and making our way down. "The grounds of the palace are huge. I've lived here most of my life and still I don't think I've seen everything within the gates. There's so much." He took me along the back wall that eventually met the rocky ledge of the mountains behind it. The walls were made of the same stone as the mountain itself, grand and dark, with jagged shelves. "This wall was designed by the first king of Deshan after the Great War," Hendrik said as we passed. "The very war in which the Savians became subject to the Brockans. His name was Louk, and he believed that this wall would connect with the strength of the mountain. It was symbolic of how he viewed his kingdom. King Louk vowed to never leave the palace walls, not willing to risk any dangers that might exist outside. He hired scouts and messengers to patrol the kingdom for him, believing that his own life was too precious to the nation." I nodded, the story familiar to me. Every Savian child knew of the Great War and King Louk. It was hard to forget the name of the man who made your people slaves.

"Ever since then, the kings of Deshan have done the same. Of course there are exceptions. Hunts, diplomacy trips, and so forth, but nothing that would take the king away from his duties here. The kingdom is divided into sectors and an ambassador reports weekly to the king on what is going on in each." I absorbed this bit of information, not aware until now that the king *literally* never ventured out to see his people. Would Corban do the same?

"How can the king really trust his ambassadors? Could he possibly be receiving false information from them?"

Hendrik shrugged as we passed beneath a low hanging bough. "Of course, as with anything else. The king just has to be sure to choose ambassadors and messengers he really trusts. That is how he rules his kingdom."

I frowned. Did Corban even know what was going on outside of these walls? If he wasn't there to see the conditions of the Savians in the orchards, wasn't able to see for himself how terribly they were treated by the soldiers, wasn't able to even meet them besides those few servants in the gates, how could he really make decisions? No wonder the queen told me in her room that she hardly knew any Savians. Without leaving the palace grounds, she wouldn't have a chance.

We entered a large training field after we passed through the grove of trees along the wall of the palace. Dozens of soldiers were lined up on the field, running drills as captains walked up and down their rows. The whiteness of their hats and cloaks hurt my eyes in the sunlight. They were far enough away from us that I could not see their faces, but I could see what a lack of variety there was. They were all around the same height—tall and muscular, holding their swords in front of their faces as they marched. "These are the palace guards," Hendrik explained. "They live here on the grounds and train here. Their only duty is to protect the royal family from harm. There are other barracks outside of the grounds where civil soldiers train, but these are the very best. It is an honor to be chosen to serve the royal family." I blinked at the sight of them, so many marching with nowhere to go. It seemed a waste that the palace employed so many of them when areas outside of the palace were riddled with crime. Surely we could use the best soldiers and their influence there.

I nudged Riushka on with my knees, eager to discover the other parts. Hendrik led us around the training fields along the wall where the tailor and the clinic were. He nodded toward them as we passed. "You already know about these buildings," he said. "The clinic in particular is one I know you are accustomed to." I opened my eyes in surprise. What did he know about me being at the clinic?

"What do you mean 'accustomed to'?" I asked slowly.

"Kirt told me that you occasionally visit him there is all," Hendrik replied, avoiding my gaze. He positioned his horse forward as we rounded the wall and came toward the main palace.

"Gorgeous, isn't it?" he said as we stopped behind it, our horses pawing the ground and snorting into the grass. "The whole plan when it was built was for it to contain everything necessary within the walls. That way there would never be a reason to have to venture out. Most of the palace staff lives and works here. The courtiers have housing within the palace as well—special friends of the royal family. It is its own world. A universe in and of itself."

I nodded, squinting up at the turrets that were so high they seemed to disappear into the clouds. "It is," I agreed. "Hendrik, can I ask you something?"

He nodded and directed his horse toward the mansion now. "Of course you can."

"If you were Corban, and you were given the chance to rule a country like Deshan, what would you change?"

He looked surprised by my question, frowning as he steered his horse away from the palace. It was a few minutes before he spoke. "What would I change?" he mused. "There are a lot of things I might change. Less defense within the palace, more resources on the borders, a larger team of advisors, and more ambassadors in smaller districts . . . ," he said, drifting off. "Why do you ask?"

I shook my head as we passed the large pool, a half dozen courtiers waving at us, unamused as they floated on rafts. The water was a perfect blue, the bright colors of their swim dresses and trunks stunning against the color. I wondered how it would be to swim every day on the palace grounds—nowhere to be, nothing to do, no one to answer to. I wasn't sure how long I would enjoy it. Not if I knew what was really going on outside the gates. Maybe that was why they stayed inside. Maybe it was easier not to know.

"I guess I'm just curious," I responded after awhile. "This kingdom is so great, so vast . . . more beautiful than anything within these walls. I realize that they were built to be a protection, but I can't help but feel that they do more harm than good. With them and that old tradition, Corban will never see what else is out there. How does he even know what to do when all he can rely on is the word of the ambassadors he probably didn't even choose himself?" I thought specifically of Marley. He had been around since Corban was a child. I frowned as we rounded the corner toward the mansion. The sun was beginning to set and my legs cramped from riding so long.

Hendrik nodded and opened his mouth more than once but did not say anything. Finally as I dismounted and handed him the reigns he replied. "I agree."

With a smile he nodded toward the house. "I'm not sure why I brought you on this ride," he remarked. "I just felt that it was important for you to see how and why things are done the way they are here." I couldn't figure Hendrik out. So many of the things he said seemed to contain hidden meaning.

I forced a grin, trying to convey happiness that wasn't real. Had Marley been able to hide the truth from Corban and possibly his father because of the way the kingdom was organized? I wondered who would have the courage to tell Corban what was really happening—or did he already know? I waved good-bye to Hendrik as I entered the mansion for dinner. These walls felt as restricting as the village boundaries. Maybe I was wrong, but a nagging part of me knew that us girls in the mansion weren't the only ones who were prisoners.

* * * * *

The night I went to meet Corban was overcast—a rarity in Deshan. I decided to leave right from the stables and planned on telling Hortense that Hendrik kept me late. I wasn't sure if it would work since usually guards escorted me back to the mansion after class, but I told Corban I would be there, and if I didn't show, he would be left waiting for me. Besides, if I could be alone with him I could put off his feelings for me. Single in on one of the other girls— someone I liked. Jessra or Olia. Possibly suggest he meet one of them instead of me next time. It might not work, but it was worth a shot. I had to let these feelings for him go if I was going to live.

I wasn't worried about getting home. It would be night, and dressed entirely in my black riding clothes, I was certain I could sneak back to the mansion unnoticed. The dogs had not been out patrolling the yard since the first week we arrived, and the soldiers were so bored of watching the mansion that most of them dozed off on watch.

Getting there would be a different scenario. Corban had asked me to meet him at sunset, which meant I would be in the light on my way there. I studied a map of the grounds that Hendrik was kind enough to leave for me. The grove was near the clinic—on the other side of the grounds from the stables. But if I could get to the clinic, I could also get to the grove. By walking along the back wall of the grounds through the fields, I might be mistaken for a stable hand, especially if I could pull my hair up in a cap. Looking out the stable window I saw the sun beginning to sink slowly, lighting up the sky with pink and gold fumes. Hanging on the wall in the stables were a row of hats. I picked a dusty one off of the nail it hung on. Pulling the brim far over my face and tucking my hair into the hat, I looked just like a stable hand.

Getting to the rear wall was easy—most of Hendrik's staff was eating dinner in the back barn, and I crept by unnoticed. From there I ran as fast as I could, taking advantage of the fact that the grounds were quiet in the evening. Hugging the wall, I made it to the clinic without incident, drenched with sweat but happy that I had made it this far. I crouched in the bushes near the side door, attempting to locate the grove Corban had spoken of, pushing aside the excited rustling that was forming inside my stomach. Right as I began to stand, the side door of the clinic opened and Kirt walked outside with a man. I couldn't see whom from behind.

"You will remember to rest. A wound like that one can be infected easily if you are not careful," Kirt directed. "Come back tomorrow, and I'll look at it again. Once again, you said that you fell?" Kirt prodded. "Onto your own sword?"

The man turned to Kirt and I almost gasped out loud. Marley! "Something like that," he grunted. "But the fellow who left it there was thrown in prison. He and the rest of his dissenting group. Disloyal to the crown . . . ," Marley grumbled.

"You threw him in prison because he left your sword out?" Kirt sensed the unlikeliness of his story. I shivered and leaned my head closer to hear Marley's response.

"It's none of your business how it happened!" Marley snarled. "Forget it!"

Kirt frowned, "Marley," he began, then stopped, rubbing his face lightly with the back of his hand. "I . . ." His voice trailed off.

"Get on with it," Marley growled, stepping closer to Kirt.

Kirt looked at the ground. "I've been meaning to ask you . . . When can we make the antidote more widely known? It is . . . ," he paused, "it's painful to me to watch so many infected by it when we could so easily help them." Kirt's voice shook.

Marley turned toward him and thrust his jeweled finger in Kirt's face. "You're no better than those lousy dissenters! I've told you before to let it alone. If I'm asked again, I'll see to it that we find another royal healer. You ask too many questions and have too many requests. I've had enough!"

Kirt frowned. "I'm a healer, sir. It is my responsibility to cure our people if I have the resources to do so. Which I do." He raised his eyes bravely to look at Marley. "We can't just let them die."

Marley stepped closer to Kirt, towering over him. "I can make you disappear," he warned, his voice low and rumbling. "I've done it before to people much more important than you." I covered my mouth with my hand. First King Jairus and now the entire Savian race. What else was Marley capable of?

Kirt nodded, stepping back inside the doorway, his face crumpled in fear—or possibly shame. "Forgive me, my lord. I will not ask again."

"No, you won't," Marley snarled.

Kirt bowed politely in response, and Marley cursed and stomped on his way back to the palace, holding his wounded arm and kicking at everything in his path.

Once he was out of sight, Kirt stood for several more minutes and sighed deeply, his hands folded in a prayer, held against his chest. Then he shook his head sadly and entered the clinic. I waited for several minutes until my legs grew numb. Crouching there, I wondered how many people Marley had made "disappear." If he could do it to someone as important as Kirt and the king himself, he could definitely do it to me.

* ✳ * ✳ *

I located our meeting spot easily and waited patiently for Corban, sitting in the grove against the trunk of a large palm, my eyes closed, replaying the scene with Marley and Kirt over and over. Any excitement I felt for seeing Corban again was overshadowed now by the seriousness of my situation. I had to focus if I were going to aid my people and live. Before overhearing the conversation with Marley and Kirt, I planned to use tonight to encourage his feelings for the other girls. But now there was more at stake. I needed to figure out what Corban's sympathies were towards my people.

"You made it," I heard a low voice behind me. Corban ducked under a low hanging palm, smiling at me. "I wasn't sure if you would be able to." I stood to curtsy awkwardly in my riding clothes, but instead was greeted with a hug. My heart stopped momentarily. "I've been looking forward to seeing you again since we last spoke, wondering if you would remember or if you would find a way to be here."

"It wasn't too hard," I admitted truthfully. "I just came right from the stables. I apologize for my clothing though; there was no way I could walk in a ball gown across the fields unnoticed. I might also smell a bit like horses," I confessed.

He chuckled and pulled me down to sit with him against the trees. "I should have known you would be coming from the stables. Fortunately, horse is my favorite scent." We laughed and then faced each other. Why was it so difficult to push him away? In the approaching dusk I could see the outline of his features, his curls framing his face, his white teeth almost floating in the darkness.

He smiled at me, inching a little closer. "Larken, I have so many questions to ask you. A million things I want to know—and we do not have time at the balls." He laughed lightly. "Especially when you run away from me in favor of linen closets." I loved his laugh— so uninhibited, so comfortable. "So I thought this would be a good opportunity to talk. No distractions, no other girls. Just us." He had such easiness about him. It was contagious.

"How well do you know the other girls though?" I prompted. "There are so many amazing and smart girls." The words sounded forced coming out of my mouth. It wasn't that I didn't mean them. Jessra was amazing. So were many of the others, even if they did hate me. It was just that I knew that he didn't ask me to come here to talk about them.

He shrugged. "Of course there are some amazing girls. But I want to get to know you. So let's play a question game. You ask me one, and then I'll ask you one. The loser will be the one who cannot—or will not—answer the other's question."

I nodded. It was a game I used to play with Cen on slow days in the clinic. It was how I learned so much about my mother. Lucky for me, Cen is as competitive as I am and hated to lose even a simple game like this one. Thinking about him stung as always.

"Ladies first," Corban said, nodding to me.

I tried to start off light. "Prince Corban, have you ever lost to a lady in a duel?"

He laughed. "I have never been matched against a lady, although after seeing your skills against Hendrik, I'm afraid I might lose to you in a duel."

"Probably not," I replied, beaming. I couldn't help it. It felt so good being around Corban. Most of the time I forgot he was the crown prince, the future ruler of Deshan.

He smiled back at me, pushing his hair to the side of his face. "My turn. Larken—if you could travel to any foreign country within our continent, which would you choose?"

I didn't have to think long before responding. "Sansikwa. I have been practicing that language for years. Besides, I would love to see their frosty mountains. The idea of 'snow' is completely foreign to me and I want to see that it actually exists." I thought of Kirt's trek there to discover the cure for vox. "I have had to rely on pictures for too long. It is time to witness it for myself."

Corban laughed, responding in Sansikwan. "I have seen pictures of the snow as well. It looks amazing—so white, so clean. If my circumstances were different, I would also love to go there." He cleared his throat uncomfortably, then looked up and offered me a smile. "Your turn."

I swallowed, delving into a more serious topic. "Corban, how many of the other ladies in the program have you met individually outside of the balls?" If I knew he had another interest, perhaps I could persuade him in her direction—as much as it would break my heart to do so.

His face grew serious and he looked at the ground, beginning to pull up small clumps of grass and setting them next to his knee in a pile. "You are the first and only, Larken. I would have thought that you knew that. You are the only one I have seen outside of the balls. From the very first time we met in the stables and you plowed me over, to the hunt, to the linen closet . . . Do you really believe that I ask all of the girls to meet me privately?"

"Is that your question?" I asked him jokingly. I hadn't meant to change the mood so drastically, but I needed to know that Corban was loyal to me before I could discuss the Savian issue.

"No," he said, burying his face in his hands. I waited silently for him to speak again, stiffening as some soldiers marched nearby us. Fortunately, a chorus of crickets masked our conversation. Corban made a face at me as the soldiers passed, and I had to bury my own in my shirt to keep from laughing.

When we were certain they were gone, Corban inched closer to me, whispering this time. "Larken of Canton, have you ever been in love?"

I stared at him, my face growing hot. Jessra had asked me this once before, in the pool. My answer now, I assumed, would be the same. I had never given much though to love, seeing only the clinic and the safety of my people in my future. But looking into Corban's earnest eyes . . . I thought of his laugh, of his way of making me laugh. Of his kindness and attentiveness. Of the way I thought about him throughout the day when I should be thinking about other things.

"I'm . . . not sure," I finally replied. It was the truth.

"That's not really an answer," he replied, his eyes twinkling.

"It's okay if you have been . . . that's why I asked. I just wanted to know."

"That was an honest answer," I insisted. "Suppose I have felt it? How do I know what it is supposed to feel like? I have felt missing. I have felt affection. I have felt the joy of care and the pain of loss. I have felt envy, I have felt protective, the fear of missing love. I have felt those things."

"Oh, Larken." Corban surprised me, kneeling and lifting me up to kneel with him. He embraced me fully without inhibition, his arms pulling me deeply into his, my face burrowed in his chest. In his arms I wanted to laugh from joy and cry from fear and he held onto me as the crickets sang for us and the stars fought their way through their blanket of clouds and our shelter of palms to give us some light.

When he finally released me, I looked up in his eyes and saw that they were wet. "Corban, I'm so sorry," I said quickly. "Don't think that my answer means I do not have feelings for you. I do—I just cannot tell you if they are love or not. Not now. Not yet. If I do feel that . . . at some point, I want to really mean it. You deserve that."

He gave a muffled laugh, rubbing his eyes with one hand and keeping the other on my waist. "It's not that, Larken. I am not asking you to confess any feelings for me. It was an honest question and I received an honest answer. You cannot imagine how much it means to me to hear the truth." He sighed deeply, pulling me toward him, until we were face to face in the grass, our hands touching, our shoulders, and our sides. Every part of me that touched him was awake. He reached out and brushed a wisp of my hair away from his face. "Before this began, I hoped to find someone who did not feign affection out of desperation to be made queen. I didn't want anyone to make it something that it's not. I appreciate you telling me the truth."

"I will always tell you the truth, Corban," I murmured. And I would. I would tell him everything. The truth about my race, my desire to stop the vox from spreading, my real reasons for wanting to ride and train and fight. What really happened to his father, what Marley was doing to him and the rest of the kingdom. In that moment, if he asked me, I would tell him anything.

His arms folded around me, and we sat in the tall grass, his chin burrowed into my neck, his cheek against the side of mine. This was definitely not diverting his attention, but I didn't care. The crickets seemed to stop their song and the moon hid behind the trees.

He stroked my face and then laughed his same familiar laugh, although it sounded a bit embarrassed as he broke away from me and I turned to face him. "You know, it's your turn to ask a question, and you better make it a good one."

I released my elbows, sinking in deeper to the grass as the moonlight came back into our view, lighting up Corban's face. "I think we better stop here. I have so many more questions for you, but I am a bit worried that Hortense will send the dogs to sniff me out if I don't return to the mansion soon." There were so many things I wanted to ask Corban. After my ride around the grounds with Hendrik, I wondered more than ever how much Corban actually knew. Part of me felt like I was falling in love with a man that was involved in all of it—was knowingly sentencing his own people to death—but a deeper part of me felt like he was completely innocent about what was really happening. Was that love? Believing the best in someone? Giving them the benefit of the doubt?

Corban nodded, standing up. "Of course. I forgot all about that, I was enjoying myself so much. Will you meet me here again? In two weeks, same time? I would ask you to come next week but it is the ball. We can continue our game then, if you'd like. I still have so many questions I want to ask you. I'll find a moment to sneak away."

I nodded in response. "Of course."

He reached for my hand in the darkness and held it briefly before turning to go. "I've been to this spot dozens of times. It is where my parents would meet, and it has always been a special place for my family. Our home within our home, if that makes sense. I was a little worried about sharing it with someone, since it is the only place in the castle grounds where I feel I can truly be alone." He paused and brushed his hair back, dropping my hand.

"I never planned on bringing anyone here. But I'm glad that I did." He locked eyes with me. "And I'm glad it was you."

21

So I've been thinking," Jessra said as we swam the next evening. "I want you to come to fashion class with me. Just once. There's something I want to show you there."

I looked at her, waiting to see if she was serious. I hadn't been completely transparent with her—or any of the girls for that matter—about how important my time at the stables was to me. She would be surprised to find out how hard it would be to miss even one day there. "Are you forgetting how embarrassing my taste in fashion is?" I asked jokingly, hoping to deter her.

She giggled. "No, I haven't forgotten. But I really love fashion class. And I want to show you some of my designs, and . . . I miss you. We don't see as much of each other since we all split up for afternoon classes." She was right. The only times we really had to spend together were meals and our late-night swims.

"You know, I've actually been considering a change in my wardrobe if you can imagine," I teased, gesturing to the swim dress Jessra lent to me months ago. "I mean, I cannot decide though, is white still the new color? Or is it now dingy gray from being worn so much? It's just so hard to tell sometimes!" I held a hand to my face in mock anguish.

Jessra splashed water in my face with a giggle. "Don't tease! We might not be fencing with grown men and riding horses, but we have a good time!"

I splashed her back, and she retorted. Soon the other girls joined in, all of us half-drowning and laughing so hard we did not even realize Hortense was standing above us outside the pool, tapping her foot impatiently.

"Are you quite finished ladies?" she asked scornfully. "A queen would never—" To my surprise, Jessra ignored Hortense and went under water, rising quickly with her arms outstretched, splashing her. Hortense stood staring into the pool, water plastering her thinning hair to her face in disbelief, so I spread my arms and splashed her too. Now Jessra wouldn't be alone. One by one all of the girls joined in, while Hortense fumed. Finally she had the sense to walk away from the pool and threw her hands in the air as she returned to the mansion, her shoes squeaking every time she took a step on the marble walkway.

We laughed until we cried.

*　*　*　*

I attended fashion class the next day, much to Younda's disappointment.

"Ugh. I thought you learned your place, as an animal in the stables. Besides, you always smell like horses, or worse. Please tell me that your attending this class will not be a daily occurrence," Younda scoffed on our walk to the tailor's. Her usual group of minions surrounded her, holding their hands up to their mouths with a giggle when she mentioned horses.

Jessra clenched her fists at her sides, but I ignored Younda and pulled Jessra away from her. "She's just jealous of me because I have fashion sense she can't compete with," I said loudly to Jessra, mocking Younda's conceited voice. Then we ran further ahead so we would not have to hear the onslaught of insults I was certain would follow.

Rows of white desks were set up in a spare room in the tailor house. On the far side of the room stood white shelves lined with gold foil notebooks. "We keep our designs over there." Jessra pointed to the shelves. "Would you like to see some of mine?"

I nodded encouragingly. "Of course! Why do you think I decided to come?" I asked. "Let me see!"

Jessra retrieved her folder and opened it timidly. "Now these are just first drafts . . . They're not very good," she mumbled, pulling out some of the gowns she sketched.

I expected to give her false encouragement, but the drawings she pulled out of her folder were better than I anticipated. The gowns were elaborately sketched, and Jessra had not missed a detail. A swan inspired one of her sketches. White feathers cascaded down a full gown on the sleeves and bodice. Another looked like water, with swirls of blue rippling down the dress and sweeping to one side.

"Jessra, these are excellent," I flipped through the pages one by one. "Really, I had no idea."

She pulled the folder back shyly. "They're all right I guess. There's still so much that I need to learn. But I have one that I wanted to show you." She ruffled through the pages to the back, retrieving a sketch and handing it to me carefully. It was some sort of suit of armor. Black leather leggings and gold plated armor that looked like fish scales covered the knees and ran along the sides. Tall black boots were fitted and came over the leggings, with gold tassels and spurs on the foot. The top was a simple black tunic with a shield embroidered over the heart. A red cloak fanned out across the page. Jessra even sketched the arrow sheath, liquid black feathers protruding out of the top. "It's you," she said softly. "Well, I designed it for you anyway. It's armor made for a queen."

"It's really beautiful, Jessra. You didn't tell me you were so good," I whispered, "I would love to wear something like this. I've never seen anything like it."

She shrugged. "It's nothing too great. I mean you should see the designs the tailors put out—especially Veda. But it made me happy to do it for you. I wish it were real so I could see you ride while you wore it."

By then the rest of the girls had arrived and retrieved their notebooks. Veda stood at the front and clapped her hands to call us to attention. "Good afternoon, ladies! How has your day been?"

The chorus of girls murmured, "Good," while Jessra turned to me, pointing at the front. "That's Veda, in case you forgot."

Veda wore a vivid red dress that tumbled to her feet. The sleeves seemed to be made of stiff, gold lace. Her voluminous hair was pulled in a messy knot at the top of her head and she wore glittery gold sandals. Her smile revealed the sizable gap in her front teeth.

She spent thirty minutes discussing how to balance textures with us, explaining why it is important in any design to employ multiple textures. Surprisingly, I didn't hate it. Although it was not nearly as exciting as riding or training, it was more interesting than I expected it to be. After her lecture, she clapped twice and two servants brought out a large gold tray full of colored ink and quills. "Let's practice drawing with texture," she directed, motioning toward us. "I'll come around and see how you are all doing."

Jessra handed me a sheet of parchment and we walked to the front to retrieve some ink. After sitting down, I started to sketch, looking over at Jessra's paper to study her techniques. Drawing and sketching came so easily to her, it was amazing how quick she was.

"Ah, I don't believe I've met you before," Veda said, stopping at my desk. "What's your name?"

I stood. "Larken of Canton. I usually attend my afternoon classes at the stables. But Jessra spoke so highly of you and your class that I decided to give it a try." I smiled back at her—it was impossible not to.

She beamed. "Well, I'm so happy you did. I've heard of you, Larken. You're the girl who saved Prince Corban's life on the hunt, right?"

I felt my cheeks grow hot. "Yes. But it was nothing really. I was just in the right place at the right time." I turned back to my desk to avoid talking any further about Corban.

She shook her head, still smiling. "Oh, it was far from nothing. The queen told me the story herself. Some of us have been watching that boy grow up his entire life. Why, he's like family to me! What a blessing that you were there."

I nodded. "Thank you, Madame Veda." I could feel the angry stares of the other girls in the room.

She smiled even wider and gave me a little wave. "I'll come back and talk to you later. I look forward to seeing what you create."

I sat down and looked over at Jessra, who was grinning uncontrollably at me. "She's brilliant, right? Now can you see why I love this class so much?"

"She is great. But wait until you ride the horses through the fields," I teased. "It's even better."

Younda took her opportunity to pipe up, "Only Larken would bring up horses in a class about fashion."

I heard a few girls giggle, but I continued working on my sketch, doing my best to ignore her.

"I heard," she continued, "that Advisor Marley sent some soldiers to Canton to find her father. To see what she was all about, you see." My back stiffened. "It turns out that they couldn't find anyone in Canton named Larken, and no one knew who her father was. She's a fraud. A total fraud."

Jessra turned around. "Shut up, Younda. You don't know what you're talking about."

Veda came over and shushed us with her finger. "Ladies, back to work. Please help maintain the creative energy in the room."

I looked gratefully at Jessra and turned back to my sketch, but Younda wouldn't stop whispering loudly to Keisha, Nadia, and the other girls sitting around her. "I've said it before, and I'll say it again. There is something strange about Larken. Not only does she sympathize with Savians, but no one can seem to locate her father in Canton. Maybe he's dead just like her mother. Though, if I were her father, I'd disappear too."

Jessra stood up then, flinging ink all across the room. I stood, too, tears springing to my eyes at the mention of my mother. Veda stopped Jessra before she could do anything, putting her arms on her shoulders and turning her toward the door. "Miss Younda?" Veda said, stepping in front of Jessra. "I will not tolerate bullies in my classroom. Apologize now to Miss Larken, or you will not be welcome here again."

Younda looked up at Veda with innocent eyes. "But Madame Veda . . . ," she whined, "I didn't say anything I should apologize for."

Veda shook her head and cast a concerned glance in my direction. "I heard every word."

Younda's cheeks blushed a deep red, and she turned anxiously to look at Keisha and Nadia on either side of her for support. They were giggling before, but now that Veda was involved they were quietly sketching and avoiding eye contact with her. "I'm sorry, Larken," Younda offered pathetically, her voice flat.

"Thank you," Veda said, returning back to her desk, her lips pulled tightly in a grim line. "Now, no more trouble girls. What an unkind way to welcome Larken to our classroom."

But as soon as Veda was out of earshot, Younda turned to her friends and whispered just loud enough for me to hear, "I'm sorry that you're a Savian and your parents abandoned you."

* ✱ * ✱ *

I wrote Cen a long letter that night. I knew he wouldn't write back—I hadn't heard from him in months now. At times the pain of missing him felt so deep, so encompassing and nauseating that I had difficulty doing much else but think of him. I couldn't listen in classes and had difficulty making myself stand some mornings after I dreamed about him. I wondered what he would think of me here in the palace with all of these girls. If he would be proud of me or disappointed in me for the time I spent at the stables. He was so against violence of any kind. Would he be sad to see that I was learning to fight? Or would he be proud of my hard work and progress? I thought of Younda and what she said at fashion class about me being abandoned. It hurt so deeply because it wasn't true. I had Cen. He was the only parent I ever needed.

Some days it would be lunchtime before I even thought of Cen. Those days were the hardest, because when a memory or a fleeting image of my past entered my mind, I felt shame for leaving him at all. I felt guilty for allowing so much time to pass without thinking of him and wondering if he was all right, if he was safe, if he—and this was the hardest for me to imagine—was even still alive.

It was the night before the next ball, and instead of chatting with the other girls about it at the pool I had come upstairs to write. Cen may not even receive my letter, but writing it might help me deal with my own pain. Sometimes, I was learning, the process was more important than the end goal.

> *Dear Cen,*
>
> *I haven't heard from you in months. Not since you wrote me about Maddock and his recovery. I don't know where you are or what is happening or what to do. I know there is danger in the orchard villages. I know that what happened to Maddock's village is not an isolated incident. I know that it is not safe for me to know any of this, much less share it. But then again, I know that every day I spend here is uncertain and that if I do not write it now you may never know how much I really love you.*
>
> *I was never an orphan. My mother was killed but even before that you made the decision to take me in. I have never been alone thanks to you. I have never felt like an orphan, never felt abandoned. Your prayers for me, your teachings, and your never-ending compassion have been the guiding compass in my life. You are my north star—you point the way to everything I want and everything I hope to be.*
>
> *I also believe in medicine and healing because of you. I believe that what we do as healers is the most important work because we prolong life—we enable it. I never realized before this experience in the palace what a gift*

life is until everything I knew before was taken from me.
I want to heal for the rest of my life. I want to carry on
your work.

    Please be alive, Cen. I need you.

    Love, Emi

I wrote in desperation, with all of the love inside of me. Maybe he couldn't feel it from this distance, maybe by leaving him I broke his heart, but I would find my way back to him. As soon as I finished what needed to be done here.

22

"Ruldet, I . . . what is that?"

Hanging in front of me was the flashiest dress I had seen yet. It was made of cherry red silk and was draped dramatically in the front. The back sported matching red lace, with a strip of silk racing down my spine.

Surely this was meant for one of the other girls. Hadn't Ruldet heard me when I'd told him "nothing too flamboyant"? I turned to stare at him, my eyebrows raised.

"I know it is a lot," he said, blushing. "But when I saw the fabric I felt that it was made for you. Such a powerful, strong color." I noticed, behind his blush, that he looked tired, and I wondered if he had stayed up all night sewing to finish it in time. "Do you like it?"

I turned again to stare at the dress, trying to force away the lump in my throat. Writing that letter to Cen last night had been difficult for me, wondering if I would ever return to my old life. The dress was loud, yes, but that wasn't the problem—it was a beautiful dress and I would be lucky to wear it. I just wished my mood could match its cheerfulness.

"I love it," I reassured him, sensing his concerned eyes on my face. He beamed in relief.

Later that night, I stepped into the ball and spotted Corban immediately. He was dressed in gray from head to toe, the mono-chromatic look making him appear taller somehow. He looked darker than usual from the sun, and his hair was slicked back smoothly— a change from his usual sweeping curls. Several of the other girls swarmed around him, and he welcomed them each individually. Petra said something that made him laugh. I stood watching him, and for a moment he caught my eye, his expression alight when he saw me. "Nice dress," he mouthed, showing his familiar, calming smile before Petra pulled him aside, and he extended his hand for a dance with her. Seeing his hand on her waist stung a little, but I brushed the thought off and made my way over to the glimmering buffet on the opposite side of the orchestra. *He needs the other girls*, I reminded myself. I could not bring all of the attention to myself.

The food at the balls was impeccable and original. Tonight I loaded my plate with piles of green candied grapes, strawberries del-icately sliced with cream custard oozing from their hollowed insides, and bacon wrapped tarts filled with sour cherries and spiced cheese. After our conversation in the grove of trees, I wasn't terribly wor-ried about getting my chance to dance with Corban. I knew where I stood with him; he had made it clear that he had feelings for me. I just wasn't sure how I felt about him. Perhaps by entertaining his affection I was going to make life harder for myself. I walked to the edge of the room and sat at a table nearly in the dark with a few candles flickering to light up the space.

Laughter erupted from a table in the center, and the orchestra began a slow, steady waltz. I finished my plate of food and rested my head on the table, letting myself relax and enjoy the peace and quiet. The soft thrum of the crowd moving in and out around me was comforting. No one stopped to see who the girl in the corner was this time; no one came to me with questions about the hunt.

A few hours into the ball, two women sat down at my table, nodding to me curtly and sipping from their goblets. One wore a hat made out of purple ostrich feathers, and the other was plump, dressed in pumpkin orange. I could tell they were trying to keep their conversation private—no doubt why they retreated to this corner of the ball to begin with. I kept my head on the table, still enjoying the music when I heard one of the woman's whispers.

"They say one is a Savian! The horror! A Savian girl in these gates, in this room!"

I sat up suddenly, nodding to them politely when they stared at me, and then looked toward the orchestra, as though disinterested in their conversation.

They were silent for a moment, eyeing my reaction and then turned toward each other again. "Who's your source?" pumpkin dress asked, her mouth hardly moving as she spoke.

"It comes from a soldier in one of the outer villages. Danton's boy. He said that there is talk there among the Savians, and the soldiers picked it up somehow and alerted the palace. It makes sense of course, what with there being twenty-one girls in the program this year. They usually only take twenty. It's a wonder no one accounted for the extra girl. Of course they attributed it all to a mistake with the books, and they were all so lovely. How could they have sent one of them home without knowing?"

Pumpkin dress shook her head in disgust. "Well, that girl better be careful, because she will be facing dire consequences if she is found out. An entire nation will be outraged at her. Defiling these halls, these palace walls with her presence! Living like a queen! Can you imagine?"

Ostrich feathers snorted. "It is despicable to think about. Dancing with the prince and sleeping in the same room as the future queen! What if she is chosen?"

"They will catch her by then," pumpkin dress said firmly, finishing off her glass and hitting it on the table with a bang. "I have full faith in that."

I forced a coughing fit then, my stomach churning as they spoke. They both looked up with concern, and I held up my hand and smiled, curtsying to them before excusing myself and coughing my way out of the room.

Gasping for air, I lifted my skirts once I was out of sight and ran down the hall, tears springing to my eyes. I ran to the linen closet, hoping that I might be able to devise an escape plan there. For a moment here and there, I thought it was possible for me to be queen of Deshan. Thought I could make changes. But overhearing that conversation made me realize how wrong that was. The Brockans would never accept me—a Savian orphan as their queen. And now that sources within the palace knew of a Savian, the truth of my identity was bound to come out. Younda was telling the truth in fashion class. She knew who I was. How many others did too?

I flung the door open and slammed it behind me so quickly that I almost stepped on Corban, who was sitting with his back to the wall. The force of the door rattled the candle that he set above him.

"Corban!" I exclaimed, grasping the back of the door to steady myself.

"Hello," he said, standing to greet me with a smile. He bowed formally, even here alone in this closet with no one watching him. It struck me how different we were. He had been raised in the palace, brought up with a lifetime of formality, while I was born to a prisoner mother and thrust into poverty—into slavery really. No matter how comfortable I felt around him, we were from two different worlds.

"You're shaking," he said with concern in his voice, stepping back to observe me. "Larken, you are absolutely shaking! And you rushed in here—what's wrong? Did something happen?"

I swallowed the lump in my throat and shook my head, still inhaling big gulps of air to calm my system. "No, no—everything is fine," I said. "I'm not sure what's wrong. I'm fine." But I wasn't fine at all. My identity was unraveling—how many others knew who I was? I felt my stomach sink as I thought of Marley. He definitely had to know, and it was just a matter of time before he made my identity public knowledge.

Corban eyed me nervously. "Do you want to sit? I've been looking forward all night to meeting you here. It was more difficult than I thought it would be to steal away."

We sank down together, our backs against the shelves and he lifted my hand comfortably, grasping his own around it. I thought I would be surprised by how easy it was between us, but I wasn't surprised at all. It was always this way with him.

"Do you want to finish our game?" he asked with a small grin, evidently trying to lift my mood. "I believe it's my turn to ask you a question."

I nodded, still fighting back tears. "Yes. Let's continue."

But instead of asking a question, he brought his hand to my face, brushing his knuckles down my cheek softly. "Larken, something is not right. Please tell me what it is. Did someone say something to offend you? Were you hurt to see me dancing with other girls? Please, tell me and I will do everything in my power to make it right." His voice was clear and even, no guile or mocking in it whatsoever.

I watched his expression in the dark, the candle flickering its shadows across it. Could I trust him? Before I could stop myself, I asked the question that had been pressing me for months. "Corban, what happens at the end of all this?" There was fear in my voice, and I knew he could sense it.

His face registered surprise, but he kept his arm around me. "What do you mean, at the end of this?"

I inhaled slowly. "What happens in a few months when you make your decision? I know you don't want to talk about it, but what happens?"

When he spoke, his voice was serious. "You know what happens. I make my decision. There will be a ceremony . . . a wedding." His voice was bleak and hopeless as he replied, and I wondered why when he seemed so happy to be here with me.

"But what happens . . . if you don't choose me?" I bit my lip to keep it from trembling and turned my face away from him, focusing instead on the shadows dancing on the wall. What I really wanted to ask was, what happens to my people? Do we all die? Does Marley win? Without me here, will my people even have a chance? Will I ever see you again?

He finally spoke, and when he did his voice was deep and hollow, the saddest I had ever heard. "Oh, Larken. Why would you even ask me that?"

He pulled me closer to him, his hand behind my back. Before I could say another word, he interlaced his hands gently around my neck. Our faces were so close I could feel his breath on mine, could smell his boy scent, could see his smile beginning to form.

Right as our lips were about to touch, a voice yelled down the hall. "CORBAN!" Marley's voice echoed, getting closer to the door. "COR-BAN!"

I stiffened immediately, and Corban stood before I could move, brushing his hair back quickly. "Come join me for a dance, please," he whispered, before exiting the cupboard and closing the door tightly behind him. I heard muffled shouts and then the clacking of footsteps getting farther and farther away.

My heart was still pounding from the shock. I couldn't let Marley know it was me inside the closet with Corban—not after I heard what those women were saying. Marley knew I was a fraud—the only question was how long he was willing to keep me around. He would use this information to his advantage. He would find a way to extort me—to use me just like he used everyone else, including Corban, to get what he wanted.

Bravely, I exited the room, walking swiftly down the dark hall into the ball again. My red dress rustled as I walked, each step leading me closer to the ballroom that seemed flooded with candles, the light emanating from the doorways. Corban was waiting for me at the door and reached for my hand. His face was serious.

"Please honor me with a dance," he said in a low voice.

Marley hovered nearby, frowning as he watched us. His black gaze never left me. Corban didn't seem to notice at all. We didn't say a word, which was not like us. Instead, he held my hand tightly and we danced, the faces and lights around us a huge blur. I knew I shouldn't be dancing with Corban like this. I knew I should be following Kirt's advice and diverting his attention to other girls. But after the first dance when I curtsied and tried to pull away, Corban shook his head and asked me to join him for another.

The lights above us twinkled just like the stars beyond them, and I thought about the impossibility of my life. I was a Savian orphan and I was in the arms of Prince Corban—the most influential man in the world. We could never be together, not really. For the first time that realization hit me. Corban would never really be mine.

We danced all night, even when Marley urged Corban on multiple occasions to dance with one of the other girls. His arm gripped my waist fervently, his eyes steady and constant. I tried to fully enjoy my time with him, to forget that there were hundreds of eyes on us, but it was difficult with Marley constantly lurking nearby.

I knew while we danced that I was Corban's favorite, and by refusing to dance with anyone else, he was making that clear to the entire royal court. I should have been happy, thrilled that the man I was beginning to love was choosing me back, but all I could think about was that by choosing me so publicly, Corban had made my situation even more dangerous than it had ever been before.

*　*　*　*　*

We didn't stop dancing until the orchestra began to put their instruments away, and an angry Marley whisked Corban away. I turned to face the wrath of the other girls, who stood in a circle near the door, casting incensed glances in my direction.

Jessra pulled my arm toward the door, hugging me tightly around my waist. "Larken, I can't believe that you danced with him for close to an hour. An hour and he didn't ask anyone else! You've got to understand that the other girls are furious. Not that I blame them, but luckily I had a dance partner. What did he say to you?" I scarcely heard her. My mind was somewhere else.

"I'm sure they're a little mad," I replied with my eyes on the ceiling. "But they all would have done the same thing."

She shrugged with a laugh. "Can't say I disagree there."

"Did you dance with the boy in the purple suit?" I'd caught her gleaming eye multiple times while she danced nearby.

Jessra blushed. "Of course. All night, except for the two dances I had with Prince Corban before you. He told me all about his dogs. It might sound boring to you, but it was actually quite interesting."

I giggled, raising my eyebrows. "How?"

She pushed me playfully, "When a cute boy is talking to you, it doesn't matter what he's saying, Little Miss Dance–with–the-Prince-All-Night."

Tulia called for Jessra to come up and join her. "I've got to tell her about my night. Do you mind?" Jessra asked. I shook my head and she skipped down the path to join Tulia and the other girls, telling them all about the purple suit boy and his dogs.

I slowed until I was at the back of the group. For some reason it was important for me to spend as much time as possible outside under the stars tonight. The soldiers patiently followed me as I walked slower and slower, my head turned upward.

While the rest of the girls filed into the house, I stood a little longer, lost in thought—thinking about Corban and Marley and my place here. I thought about Cen and where he was. I thought about Maddock and where he was. I thought about the fact that I was falling in love with a man who didn't even know who I was.

I stared at the stars until a soldier cleared his throat, obviously tired and eager for bed. I curtsied politely and entered the house alone, beginning my solo walk to the stairs. It seemed eerily still inside the mansion. The only sound I heard was the shuffle of my skirts rubbing together. I put my hand on the stair railing then suddenly heard a loud squeak on the mansion tile.

I whipped around in a panic, but before I could see anyone, I felt a hand cover my mouth so I couldn't scream while the other held my flailing arms. I struggled, kicking and beating my arms, but the grip was iron strong. Marley had sent someone for me much sooner than I anticipated. My heart racing, I bit down hard and turned to face my opponent. Even in the dark, it didn't take me long to identify the face.

It was Maddock.

23

Once I saw who it was, I stopped struggling and he released me, his eyes darting back and forth to make sure no one heard us. Silence. Then he opened his bony arms and I pulled him to me tightly.

"What—what are you doing here?" I whispered as the shock began to wear off. Relief filled me then. He wasn't one of Marley's men sent to carry me off like I thought. Then I realized how much danger Maddock was in for being here. "You're going to get killed! There are soldiers at every door!" He looked different. He lost a lot of weight with his illness, but now he was so thin that his limbs just looked like muscle with a blanket of skin. His dark hair had grown out and was knotted at the nape of his neck. A rusted knife was pitifully gripped in his hand, as though that would form any protection from the soldiers.

"We can't talk here," he whispered, his eyes wild with urgency. "Is there anywhere we can go?"

I nodded, dozens of questions racing through my head and none of which had a logical answer. After living in the mansion for months by this point, I was familiar with every closet and nook of the place. There was a small storeroom in the far end of the mansion that Jessra and I found one afternoon while exploring.

He followed me, both of us attempting to be as quiet as possible. It wasn't difficult for me with slippers on, but Maddock's riding boots treaded heavily on the marble tile. We passed Hortense's quarters and I turned to shush him with my finger, even though through her door we could hear her loud, rumbling snores. Finally we made it to the closet. I allowed Maddock to pass through before closing the door quietly behind me.

"Maddock, what are you doing here?" I hissed. "This isn't safe!" I crossed my arms, processing his sudden appearance. I paused for a minute. "Is this about Cen? Is he okay? Is he hurt?" I sank to my knees, the red dress billowing out around me. "It's Cen, isn't it? It's been months since I heard from him."

Maddock took off his sheath and knelt down, his voice patient and hushed. "Emi, this is so much bigger than you or Cen."

I looked up, fear rising in my voice. "Maddock, what is going on? Tell me why you're here. How did you get in? How will you get out? These grounds are swarming with soldiers. You'll never get out alive."

Maddock gave me a soft smile. "Don't worry about me. There's a huge willow in the corner not too far from here. I just went from tree to tree until I got inside the grounds. I watched all day and figured out where you lived from up there. You see a lot when you're up that high," he said with a smirk.

"But why are you here? We may not have much time before someone realizes I'm missing." I thought of Jessra, the only one who would really miss me. I hoped she was too tired to wait up.

He nodded. "Right. I'll jump right in because I don't know how much time we have," he began, "there's much more going on than just a sickness to wipe out my village. Several more are falling under the same plague and only after the walls are built! Emi," he said, his eyes locking with mine intensely, "they're finished building the walls on your village now."

"Maddock, what are you saying?" I asked him warily. "The vox? Is that what you mean? What other villages are infected?"

There was a creak overhead. One of the girls was awake; I could hear her walking around the room. He looked at the ceiling and stopped talking, holding a finger to his lips. The footsteps stopped for a moment, and I took the chance to break the silence.

"Maddock, you're not safe here. I gave up too much to save you to watch you get caught right now." I exhaled slowly. "You're the reason I'm here to begin with." I could see his scar from the antidote peeking out just above his ratty shirt. Gently I reached out to him, tracing its outline with one finger. It amazed me how a simple treatment could save a life. A whole, human life. As nervous as I was that he would be caught, it was a miracle to see him. He was family—the closest thing I had to family besides Cen.

He nodded slowly, pulling his shirt down a little to reveal the entire scar. In the dark, he seemed much older than he really was. It was the same maturity I saw the first day he stumbled into the clinic. He had seen too much. "I will always be grateful to you for this," he said softly, nodding down toward his scar. "But the fight isn't over yet."

I stood quietly, trying not to rustle my skirts. "Please just tell me Cen is safe."

Maddock hesitated. "Emi, Cen is in prison." I gasped, feeling tears well up in my eyes as Maddock continued. "There was a Savian kid dying of fever and he treated her instead of the soldier that was waiting on him. They threw him in prison for it."

"Prison," I repeated as though it couldn't possibly be true. I slumped against the wall, my ears pumping with warm blood.

"I went to visit him," Maddock whispered, "disguised, of course. I've been in and out of your village when I can, but I still have some friends to take care of in my village. I'm the only one there who can take care of the sick really. Cen has been treating his fellow prisoners while he's in there. He complained about medical resources, but otherwise he is fine. The guards have treated him better than most because of his skills. I guess the Brockan soldiers miss him treating their little scrapes and bruises, so he'll be back to the clinic soon. I wanted to tell you sooner, I really did. I just didn't know how."

I buried my face in my hands. "So you came here tonight to tell me? Maddock, you shouldn't have done that. You're really not safe here. You should have written."

"I had to come," he replied fervently. "Because I get the feeling that no one is telling you what's going on and someone has to. I've already lost my brother! If they take my life? Fine. Your life is the only one that can save us."

"Maddock, what—" I shook my head, afraid of what he was about to say. "What are you talking about?"

He frowned and then whispered, "Let me start at the beginning. Just so you can know why it was so important for me to come in person." He paused. "For years there have been rumors that the Brockan government was growing tired of so many of their resources going toward us Savians. They think they can't expand with us. Instead of focusing on trade the government has been focused on us. On making sure we do not revolt."

I nodded. I already knew all of this. I'd heard it myself from the soldiers in the orchard and Marley too. But how did Maddock know?

He continued. "The government doesn't trust us enough to hand over our freedom. They think our numbers will overpower theirs. Instead of working for peace, there are men within these walls," he made a circle with his finger, "who would rather destroy us completely."

"A genocide," I murmured, thinking of Marley's book—of *Project 11*. "A mass annihilation."

Maddock nodded. "Right. A massacre like that would do two things: First, it would allow for government expansion. All resources could go to getting more land—making Deshan and the Brockan government even more powerful. And second . . ."

I spoke up. "Second, it would get us out of the way so any future battles would not be from us. It would clear out the people who have the longest history of hatred."

Maddock nodded. "Exactly."

"I know this already, Maddock. You didn't need to come to tell me."

"No, stop," he protested. "Emi, you don't see what's going on outside the walls right now." His voice shook a little, but I couldn't tell in the dark if he was crying. "They're isolating us," he whispered intensely. "I've been going from village to village at night, and I've seen it. They're building walls around one village at a time. Then, once their forces overpower ours, they are killing us. One village at a time."

My voice caught in my throat. The reality of Marley's plan—the orchard restructuring he had told Jessra and Younda about—was being carried out. I wondered before if it was happening, but it was hard to know from within the palace walls. Again, I considered how dangerous it was for a king to be behind closed walls—completely unaware of what was actually going on in the kingdom. "They're killing everyone?" I thought back to something Maddock said earlier about the walls around my village. I imagined soldiers building walls and lighting fires, killing men, women, and children without hesitation—the people I loved. I felt like I might be sick.

"We can't fight back, we can't get organized and revolt because there is no communication! For years this has been in the works. They cut us off from each other, so that the other villages don't even know that this is nationwide." I closed my eyes in pain. He was right.

"Disease," Maddock whispered, giving me a moment to figure it out myself. "Vox. They're using the disease to kill us. Much more subtle than the sword. Quieter too. I don't think most Brockans even know that it's happening. It's just a matter of time before Kalvos starts getting the vox."

I held my hands to my face and tried to breathe deeply. How could I not have realized this was *Project 11* before? Entire villages destroyed by a rare disease; the royal healer searching for and stockpiling a cure for the soldiers deported to the villages. This was the plan. Marley's "experiment." And it would work. Of course it would work. Kirt was the only one in Deshan with access to the antidote, and a fleet of royal guards protected it day and night.

"But how is it spreading?" I asked. "It's not like they can infuse it in the air. Walls wouldn't do anything if that were the case."

Maddock shrugged. "I don't know how it's spreading, but many already have it. We can't just stop it at this point—we need to reverse it. To save as many lives as we still can. It might be too late for some of them, but it's not too late for all of us."

I shook my head. "Maddock, I don't know what you want me to do about it."

He took a deep breath and inched closer to me. Our legs were touching now. "Emi, rumors have been circulating in the Savian villages, mine and yours and several others I have been visiting. The marketplace is buzzing about it too. They're saying a Savian girl is in the program. That she is the closest to the prince." I shook my head, my face flushing as I thought of the two women at the ball.

"Emi, the Savians—our people—know about you somehow. Maybe servants have spread the news, I don't know. And they know something is going on in the villages. Everyone is sick. They're all sick and every antidote in the world can't save us if the government wants us dead." He paused. "You're the only hope any of us have of surviving. We have no resources to fight back. We have no weapons or skills."

"Even if our people do know I'm here, what am I supposed to do?" I cut in. "I have no say! I'm no one here!"

"You have the prince's ear!" Maddock exclaimed. He clamped his hand over his mouth at the outburst and looked nervously at the ceiling above. "You could do something more than just stop it—you could change things! You have to try, Emi." His voice was pleading, borderline begging.

"How could I do anything without giving myself away?" I demanded. "What do you suggest? I'm already being watched, I'm already suspicious enough!" I felt my heart sink with the realization of my helplessness. "I wish I could stop it but I can't! Marley has too much power. I'm pretty sure he already knows who I am! He'll throw me in prison, he'll kill me and Cen and anyone I am close to! I can't do anything!"

He was silent after I spoke, his eyes closed as he held his fingers on his chest, tracing the outline of the scar. I believe it is possible, even for just an instant, to feel the pain of another, and in that moment I felt the pain of Maddock. We had both lost so much to the Brockans already—my mother, his parents and now his brother. Of course he would do anything he could to stop that cycle; of course he would risk his life to ask for my help.

"Emi, you have to try," he finally whispered, tears welling in the bottom of his hollow eyes and falling silently down his face. "You have to deliver us. You're our only hope."

I began to cry then too, for my loss and his loss, and for Cen, and for every fear I harbored inside. I held him while we cried, my hands brushing through his hair, my arms pulling him toward me like the mother he no longer, and I never, had.

"I don't think I can," I said to him when we both regained our composure. "I want to. I'd like to think that there is something I could do to help, but you don't know what it's like. I'm already being watched. They'll kill me if they find out who I am." It was so late that I was almost incoherent, could hardly remember a thing I had said or done tonight.

"I have to go now, before the sun comes up." He reached for me and hugged me fiercely in his bony arms. "Deliver us," were the last words he said before disappearing into the dark night.

He left his rusted knife on the floor of the closet.

*　　✦　　✳　　✦

I slept until noon, and when I woke up I saw three or four other girls still asleep too, their hair peeking out of piles of blankets. I yawned loudly, forgetting for just a minute that my people knew I was there and believed I was the only one to deliver them. That Maddock was here last night in the palace and confirmed Marley's plan. Everything just felt like a dream. It couldn't be real.

Classes dragged on that afternoon and more than once Hortense had to clap her hands to wake one or more of us up. "If you can't remain alert during class, I may be forced to tell the queen to cancel the next ball," she threatened. But when it kept happening, she canceled classes for the rest of the day, throwing her hands in the air, fed up with us. I didn't even care that she canceled my time at the stables, Maddock's conversation still ringing in my head.

"So what really happened last night?" Jessra asked me a few hours later in the pool. We ate an early dinner, Hortense suggesting that we all get to bed right at sunset so we would be rested for classes the next day. The water was refreshing tonight—cooler than usual. The seasons never changed much in Deshan. It was always hot, but once in awhile a cool wind blew through and the heat seemed to lift, if only temporarily.

"What do you mean?" I asked her back. "I told you. I ate some food and then danced with Corban. Nothing else happened."

Jessra rolled her eyes. "Larken, you dance all night with the prince and you expect me to just let it go? And then what happened after the ball?" She looked at me incredulously, her long hair floating behind her in the water. "Nothing else you want to tell me?" She was fishing, but I wasn't sure for what. We had spoken after the ball, and she had seemed to accept my answer just fine then.

I shrugged. "No, there's nothing else." I was irritable from lack of sleep and worry about Maddock. Not that his knife would have protected him much, but the sight of it alone on the floor wouldn't leave my mind. Maybe it could have helped him. Where was he?

"But what about the prince? He was looking around the ballroom all night and disappeared for almost half an hour. Then when he came back he danced every song with you. Every girl complained after her dance that he seemed to be preoccupied—always looking around, never hearing what they said—and that was before he danced with you for so long." She paused, shaking her head. "You act like its nothing. Larken, is there someone else? Another boy?"

I gulped. Had she seen Maddock somehow? "What? No! Why do we have to talk about this? Can't we talk about the boy with the purple suit? What's going on with him? Does he have a name yet?"

215

It didn't work. "Larken, I know what you're trying to do. Switch the attention back to me. But it's not going to work this time. And, no, he has not told me his name yet. He's saving it for the last ball."

For a minute I thought I had her, convinced she would start talking about him again. I waited as her eyes glazed, focusing intently on the light behind my head. But it didn't work. She shook herself out of her daze. "No—no. I refuse to answer any more questions about him until you answer mine. Is there someone else you care about? Do you even want to be queen?"

I floated on my back, water rushing in my ears while she spoke. "Jessra . . ." I submerged myself and came up again, annoyed that she insisted on dwelling on this subject. "Why do you keep asking me that? There's no one else!" My words came out harsher than I meant them to.

She grimaced sadly and hoisted herself out of the pool, folding her huge, white towel around her like she were a bat folding up her wings—first one arm, then the other. I stayed in the pool. By now the rest of the girls had filed out and were probably getting ready for bed.

Jessra stared down at me, her long hair dripping like a spout onto the stone. "You know what he told me, Larken? The prince? During our dance?"

"What?" I asked, lifting my eyes to meet hers.

"I told him I was still homesick and he told me that he was sorry we have to wait a year here. He told me if he had it his way we would end things early and he would make his decision tonight."

"Why would he say that?" I asked, my heart thumping with hope.

"Because he already made his decision, Larken. Because he has already picked you. The one girl in the program who doesn't even want this."

She shivered a little into her towel and then walked away, leaving me in the pool. It was the first time we had ever left the pool separately and for some reason, even with everything else going on, it made me feel like I was completely alone.

24

Sunlight brazenly flooded the room, and I groaned, my eyelids fluttering listlessly. Hortense stood at the window, her fists around the curtain with a smug grin. Ignoring the gasps and cries, she stomped her feet. "There will be a special meeting this morning in the Great Room of the palace. Your attendance is mandatory and you must all look presentable. We will be leaving in thirty minutes." She paused, waiting for us to jump up. "And Prince Corban will be there."

That was all it took to get us out of bed. Screeching and scrambling over one another, the girls dressed and braided their hair, heavy bags resting under our eyes from lack of sleep. The room was full of chatter about our meeting at the Great Room. We had been in the palace for months and had never been asked to attend anything like this before. I dressed quickly, braiding my hair loosely as I walked down the stairs to find something for breakfast before we left.

Hortense was the only one at the table when I came downstairs, slumped over the table and slurping her tea—breaking every rule of etiquette she demanded we learn. "Miss Larken," she said between smacks, "did you enjoy yourself at the ball? I never had the chance to ask you about it."

"Yes, madame," I replied.

She frowned. "Your behavior was completely inappropriate. Dancing with the prince that long without giving the other girls a chance? It's rude, and it was embarrassing for me. I hoped that I had taught you better manners." She scooped some sugar in her teacup, not even meeting my eye.

I swallowed hard. "Madame, I am sorry for embarrassing you, but any girl here would dance with Corban as long as she had the opportunity to."

"It's *Prince* Corban to you," she replied snootily. But before she could say another word of scolding, a trail of girls entered the room, each one yawning and rubbing her eyes.

She stood up, clapping her hands together. "Ladies, we do not have any more time. Those of you who came down late will have to wait until lunch to eat. It is time to make our way to the Great Room."

Instead of groaning or complaining like I expected, the girls lined up obediently and began to file out in a single line. I grabbed an apple from the bowl on the table and concealed it in my dress for later. On our walk there Jessra, clutching Tulia's arm protectively, was still not talking to me.

The Great Room really was great, crafted almost entirely out of the gold-flecked marble that lined the floors. In the center of the room was an enormous stage surrounded by marble benches on all sides. Three golden thrones overwhelmed the stage and on them sat the queen, Corban, and Marley. I expected courtiers to be in attendance, but as we filed down the steps I realized that no one else was there besides the soldiers flanking each entrance.

As soon as we sat down, Marley stood to speak to us. His slick voice sounded especially icy today. "Ladies, it's good to have you here. Thank you for joining us in the Great Room. This room is a special place for our country. It's where the laws of our beautiful land have been made and announced, where the ancient and contemporary kings have been coronated and where, yes, royal weddings have taken place." Several girls giggled, bringing their handkerchiefs to their faces. I did my best to catch Corban's eye, but he was focused intently on the floor by his feet.

"Now, on to my first point of business," Marley continued. "There will be a bit of a shift in our protocol within the castle. As many of you may know, we employ many Savian servants in our halls." His face turned red. "They make your beds, your food, and even teach some of your classes." I covered my mouth, my cheeks growing hot.

"Until now. As of today, it is not only prohibited, but it is unlawful for a Savian to live within the palace walls. Those working on the staff have been dismissed." He coughed, and I knew what he meant was much worse. "This is one reason why we have called you all here. If you know of any Savian within the palace walls, it is your duty to report it to Madame Hortense, who will report it to me. From here on out, it is a crime punishable by death for their nationality to mingle with the royal family within these walls. I expect your full cooperation on this." I buried my nails into my palms, my knuckles turning white.

Younda turned to look at me, her eyes bloodshot and manic. For a moment I wondered if she actually knew my secret or if she was just using her speculation to intimidate me. I inhaled sharply and averted my gaze from hers.

"Oh, and one more matter of business on a brighter note!" Marley exclaimed, his eyes brushing past mine. "Prince Corban has an announcement to make."

Every girl sat at attention, eyes fixated on Corban, who stood up slowly and brushed his hair from his face. His expression was unmoving and serious as he made his way to the front of the stage. He kept his eyes focused on the marble tile at his feet when he announced, "This morning I was promoted to chief commander for the Brockan Army. It is a great honor, and one that I accept with gratitude." He didn't smile during his announcement and returned to his seat quickly, his mother reaching out for his hand.

The girls erupted in applause, and Marley beamed proudly at our reaction. He turned back to smile at Corban. "Yes, yes, we are very pleased. He is a fine warrior and will be a tremendous asset to the Brockan military. Under his leadership we expect only victories! Not that Deshan knows anything less. Now, I believe we have covered everything we need to. Please remember to keep your eyes open for any Savians in our midst, as they may be dangerous to our royal family and safety within these walls."

I shook my head in disgust. This was Marley's way of letting me know that he knew who I was. I could feel it. But why would he allow me to stay if he knew?

We were dismissed after that for class. I scarcely heard a word as Hortense droned on about the rules of foreign trade. I knew Corban was a Brockan, but until now I hadn't internalized how far on their side he really was. I thought of him as a friend—well maybe a little more than that. Or a lot more. And while I knew he was the Brockan prince, I never thought of him as a Brockan or a Savian or anyone but Corban. After his announcement though, I realized how dangerous it really was for me to get close to him. Corban was in charge—the commander of the people that were trying so zealously to destroy mine.

* * * *

I ran to the stables after class, eager to escape the mansion and the other girls. It would be a relief to get away from them all—even Jessra, who was still avoiding me. When I couldn't find Hendrik outside, I raced past his aides up to his gatehouse.

He was writing a letter at his desk when I came in. "Well, hello Larken!" he said, tucking his letter under a stack of papers. "How was the ball?"

I half smiled at him and sunk into one of the armchairs facing his table, not realizing until then how tired I was. Between dancing all night at the ball, then Maddock's visit, then my worrying late at night, I was behind on my sleep. I doubted the new information we received at the Great Room that morning would help. That, and Marley's threatening eyes on mine. Every night I wondered if I would be taken from my bed by some soldiers, never to be seen again.

I shrugged at Hendrik's question casually. There was no reason to involve him in my fears. "The ball was wonderful. I danced all night. And we had a meeting in the Great Room this morning." I paused, unsure about how much I could actually tell Hendrik. I trusted him but reminded myself that he was still under orders from Marley and Corban.

"Did you? I hadn't heard about any meeting." Hendrik edged closer to his desk curiously. "What did you discuss? Whatever it is, it seems to be upsetting you."

I released a sigh and told him everything Marley told us—about the Savians and their numbers at the palace, about Corban's new title and position as chief commander. He listened with wide eyes, nodding his head but not interrupting me ever or asking questions. "I guess I just feel afraid," I said slowly. "Not for myself but for this country. What's going to happen to us if we continue believing that Savians and Brockans are so different?" I looked up at him, gauging his reaction. I had said too much. I expected him to look suspicious, but instead his eyes looked eager—maybe even a little sad.

He blinked deliberately and allowed several moments to pass in silence. My heart beat. I shouldn't have been so careless! "Larken, I need to tell you something," he said flatly.

I looked up at him, and somehow I knew what he would say before he said it. "Kirt told me about your secret," he said. "Back at the hunt we speculated together about it, and later he confirmed it."

I inhaled sharply, stunned. Hendrik knew my secret all this time? I opened my mouth to deny it before I realized that he had never said anything about me being Savian.

"I only bring that up," he said quickly, before I could speak, "because I am a Savian too."

Warmth spread throughout my body. "No," I stammered, "that's not possible. They would never allow that." The words seemed to rattle out of my mouth. "You've been employed for years! You look nothing like a Savian." I shook my head, confusion replacing my fear. "I don't understand. Hendrik—how?"

"You don't look like a Savian either," he pointed out. "I hoped you would come to the stables for classes so that I could look out for you. You are safe as long as I am here." He paused. "Larken, there are many people counting on you. More people than you would believe, who somehow know that you're here and are praying for you to deliver them. Just because the royal family never ventures outside of these walls doesn't mean the rest of us don't."

"I know that," I whispered. Hendrik was just one more person who I would eventually let down.

We sat in silence for several moments. I didn't expect Hendrik to react this way. He knew—like Maddock—that there were Savians out there who knew I was here. He had confessed his own identity nonchalantly, as though it were nothing. As though he couldn't be killed for it. I heard horses snorting outside the window, and the stable hands calling back and forth to each other. A clock on Hendrik's wall ticked loudly.

He grimaced, his eyes level with mine now. "I have wondered when I would tell you. And how you would react to it, knowing that for months I knew exactly who you were and said nothing to you." He looked out of the window, his hands placed delicately on his table. "I thought it would be when you left, when the program ended. But now seems like as good a time as any. You need to know that you have an ally. You have always had one in Kirt, of course. And now in me—whether you knew it or not."

The shock was wearing off and I forced a smile, even though I still wasn't sure whether I could trust Hendrik. "So are you in danger here?" I asked. "You seemed so unafraid to tell me who you really are."

He shook his head. "I don't think I'm in danger, and I trust you." He looked at me pointedly. "There are some, of course, who have worked in the palace longer than I have, but we have been friends for so long that I think they have forgotten the issue of my race entirely. I doubt that I'll be in trouble with Marley's recent announcement, although I will definitely be on guard."

I shook my head. How many more Savians were inside these gates that I wasn't aware of? Had they spread the word that I was here? That I was close to the prince? "Hendrik," I stammered, "how are you here at all? How did you get this position? How many more of us are there?"

He twitched his lip. "It's a bit of a long story."

I smiled and shrugged my shoulders. It felt good to know that he was on my side all of this time.

"Of course I'll tell you," he said slowly, his eyes on the door behind me. "But I ask that you listen with unbiased ears. I would have done many things differently in hindsight."

I looked him in the eyes, nervous about what he was going to say. "I understand."

"Before I begin"—his voice shook with each word—"let me say that I care deeply for Corban and his family. They have been the closest thing I have to a family for most of my life."

He paused again for several long moments. "Years ago, I came to the royal palace as a servant. Well, actually, more like a slave. My parents died when I was young and I was rounded up from the orphanage to work in the palace as a kitchen hand. King Jairus was young too, although he was a few years older than me. He used to sneak away so we could play together. We would fence and when I had some free time, we would climb trees in the fields." Hendrik's eyes were vacant as though I was not there—as if he were currently living in the memory. "One day we were playing in the woods behind the palace and he fell and hit his head. I carried him, even though he was much larger than I was at the time, to the clinic. When we got there, he had lost a lot of blood. The healer was able to save his life though. Jairus promised me that day that he would repay the favor." He paused, wiping his forehead with his sleeve.

"Jairus convinced his father to send me to a battle training school in West Deshan. His father, King Iliok, was not a kind man, but Jairus convinced him that by investing in my schooling, I might become a great general someday for the Brockan army. Jairus never told him I was Savian. He could have, but at the time he didn't think to. We were so young then that it didn't matter to us."

He took a swig of water from a glass on his desk. "I spent the next ten years at the barrack school, learning how to ride—to fence—to kill. And when I returned, King Jairus was crowned and welcomed me with open arms. But he told me that some things had to change. 'Never reveal your race while you live in these grounds,' he warned, 'And never speak to my son about your people either. That is all I ask of you.' I pleaded with him, 'But I cannot be your general and plan out strategies for you to kill my people. You cannot expect me to sit in your battle hall and watch them suffer! You sent me away, but I will always be a Savian.'" Hendrik rubbed his eyes, his voice laden with emotion.

"So then he told me, 'I would never ask that of you. You will never sit in my battle hall. Your one job is to train my son. Train him to be a great warrior. Train him to defend and lead his country if the time comes.'"

"Corban?" I questioned. "He asked you to train Corban?"

Hendrik nodded. "I thought nothing of it then. Corban was just a young boy who loved to fight. He learned quickly and I enjoyed spending time with him. But as time went on, I began to see that he was capable of much, much more.

"He was so good at riding and at fighting. He learned battle strategies quickly and often came up with clever ideas of his own. Yet he was raised with the same biases as his father—that Savians are second-class citizens who cannot be trusted." I cringed when Hendrik said that. I knew he was right, but it hurt to hear that Corban was raised to hate my people just like the rest of the Brockan children. Perhaps even more.

"Marley was Jairus's advisor," Hendrik continued, "and conditioned both of them to think with his same opinions. He always said that Jairus was too soft, but that Corban has the strength his father lacked to completely annihilate the Savian race and to expand the country's borders. In many ways, he is completely right about that. Corban has the training and intellect his father never had."

The Hendrik that was usually so stoic seemed to melt as he spoke of Corban and Jairus. "I cannot talk to Corban about his loyalties because it pains me to see any sort of hatred toward the Savian race that he might harbor. And also . . ." Hendrik stopped talking, and shook his head. After several minutes of silence, it became evident that he was not going to continue.

"Hendrik," I murmured, standing and putting my hand on his. "You cannot blame yourself. You did what his father asked of you."

Hendrik shook his head as he stared out the window. "You don't understand," he offered in a hoarse whisper. "I deserve to feel this guilt for what I've done. I knew that this day would finally come. I knew that he would be given this new title and responsibilities, but now that it has actually happened, you can understand that it is difficult for me to accept."

"What do you mean?" I asked, as Hendrik stood and pressed his face against the cabinets behind his desk.

"I have single-handedly created the most powerful weapon the Brockan army has to destroy our race."

"What's that?" I whispered, even though I already knew the answer.

"Prince Corban."

25

"We're going to the clinic," Hendrik told me when I arrived at the stables for training a few days later. I knew who Hendrik really was, and it made things easier somehow. Even though Jessra was still not talking to me, I had a confidant.

"Why?" I asked anxiously at his announcement. "What's at the clinic?"

"Kirt," he said. "Kirt's at the clinic, and he has something for you. I'll take you over there as soon as you saddle up."

My heart raced wildly on our ride there, and every fear I could imagine about Maddock and Cen came to surface. It had to be them—why else would Kirt summon me? I blinked away tears and straightened my shoulders, doing my best to be brave, but realizing that in just moments my entire world could be shattered.

Kirt stood at the entrance to the clinic with his arms open wide for me as we rode toward him. I dropped from my horse, began to run, and jumped into Kirt's arms. His turban was wrapped tight, and his face looked thinner. His spectacles had difficulty staying on his nose. "Thank you for bringing her," Kirt said to Hendrik. "I'll walk her back to the stables when we're finished."

Hendrik nodded. "Fair enough." He turned to me. "See you soon, Larken."

I waved good-bye to Hendrik and followed Kirt to his office, trembling. "Is something wrong? Is it Cen?"

Kirt gestured to a chair in his office and sat down at his desk facing me. "I have something that I feel may be of value to you." He reached into the folds of his robes and retrieved a letter.

Quickly tearing it open, I tried to slow down, to absorb all I could from Cen's familiar script.

> *Emi,*
>
> *Before I pen another word I must reassure you that I am safe and well. Maddock told me that he informed you about my little visit to the prison. I hope you did not worry. It was a wonderful experience. I was able to treat many there who otherwise may not have survived. I asked the guards for better supplies for the sick. The conditions in the prisons are terrible, and many need help. The only downside to being there was not being able to treat those outside the prison or being able to write you.*
>
> *The guards are surrounding our village here, building high walls to keep us inside. They have closed the orchards so no one has work to do or anywhere to go. Before I entered the prison, they had just begun building. Now, they are near completion. I'm not certain why they're shutting us off from the rest of the world. My only hope is that by locking us in, they're not also locking you out. Maddock has not been to see me in weeks. I worry that with these new walls, he'll have difficulty reaching me.*
>
> *Emi, I didn't tell anyone about you, but somehow every patient we have seems to talk of a girl in the palace who will save her people from destruction. It is you. I understand the responsibility may seem overwhelming, but instead I ask that you look at this time as a brilliant*

opportunity. Our people will perish unless you help. We absolutely need you. Which is a good thing, because you are the bravest person I know.

I love you every day. Be safe.

Cen

Kirt said nothing about the streams of tears that fell down my face. I wiped them with the back of my hand. They were tears of relief, of course, but also of concern. It was one thing to have the entire Savian race depending on me, but Cen—his opinion mattered more to me than all of theirs combined. The weight of my responsibility and the realization of my powerlessness here seemed to collide. I could do nothing. I could do everything.

Kirt studied my face. Then without saying another word, he offered me a candle, tipping it toward me. It was a command, not a suggestion. Reluctantly I held out the letter, releasing it only as the flames licked my fingertips. The burning envelope fell into a bowl on Kirt's desk.

"He's alive," Kirt said simply, his eyes not moving from mine. "I sent a trusted aide to your village to locate him. He was uncertain how to contact you ever since he got out of prison. The aide made it clear that he could write to you freely, that your letter would not be censored by the palace. I told Hendrik as soon as possible so he could get you here."

I nodded. "Thank you," I murmured. "And thank you for calling me here so soon. This news is the best I have heard in some time." There was some truth to those words of course. Cen was alive, but his letter also made me fear—not just for my race, but for my village, for my loved ones in Kalvos.

"Of course." He paused, his expression still and unmoving. I reached toward the pulse at my neck, inhaling deeply and feeling the beat slow as I calmed down. "I only wish I could do something more," he said. "I understand that the situation in the villages has gotten much worse."

His offer pricked an idea inside of me and I leaned forward and rested my elbows on his desk. "Actually," I said, fighting a lump in my throat, "there may be something more you can do."

He nodded at me, "Anything."

I chose my words carefully. "Kirt, I want to talk to you about the vox cure."

"I am not at liberty to discuss that cure," he murmured, gazing toward the wall. "I have been given strict orders—"

"By Marley?" I interrupted.

Kirt sat up now. "What are you saying? How could you know that?"

I'm not sure if it was Cen's letter or Maddock's pleading, but I felt brave right now. "Kirt, I overheard your conversation the other evening. Outside the clinic." Shock spread throughout his face, but before he could open his mouth I continued. "Kirt, he's trying to kill us. To kill every Savian—and he's doing it by spreading vox among the villages. I don't know how he's doing it, but he's cutting us off and building walls and releasing the disease somehow . . ." I bit my lip nervously before continuing, "It's true. I swear it's true."

He lifted a trembling hand to his face. "Larken, you should not speak of this," he pleaded. He glanced at his door nervously, as though someone could be overhearing us somehow. "You could be killed. We both could. You don't know what they're capable of."

"I'll be killed regardless!" I said, much louder than I intended. He eyed his door nervously, but no one came. "Why should I care if Marley does it now or later? At the end of this I'll return to my village and suffer the same fate . . ." Sweat pooled around my hairline. "Unless," I said, pausing, "you do something about it."

He removed his glasses and rubbed his eyes. "You want the antidote? Fine. I'll give it to you. I actually thought about doing this as soon as I learned of your identity. You'll be much safer once you get it—now is a good time. You'll have to keep the scar hidden, of course, for the time being but that shouldn't be too difficult." He gave me a look that was both pitiful and angry. That wasn't exactly the offer I was hoping for.

I shook my head. "Kirt, we need much more than that. I'm one life. There are thousands more to save. We need to mass-produce the antidote. We need as many healers as possible to stockpile it for their patients."

He scratched his beard roughly, avoiding my eyes. I knew I was asking a lot. "Can you do that?" I asked. "Cen can help us! I can help too!" My heart was pounding wildly again, but not from fear. "And do you know how it spreads? Did the Sansikwan healer . . . did she give you any information about that? Or did she just offer a cure?"

He shrugged, removing his spectacles. "We did not discuss that," he said. "Not much is known about how diseases are spread from one person to another."

"The starter," I offered. "The bacterium. Does it have any properties that might give us a clue?"

Kirt considered this momentarily. "It's a yeastlike bacterium. It could be through touch . . ." He drifted off, deep in thought, but when he turned back to me, his eyes were sure. "Give me some time. I'll try to help you. But first, if you're going to return to those villages when this is over, you should get the antidote now. It may be difficult even for me to get it. It's guarded heavily and Marley receives a report on each person who receives it . . . But I think I can do it. I can't send you back there knowing what I know now."

I was surprised by his reaction—his immediate promise to help my people. "Thank you," I replied sincerely. I wasn't sure what else to say.

"I'll be right back," he said, heading toward his door. "And then we'll finish this discussion."

"Wait, you want to give it to me here, right now?"

He turned around to look in my eyes. "Miss Larken, I have been around long enough to know that sometimes we must act on our instincts. I cannot let you return to your village at the end of this program and contract the disease. Your people need you too much." He paused, and when he spoke again his voice was brittle. "We all need you too much. It will only take a moment."

I waited for him in silence for almost a half hour. The wind blew a branch against his window, scraping like a claw. I thought about what my people could do with Kirt's help. Maybe I could take some of the antidote home to my village. But would it be enough? And would I still be killed in some other way if the vox didn't do it?

Kirt entered the room, holding a vial of bubbling white liquid as well as a standard kit. "I would have Natty prepare a room for you," he apologized, "but that may cause too much suspicion, and a chart would need to be filled out."

I knelt down on his floor, watching as he arranged his instruments across the marbled tile. "I'm going to make a small incision right here." He motioned to the space above his heart. "You'll need to remove your tunic so I can get to it. Once I have the open incision, I will pour the antidote into your bloodstream. It will froth quite a bit and hurt, but the pain won't last long," he reassured me. "You'll need to be careful not to cry out."

He held up the vial so I could see it more carefully. "The antidote cauterizes the blood, so there won't be much bleeding. From there, I simply stitch it up. A simple and quick procedure."

I nodded in gratitude and lifted my tunic over my head. I lay on the floor in my undershirt and watched everything he did—the sterilization, the placement of the incision, the actual cut. He was incredibly precise, his fingers attuned to each action. It didn't hurt—at least not until he poured the antidote into the opening. I shoved my fist in my mouth to keep from crying out, my teeth bearing down on my clamped knuckles. It was both scalding hot and freezing cold at the same time. The pain electrified my entire body. I felt my back seize uncontrollably as I wrenched in insufferable agony until, almost as quickly as it began, it ended. Relief washed throughout my body like a wave.

"You were much braver than most of the soldiers," he said with a smile, beginning his stitches effortlessly. I winced when the needle first pricked, but otherwise I couldn't feel a thing. I brushed the sweat away from my forehead as he worked. I was in the best hands possible. Kirt was silent when he finished. He lifted me up and handed me my tunic. One by one he put his tools away as I sat in one of his chairs, fingering the bandage carefully.

We didn't speak for several minutes, both of us intently focused on the branch scraping across the window. When he finally spoke his voice quavered. "It's a terrible thing I have done."

"Saving me?" I asked. "Are you worried about what Marley will say if he finds out?"

He shook his head and lifted his hand, "No. No. It is more . . . It is more." His voice shook. "Unknowingly I have provided a way for this great evil to happen. How could I have known what Marley had planned?" He frowned, setting his kit on the desk. "I thought that in finding a cure I would save lives. But it seems as though I just provided a way for more to be lost. At least now I have the comfort of knowing yours will not be one of them."

He walked me back to the stables later, asking the soldiers if we could have some time alone. We walked wordlessly, both of us tortured by the knowledge we had. The burden rested upon us almost tangibly—a physical weight strapped onto our backs. We had to stop this disease before it took any more lives. We had to stop Marley. We were the only ones who could do it now. I almost felt more pressure now that I was inoculated against the disease. I felt guilt—guilt that I would live when so many others would die.

When we reached the stables, Kirt bowed as always, before walking away. He hadn't gone far when I called after him. "Hey, Kirt?" He turned slowly, his hands clasped behind his back. "Thank you!" I yelled. I hoped he heard my sincerity.

He bowed in response and continued along the path, his shoulders hunched over, turban bobbing. I watched him for a moment and realized then, with everything in me, that Kirt was the bravest person I had ever had the pleasure of knowing.

＊　＊　＊　＊

Cautiously I put on my swim dress, the heat finally winning out. You could still see the incision Kirt made, but at least it was completely closed by now. For the next few nights I studied Marley's map while the other girls swam, their splashing and voices echoing up through the balcony doors. The map and its details were so familiar to me, but I still didn't have a plan. His plan, however, was clear to me. Isolating the villages and farms, building walls, releasing the vox. But how could I stop it? Corban seemed to be the answer, but I didn't want him to be. I felt that a swim would help clear my head.

I was careful to keep my chest under water even though my swim dress covered most of the stitching. Floating on my back with my ears beneath the water, the girls and their chatter drifted away. This might be one of my last quiet moments before everything changed. I couldn't stay, not with what I knew. I would see Corban tomorrow at the grove for the first time since the last ball, Maddock's visit, and Corban's new promotion, but this visit wouldn't be like the last. I couldn't keep wasting my time here while my people died. It was strange really. If I were brave enough to tell him the truth tomorrow, I would be starting a war—perhaps literally—against Marley. Maybe even Corban. Before I did that, I wanted to enjoy one last night of peace.

The mood was changing with the rest of the girls too. They were nervous, each of them analyzing their last conversations with the prince. Who would he choose? Who had the best chance? I drifted in and out of their conversations, paying particular attention to one I overheard from Younda.

"My father . . . weapons . . . Savians . . . war." It was nothing new to me, I'd heard her speak that way before, but something about it tonight seemed more threatening. I swam closer to her and Sasha, but they didn't speak much longer before pulling on their white robes and going back inside.

The rest of the pool emptied shortly thereafter. Even Jessra went inside, much to my disappointment. I swam laps in silence, my muscles enjoying the stretch and the lack of resistance the water offered. They had grown substantially since I started training. What used to be limp rags were now lean and sculpted. I was still short, but no one would call me small anymore. I felt and looked strong. It didn't hurt either that for the first time in my life; I had consistently gone to bed with a full stomach.

When I was midway through the pool, I heard a splash at the far end. Frantically I floundered up to see Jessra's head bobbing at the edge. My heart surged. Even if she refused to talk to me, it was good to see her. My strokes were timid, hesitant as I swam toward her. She held my gaze instead of turning away or averting her eyes like she had done before. "Hey," I said.

"Hey," she replied back with a soft smile.

I started in quickly. "Look, I'm sorry about how our last conversation ended. I didn't want it to be like that." I paused, treading water while I spoke. "I'm sorry that I was unkind to you."

She nodded, considering my apology, and then twitched her lip before speaking up. "It's more than that, Larken. All of this is more than just that." She paused. "I've been meaning to ask you this for a while but I was waiting for the right time . . . is there anything going on that you're not telling me about? I'm not the only one who's noticed that you're always missing somewhere. At the stables late at night, getting pulled out of classes to go to the clinic . . . When everyone else is there, you're always gone. You can tell me anything," she emphasized, her eyes heavy. "I just want to know. I want to help you—however I can."

I was lucky to have a friend like Jessra. She had a bigger heart than anyone. But I couldn't tell her the truth. Not now, when I was preparing to tell Corban. The knowledge could endanger her. I bit my lip. "Thanks for the concern, Jess, but you know I've been busy at the stables. Hendrik takes my classes pretty seriously . . . And I get called out to the clinic because in my training I sustain a lot of injuries." I felt around for the cut above my heart. If only she knew.

She released her long hair into the cool water. "You know, it's okay if you have a boyfriend," she offered, twirling a piece of her hair nervously. "That boy I was talking about earlier? I saw him. After the last ball." I felt my heart began to pound. She saw Maddock?

"When you didn't come up for bed," she continued, "I came downstairs and heard voices coming from that closet we found together. I couldn't hear much of what was said with the door closed, so I went back upstairs and waited for you. Eventually I saw him leave outside the upstairs window, and I pretended to be asleep as you came in. I didn't bring it up until now because I was hoping you would come to me about it. But a lot of girls here want the prince to choose them. They really think they love him. And if you have someone else, it just seems like you should tell him. Not just for him, but for them too."

My heart began to pound. Jessra had seen Maddock! "Jessra, he's not my boyfriend. I promise you that," I said with an urgent whisper.

"Well, then, who is he?" she asked, her voice steady and controlled. "Is he the one you keep leaving to meet? Is he the reason you're missing from classes and balls and dinner and everything else? Is he a servant or a nobleman's son or what? I need you to tell me so I know how to cover for you. I keep trying with the other girls, even with Hortense, but I don't know how much longer I can do it." Her eyes filled with tears, and she flung her hands in the air helplessly. "I consider you my best friend in this house, and the sad thing is, I hardly know anything about you." My heart sank. I knew how hard it was for Jessra to tell me this. She was loyal, almost to a fault.

"Jessra, I promise, he's not my boyfriend . . . ," I stumbled, "but I can't tell you who he is. I will, though. I will tell you everything when all of this is done, when the program ends, but just know that it's not what it seems. I wouldn't do that to Corban—please know that." My voice choked up as I spoke and I reached toward her, before realizing that if I did, she would see my incision and have even more questions.

Tears fell freely from her face now. "I'll never betray you, Larken. Not ever. But I'm not sure I can do this anymore. Until you can tell me the truth, I can't keep protecting you and lying for you when I don't even know who you are."

I began to cry as well, my tears hot like acid on my already wet face. "Please don't do this. Please don't say that. Can I just ask you to trust me? I'll tell you everything when the program ends. Everything," I pleaded.

She shook her head. "I can't . . . I can't do it. I'm sorry." She hoisted herself out of the pool and grabbed her robe before walking inside slowly.

I folded my arms in the water and cried. I thought about how I would continue this experience without Jessra. I needed her friendship more than I cared to admit and who knew how much more I would need her after I spoke to Corban. Still, I couldn't risk telling her the truth. I saw how she reacted to even the word *Savian*. She would hate me. She might even turn me in.

I floated under the stars, letting my tears mix with the water of the pool, until a soldier motioned for me to go inside. I was meeting Corban tomorrow night. I would tell him everything then—everything that I couldn't tell Jessra tonight. There were so many sacrifices I had to make to keep my identity a secret. So many relationships I damaged along the way. I guess it hurt me more than I cared to admit that my friendship with Jessra was one of them.

26

My stomach roared as I stepped into the grove the next evening. I considered not coming. I thought it more than once throughout the day, but I also felt the truth poised within me, ready to spring. Corban was waiting in the shadows of the trees. It was a few minutes past sunset as I entered, but I felt lucky to be there at all. Hortense wasn't happy when Hendrik wrote her and said he needed me to stay late. Kirt and Jessra were right—she was definitely growing suspicious.

"Larken," Corban greeted me softly, enveloping me in an embrace. "I was worried you wouldn't make it. Thank you for coming." He rested his head on mine, and I felt the warmth of his arms immediately. How could they feel so right? If I held my tongue, could I stay in them? Was that the choice I was making?

"Of course," I responded. He released me and I reluctantly allowed him to, sitting gingerly against the tree with my riding boots tucked up under my skirt. "I wasn't sure if you wanted to see me still . . . We haven't spoken since you received your new position. Chief commander is such an honor." I gauged his reaction, seeing how he responded to that title.

He nodded. "Of course I wanted to see you. I have thought of little else. Please—" he said, gesturing toward me, "please come sit closer to me." He had not mentioned his new position. Evidently it was a delicate subject.

I inched over and sat beside him, my braid falling across my shoulder and touching him. I let it stay there. "It's such a nice night. I love this time of year."

A bright-green bird hopped in the palms above us back and forth from tree to tree. "I think so too," he replied. "My father loved this time of year. He used to say that this season was why there have been so many battles over this land. 'It's the breezes!' he used to say. 'These breezes are enough to start a war. Who wouldn't want to live here?'" Corban chuckled in a sad sort of way.

I sat quietly next to him, absorbing his information about his father. "Are you ready to resume our questions?"

He nodded, exiting his daydream. "Yes. There are some questions . . . I've been eager to ask you." His voice was uncharacteristically serious.

"All right," I started, trying not to let the hesitation in his voice bother me. "Corban, what's your favorite palace dish?"

He coughed. "Excuse me? Are you talking about food? My favorite food?"

I smiled as though this were a perfectly reasonable question to ask. "Yes. The food in the palace is like something from a dream. I've never eaten so well in my life. I want to know what you think is the best dish since you've grown up here."

He shook his head with a laugh and put his hands behind his head, resting back on the tree. "That's easy. A roasted corn and chicken soup. It is served with purple grapes and a fresh crust of cheesy bread. I cannot think of anything I like more." He laughed. "And for dessert, chocolate-covered figs with salted gravy on top. It sounds strange, but it is superb. Nefra, my cook, makes it for me on special occasions."

"I hope to taste it someday," I said with a laugh. "Your turn to ask a question."

He linked his arm through mine softly. "I'm afraid my questions are a bit more serious." I swallowed hard as he continued. "Marley let me know that there was some question about your eligibility to be here. He sent a scout to Canton to meet with your father. The only thing is, no one knew of a Larken or her father in Canton. They searched high and low."

I inhaled sharply, his candidness surprising me. *Younda was telling the truth in fashion class that day. She knew.*

"There's also another rumor circulating . . . That a Savian girl is in the program. That she snuck in somehow. Marley seems to think it's you, since they couldn't verify your father in Canton. He wanted to officially have a hearing"—he stumbled over the word—"but I told him absolutely not, until I got a chance to talk to you first. I could never make you go through something like that."

My breath quickened and I nodded my head slowly, internalizing what he said. Maybe I wouldn't have to be brave. Maybe he already knew everything.

He gauged my reaction and then continued. "Of course I told him that was preposterous. I told him you could verify everything. Not only who your father is, but also your mother, and that he should let me talk to you about it myself." He frowned slightly. "I've been waiting for the right time, since he has been pressuring me, and have come to the conclusion that there will never be a right time. It will always be a hard question to ask."

He shifted, retrieving his arm from mine and brushing back the hair that fell into his eyes. "I have to know," he whispered. "We are so close to the end, and Marley's persistence makes me feel uneasy. The rest of my advisors are also concerned. I need to hear the truth from you." I could tell it pained him to ask me this. He looked stiff and formal. So different from the Corban I knew.

I bit my lip. I could never answer this question and live. I was so close to the end—so close to leaving the palace and joining my people again. I could fight for them there. It didn't have to be here in the palace. It would be easier to petition for them without him knowing I was one of them. That was my plan all along. Still, I promised myself I would never lie to Corban. That if he asked, I would tell him anything. I didn't speak, avoiding his gaze. Some truths were heavier than others, and this one had the potential to destroy my life. Still, it was the truth. As scary as it was, I wanted Corban to know the real me. I had wanted him to know for a long time.

"Marley is telling you the truth," I said softly. The breezes around us continued to blow, pushing my hair in front of my eyes. I brushed them away and in doing so, felt tears that I did not know were waiting there. "I am not who I say I am."

He turned to face me and I forced myself to meet his eyes. I expected to see anger in his face but instead I saw something else—confusion perhaps or maybe denial. "I don't understand," he said, his voice deflating. "I thought—"

"My name is Emi, not Larken," I said bravely. "The way I got into the program—it was an accident. I came to the palace to save a friend's life. Entering the program was the only way I could get to the palace to find the cure I needed. I did not mean for things to get this far. I am not Larken from Canton. I've never even been to Canton. I don't know who my father is, and my mother was killed following my birth. She was a Savian." My mouth was so full of emotion I could barely speak. "I—am a Savian." I was expecting to feel terrified of his response, but instead I felt liberated. Tears continued to streak my face, but not because I was afraid or sad. They were tears of freedom. The truth felt good on my tongue.

I kept going before he could interrupt. I needed him to hear. "I didn't know what to do. I had to get an antidote that would save a friend's life, and I knew it would mean death if I told the truth. So I lied to you and I lied to Jessra, and everyone else I care about here because it was the only way I could think of to stay alive." He was fidgeting, finding his own courage, so I continued quickly. "But I care about you, Corban. I wasn't expecting that. I don't care about the title or the land or any of it. I just care about you." Tears were streaming down my face. "I want to be with you. I don't know how we ever could, but it is all I want."

I stopped talking, my emotions overwhelming me. I continued to cry, tears racing down my face, but at the same time, I couldn't help but smile. It was the right time to tell him the truth—to face whatever repercussions may come from it. I was tired of lying.

He didn't say anything for several moments, though he opened his mouth more than once as if he had something to say. I analyzed him expectantly, hoping to see understanding. Birds hopped around above us, the wind continued to blow. It was as though they didn't understand that this moment was potentially the most important moment of my life. I watched Corban's face cautiously, not sure what he would do. For a long time he just stared at the grass.

Eventually he stood up, leaving me on the ground. His face was stoic as he smoothed his tunic down. "I appreciate your honesty," he said with a flat voice, "although I think that it is too late."

"Corban—" I pleaded from the ground. "Please."

He shook his head at me. "How dare you address me in such a casual manner?" I stiffened. "I am the crown prince of Deshan! The chief commander of the Brockan army. I expect to be treated as such. Now stay here," he ordered. "Don't move." He squared his shoulders back tautly, suddenly transforming from the man who loved me to the prince—the chief commander, the one with all of the power.

I couldn't breathe as he left.

Tears rattled down my face. They did not just fall out of fear, although I definitely felt that. I cried because I had already lost so much because I was a Savian, and Corban would be one more casualty. And if Corban didn't love me, if he wasn't willing to help me, there was nothing I could do for my people. It was hopeless. When the tears stopped, I stared at the stars above me and hoped that if I couldn't have Corban, he would find someone else who would love him. I hoped that maybe, because he knew me, he would have compassion on my people. I hoped that he would not take his anger with me out on them.

Almost an hour later, Corban walked back into the grove, his arms folded. "I've made arrangements for you to return to your village. The punishment for treason is death—which is what you deserve. But out of kindness to you, I have arranged for you to disappear. I will have Kirt let Marley and Hortense know you were ill and sent home. Marley will not be able to find you. Hendrik will accompany you there. I let him know who you are and he has sworn to keep your secret and deliver you home safely." He stared ahead, avoiding my eyes. "You cannot ever come back, Larken." He shook with anger. "Or whatever your name is. I have shown you this kindness, but please do not test me. If you return somehow, I will have to punish you to the full extent of the law."

I heard his voice crack when he said that, but his face was resigned.

"Corban, I promise I'll leave," I told him, barely able to see his face through my tears, "but first, please hear me. My people are in danger! We need you! We need your help!"

He held up his hand. "Stop it," he ordered. "Not another word."

I stood then, a sob caught in my throat. "Corban, please believe me. I never meant to hurt you. I never thought it would go this far. I'm still the same person," I pleaded. "It is still me. That part wasn't a lie."

"It was all a lie," he corrected me, stepping around the tree and exiting the grove.

I stood there for several more minutes with my arms at my sides, my chest heaving in and out. I never thought my arms could feel so empty.

27

*H*endrik led me to the stables and let me cry in his gatehouse before we left. It was the only thing I could think to do. He did not push me for information or express disappointment. I knew he was disheartened though. I had planned to tell Corban everything I knew about Marley, but he hadn't given me the chance once he found out who I was.

I trusted Corban. I thought he loved me—really loved me. What could I do now to help my people from the village? I would be corralled back inside and kept there while everyone I loved died around me. I could not think of a worse fate.

"I told him everything," I murmured as the moon shone through his gatehouse window. "I told him who I am." Hendrik nodded patiently, still not saying a word. "How foolish I was," I cried, rocking back and forth. "How could I tell him the truth?"

Hendrik waited so long to answer me that I didn't believe he would. When he finally spoke, I expected him to offer comfort of some form. Instead, he stood and said simply, "Because he loves you. He deserved to know."

When I finally settled down—more out of exhaustion than relief—Hendrik pulled a soldier's uniform out of his closet. "It's time to go. Corban gave me strict orders. I'll be waiting outside once you have changed and will escort you myself."

Dazed, I nodded and dressed in the white pants and top, the long cape, and finally—the hat. With a sigh, I pulled Marley's map from my dress pocket and tucked it into the folds of the uniform to bring with me back to my village. It seemed like the last clue I had left to thwart his plans, which was now looking more and more impossible. Hendrik knocked and then entered, looking me up and down in my full apparel. "We'll leave immediately," he said, "but first." He pulled a black bag out of his pocket. "Corban wanted you to have this to take home with you."

I could hear the coins clanking against each other before I opened it. The bag's weight jerked my wrists to the ground. I pulled the black drawstring, revealing mounds of huge, gold coins. Obols. I had never even seen one before. In fact, I doubted whether they were any use to me in the village. No one would accept such a valuable piece without causing suspicion. Hendrik stepped closer to me. "He wanted you to have your sword too. Just in case."

I felt my throat close with emotion and gripped the bag tightly before I could cry anymore. Hendrik led me to the stables, the night completely dark. He motioned to Riushka, who was saddled. She snorted into the ground, clearly upset about being woken at this hour. "I thought you might want one more ride," he said with a sad smile. "I want you to know, Larken, that none of us are disappointed in you. None of us Savians. You are brave. You did the best that you could."

I hardly heard him, the pain in my head and in my heart so overwhelming. I mounted her slowly and rested my head in her mane, hugging her neck and patting her tenderly. There were too many good-byes to say. We rode through the grounds, soldiers nodding up to us as we passed. The mansion was in the distance, the light still on around the pool. I thought of Jessra and how she would feel when she found out I was gone. Would she even care? The other girls would be overjoyed, I knew that much. We passed the main palace next and I prayed for a glimpse of Corban—a wave good-bye, even a frown—anything that could tell me that he cared enough to see me go. But the only thing I saw were patrolling guards, their white capes catching in the breeze like ghosts.

Once we reached the gates, two guards held a torch in front of our faces. "Who goes there?" one barked.

"It's Hendrik," he said. "And I am accompanied by one of our guards. I am doing official business for the prince himself."

The guard nodded and cast a curious glance in my direction. I tilted my head down. "Very well. You may pass."

"It's easier to get out than in," Hendrik whispered to me as we passed through.

We rode through the square and across the capital, passing only a few people out at this hour. Everyone was home, eating dinner with their families. I was heading toward the only place I had ever called home, but for a brief moment I strangely felt as though I were actually leaving my home behind. Hendrik let me lead the way to my village. We rode into the night, dark shapes beginning to form where trees once stood. The heat of the dusk settled in but our pace never slowed. *You will get there*, I told myself to keep my mind occupied. *You will reach your village and you can still help. You will see Cen.*

I urged Riushka forward. The wind whipped my braid into my face as she ran, wisps of my hair flailing around. "Good girl," I whispered in her ear. "Faster."

We rode through the orchards behind the palace away from the city. I dared to turn back for a moment and saw the palace. I focused on Riushka and the trail ahead of us.

When we arrived at Kalvos, I patted Riushka softly and slowed to a walk. Maddock was right about the wall. It was complete, standing close to ten feet tall. Half a dozen guards sat lazily on the ground near the entrance.

"Gentlemen," Hendrik called out, startling them from their sleep.

"Who is it?" one asked nervously as they clambered to their feet. "What are you doing here at this hour?"

Hendrik dismounted and motioned for me to stay behind as he walked toward them. "I come in the name of the crown prince. He sent me to investigate the happenings of the soldiers here. It seems that perhaps I'll have to report that the soldiers posted at this village sleep during their shift." His voice was stern and confident. "What a disappointment."

One of them stammered, "But it's the middle of the night! Who are you? How do I know you're not lying?"

Another soldier stepped forward. "The capital always sends you in groups. Two measly soldiers doesn't mean a thing to me!"

Hendrik stepped closer to him, his broad shoulders widening. Without saying a word, he opened the sleeve of his cloak, revealing a gold crest. "I am the chief stablekeeper and weapons master of the palace, and I trained Prince Corban myself. I am his most trusted advisor."

The men stood back with wide eyes and nodded eagerly. I could see them blush even in the dark. One bowed until his comrade pulled him up with a disgusted glance. "What is it we can do for you, Chief?" he offered.

Hendrik stepped back. "Tell me how supplies are delivered here. What time of the day? I need to provide supplies to you, but it does not seem that this wall has any entrances but this one. Is there another one should I have the need to bring in something inconspicuously?"

The soldier who bowed earlier stepped forward. "Sir, there is a back entrance on the far northeastern corner. If need be, send a messenger ahead of time and we will have men at the ready to receive your delivery."

Hendrik nodded, stroking his beard with his free hand. "Excellent. Tell me, what is the state of the village here? Others are falling swiftly. Is this one infected as well?"

The soldiers looked at each other uneasily and I felt my heart surge. I had the feeling Hendrik was not acting on Corban's orders right then. "We have not had orders to begin the plan yet. We expect to begin in the next six weeks."

Hendrik turned back to look at me with knowing eyes. I nodded to him and circled Riushka, turning to the main road one last time. I may die within these walls—but at least I would be with Cen when I did.

"Thank you," Hendrik replied. "My colleague and I have need to inspect the village while its occupants are sleeping. We will exit out of the northeastern gate when we're finished."

"Anything you need," one soldier replied with a cock of his head.

Hendrik walked back to me and after mounting his horse, led the way through the gate. The soldiers stepped aside to let me pass, all gazing up at me curiously as I kept my head down. Hendrik let me take the lead once inside, and I took Riushka through my streets, the village I had lived in my entire life. We passed Kiefer's bakery, its red door shabbier than I remembered. He always saved me a roll at the end of the day if I stopped by to see him. We passed Lakshna's house. She was a widow who raised three sons on her own.

Finally we reached the clinic. I looked around at the dark shadows to make sure no soldiers saw me enter. The night was still, the moon hidden behind a row of clouds. Hendrik and I were the only ones here. I patted Riushka softly before dismounting, trying to absorb the feel of her hair, the warmth of her body. I would miss her too.

"Stay in close communication," Hendrik said, breaking the silence. "Kirt and I will do our best to keep you informed on what is happening and how we can assist you and our people. I can't make any promises. You know how powerful Marley is. But we'll try. We haven't lost this fight yet." Hendrik's voice broke.

I nodded and forced a smile, but he knew and I knew that it wasn't real. It was hopeless now. Corban had been our best bet at overcoming Marley and his soldiers. I thought the truth would be enough, that Corban would accept it. I trusted in his love, believing that it would also be enough, but I was wrong. We were in two different worlds—the Savians and the Brockans. How foolish I was to believe otherwise.

"Thank you, Hendrik," I whispered. "Give Kirt my love and gratitude please. And tell Jessra—tell her that I love her too."

He smiled sadly at me and dismounted, embracing me in his brawny arms. I felt his tears fall onto my scalp. "For what it's worth, I think you would have made a wonderful queen."

I buried my fist in my mouth and bit it to keep myself from crying out. Then I opened the door to the clinic where I had lived my entire life, back to the home where I actually belonged.

* * * * *

Cen kept me occupied over the next several weeks, sending me on errands around the village, giving me the most interesting and time-intensive patients, and calming me down when I awoke with night terrors. It was so good to see him again, to be around him and know that he was safe, but prison had changed him. He was thinner than I had ever seen him, his skin just wrinkles around his bones. His mess of eyebrows shadowed his gaunt eyes, and he shook even when performing the smallest tasks. It seemed that he had picked up a cough from one of our patients, and the sound rattled through his lungs as if there was nothing inside of him at all. Like he was a reed and the wind could sweep right through his body. I assessed him on multiple occasions, trying to discover what was ailing him and how we could fix it, but there was nothing to be done, and whenever I suggested a particular course of treatment, he shrugged it off as though it didn't matter. What he didn't realize is that after losing everything, I couldn't lose him.

He was patient with me like he had been my entire life, letting me cry when I needed to and allowing me to take Lexon for long rides in the evenings before sunset within the village gates. It was on those rides that I began to notice the change in my fellow villagers. I knew life had been hard on them since the soldiers closed off the orchards. At least working there they had something to do. Now, within these walls, many of them stayed inside during the day, unless they were waiting in the long lines at the well for water or rations of food. Many of them kept their heads down, their eyes on the ground instead of the sky. A few waved at me, but no one said hello anymore. There were patients at the clinic that began to request that Cen treat them instead of me—even in the state he was in.

"Why won't they let me help them?" I asked Cen every time it happened, my feelings sensitive and my anger teetering on the edge. "I can take care of them as well as you can. You should be in bed!"

He shook his head and shrugged, never offering me an explanation. But I knew what he wasn't saying. They didn't know me anymore. Cen was the one they trusted to heal them.

Knowing that, it was difficult to find joy in the same tasks I performed before. While I still loved healing, I found myself daydreaming about my classes at the palace. I had no one to practice my Sansikwan with, no books about foreign policies, no history. I even found myself missing poise class more than once and reminded myself regularly to keep my shoulders back and to walk softly. I buried myself in the books we did have, searching them by candlelight when I couldn't sleep and drinking large glasses of water to keep my belly from growling. I had forgotten what it felt like to be hungry.

On multiple occasions I pulled out Marley's map, searching for something, anything, that would stop his plan before he destroyed my people. I thought I knew what the red circles on the map were after comparing it to the maps we had—the villages that dotted Deshan, more in number than I ever imagined there could be. But what I couldn't decipher were the green dots within the red circles. There were even more of them than red circles. Some of the larger circles were littered with them. Was it the number of soldiers? The prisons?

I wrote several letters to Kirt and Hendrik, asking them for any news and progress on mass-producing the antidote, but I wondered if they were even receiving them. Were the soldiers cutting off our ability to send and receive mail? I guessed that was the case. I hadn't heard from them since I came here, and as much as I hated to admit it, I felt that all hope had abandoned us.

* * * * *

One night we received a knock at our door. I sat up in bed quickly, throwing on my tunic and clammering down the steps before Cen could awaken. His loud snores rattled just like his coughs, hollow and stubborn. Carefully I cracked the door open. A young woman, tears running down her face held a child—no older than three. Her son was asleep in her arms, his face disturbed and heavy. "Please help," she said desperately as I took him from her arms and carried him over to the cot.

I gestured for her to sit down as I hovered over him, observing his breathing. He was feverish, moaning in his sleep. "What is it?" I asked. "What is he complaining of?" I rushed to the cabinet for a pot of jusen to rub around his temples.

She buried her face in her hands, too overcome with emotion to respond. "I don't know," she finally said. "He's been sick for almost two days now. A fever that I can't seem to cure no matter what I try. This morning he blacked out on our walk to the well." She stared up at me, her dirty face streaked with tears. "And his feet."

With trembling hands, I pulled the boy's stockings off. A dozen purple rings intertwined from his heel to his ankle. Hot tears sprang to my eyes.

"Vox," I murmured. "It's here."

28

"ome back every day," I told the young mother, while offering her son the temporary treatment of farknon and lucius paste we gave Maddock when he first arrived. "This will be an ongoing treatment." It reduced the swelling and fever temporarily, but there was only one cure, and it was locked in a vault in the palace clinic.

Since that evening, we had several new cases of vox daily, knocks sounding at all hours. It was mostly the young and old that were infected, although after a week the adolescents and middle-aged began to show up. All had rings forming on their feet accompanied by a high fever. I worked tirelessly, waiting for brief interludes when the clinic was slow so I could catch fifteen, thirty, sometimes sixty minutes of blissful, uninterrupted sleep.

Cen's condition worsened. His eyes seemed more sunken in their sockets almost every morning. "I'm sorry," he apologized to me profusely. "This isn't fair. I shouldn't allow you to do so much." But I knew and he knew that he was doing the best he could.

One night after providing temporary relief to an old woman, I closed the door and sat down on a stool, staring aimlessly at the candle that was melting slowly before my eyes. I thought about how strange it is that you do not recognize your own exhaustion and emotion until you stop moving. At least it distracted me from thoughts of Corban. The flame hovered over the wick, forming a bell shape. Black, then blue, then gold. But somewhere in the middle of the blue and gold, a gray U formed, dancing with the weight of the candle. I stared at the U, focusing on its movements. My mouth hung open but I was too tired to sleep. *Your life at the palace wasn't real,* I told myself, mesmerized by the weight of the flame. *It was all a dream—a long dream. And soon it will end. Not just your dream, but the dreams of your people.* I wondered what they would do to me when I didn't die with the rest of my fellow villagers. What death would await me? What if I went back? That thought had crossed my mind before, but it was fleeting. I couldn't possibly. But what if I did? What if I could find a way to get the antidote into as many hands as possible? What then? Cen coughed loudly in the loft above me, and I let my hand rest on my elbow, the flame awake in my mind even after I closed my eyes.

When I woke up the next morning, I was hunched over my legs, bent at my waist and still sitting in the stool. My muscles ached, especially my neck, and I twisted from side to side, stretching my back on my way over to the cupboards. I was angry at myself for not at least curling up on a cot. I opened the pantry and pulled a water pitcher and a glass from a shelf, drinking until my belly felt round and taut. I kept drinking, even after I was full because I couldn't seem to get enough water. Some of it dribbled down my face, and I let it because it felt good in this heat to have something cleanse my face of the lingering sweat. I set my glass down on the table and jumped at the sudden idea that my empty glass gave me.

My feet thundered up to the loft as I tugged Marley's map from underneath my bed, sandwiched between two of our books. Once I located my village on the map, I startled Cen by yelling that I would be back soon and ran outside the clinic door, not even bothering to close it. In my bare feet I ran to the center of the village, the sun spreading thinly across the horizon above the gates. I passed several soldiers huddled in groups, conversing before they started their shifts. They didn't care what we did anymore. Cen told me they lightened up on discipline once the walls were built. I wondered if they felt sorry for us at all. We were helpless and they knew it.

Once I got there, I opened the map, determining the location of the dot compared to the compass on the map. And then I confirmed my suspicion. The wells. The green dot signified the wells at the center of every village. We drank that well water, bathed in it, cooked with it.

Marley was contaminating our water source with vox.

I gripped the map tightly and returned to the clinic, running up the loft two steps at a time.

"The wells!" I yelled to Cen. He jerked up as I entered. "The vox is spreading through the wells! Those are the green dots on the map." I spread it open for him to see. He sat up groggily but eagerly, looking down to see the map. I had shown it to him multiple times, of course, but he couldn't find anything noteworthy about it. In fact, I think he had forgotten about it completely until I held it in front of him now.

"Let me show you," I said, trying to control the intensity in my voice. I did not want to cause any more suspicion from my neighbors or the soldiers than I already had.

I sat on the bed beside him and pointed to the placement of the well in our village. "The green dot is in the center in most villages," I explained, "but in our village it is closer to the east, just like it says here with the compass at the bottom." Cen nodded, his unruly eyebrows furrowed tightly.

"Marley's plan is to build the walls and contaminate the only water source available! He provided the soldiers with the antidote, which protects them but also keeps them from causing suspicion if they drink water from the contaminated well." I thought of the soldiers who stood by our well, always patrolling nearby it. "They drink the same water we do, but they are immune to the disease."

Cen pulled his blanket up tighter around him, even though it was already extremely hot in the loft. I held up my hand, surprised my brain could still function even with all of the emotion and stress. I slowed down. "But we can't just avoid drinking the water. We'd all die from thirst as fast as we would from the vox." Marley's plan was perfect. He knew where we were weak. We need water to survive and the wells are the only source—especially after building the walls. We have no chance to find it elsewhere.

Cen nodded, his voice raspy from his coughing. "Before we use water to treat patients, we boil it," he said. "That was one of the first rules I taught you about cleaning wounds."

I shook my head excitedly. "Yes! That's what I thought. We'll have to boil it in secret before we drink it or bathe with it and warn the rest of our people to do the same. I think that will stop the disease from spreading."

Chills raced down my body. "It's not a complete solution of course," I admitted. "Eventually Marley will catch on, but it will buy us some time. And Kirt promised he's going to find a way to distribute the antidote. He won't forget about us. But until he can get here, boiling water might prevent new cases of vox, so we'll have less to give the antidote to when he does come." *And less to bury*, I thought.

Cen reached toward me and rubbed my face with the back of his trembling hand. "You did it," he said softly. "Now how are we going to spread the word?"

"We need Maddock," I said. "He's the only one I know who can get in and out of the gates to warn the other villages. How often does he come by?"

Cen raised his shoulders in a shrug. "Not often. It is difficult with the gates, and he told me he's visiting other villages, trying to spread hope and may not return to Kalvos for a while. But he told me—" An abrupt round of coughing stopped Cen from speaking for several minutes. "He told me," he finally said, his voice sounding raw, "if I ever needed him to tie a white towel on one of the turrets near the back gate. He said he would see it from the forest and know to come." He attempted to get out of bed, but I gently pushed him back down.

"Stay here," I said, unable to contain my excitement at my discovery. "I'll find a way to spread the word."

He nodded gratefully and rolled to his side. "You're brilliant, Emi," he murmured. "I'm so proud of you."

Even though he had said those words to me hundreds of times before, this time I actually believed him.

* * * * *

Before I did anything else, I closed the clinic and ran to the northeast gate to tie the white towel. It took some climbing and a skinned knee, but fortunately no soldiers were in sight when I did it. I was proud of myself for discovering how the disease was spreading, but there was no way for me to truly stop it. To do that, I would have to return to the palace. Until then, though, I had to warn my village.

The first house I went to was widow Lashkna's. She was the town gossip and everyone knew it. Her tendency for telling stories was exactly what I needed. She was forming cakes with just cornmeal and water when I arrived, and continued doing so as I talked to her. It took the better part of an hour to explain everything to her about Marley, his plan, and how I knew. She was furious by the time I finished. "Alerting the village will not be an issue," she said matter-of-factly. "Everyone will know within the hour. I'll use my network."

"Excellent," I replied. "Remember to tell them to boil their water in private. We don't want any of the guards to catch on."

I went back to the clinic feeling happier than I had since I arrived here. My sense of purpose and my ability to help was renewed. But as I turned the corner to reach home, I realized how transient that feeling was. A line stretched from the clinic door around the back to Lexon's stables. Forty or fifty men, women, and children stood waiting at the door, some of them slumped on the ground in exhaustion, others sniffling and holding their sides, and at least ten children and babies whimpering. The vox had spread.

Of course it had, since everyone drank water. I hadn't found a resolution; I had merely delayed the inevitable. Many were sick already even if they weren't showing signs of the virus and those would all suffer without the antidote. If anything, all I had done was distract myself from the end goal. We would still all die eventually.

I spent all day and most of the night mixing farknon and lucius and administering the paste. Cen came down for an hour at midday, but he was so sick that he retreated back to bed shortly thereafter because the noise and the chaos only worsened his cough. The one benefit to treating so many on my own was being able to discuss the disease openly with my patients. I instructed them to boil their water before drinking it. Most were understanding and hopeful, but others cried in despair when I told them what the disease would eventually do. Soldiers trickled in and out, and when they did, the chatting ceased completely. As soon as I got the soldiers on their way, though, it resumed.

The young mother who had brought her boy to me was the last to leave. I took him from her arms and sat him on my lap as I administered the paste, brushing his sweaty hair from his eyes. I was so tired that I was almost delirious. I sang to him as I fed him the paste and rubbed his feet with my hands to improve the circulation. She thanked me when I was finished and was halfway out the door when she stopped and turned around.

"You're the girl, aren't you?" she asked pointedly, her eyes heavy. I wondered if I looked as tired as she did.

"Pardon?" I asked. "What girl?"

She stepped closer, hoisting her child up on her hip. "The girl who was in the palace. We all heard one of our own was there but figured it was a girl from a distant village. But it wasn't," she said knowingly, her eyes brightening a little. "It was you. It had to be you."

I nodded slowly. "A friend came to me months ago with vox," I explained. "I went to the palace because I didn't know how else to heal him. I spent months there living among the girls who would eventually become the queen before I was discovered and sent home." It sounded so simple when I told her the story, but it wasn't. I left out my feelings for Corban, my anger toward Marley, my friendships with Kirt and Jessra and Hendrik, the aching hole left in my heart. I bit my lip and looked at her standing in the flickering light of a candle on my desk. It was hard to admit my failure to a woman whose son was dying. "I thought I could do more . . ." I drifted off. "I'm very sorry about your son."

She looked down at him and shook her head in despair. "So there is nothing left to be done?" Her voice broke. "I just go home and wait for him to die?"

I shook my head wanting to tell her that there was still hope, that an antidote existed which would save him and the others. But I knew that I could never promise that. Kirt and Hendrik may not come—and even if they did, the solution was much bigger than me or any one of us. "I'm sorry," I said simply.

She stared at me, her eyes brimming with tears. It was an honest stare, full of premature grief for the fate of her son. Cen once told me that grief is the worst kind of pain, because it is not the pain of anger or fear or hurt. Grief is the pain of love. She held my gaze for several minutes and allowed the tears to fall steadily down her face before nodding bravely and turning to go.

I had considered returning to the palace before, but only momentarily. Corban warned me never to come back, and there was no way I could get Lexon out of these gates. I wasn't sure there was any way *I* could get out of these gates. But as I stared into the eyes of that mother whose grief was so deep, I knew that I had no other option. No matter how difficult it would be or what dangers stood in my way, it was time.

I had to go back.

*　*　*　*

This time I warned Cen before I left. "I wondered when you would," he said weakly, his blue eyes watery. "Tell me what I can do for you here."

We made plans. If everything went right, Maddock would be here within a couple of days to help Cen run the clinic. Making the paste was simple enough and Maddock could administer it without me.

I decided to enlist more help in the meantime and paid a visit to the young mother. Her name was Fretta, and she was willing to help once I told her my plan. I taught her how to make the paste, and she spent the entire day with me in the clinic so she could take over for me and treat the patients who came in. There were more coming in every day. I wasn't sure how long I would be gone, and she promised she would stay as long as necessary and help look out for Cen. Cen would help when he felt well enough, but we both agreed that it was better not to count on him. It was an ordeal for him to even walk up and down the clinic stairs.

"I'll see you soon," I whispered to Cen when he went to bed. I kissed his forehead tenderly. I loved Cen so much, but I couldn't save him by staying here. My fear was that I couldn't save him at all, but maybe in saving so many others I could return the favor of him taking me in all of those years ago.

"I love you," he whispered back. His lips were so dry he could barely move them. My heart ached with his words. I left him then to go downstairs to the clinic, because one more word from him and I might lose any courage I had left.

Fretta helped me close up for the night; Judah, her son, sprawled out sleeping on the table. I asked her to stay the night with Cen until I left and set up a small sleeping area for her in the clinic downstairs. She agreed wholeheartedly, and I knew that between her and Maddock, Cen and the rest of our village were in good hands.

I lifted up the floorboard where we hid our valuables. Usually we had two or three finlas if we were lucky. Tonight I pulled out the huge bag of obols Corban had given me, the white soldier's uniform and, last, my sword. Fretta's eyes widened as I took off my tunic and boots and began to dress in the uniform, sheathing the sword at my waist and putting the bag of money in a pouch inside the cloak.

"How are you going to get in the palace?" Fretta asked me as she watched me transform from a Savian healer to a Brockan soldier.

"The same way that I got out," I replied.

29

I left in the dark and headed toward the back gate, my long hair tucked into the soldier's cap. Guards should be there at this time of night, but fewer than there would be guarding the front. At least that is what the soldier told Hendrik when we came back in. I squared my shoulders and tried to look broader and taller than I was, but I was drowning in this uniform. The white cloak almost reached my ankles when it brushed the knees of the soldiers. The bag of obols jingled on my side and I kept one hand on the sheathed sword.

"Who goes there?" a soldier called as I rounded the corner to the gate.

"Leon," I said in the deepest voice I could muster. Leon seemed to be the most common name among the soldiers at the mansion.

"Leon?" the soldier asked, walking toward me. "We don't have a Leon in our division."

I coughed a little. "I don't report to your division. I report to the crown directly. Special business. I need to return to the palace immediately. And I'll need a horse."

The soldier laughed a little. "On official business from the crown, eh? I've heard that one before." He stepped closer. "You look a little small to be a soldier, don't you think, boy?"

I squared my chest and pulled the cloak more tightly around me, still hiding my face in the shadows. "I would ask you not to speak to a messenger of the crowned prince himself in such a disrespectful tone." Hortense would have been proud of my language choice. I lifted my head, remembering everything she taught me in poise.

"I don't think yer anyone at all," he spat back. "You should be the one showing me some respect! I'm yer elder! I'm of a higher rank!" He charged toward me, his hands outstretched. I opened my mouth in surprise. I didn't expect to pass through the gates without questioning, but I didn't think it would come to this either. I unsheathed my sword and stood my ground with my feet firmly planted until he was right in front of me. Then, using his own momentum, I stepped on his foot to pivot myself around him, pushing him on the back. He stumbled forward, his arms outstretched. With a growl he turned around and retrieved his own sword clumsily. I swallowed hard. I had never dueled with anyone but Hendrik, and I knew that he had gone easy on me most of the time.

"We can end this easily," I said loudly. "I have almost a hundred obols in my cloak."

His eyes widened and he paused for a moment, considering it. Abruptly he shook his head. "Well, then, I can finish you off and keep those for myself," he said. "My commander will have my hide if you take one step out. No one goes out, and no one goes in under any circumstance without his permission. The fact that you came to this gate means yer trying to hide somethin'. If you were part of our group, you would have exited the front."

"Well, let's end this like gentlemen," I said, trying to control the quiver in my voice. I bowed with my sword in one hand, and he charged toward me with both hands on his sword.

I blocked his first blow from above, but only barely—his sword was much heavier than mine, and he was much stronger. He came at me again from the side and I deflected that as well, but I stumbled forward from the pressure of it and barely had time to turn around before I held my sword against his from the back. My heart beating frantically, I faced him and then ran toward him. My sword nicked the side of his arm.

"Yow!" he yelled, reaching for his arm. "Yer dead, boy."

"We can end this another way," I offered, completely out of breath now. "It would be a grave consequence to have killed the most trusted servant of the prince. I have money. I will pay you for exit and safe passage to the palace."

He shook his head and looked down at his arm, then turned to me with fire in his eyes. "Well, now I want yer blood and yer money."

He ran toward me again, but right before he got to me I remembered what Hendrik told me. With my size, it wouldn't be my fencing that won the duel; it would be my wit. Just as he came toward me I ducked under his sword, knocking it out of his hand with mine and stepped on his foot, swiveling around him to pierce him from the back. It was one of the first disarming tactics Hendrik taught me, perfect for a warrior who is smaller than his or her opponent. Right before I got around completely, though, he yanked off my hat. My long braid escaped from underneath it.

"A girl!" he yelled. "Yer a girl!" He bent forward to retrieve his sword from the ground, but I pushed my sword more firmly against his back, tearing his coat but still not drawing blood.

"Quiet!" I whispered. "I may be a girl, but I'm a girl who could kill you at any moment." My breath was heavy and uneven, but I wasn't afraid of him anymore. He was a sloppy fighter. My guess was that he grew up in a small town and was trained in the villages. He was just a guard—not a professional soldier of the king.

"You're a coward," I hissed in his ear, pushing the sword deeper against him. "Now march toward the gate." I struggled to retrieve the ropes I had in my pack with my free hand. He shook his head no and grunted, refusing to take a step.

"I'll call for help," he threatened weakly. "I'll yell as loud as I can that there's an intruder at the back gate. There will be ten soldiers here before you could blink an eye."

"Do that and you'll never hear the end of it," I replied. "A soldier outwitted and outdueled by a girl? The only posts you'll be getting after is in the kitchens. You'll never be given another guard position. Now move." My confidence surprised me. For years I had quivered with fear in the mere presence of a soldier, but now I was in control. Perhaps my time in the stables had done more than teach me how to fight. I held the ropes in my mouth, so I could position him with one arm and hold my sword in the other.

He took a couple reluctant steps forward. "You could be hung for treason," he threatened again. "Impersonating a soldier? Yer just a girl! A Savian! You'll be killed fer sure!"

"I'll already be killed," I replied, surprising myself with my admittance. Yes, I could absolutely be killed for what I was doing and I probably would be, so what did I have to lose? "Now march."

He stepped forward, cursing as he did and kicking angrily at the pebbles at his feet. Once we reached the gate, I pushed him to his knees and bound his hands and feet tightly, leaning him against the wall. Hendrik never taught me how to tie knots, but I'd secured enough ropes in the stables to know what to do. "Where are the keys?" I asked, once I was confident the knots would hold.

"Like I'll tell you"—he spat at me and a spray of saliva hit my cheek—"you're going to hang for this."

I placed the point of my sword against his heart. "The keys."

When he refused to respond, I pulled a handkerchief out of my pouch and stuffed it in his mouth. Then, while he wriggled and fought against me, I removed his weapon belt and retrieved the keys from inside.

"Thank you," I said and walked back to get my hat.

When I returned I inserted the key, and, with a twist, the huge gates opened. Before I could forget, I shimmied up the other side of the gate and tied the key to the white towel I'd left for Maddock. He may not need it, but it could make his trips in and out of the walls easier. While I was up this high, I could see most of the village.

The clinic doors were closed, which was good, and I could see no villagers. Soldiers were pacing the grounds not far from me though. I didn't have much time before they discovered their friend.

I whistled loudly, and several seconds later watched Fretta lead Lexon out of his stable, holding his bridle to keep him from whinnying. It was our signal in case I couldn't secure another horse. I climbed back down and waited until I saw her approach, holding up my hand for her to stay where she was before skipping toward her. I couldn't let this soldier see her and report her later. "Thank you for your help," I whispered.

Her eyes widened when she saw the soldier with his back against the wall but she nodded in response, handing Lexon's reigns over to me. "Good luck, Emi," she mouthed before running back toward the clinic. I sang softly to Lexon as I led him through the gates as the soldier continued to writhe in anger. As an afterthought, I tossed him an obol from my bag to compensate for his embarrassment.

The gate closed behind me with a clang much louder than I expected, its noise echoing across the perimeter, so I quickly mounted Lexon and spurred him toward the palace. We rode around the huge wall and through the orchards to the west to avoid the main gate. The stars lit our way all the way to the capital.

* ✳ * ✳ *

It was the middle of the night when I arrived at the palace. The marketplace was still, the booths still set out but all of the wares and sellers gone for the night. The scent of fish and herbs lingered as though the heat contained them mid-air.

Lexon's hooves echoed across the square and I quickly jumped off of him, steadied his whicker, and walked over to the huts where I left him where I left him before. I wandered up and down the huts until I thought I reached the one from that day almost a year before, and then pounded on the door three times.

I could hear cursing and shuffling inside. I squared my shoulders, my uniform covered with a dusty film from the ride. A man holding a candle opened the door, his face drawn up in a sneer.

"What is it at this hour?" he barked. It was definitely him. He had the same shifty eyes. Once he saw me in my soldier's uniform though, his face softened. "Oh, I see. How can I help you? Is this about the manure? You know, we try to keep up after the horses we stall but it can be difficult. They're real animals, heh, heh," he stammered. "We'll try harder. Really we will."

I suppressed a smile and spoke deeply. "No, I require your assistance." I gestured to Lexon. "My horse is in need of a few nights' feed and shelter."

He looked Lexon up and down. "Can't you house him in the royal stables?" he asked, "He doesn't look like a palace horse, but—"

I shook my head. "No. I need him to stay here, and I'm going to rely on your discretion about this encounter."

He frowned. "Well, I don't know how comfortable I am with that." I reached into my cloak, retrieved a handful of obols, and put them in his hands.

"Perhaps this will help you to feel comfortable?" I asked. "Keep him until I return."

The man's eyes widened. This much money could probably buy him a new life. "Yes, yes of course that is more than fair. Yes, until you return." Rubbing his tired eyes with his free hand, he came outside in his robe and reached for Lexon's bridle. "Come on, pretty horsey. I'll take good care of you, horsey."

"Thank you," I replied. I cut across the marketplace toward the main gates. While I was still a safe distance from the huts, I found an alley and walked a few steps into it before kneeling and spreading out my supplies: I had my pouch of obols, in case a bribe was necessary, and my sword in case of a fight. I unsheathed my sword quietly before pulling out a small piece of glass that I used at home as a mirror. I balanced it on a rocky shelf of the wall until I could see myself in it. Using the light of the moon, I did what I should have done earlier. My braid fell to the ground in a heavy thump, dust gathering already in its plait. The rest of the hair I cut off with a knife until it fell around my ears. I expected to feel something after cutting it off, some sort of loss, but I felt nothing at all. If this was going to work, cutting my hair was a necessary step. Getting into the palace would be harder than getting out of my village gates.

I held the knife up again, this time to my face. Using the mirror I cut a shallow scratch near my left eyebrow. I blinked once in pain as blood trickled down my face. I reached to the ground for some dirt and patted it on my face, mixing it in with the blood but carefully avoiding the cut itself. Two deep breaths later, I was on my feet. The sun would be out in a few hours, and I had no time to lose.

I walked with a limp as soon as I caught sight of the golden palace gates, their presence the only obstacle keeping me from Corban and the vault with the vox antidote. Ten guards stood at attention near the entrance, two patrolling each side and six in a row blocking the front. Their swords were drawn in position. One called out to me as I came into view, "Who is it?" My heart jumped in my chest, rays of fear shooting down my arms, my hands, my fingertips.

I said nothing but walked closer, smearing more blood on the white edge of my cloak.

"It's a soldier!" I heard one say to the soldier in the center. "It's one of ours!" He left his post and ran toward me, his sword still outstretched.

The soldier in the center called out to him, "Stop there!"

The soldier stopped immediately, about ten feet in front of me. I lifted my eyes to meet his. "It may be a threat! A trick!" the center soldier called out. "Return to your post. We have no scheduled arrivals!"

I waited for the soldier to return to his post before continuing forward, making each step jolting and heavy. When I finally reached the gate, the center soldier stepped forward, nodding at his men behind him. "Are you a palace soldier?" he asked, his frown stark even in this darkness. "I did not receive a report that any were arriving this evening."

I nodded and spoke in a deep voice. "I was on assignment in an orchard village on the outskirts. There was a huge riot. A Savian uprising. I was wounded but escaped. I have traveled for several days on foot to warn the prince himself." I heard my voice shake, attempting to steady it. The soldier did not seem to notice.

"There was a riot," he repeated. "And you were wounded."

I nodded, forcing myself to grimace. "I need medical care, sir."

He looked me up and down warily. "Where is your identification badge? I cannot let you inside without it."

I swallowed at this realization. I had wondered if proper identification was required, but seeing as how I had only ever come out of the palace as a soldier, I didn't know the process. "I lost it in the riot," I stammered. "Please, sir, I need to see the healer."

He shook his head. "I'm sorry. Chief Advisor Marley has increased security measures here recently. No identification badge, no entrance to the palace. If you cannot produce yours by morning, I'll alert the chief officer and have him check your name in our records. Otherwise, you cannot enter at this hour. I'm sorry—I can see that you have been through a lot." His face was remorseful, but he held his stance. A bribe would definitely not persuade him. He was on Marley's force.

I touched my head where the blood was beginning to clot and nodded, completely defeated. I was so foolish to come, to risk everything for a scheme that was so poorly planned. I was lucky to have gotten this far. The chief officer would not find my name on the ledger. I would be imprisoned. And after what I did in my own village to the guard, I could no longer return there.

I turned to go with my face down, feeling the eyes of all of the soldiers on me. The next resort was going to the back gate—across by the mountain like Maddock had done. But that would take hours. Maybe even a full day.

I turned suddenly, feeling my face light up. "Sir," I said strongly, "months ago every soldier was taken to the royal healer for a procedure." He bit his lip nervously but said nothing. "I have the scar to prove that I was there for that."

He watched me carefully for several moments before motioning me forward. Awkwardly I pushed my torn cloak to the side and reached toward the top of my uniform, unbuttoning only as far as necessary. I pulled the collar down just to my clavicle. "Here it is, sir." He stepped closer to examine it and nodded slowly. I was certain that he wore the same scar above his heart.

He frowned, glancing around the square anxiously. "These circumstances are extreme," he said in a lowered voice, stepping closer to me. "But you are young and in need of help. I'll make an exception for one of the country's brave soldiers. Only a true soldier would have received that scar." He nodded toward one of his men. "Rajhim, take him to the royal healer. I'll follow up with him in the morning."

The soldier who ran toward me earlier nodded and stepped toward the gate, pushing against it with all of his weight.

"Thank you," I murmured to the center soldier. "Thank you very much."

He nodded curtly and broke his stance only long enough for me to enter the gate. We made our way slowly to the clinic, my fear subsiding with each step. I knew my way around here almost like my own village.

Corban, Kirt, and Hendrik, whether on purpose or not, had given me every tool necessary to return. The soldier's uniform, the money, the sword, and the scar.

30

Kirt wrapped his robe tightly around him and blinked tiredly in the night, as though this kind of disturbance was routine for him. If he recognized me, he did not show it, but instead thanked the soldier and told him he would report to his commander on my treatment. It wasn't until we reached a patient room in the clinic that he looked at me again and circled the cot slowly, his hands behind his back. He removed his glasses more than once, cleaned them on his robe, and put them on again, his face creased with concern. I removed my hat, forgetting momentarily that a braid would not tumble out of it.

"Larken," he said simply. It wasn't a question; it was a realization. The exact moment in time when he made the connection that this ratty soldier in front of him was the same girl I was in the mansion.

It was strange to hear that name, but I nodded. "It's me, Kirt."

In one swift motion he fell to his knees with his hands clasped together, his shoulders shaking for minutes before I heard the sobs heaving in his chest. "We thought, I thought . . ." he trailed off. "So many are dead. I tried. Larken, I tried." He repeated these words over and over, until I felt emotion rise in my own throat. "We wrote," he said once he gained composure. "Hendrik and I even rode to your village several weeks ago but they wouldn't let us in. They said no one could go in or out . . . How did you get here? How did you manage it?"

Tears pricked my eyes. They came. They had tried to see me. For weeks I had felt abandoned, but there were still those who cared about me, who hadn't forgotten my people and their plight.

I closed my eyes slowly and shrugged my shoulders. "I had to come," I finally said. "I know Marley's plan and I couldn't stop it from where I was. So many are dying in my village. I came for you of course, but more than that I came for Corban. He is the only one who can undo what Marley has started, and I am the only one who can plead our case to him." Saying those words made it all seem real. They validated my reasoning for leaving Cen in the state he was in—for leaving the people in my village at all. I couldn't have done it unless I knew it was my only choice.

From there I unfolded everything to Kirt. He cleaned the wound on my head, his face both fearful and proud. He gasped when I told him about the wells and how Marley was using them to spread the disease. "I hadn't even considered," he said, over and over. "I hadn't even considered."

When he finished stitching up my head, he bandaged it and sat on a chair with his legs crossed, watching me intently as I divulged my plan to him. "I'm going to find Corban. He told me not to come back. He said that if I did he would make me pay for being a traitor, but I would rather die than spend one more day in that village watching so many others die in front of me."

Kirt nodded, brushing away another tear. "You're brave, Larken."

"Emi," I corrected him. The name Larken was a part of a life rampant with denial and lies. I was done lying and I was done hiding.

"Emi," he said with a smile, trying it out. He twitched his lips and looked at the ground. "Unfortunately, things have changed here as well. You may not have much time to speak to Corban."

I stood up and subconsciously touched the bandage Kirt placed on my head. "Why is that?" I asked, my throat dry.

He frowned. "After you left, Corban locked himself in his quarters. For days he didn't come out. I only know because I was sent to him on the fourth day. His mother was concerned that he wasn't eating. After my visit his temperament seemed to improve, but he seemed to have let go of all of the morals he so strongly believed in. He did not protest when Marley rounded up hundreds of Savian servants and sent them to the outer provinces. He goes nowhere without Marley by his side—he has been called Marley's Shadow behind his back. He cancelled one complete ball, saying that he preferred to keep to himself. Many of the girls in the program have visited me with upset stomachs and nightmares—all stress induced. I think they're as aware of the unrest in the kingdom as we are." Kirt paused, rubbing his face with his knuckles. "I have never seen Corban like this in all of the time I have known him." He looked down. "I think he understands what is happening and feels helpless to change it. I hope that your coming here was not in vain. He may not be as receptive to your plea as he might have been before."

I nodded, absorbing this new information. "But you said I may not have much time. What does Corban's behavior have to do with that? The girls still have more than a month left in the program."

He shook his head. "Corban made a decision to end the program early. He will make his decision in two nights, and he has opted to do it in front of the entire kingdom at the gates instead of in a closed ball. He said he wants to announce his decision with everyone there to hear it."

I pushed my chin toward my chest and stared out the window. The sun would be coming up soon. I would have to speak to Corban tomorrow night. It was the only day left to get to him before everything changed. I should have felt nervous, but instead I felt a flutter in my stomach at the thought of seeing Corban again—even given the circumstances. "I never thought so much could change in just a matter of weeks," I said to Kirt.

He nodded in agreement, eyeing the growing light outside the window. "Let's get you to a more private place so you can sleep. The commander will be back in the morning to verify that you're a soldier. You need to be hidden before then. I'll tell him that you escaped in the night after your treatment. After all, that won't be too far from the truth." He winked at me.

"Where should I go?" I asked.

He stood and gestured. "Follow me." I rubbed my eyes anxiously, in no state to leave the room. But he stood and exited so swiftly that by the time I got out the door he was halfway down the hall. I had to run to catch up with him.

Dazed, I followed him through several halls until he led me into a small room, almost the size of a cupboard. A map of Deshan hung on the wall with marks indicating the various clinics that were stationed at the barracks.

"You'll be safe here." I waited for him as he retrieved a cot and several blankets for me. "I'll bring food for you when I can," he whispered before he left.

I was so tired that all I could do was nod at him gratefully before falling into a much-needed, dreamless sleep.

*   *   *   *

I woke several hours later when Kirt stepped into the room to leave some bread and eggs, and then a second time when Hendrik stepped in to greet me.

I sat up uncomfortably on the cot, rubbing my eyes and brushing my newly shorn hair out of my face. I told him the same story I told Kirt while I ate my breakfast—or maybe lunch. It was hard to tell which. He cheered loudly when I told him about my fight with the soldier at the gates. Standing and knocking Kirt's map off the wall, exclaiming, "I knew I trained you right!"

When I told him about the vox infecting my village, he nodded somberly. "It is everywhere. You're not the first to tell me this, but you may be the only one in a position to stop it." When I told him about how I got into the gates here, he smiled. "You know, I've actually thought about that since I took you to your village at his command. I think that unknowingly, Corban intended for you to come back here. The sword, the money . . . Maybe he knew that you're the only chance the Savians have." He tousled my hair before he left to prepare the horses for the queen's ride, promising he was at my service for anything I might need.

Now that I was up, I quickly became bored in the tiny room. It was hot, so I created a makeshift fan for myself out of some papers Kirt had stacked on the floor. I went to reposition the map Hendrik knocked off the wall. There was an intricate design behind where the map was, and I stepped forward to examine it more closely. The candles had burned out, but if I got close enough to the page I could just make out some details. Thousands of tiny words were written onto the wall—all connected with small lines and brackets. I had to stand right up against it to read what was scrawled in Kirt's familiar hand. I could tell that they were names, although there weren't any that I immediately recognized. "What is this?" I whispered, a feeling of wonder absorbing into my skin. Somehow I knew it was important, even if I wasn't sure how. I studied it most of the day, until sleep overcame me again, and I napped on and off.

Kirt came to me in the late afternoon, his sleeves rolled up and his expression gaunt. "I'm so sorry for leaving you alone for so long my dear," he said, squinting his eyes. "Busy day at the clinic in preparation for tonight's event. A lot of dehydration and fatigue with this heat." He carried a large pitcher of water in one hand and a small loaf of bread and meat on a plate in the other.

"I understand." I gratefully accepted the pitcher. "Thank you for coming to me at all. It has been good for me to rest. I didn't realize how hard I had been working at the clinic until now."

He sank down with his back against the wall, crossing his legs casually. The folds of his robes billowed out around him. "I understand that. The caretakers never take care of themselves."

I gestured to the wall between bites. "Kirt, I've been staring at this all day. Hendrik accidentally knocked your map off the wall and I've been trying to make sense of your scribbles. It doesn't have to do with medicine, does it? It seems to be more proper names than medicinal terms."

Kirt stepped back to look at the wall and nodded slowly, a smile spreading across his face. "You, my dear, are looking at my life's work," he replied. "And the reason why I as a Brockan would do anything to support you and your people."

I smiled gently, touched by his response. "But what is it? It looks like a big tree—a big, messy tree."

Kirt nodded. "That is not too far from what it is." He stood to face the wall, his hands behind his back. "This project of mine started after my years of working with the Brockan military as a medic. I treated so many Brockans who looked like Savians and so many Savians who looked like Brockans. I began to feel that there was not such a big difference between us. At what point did our races become so separate? So I began to create links. After the last Great War, the Brockans obtained the Savian genealogy records. Because of my position here, I have been able to compare both the Savian and Brockan records. From there I have been able to uncover the traits and genes that make up a 'Brockan.' Once I understood their genes, I did the same with the Savian line. Starting at the top, I made connections—genetic links between individuals and families, most of them royal. My research is still incomplete. I have years left until I will have a clear understanding of what it is that sets us apart. But what I have found basically is that genetically our people are not different at all. I think I have tracked back as far as possible. Through my research I've discovered that our people began with two brothers. Brothers, Emi!"

I felt my eyes widen. "But how is it possible? Our entire lives we are taught to categorize Brockan or Savian traits. Should we ignore that those exist?"

He shrugged. "It is just what has been traditionally taught. You have blue eyes but you're considered a Savian. The prince has brown eyes yet he's considered a Brockan. Both of you break the conventional rules. What we are taught is not always the truth. These beliefs, this struggle—there's no basis for it. We're all humans, are we not?"

I swallowed hard, doing my best to understand it all. This finding was not earth shattering. Of course to live in the same land we had to have shared family anciently. But this kind of proof was a good start. The fact that someone cared enough to put in this amount of effort was a good sign. We could work toward peace. "So that's why you are willing to help us?" My voice sounded hoarse.

He nodded. "In a sense, yes. We're not so different from one another. Well, to be more precise, we're not different at all. We're all brothers and sisters and have wasted hundreds of years contending against each other. Can you imagine what we could be, what we could create, if we decided to let go of the false beliefs our fathers instilled in us?"

I nodded, feeling more inspired than I had ever been to fight, not just for the Savians but also for the Brockans. "Are you going to tell the queen or Corban?" I asked. For some reason, it was important to me that Corban know this.

He nodded, rubbing the back of his hand across his face as he stared at the map. "I plan to tell them," he replied. "When the time is right."

Kirt and I sat in that little room staring at the map until he had to return to his duties. I knew what I needed to say to Corban tonight. Last time I had words to say, he wouldn't listen. This time it was truly a matter of life or death. He had to hear me out.

* * * * *

It was almost dark when Hendrik returned. "I did what you asked," he said as he came in. "I sent the private letter to Corban. He thinks he's meeting his mother at the grove tonight to discuss his decision for the coronation without Marley."

I nodded anxiously. "How did you manage that?"

"I have some connections in the palace," he replied with a smile. "You forget that I have lived here almost my entire life. I know how things run."

I wrapped my arms around myself, resting my palms on the curves of my shoulder blades, my teeth chattering. I had minutes before I met Corban at the grove to plead for my people. I had minutes before I saw the man that I loved—a man who had changed, according to Kirt. It was agonizing and thrilling all at once.

"Hendrik, what if he tries to kill me?" I asked suddenly, realizing what a trap I was sending myself into. Corban might have forgotten everything about me except for the fact that I was a Savian who had lied to him. "What if he turns me in to Marley? What do I do?"

Hendrik looked at me earnestly and stroked his beard. "You die knowing that you did everything you could to save an entire people. You die with thousands of us knowing that you did the best you could." He shrugged as though what I was doing was the easiest thing in the world.

"Thanks for the encouraging words," I said with a half grin. I appreciated his honesty at least.

"Oh, I almost forgot," he said, handing me a parcel tucked under his arm. "I asked Veda for a change of clothes for you." My eyes widened. "Well, she doesn't know it's for you, of course, but she was happy to help me and didn't ask questions." He grinned. "I figured you wouldn't want to be wearing a dirty soldier's uniform when you saw Corban for the first time again."

I nodded gratefully, accepting it from him. "You'll be nearby, won't you, Hendrik?" I asked. "Just in case?" I would feel better knowing that Hendrik was in earshot—whether or not he could defend me.

"Yes," he said, "but you won't need my help." He left me alone to change, and I pulled off the soldier's uniform gladly, casting it in a white heap in the corner. Veda made me a simple black tunic and leggings, along with some leather-riding boots, not unlike those I always wore. I smiled at Hendrik's choice. I wouldn't look glamorous or beautiful or radiant in these clothes. I would just look like myself. I thought back to that moment months earlier when I knelt in front of the mirror in the mansion and made myself promise not to change who I was. To never forget that I was Emi from Kalvos, daughter of Cen, healer's assistant. But I had changed. I hadn't lost sight of myself; I had discovered who I really was.

I wasn't different like I was afraid I would be—I was new.

31

I smoothed down the hairs escaping from the tiny knot at my neck while I waited for Corban to come. The crickets were out tonight, their noisy voices blaring from every direction. I sat in silence, pondering what he might say, doing my best to rehearse everything that was said between us the last time we spoke. There were a thousand things to say and even more emotions to express. More than anything, I was afraid that I wouldn't get the chance to tell him everything I needed to. I'd learned the hard way that nothing is as haunting as the words we leave unsaid.

I was so absorbed in thought that when he stepped in, rustling branches softly, it startled me. For a while he didn't see me in the dark, and I waited before saying anything to him, preferring to see him like this, no matter how fleeting the moment was. He looked so different than he had before—taller and even more handsome somehow. His hair was longer, falling below his ears, just barely shorter than mine was now. He wore riding pants and a loose fitting shirt, his sword dangling by his side. I closed my eyes tightly before opening my mouth, mustering all of the courage I had left.

"Corban," I whispered, standing to greet him.

His eyes looked serious, their usual light missing, as he turned to face me. From the front, dark curls fell across his forehead. I expected him to yell or draw his sword, or to respond in anger when he saw me, but instead he just stared, his mouth open slightly. His expression was unmoving as it had been at our last meeting with each other. We never said a proper good-bye, and that was making this moment even harder.

"Larken," he whispered finally, taking another step toward me. "Larken, is that you? What are you doing here?" His voice was interested but also serious. He wanted answers and nothing more. "I thought I told you not to come back." He said the last bit like it was a fact, not a threat. His tone was soft.

I ignored his words and stepped toward him, my arms out. Without hesitating, I stood on my tiptoes to embrace him fully. He winced at first, his arms close by his sides but then as he pulled me close to him, his hands shook on my back.

"How can you be here?" he whispered into my hair. A chill raced from my ear to my feet. He didn't say that I shouldn't be here.

I stepped back and studied his face—it was stressed, deep lines running through it that I hadn't seen before. His eyes were puffy from lack of sleep, black circles hovering. "I had to come back," I responded. I felt a painful lump swell in my throat. It would take everything I had to control it.

He looked so flustered that I don't think he heard a word I said. "How did you get in?" he asked. "You look . . . different." I smiled a little. I knew I looked different. I'd lost weight since returning to the village, cut my hair, and had a bandage across one side of my head.

"So do you," I replied.

He stepped away from me. "Larken, you have no idea how happy I am to see you alive. I worried every day that by ordering you to leave I was sentencing your life. Especially—" He stopped talking and bit his lip, shaking his head bitterly. "Especially . . . Never mind."

"Especially since you found out about Marley's plan?" I asked, breaking the tension.

He looked around as though he was afraid that someone might be listening. "What do you know about it?" he asked warily. "Larken, you have to believe that I tried to stop him. I never wanted to relocate the Savians, but he has made it clear that there is no other way. Your people will be safe in Sansikwa." He gestured with his hands. "Their government has agreed to take you with open arms. You'll no longer be slaves! This could be a good thing for them—a new life!"

I covered my mouth, and felt hot tears of anger prick my eyes. So this is what Marley had told him. More lies. It was several moments before I could respond.

"Corban, how can you be so ignorant?" I asked before I could stop myself. "You're the chief commander of our people—*our* people. Brockans and Savians alike. Marley's plan isn't about relocation." Corban opened his mouth to protest but I cut him off. "Corban, he's not relocating us. He's *killing* us. He's isolating us in our villages, building walls, and spreading a disease that only he controls the cure to. My people are not being transported; they are being murdered!" I spat out the last part, my face streaked with tears. "And you're letting it happen."

His face transformed as I spoke, softening and then hardening again. He sunk to the grass, his legs tucked beneath him. "You don't know what you're saying. You've been given the wrong information—" He shook his head, his dark curls falling in front of his eyes. "That's not right."

"Not right? Corban, I was there!" I protested. "I watched it happen in my own village. The only reason I came back here was to see what you could do to save us. Marley has been lying to you!" I stopped for a moment to breathe. "Corban," I said slowly, "Marley cannot be trusted."

I took a deep breath, attempting to compose myself, but my next words came out as sobs. "I can help you! We can do this together, but you cannot trust Marley. He wants to destroy my people. He has a plan, and it's working. We're all going to die—" My voice broke. "So many have already died."

When these words came out, this plea for my people, I realized they were as much out of love for him as they were for them. This wasn't the Corban I had come to love. That Corban would never do this. It wasn't just a matter of Savian or Brockan—it was a matter of freedom for him too, freedom from the voices that had manipulated him his entire life.

"How do I know you're telling the truth?" he asked, his face streaked with pain. "You lied to me once. How do I know you're not lying to me again?"

"What do I have to gain?" I retorted. "I risked my life, disguised myself as a soldier, escaped those walls, and came here because *you* are the last chance we have." I heard the intensity in my voice: it was desperate, but it was also full of love. My people were worth this—each family, each life. I realized then that I would do this all over again for just one of them. Cen had taught me the value of an individual life.

He nodded in understanding. "I thought that you came back for me." There was a twinge of sadness in his voice. I reached toward him, but he pushed my hand away gently, shaking his head sadly. "Marley was an advisor to my father. My mother never trusted him, but he has so much power and respect in the kingdom . . . He has always been so good to me, never given me a reason not to trust him, so I told my mother it was fine. I never thought that he would do something like this." He clenched his jaw. "How could I have known?"

"There's more, Corban." I continued, feeling my fingertips press into my palms. "Marley planned your father's death. Whether he killed your father himself, I don't know. But he planned it." Shock appeared on Corban's face as I briefly told him about the conversation I heard in the orchard so many nights ago, back when I was a forgotten Savian girl, haunted by words I should never have heard.

For a moment after I finished, Corban just stared at me, his face blank—except for his eyes. They were full of fire. In one motion he stood up and began to pace the small grove, his hands behind his back. He kicked angrily at the bushes nearby, releasing the anger that comes only from realizing you were lied to over and over again by someone you trusted. I watched him patiently, knowing that at any point we could be separated. It felt like a gift to see him again—even under these circumstances.

He looked at me eventually, calming down, and motioned for me to sit. I nodded tensely, brushing the tears from my face and sinking down into the tall grass. He raked his fingers nervously through his hair. We sat quietly as the crickets screamed in the night and the hot breezes blew like they had the last time we met here.

"Larken, I believe you," he said simply. "I believe what you say." I tensed up, leaning forward. "I believe you even though everything before was a lie. Because when you spoke just now, I felt the truth." He shook his head. "I will be crowned king tomorrow after my announcement, and I'll have the power to overthrow any policies and individuals that may be in place. From there I will do whatever I can to stop it. No more lives will be lost." He cleared his throat. "In fact, I'll put an end to it immediately. But Marley can't know anything until tomorrow night . . . He holds too much power now . . . It wouldn't be safe. It wouldn't work." He closed his eyes and I knew that he was already formulating a plan to stop Marley.

I reached toward him and this time he let me embrace him, both of us kneeling on the grass. "There's more," I whispered. "There's an antidote that can stop the disease. We need to distribute it to as many villages as possible. Kirt can help us—he developed it." I pulled my tunic down to reveal the scar above my heart. "He gave it to me before I left," I explained. "It's a long story. But I can help too. I know how to do it. Just give us the resources and we'll get to work." I sensed the eagerness in my own voice. "Corban, thousands are suffering in your country right now, but we can put an end to it. We just need your permission."

He looked around nervously. "Larken, I don't have time to hear it all right now. I want to hear it—need to hear it—but I can't stay much longer. They'll come looking for me, and they cannot find you." He paused. "Especially Marley. You're not safe here. I'll get Hendrik and he'll escort you back to your village where you'll be safe." He scanned the perimeter of the grove and then touched the side of my face. "I promise you that no further harm will come to you or your people. Please trust me."

I nodded, feeling the honesty in his words. He would do what he said. But for some reason, even though I got what I came here for, there was more I had to resolve. "Corban, this cycle, this tradition of slavery has to end," I said softly. "My people are only safe until the next time Marley or some advisor like him decides to be done with us. You have to change things," I urged. "You're the only one that can."

He rubbed his eyes and looked away, resting his palms on the grass. I couldn't tell if that made him angry or not, but I had to say it. I had to say everything.

"You ask for too much, Larken," he said finally. "I cannot just free an entire race."

I swallowed, considering this. He agreed to save my people, not to free them. Isn't that what I came here for? They would be spared, but was that enough? I would live my life in my village working for the Brockans. There would still be soldiers, there would still be hungry bellies and low supplies and early death. How had I not considered this until now? We would not be free. We would never be truly free.

I shook my head. "They may be more forgiving than you think. They want the freedom to live their lives. So many could strengthen this kingdom. Marley believes expansion will do that, but I disagree. Thousands of lives could contribute so much good to this country. They just need the chance to do it." I thought of Cen and the good he could do if given the resources. Of Maddock and his passion to serve others. Of the people I had treated throughout my lifetime. Good people. They deserved this chance.

He looked at me bravely. "You would have made a wonderful queen, Larken. Always thinking of others, not afraid to speak your mind." He paused. "You know, after you left I considered coming to look for you. I wanted to speak to you one last time . . . I wouldn't have blamed you for never coming back. After all, I told you not to."

He sighed and lay back on his elbows, his head tilted toward the stars. "They told me at the beginning of this that I could have my pick of any girl in the kingdom." He shook his head sadly. "But it turned out to be every girl but one."

"I know you still have a decision to make tomorrow." My heart broke with each word I said. "I know you cannot choose me. I didn't come back to ask for that too."

"You don't understand. I *want* to choose you." He looked at me then with full eyes, unblinking. "You have always been the one. I have been sick with worry since I sent you away. I have gone mad thinking about a future without you in it, Larken." He inhaled deeply, clenching his palms in anger.

"Emi," I corrected him, looking bravely in his face. "My name is Emi."

"Emi," he said, trying it out. "Emi, please know that. I wanted it to be you. I wanted it to be you since that first day in the stables. I have pictured our lives together—you reigning as the brightest, kindest queen Deshan will ever see. You make me better—you challenge me. You are all I want."

He paused. "Only you would risk your life to save your people. Only you would come to defy me—the prince—the chief commander." My shoulders shook with emotion, because his truth felt as tangible as the heavy air surrounding us.

He pulled me to my feet and wrapped me in his arms. I let myself cry then, but I wasn't sure why I was crying. I knew all along he would need to choose another; in fact, he needed to for my own safety. He had already agreed to help me stop what was happening in the villages and oust Marley. I had received everything that I came here seeking. Perhaps my tears were out of fear for his future and mine—the knowledge that our lives would never again reside in the same world.

I stepped back to get a better look at him. He was so handsome, yet so unassuming. I had expected him to be a prissy child before I came, but he had turned out to be nothing like that. He was strong and kind and intelligent. His laugh was contagious. It was the best sound I knew. He would be merciful to my people and end this crime Marley set in motion. What more could I expect?

Corban reached down and stroked my face, pulling me closer to him. Then he kissed me. And his kiss seemed to absorb all of the pain and fear I had built up inside of me. When he kissed me, he wasn't kissing a Savian or a healer's assistant from the orchard or even Larken of Canton. He was kissing me—Emi. A wave of joy spread through my body.

The kiss only lasted a moment before he let me go. I wanted it to last longer—all night—all week—the rest of my life. "I love you," I told him bravely. And finally, I knew that I meant it.

He studied my face. His looked so miserable that my heart actually ached for him. Several times he opened his mouth, about to say more but stopped himself. Finally he said, "Wait here. Hendrik will make sure you are safe until I can finish this." His voice was heavy, but it was honest.

I stood in the grove alone for the second time in my life, watching his head disappear in the dark. A few times after I returned to the clinic, I tried to picture myself loving someone else. It was too hard to imagine—and now I knew that it was impossible. I would always love him. My people would be saved, and with Corban in charge, I knew things would be easier than they had been before, whether we had our freedom or not.

Until that moment, I hadn't realized what a terrible burden I had been carrying. The breeze whistled across my face, and the weight of a thousand prayers seemed to float off me toward heaven.

32

Hendrik set me up with a place outside of the palace
for the night, a friend's vacant flat stocked with
bread, cheese, grapes, and a few blankets. We weren't sure how
long I would need to stay but he told Corban that under no circumstances could I return to my village. Not until things were
finished. I slept on the wooden floor with my sword by my side
and woke the next morning to a warm, sunny breeze blowing
through the open window. Kirt would be coming by soon to discuss my village and their medical needs.

I stood up and stretched, then pulled my hair out of my face,
tying it in a knot at my neck. I wandered through the empty
rooms of the flat. Nothing was here—no furniture or books.
Bored, I cut a wedge of cheese and sat on the bare floor when I
heard the knock.

"Coming!" I called, standing up quickly. "I'll be right there."

I swung the door open, and to my surprise, Jessra entered the
flat quietly, dressed in a simple white cotton dress with her hair
pinned back to the side. She wore the healer's white hood around

her face. "Oh, Larken," she said simply, her face furrowed with compassion. "Why didn't you tell me?"

Kirt entered silently behind her, bowing to me and then disappearing into one of the back rooms of the flat to give us some privacy.

"What—how—what are you doing here?" I stammered, pulling her in an embrace. I hadn't realized how much I missed her until then.

She stepped back with her hands in her face, tears already coming to her eyes. "I was distraught after you disappeared one night. You just weren't there the next morning and I knew it was entirely my fault. I was awful to you! The one friend you had! And then I went to Kirt a few times because I haven't been feeling well, just sick with worry about you and so anxious about being away from home this long, and I just talked about you the entire time, of course, and how devastated I was that you left, and this morning he told me the truth, and I told him I had to see you, and he snuck me out in one of the healer uniforms. Now I'm here and I'm so sorry!" She burst into tears and turned away from me. "You must think I'm a horrible person for the things I said. I've never known a Savian until you. I didn't know how wonderful your people are! If they are all like you, we're all so wrong!"

I wrapped my arm around her and held her while she cried. "Jessra, shhh. Shhh. It's all right. It's all right, I understand."

When she finally calmed down, we both sat on the floor, our knees touching. "You have to tell me everything," she said with wide eyes, sniffling between words. "All of it. How you did it, how you went home, how you came back . . ." Her breath was uneven. Kirt peeked in the door to make sure we were both all right and then he nodded, disappearing again into one of the rooms.

As concisely as I could, I communicated my entire experience to Jessra—minus a few details here and there. I figured that she already knew I was a Savian, and it wouldn't hurt for her to know the rest. I explained to her that the boy she saw that night after the ball was Maddock. That I never meant for him to be seen.

She nodded in sympathy and opened her mouth in shock at all of the right parts. She reached for my hand when I told her about Corban and how much I loved him, her eyes filling with tears.

"Larken," she murmured, pulling me toward her in an embrace, her skirt dusting the floor as she did. "I wish I had known sooner. I could have helped you . . . I could have done more to protect you."

I shook my head. "No, you don't get to be sorry. *I'm* sorry. You must have felt so betrayed, especially after seeing Maddock leave that morning. Thank you for not saying anything to Hortense or any of the other girls."

We both paused for the first time in an hour, the truth finally present in our friendship. "Did you design your dress for the ball tonight?" I finally asked, breaking the silence. "I'm sure it's so beautiful."

She smiled shyly. "Yes, I've been working on my ball gown for weeks. I'm hoping the boy will finally tell me his name at this ball. It's my last chance to find out."

I grinned. "I've missed hearing about him. How are his dogs?"

She tried to restrain her laugh, which resulted in an enormous snort—a wet snort since she was still crying. "His dogs are good. He told me he wanted to come visit me in Roding after all of this ends. I can't wait to introduce him to my sisters and my parents."

"And Corban?" I asked sadly.

She shrugged. "Prince Corban won't choose me and I'm fine with that. After living on the palace grounds I'm not so sure this is the life I want anyway." She gestured toward the palace. "I thought maybe it was. All of the parties, dancing, clothes, and power. But the truth is, I would rather live in Roding near my parents and sisters with a kind man who loves dogs and me."

"Miss Jessra?" Kirt asked timidly from the doorway. "I'm afraid we'll have to get going. I underestimated how much time the two of you would need."

I stood up. "Kirt, do you have to? I wanted to talk about my village. And I wanted to tell you more about last night." Just saying the words "last night" made my heart race in a good way.

He nodded. "I know, but I felt that this reunion was important before Jessra leaves. We have time to discuss more tomorrow and the next day, since Hendrik and I decided that you can't go back to your village until things are settled. Be careful tonight too," Kirt warned. "I have no doubt that Marley will have spies stationed in the crowds to spot you. He has been looking tirelessly for you, I have heard, since you left."

"I can stay indoors," I assured him. "I'll be careful." Watching Corban choose another girl from the program would be torturous anyway.

Jessra pulled me to her and then exclaimed loudly, "I almost forgot!" She ran to the door where she left her bag and retrieved a sack for me. "This is for you."

Inside were a pair of black leather leggings and a long, forest green tunic. The sleeves glittered a little on the tunic. A matching green cloak was tucked in as well, along with a long train and a hood. It was light but still looked substantial. It was made for long rides and rainy weather. "I designed this for you thinking that it would be good for you next year on the hunt," she stammered, "which you may not be on, but—well, I know it's not much, but I never actually thought I would be able to give it to you. I just hoped I would get the chance someday. It would be perfect for riding. Do you hate it?" Her eyes filled with emotion again.

I laughed, pulling her toward me. "I love it. You shouldn't have, Jessra."

"I'll come back for you tomorrow," Kirt said before bowing. He took Jessra by the arm and they exited together. I waved at Jessra and promised her I would visit her in Roding, if at all possible. It was good to have Jessra back on my side. It was good, in fact, to have Jessra at all.

* * * * *

I leafed through the books Kirt left for me and munched on the grapes, but nothing could distract me from thinking about tonight. Now that Corban was aware of the truth, I had to trust that he would do the right thing. My people would be under Marley's attack for only a few more hours—or so I hoped.

It was close to dark when I heard the people begin to gather, their clamor much louder than the usual market crowd. It would be hours before Corban made his decision, but I knew none of them would miss the chance to see an actual ball happen right before their eyes. The dancing would take place on the upper level, of course, but the courtiers would be all over the front lawn. There would be three thrones on the lower level—empty for most of the night until the end. If I closed my eyes, I could imagine it all.

I fell asleep on the floor and woke up much later to the strings of a full orchestra, their light trills wafting down through the open window, mixed with shrieks and bouts of laughter. Groggily I sat up and opened the shutters to see the streets below. The crowd was substantial; groups were fighting their way to get closer to the gates. I couldn't see the ball from here, but I could see the turrets of the palace—looming and ominous as ever. What would Corban say tonight?

I considered staying as I said I would. But staring at the white palace steeples I realized that soon I would return to my village where, for the rest of my life, I would wonder what Corban said and how he looked the night he saved my people. I had to see him one last time, I decided. Even if it was dangerous. Even if it would break my heart.

I dressed in the clothes Jessra left for me, the hood perfect in this darkness. No one would know it was me, and the clothes were fine enough to pass as Brockan apparel. The leggings hugged me tightly, and the cloak was the perfect length for my height. As an afterthought, I fastened my belt around my waist, tucked my sword in, and opened the door into the hot night.

I fought my way through the crowds, vendors selling their wares to the maddening throng. There were more people than I knew existed in all of Deshan. I felt invisible in my cloak as I pulled the hood over my head and made my way toward the front gate.

My eyes widened when I saw the front steps, not expecting the sight before me. The lights of the palace illuminated the entire marketplace. Thousands of candles on golden sticks were placed on each step and across the length of the gates. Massive chandeliers seemed to float from the heavens, strung through clear ropes that were held up by the colossal white pillars of the palace. The light reflected off the gold gates, dazzling in the warm night. Somehow, the inside of the ballroom was brought outdoors.

Even outside the gates people were dancing. Couples bowed to each other and performed the same steps I had learned in the mansion. Most were dressed in their finest apparel—some in ball gowns, others in silk dresses, and some in their everyday clothes, but with bright colored scarves wrapped around their heads. Groups of children ran throughout, happy to stay up at such an hour, their cries and shouts of joy the loudest sounds I heard all night. I pushed my way through the crowd, having to fight harder to get through, the closer I got to the gates.

I could see some of the girls from the mansion from where I stood. Keisha and Sasha were holding hands on the outskirts of the party, their dresses both gold toned. I inched forward a little more, weaving around a group of teenagers playing guitars. There were three thrones halfway down the steps—the same ones as in the Great Hall that morning Corban made his announcement. Before Marley had sat on one, but tonight it would be reserved for the new queen—whoever that would be. My heart ached that I hadn't thought to ask Corban when we were alone. Who would join him in ruling Deshan? The stars were so bright tonight, blending in with the top of the palace so that the lights below the palace were just a reflection of the stars above, and every surface sparkled as if it were a translucent ocean—a glass echo of light.

"Do you see her?" I heard a woman behind me ask. "Do you see our Savian girl?" She spoke softly but was close enough to me that I could hear her words. She was dressed in plain clothes, a red scarf tied around her head in a turban. Her friend was dressed the same and watched the gate with a hopeful look.

"They say she was sent home," her friend replied. "Discovered. But that may be a rumor." They gripped each other's hands tightly. I looked around the square. How many Savians were here, within the palace walls, for the first time? How many were offering prayers of hope? How many knew what Marley was doing to their people at this very moment? I thought of my friends in my village, of Fretta's tears and her little boy curling his toes in pain. Corban had to end this.

I pushed further toward the gates, spotting Jessra as I did. She was dressed in a gown that faded from red on top to pink to white on the bottom. It was magnificent. The boy with the purple suit was dressed in black tonight, and the way they danced together was graceful and sweet. They loved each other; I could see it from here. I beamed, wishing only the best for my friend. Hortense stood at the buffet, dressed in a lavender taffeta dress and stuffing her face while she stared at Hendrik hungrily. Younda observed the crowd below haughtily, and Petra bit her nails as she scanned the steps. I had not seen Corban all night or Marley for that matter.

The orchestra stopped playing a few minutes to midnight and then a loud bell chimed twelve times throughout the palace grounds. The courtiers and those outside the gates were quiet as the bells chimed. A few whispered, but most were still, looking expectantly at the steps. Even the children seemed to hush, somehow realizing that this was important. It was harder and harder to maintain my close proximity to the gates; so many were pushing their way toward them. A large chandelier ascended from navy fabric, temporarily shielding the view of the ball from those of us at the gates. When it finally rose as high as the others, it illuminated Marley on the steps with the queen and Corban seated behind him on their thrones. Corban sat up regally, his face looking surprisingly calm. The queen was nervously bouncing her leg, although a smile was plastered across her face as usual. Marley's voice boomed throughout the marketplace—a voice that was somehow broadcast loud enough for all of us to hear.

"Ladies and gentlemen, the time we have all been waiting for has finally come!" He cupped his hand around his mouth, "Especially me and the beautiful girls from the program." The crowd erupted in laughter on cue as Marley beamed across the audience. Marley wore a deep-black suit with a tie that glittered in the night. "Yes. Yes. Prince Corban, chief commander of the Brockan military and Future King of Deshan, has made his decision!" A huge applause swept like a wave throughout the marketplace.

"As you all know, Prince Corban has chosen from a group of twenty of Deshan's most eligible young ladies." I registered that he said only twenty. In his mind, I never existed. "They have spent the past year living in the south mansion learning what it takes to be queen. Our well-known and respected Hortense of Jughest heralded their dedicated schooling. Where is she?" Marley scanned the crowd. "Ah! There she is! Please give Hortense your applause and respect for her diligent efforts this year!"

I thought Hortense would explode from blushing. She tried to smile but her effort looked painful as a halfhearted applause shuffled through the crowd for her.

He continued, "I wish I could do the honors myself and announce Prince Corban's choice, but he has asked me if I would grant him the privilege. I suppose it's the least I can do." Marley rolled his eyes sarcastically. "She is, after all, his bride-to-be. But let me just say before I sit down, that I have spoken with Corban and he is *thrilled* about his decision. As are the rest of his advisors and his mother. Now enough talking from me!" Marley said. "Please welcome your future king, crowned prince, and commander in chief of your Brockan military as he reveals your future queen!"

The applause for Corban was thunderous. I scanned the crowd. For the most part these people were beaming, thrilled to witness such an important decision. Some, however, looked anxious, clutching their children protectively and looking at Corban with hopeful eyes. I wasn't sure how there were Savians outside the gates of villages, but I was glad they were there. I was not the only one who realized what was at stake here. Corban wasn't just deciding a new queen; he was revealing their whole future—our whole future.

Corban walked to the front of the stage assertively. He looked like a different person from the man who had announced his new position as chief commander. This Corban looked sure of himself. No sweating, no shaking, and no fear at all that I could sense. He stood at the front searching the crowd and then nodded twice, his eyes on the gates as a dozen soldiers moved into position.

"Thank you, all of you, for being here to support me and my family." His voice was clear and sure, broadcast loudly like Marley's. "I cannot express my gratitude for your support. Thank you, Hortense, for your patience and diligence in teaching these girls. I have enjoyed receiving your reports and I respect your opinion." I thought of my classes spent with Hortense and the other girls, practicing dances and learning poise. It seemed like a lifetime ago. Corban stepped forward a little more. "Thank you also to my team of advisors for your careful consideration and advice. I respect you and am grateful for your willingness to guide me in my efforts to choose the future queen."

He paused. "Thank you, Mother." He turned around to smile affectionately at the queen, who was now beaming with pride. "I could never do this without you. You are the source of my courage and have taught me what a true queen is. That example has been my driving force in making this decision. My father chose well, years ago. I hope that I can respect his memory and also choose the right individual to serve my people . . . someday." A soft *ahhhh* purred through the audience, and courtiers around me were already pulling out handkerchiefs to catch their tears, somehow missing his hesitant "someday."

He paused again. The only sound in the whole courtyard was hundreds of people breathing in anticipation. "However," he said, "I'm afraid I cannot present your queen this evening." A loud cry came from the crowd, individuals screaming and shaking their fists toward him. Keisha reached for her corset and passed out, and Hortense and some guards rushed forward to help her. The other girls looked as though he had slapped them across the face.

Corban ignored the crowd and straightened his tie, taking a step down. "I want to be clear that as king of Deshan, I'll always be honest with my people. I feel that honesty should start now." He paused and paced the palace steps like he had done in the grove. Only this time, he was pacing in front of thousands. "It has come to my attention that some hateful crimes have been committed against a faction of our nation." The audience swelled with chatter. I pulled the hood of my cloak further over my face. "Crimes implemented by none other than my trusted advisor Marley."

I looked at Marley, standing next to the queen's throne. I knew that if I were close enough, I would see a thin rim of sweat along his forehead. "Tonight I do not come to give you a queen. Perhaps that will come in time—I hope it will come in time—but there is a much more pressing matter to resolve. Tonight, I come to give you justice." A soft hum swept over the crowd.

Marley had slid off his throne by now and was bowing in embarrassment to the angry courtiers around him, his face red. I wasn't sure where he thought he could run. Corban must have had a meeting with the palace soldiers after I spoke with him last night.

"Stop there!" Corban ordered. "Guards, position yourselves." The guards moved, two on each of Marley's arms, their faces serious. The crowd around me buzzed, all eyes fixed on Corban. Once Marley was surrounded by the guards, Corban continued. "Marley, is it true or not true that you commissioned a project years ago for the royal healer to discover a cure for a rare disease?"

Marley snarled at Corban, attempting to shrug off the soldiers on his arms to no avail. Corban stepped closer to him. "True or not true?"

Marley turned his face and mumbled.

"Loud enough for everyone to hear," Corban stated, his voice confident and sure.

"True!" Marley said. "I did it to save our people. I did it to protect the people of this nation from a dread disease! I live to serve!" He looked toward the crowd with pleading eyes, but from what I could see of the people around me, they were not so trusting.

Corban continued. "And then, Marley, did you or did you not devise a plan to isolate the Savian villages and distribute this disease you developed the cure to, making sure the soldiers stationed there received the antidote to protect them?" Marley turned his head again and Corban stepped closer until he was standing right next to him. "Did you plan to have every Savian citizen in our nation killed in cold blood?" Corban's voice was slick, anger in every word.

Marley struggled against the soldiers at his sides. "True!" he spat. "But I didn't work alone! There are many who wish to rid the nation of that people! There are many who recognize what a burden they are to the growth of this country! A nation as great as Deshan needs a real ruler! Not a weak boy!" He was yelling, his voice echoing throughout the yard. "Join with me!" he shouted at the crowd. "Join me in my crusade!" A soldier stepped behind him and tied a scarf around his mouth, muffling him. I pulled the hood of my cloak tighter around my face.

"Gross crimes were committed against this nation at your hand. You, who should have been my most trusted advisor," Corban continued. "You'll be given a fair trial and, if found guilty, will be hung as a traitor to the crown and a conspirator to the death of thousands of Savian lives. Take him away!" Corban commanded.

The guards carried Marley from the steps, his feet flailing. By now, the crowd was angry, their voices rising. For a moment I thought they were angry that Corban dismissed Marley, but soon enough it became evident that they were angry with Marley. Several individuals spit in his direction as he was carried off. Others shouted insults. Still others watched with wide eyes, clutching their children to their chests. What would this mean for Deshan?

Once Marley was gone, Corban turned back toward the crowd and walked down with his shoulders square, until he was so close he could be almost touched by those who stood at the gates. The crowd hushed long enough for him to speak. "There is more," he said, his voice even louder. "I will be crowned your king tonight, inside the walls of the palace, but I'm not my father. I believe in change, and I believe that it begins with me. I will not be the king who sits behind his gates. As your king, I'll be there with you—in your towns and villages, hearing your concerns. I'll be involved in all aspects of the country. I cannot rule from inside these gates. I hope that you will respect my decisions and accept the changes that will make this nation great."

It seemed that half of the crowd was pleased with Corban, cheering and raising handkerchiefs to him, while others looked angry—either at Marley's dismissal or Corban's change in tradition. Regardless of their reactions, he stood his ground, watching his people unflinching. The people around me carried on, cheering and yelling, their arms in the air. I was pushed from my position as men and women swept closer to the palace. I stepped back, Corban disappearing from my view.

Eventually I saw him walk up the steps, flanked by soldiers. He waved to the girls in the program, who watched him go with confused faces. The queen waved to the people before curtsying and entering the palace. The crowd eventually dispelled, individuals returning to their villages and homes, knowing what Marley had done. Knowing what crimes were committed against their fellow Deshanians, and perhaps wondering if it was really true. After all, most of the Brockans had no idea what went on in the orchard villages. Perhaps they would never really know, but at least they recognized us as a people who were important to their king.

My heart was full as I walked through the throng of people, but in a good way. This wasn't the end, I thought as I hiked up the stairs to the flat, my cloak swinging by my side in the dark, my sword concealed neatly inside. It wasn't even close to the end of the changes that would affect Deshan now that Corban would be king, but it was a beginning. And more than anything, I felt that my people deserved that.

I lay on the wooden floor with the window open, my cloak spread out around me and my eyes on the stars. When I first came here, I had just an ounce of courage—just enough to save one Savian boy's life. But over time it had grown into this incredible chain from the prayers of thousands petitioning for help. It changed me, and

Kirt, and Jessra, and Corban. It changed the lives of thousands who would be saved because of it. It was shared courage. Something we have to use together, because often it is the courage of others that moves us to do something we don't think we can possibly do. No one person can take the credit for something as wonderful as that.

I fell asleep with gratitude on my lips for the beauty of the spoken and unspoken prayers of the thousands of people who believed. We had been delivered.

Epilogue

I went home after that, Kirt and Hendrik on either side of me. Home to my village that I knew might be ravaged because of the vox, but home to a place that could still be saved. Corban ordered all soldiers to be protectors of the people and opened the borders of the villages so we were free to travel from one to the other. It wasn't the complete freedom I begged him for, but it was progress. I choked back tears as we rounded the corner—the orchards were lit by the soft morning glow, the heat seeming almost welcome for the first time. To me, it was an indication of the earth's stability despite a nation's change. The walls were still intact, but the gate was wide open, soldiers welcoming us inside. People were walking around once we entered, toting water, holding their children's hands, carrying on and rebuilding their broken lives.

"Are you ready for this?" Hendrik asked me with a smile. "Ready to go back inside these walls?" I smiled a little, because there was always a wall—this wall and the one outside of the palace. One keeping us out, another keeping us in. I was ready for those walls to come down.

"I've waited for this day for a long time," I replied.

I looked around the clinic anxiously, searching for Maddock and Cen, when I spotted Fretta across the room. I shuffled around the people until I reached her side. "Upstairs," she said to me while spreading paste on an old woman's legs. Fretta looked tired; I noticed dark circles beneath her eyes. I wondered how long she had been treating these people by herself.

I ran to the top of the clinic, taking the stairs two at a time, and was met by the sound of Cen's cough. Maddock sat by his bedside, rubbing jusen on his temples. Downstairs I heard Kirt enter and begin to organize the chaos. He was reporting to the people what they already knew by now: that the king was putting an end to their struggle, and that with this cure, each of them would be healed. He was received with welcoming arms, a chorus of cheers echoing.

It would take some time, I knew, before the Savians would trust the Brockans—years before the walls of our division would truly fall, but this was a start. We had to start somewhere.

Cen's eyes were closed when I reached his bedside, his mouth open between his cracked, chapped lips. His face was so sallow that his eyebrows seemed to be the liveliest things on it. Maddock put his arm around me, pressing on my shoulder. "It's good that you came back," he said. Then, as if thinking better of it, he added, "But it's good that you left too." I knew he was reassuring me that it was all right that I missed some of Cen's last few days. It broke my heart, but I knew Maddock was telling me the truth. He shook his head sadly. His voice cracked. "You don't know how proud he was when he heard. We all are. You saved us, Emi."

I smiled gratefully at Maddock and reached for Cen's hand, lifting it up from his bed and pulling it to my face. He coughed with his eyes closed, so much weaker than when I left less than a week before. "Cen, it's Emi," I whispered into his ear. "It's me."

He didn't say anything or even open his eyes, but he squeezed my hand three times so faint that I wondered for a moment if it had really happened or if I had just imagined it. Tears pooled in my eyes as I stared down at the man whose love made me believe that all things were possible. He never gave up on believing that our people could have a better life. This wasn't the freedom we always hoped for. It was a small start but it comforted me that it happened in Cen's lifetime.

* * * * *

We buried Cen on a hill overlooking the orchards. The entire village came, their hands placed on the bandages above their hearts—in honor of the lives he saved. We sang between our tears for him:

> *Ring out the bells,*
> *Pull up your boots,*
> *Sing out your voice*
> *Steady and true.*
>
> *Have heart in the fear*
> *And faith in the new,*
> *Heaven's stars are fighting*
> *Their battles for you.*

Maddock returned to his village afterward, ready to rebuild whatever was left. He promised he would write. Fretta stayed at the clinic to take care of whatever minor injuries she was able to, until I could return and resume my post.

Those three hand squeezes sustained me during long, hot rides and hours of work alongside Kirt in clinics across the country. *I. Love. You.* The only language Cen had left.

* * * * *

I buried myself in my work to overcome my grief. Grief I came to recognize as pain not only for the loss of Cen, but for the loss of Corban. For a moment in the palace, I truly felt that a future with those I loved was possible—but Corban couldn't give me everything. He had completely changed the way the Savians were treated, he had Marley hung publicly as a traitor and a tyrant to the nation after his trial, and he had let me live even after the lies I told. To think that he could give me his love fully after all of that seemed too much to ask. Jessra wrote me regularly and told me that Petra was a frequent guest in the palace. She speculated that Corban would marry her once things calmed down in the nation. I couldn't think of Petra and her perfect hair and charming features without feeling the pain deepen. I buried myself in my duties to overcome the rest.

Kirt and our team worked tirelessly to deliver the antidote to as many villages as possible. We used Marley's map to determine which villages were infected first and started with those. I stitched up so many incisions that my hands cramped and blistered. We worked until we were bleary-eyed and then slept wherever we could find a place—barns, the floors of barracks, and under the Deshan stars. It had been months since that night on the palace steps and still new pockets of people and villages needed healing. So much damage had been done at Marley's hand. We treated more than just those with vox, since so many Savians had been untreated for years. Kirt implemented a healing program to recruit future village healers everywhere we went, sending them to the palace clinic to receive training.

It had been months since I had left the palace, close to a year maybe. Over the course of my long hours and haunting dreams, I had given up hope on a life with Corban, resigning myself to a future with Kirt and his team. There were worse fates, after all, than saving the lives of my people. Cen would be proud, that much I knew.

It was a hazy night at a makeshift clinic in a barn in West Deshan. I had just finished treating my last patient for the evening when a stranger entered the clinic, his hair falling just above his eyes, his shoulders broad and even. My breath caught in my mouth as I watched him step between the resting patients, shaking their hands as they looked up at him, leaning his ear to their lips to better hear them. It was dark in the barn, and his candle was one of the only sources of light, bobbing up and down around the people who were still awake. I sat back in my chair, instinctively tucking my hair behind my ears—hair that was to my shoulders, but still straggly and dirty. I wore leggings and a tunic that were clean but threadbare and ill fitting. So different from the way I dressed in the palace. The stranger caught my eye from across the room after several minutes, his eyes lighting up even behind the candle's flame. I would recognize those eyes anywhere.

I stood abruptly as he came toward me, my heart beating hysterically. "Emi?" he asked, his voice the same. "Emi, is that you?"

I felt my voice choke up at the sound of his, before I even opened my mouth. "Your Highness," I managed to say, bowing my head.

He laughed softly. "I've been looking for you for weeks, popping in and out of clinics. I finally got word from Kirt that you would be here."

I bit my lip to keep from crying or laughing or both as the patient behind me stirred. He had been looking for me? "Perhaps we could go outside?" I suggested, gesturing to the sleeping patients around us.

He grinned. "I would love that." I followed him carefully out of the large barn doors, Kirt raising his eyebrows and grinning at me as I passed him. Corban's flame was unnecessary here—the stars were out tonight. He blew it out and walked toward a patch of grass behind the barn, nodding to the soldiers that flanked its doors. My heart raced even faster as he sat down on the grass and motioned for me to join him, his arms resting on the mossy ground. He was here. Real and full. Exactly the way I remembered him.

"This feels like old times," he said with a smile as I sank down beside him.

"I didn't think I would see you again," I replied seriously, tucking a straggly piece of hair behind my ear. It was the only thing I could think to say.

He cleared his throat and was quiet for several moments before he spoke again. "Emi, things have changed so much since I last saw you." He gestured behind us to the barn of sleeping people. "I have been to almost every village in the country, stopping in to make sure the people understand that I am here to listen to them, that I am so sorry for my ignorance and the way they and their families have been treated by my soldiers over the years. I was raised with the understanding that a king never ventures past his palace gates. I've completely defied that and have met so many wonderful people. People who have been mistreated for years without my knowing it, people who are willing to forgive us for the things we did, whether consciously or not. And you know," he said, pausing to look at the sky, "I did it for them, and I did it for me, but I would be lying if I told you that I didn't do it for you too."

I closed my eyes, contemplating each word. "You made me believe that there are voices to be heard, and I wanted to find that out for myself and now I have. You were right. The nation can only become stronger if we use every voice we have. We wasted so much time keeping the Savians out that we lost sight of the fact that we need each other. We absolutely need each other." I felt fresh and raw from everything that had happened the past few months, but I knew that what he was saying—what I believed before—was still true.

"I know there may be some that are upset, but I came here because I wanted you to be the first to know that we are officially freeing all Savians. They will be first-class citizens, no different from Brockans any longer. My advisors and I have an entire plan set in motion. Schools to be built, new soldiers to train and hire, walls to tear down, land plots to divide. It's taken months, but we believe it is complete and functional. We believe it will make our country even stronger in a hundred different ways."

I nodded, feeling tears pool in my eyes. "I'm so glad you found me to tell me that," I said with a croaky voice. I wished Cen were alive to know what Corban just said. "It will change everything." We would be free.

He laughed a little and sat up so he was close to me. "Oh, Emi, I didn't come all of this way just to tell you that." He pulled me to him, brushing the tears softly away from my eyes with his fingers.

"I have been miserable for months thinking about how I could have possibly let you go. I have tried to distract myself with other girls, but I could never care about them the way I care about you." I thought of Petra dancing with him at the balls, making him laugh, and looked at him, hoping so badly that this was real.

"I don't care that you're a Savian," he said earnestly. "The rest of the kingdom might have cared—might still care—but I don't. It's taken me more time than I am proud of to reach that conclusion, but I think what matters is that I've reached it. I love you. I love you because you are Savian. I would love you if you were not Savian. I love you because you are different and real and so right for me and the people of this nation. I love you," he repeated. "I just love you."

I let the tears fall freely as he pulled me up and kissed me, the arms that I loved so much around me. Then I laughed, because this was not something to cry about. He was here. He loved me. We kissed outside the barn with the stars blazing down at us until I pulled away.

"Are you ready for this?" I asked him timidly. "Corban, there has already been so much change. Are you afraid of what others might say to you?"

He laughed softly. "Maybe I don't care."

I pulled his face toward me so that I could see into his eyes. "Why me?" I pleaded, my hands brushing away the curls that fell around his face. "Why did you choose me?"

He stared at me for a minute and then closed his eyes. "My father made many mistakes in his reign as king, allowing so many important decisions to be made by others while he sheltered himself inside the palace walls. But he did do some things right." He paused. "Before he died he warned me not to listen to those who would encourage bloodshed. He told me to fight if necessary, but only in defense of freedom."

His arms tightened around me. "Everything is changing in this country." He looked at the sword on his waist. "Boundaries, positions, and, I hope, beliefs our fathers instilled into us about how different our two people are. I can't think of a better time to have chosen you." He paused, a smile spreading across his face. "Besides all of those things, I love you. A life without you is not one I choose to live. Not without knowing if you still feel the same."

I thought of all of the people I had helped these past few months—the wounds I'd sutured, the babies I'd rocked, the healers I'd trained. I thought of that night in the orchard when I heard some soldiers discussing how they would destroy an entire race of people. But they were wrong. We were still here and would be here for years to come. It didn't make everything that happened okay, but it made it better than it was before.

"I love you," I said to Corban with all of the sincerity I had. It seemed that my joy was spilling out of me, circling me like a cloud. We kissed again, and then he pulled me toward him, my head resting against his chest.

A cry from within the barn jerked us both back to reality as a light flickered through the dusty slats. "I better check on that," I said with a short laugh, realizing that I could let him go for now; it would just be temporary.

He smiled at me, his brown eyes dancing even without the light of the sun. "I'll wait for you," he promised.

I turned to go but looked back again to make sure he was really there—to make sure that I hadn't dreamed it all.

In that moment, I think I finally understood what my mother wrote. That to have courage is to tell your story with your whole heart.

She was right. There isn't bravery without a little trembling.

Discussion Questions

1. How does Emi's character change from the beginning of the book to the end? How does she find her own voice?

2. Courage is a theme of *Star of Deliverance*. Which characters besides Emi show courage?

3. Emi feels different from the other girls in the program. In what ways is she able to identify her own self-worth despite her differences?

4. The Brockans and Savians have fought for many years. What advice would you give them in order to find long-lasting peace?

5. Friendship is a theme in *Star of Deliverance*. How is Emi a good friend? How are the other characters good friends?

6. Emi is placed in a difficult situation when she finds herself in the program. How does she learn to overcome her fears?

About the Author

MANDY MADSON VOISIN grew up reading fairy tales and knew from a young age that she wanted to write them. She graduated from Brigham Young University with a degree in English and started writing *Star of Deliverance* soon thereafter. She currently lives in Phoenix, Arizona, with her husband, Kevin. Keep up with Mandy on her website: www.mmvoisin.com.